William McIlvanney

William McIlvanney was educated at Kilmarnock Academy and Glasgow University, and now lives in Glasgow. His first novel, *Remedy is None*, won the Geoffrey Faber Memorial Award, and with *Docherty* he won the Whitbread Award for Fiction in 1975. After *Laidlaw* and *The Papers of Tony Veitch* – both of which gained Silver Daggers from the Crime Writers' Association – he published his first book of poems, *These Words: Weddings and After*. This was followed by *The Big Man*, *Walking Wounded*, a collection of stories which was awarded the *Glasgow Herald* People's Prize in 1990, and *Strange Loyalties*, which won the same prize two years later, as well as two further volumes of poetry and a collection of essays and journalism, *Surviving the Shipwreck*. The final story in *Walking Wounded*, 'Dreaming', was dramatised by William McIlvanney for BBC Television's 'Screen Two', winning a BAFTA (Scotland) Award for Best Single Drama.

The Kiln, William McIlvanney's latest novel, won the 1996 Saltire Scottish Book of the Year award.

SCEPTRE

The Kiln

WILLIAM McILVANNEY

SCEPTRE

"Come On A My House," written by Ross Bagdasarian and William Saroyan, reproduced by kind permission of MCA Music Ltd.

"Rock Around the Clock," written by Max Freedman and Jimmy DeKnight, © 1954 Edward Kassner Music Co. Ltd. for the World. Used by permission, all rights reserved.

First published in 1996 by Hodder and Stoughton
A division of Hodder Headline PLC
A Sceptre Paperback

10 9 8 7 6 5 4 3 2 1

British Library Cataloguing in Publication Data

A CIP catalogue record for this book is available from the British Library

McIlvanney, William, 1936–
 The kiln
 1. English fiction – 20th century – Scottish authors
 2. Scottish fiction – 20th century
 I. Title
 823.9'14 [F]

ISBN 0 340 65736 7

Printed and bound in Great Britain by
Caledonian International Book Manufacturing Ltd, Glasgow

Hodder and Stoughton
A division of Hodder Headline PLC
338 Euston Road
London NW1 3BH

For Joan and for my nephews and nieces and their families – theirs is the true story.

'At the moment of writing the author is fictive. Only the story is real.'

– Tom Docherty

'You must find the way to let the heat of experience temper your naïvety without reducing your idealism to ashes.'

– Jack Laidlaw

∫

IT IS AS IF, he would think, who I thought I was has dried up like a well and I have to find again the source of who I am.

HE WOULD REMEMBER THE JOURNEY back home from Grenoble through Heathrow Airport, the uncertainty of it, how it is better to travel in doubt than to arrive, and how every stage of his returning reminded him forcefully that the man who was going back to Graithnock was still the boy who had left it, and that the summer of the kiln continued to happen in him.

He would be puzzled by repeating moments of that summer, their small persistence, amazed at the disparity between the triviality of the incident and the longevity of its endurance, like coming upon an octogenarian mayfly. They came, it seemed, of their own volition. No doubt they were occasioned by some sequence of thoughts which he could not retrace. But they were for him not logically explicable. Whatever purpose he had been imagining himself to have in wandering whatever corridors of the mind, it seemed the purpose had been ambushed. It was as if a door, in some corridor down which he was passing, were suddenly to open for no reason, spontaneously.

And there in a long-forgotten place, lit by a long-dead sun or by a light-bulb which had burned out years ago, were places and people he had known. The places were as they had been, unchanged. The long-abandoned furniture was neatly in place. The people were still talking animatedly about problems long since resolved, still laughing, still saying words that he could hear, still brewing tea that had been drunk. They could be young who were now old. They could be alive who were now dead.

'OH, HERE,' Auntie Bella says.

She stops at the living-room door with her leather message-bag. She's so notorious for taking slow departures that nobody ever sees her to the front door any more. It can get too cold. She seems to remember everything she had originally meant to say just as she is leaving.

'Ye can watch the seasons change just listenin' to Bella sayin' cheerio,' Tam's father has said.

'Ah met Mary Boland at the shops there. She was tellin' me whidyimacallum's been in a car crash.'

Eventually, she finds the surname she is looking for. It belongs to a well-known and very right-wing politician. His name has for a long time been the equivalent of a swear-word in the house, about as pleasant to contemplate as Sir Anthony Eden's election win for the Tories in May.

'Oh, that's right,' Tam's mother says. 'It was in the six o'clock news. Wasn't it, Conn?'

'Well?' Auntie Bella is waiting. 'What's the word?'

'Said his condition was very satisfactory,' Tam's father says. 'So Ah'm assumin' he's dead.'

HERE HE WOULD SIT, he decided, remembering both the journey from Grenoble and the earlier summer it had reactivated, as if they were the latitude and longitude of a confused life by which he might fix where he was, beyond the physical. The physical was simple enough. It was a rented flat in Edinburgh, near the Water of Leith. The way he felt, it might as well be the Water of Lethe. For he was aging and so many of the things he dreamt would happen hadn't happened and wouldn't happen for him now. And what *had* happened, he still couldn't be sure. By the waters of Leith, we sat down and wept when we remembered Graithnock. Oy vey, with a Scottish accent.

'I have seen the future and it works' (Lincoln Steffens). He had seen the present and it didn't work. He looked round the apartment where he was holing up, surrounded by someone else's furniture. This was what he had achieved? He was a recluse among half a million people. He owned nothing but some books – no house, no car, no prospects. He hadn't just burned his boats, he had burnt the blueprint for them. He had stopped visiting old friends, owing to his present tendency to bleed verbally all over their carpets. He was trying to stop inhaling whisky as if it was an oxygen substitute. His finances were a shambles swiftly degenerating into a chaos. This was what he had earned? Lodgings in a stranger's place? Emotional destitution? The melodramatic possibility of suicide nipped in and out of the flat like a dubious friend wondering if he could help that day. Otherwise, things were fine.

He was trying to do that sum again, the addition and subtraction of experience – what did it come to? How did you quantify the dreams that died, the gifts you gave and were given, the promises you thought the world made and then broke, the remembered moments that still shone like pure gold, the wonderful faces, the death of the best, the laughter that turned banality into carnival, the purifying angers, the great dead minds that whispered their secrets to you in the early hours of many mornings, the bitter sweetness of family, the incorrigible contradictoriness of living? By remembering?

HE SITS UP IN BED SUDDENLY and says, 'Mahatma Gandhi.'

He is staring into a dimness delicately brushed with half-light from the greying embers of the fire. The furniture of the living-room has a sheen of gentle aging. The sideboard could be an antique. The biscuit barrel sitting on top of it, where his mother keeps the rent money, might as well be an Etruscan vase. The clock above the fireplace is keeping a time that doesn't seem the present. He is awake in a room he cannot recognise.

He is frozen at the sound of his own voice. Where did that come from? He has been experiencing that familiar sensation of standing at the edge of a clifftop on which the ground is crumbling under his feet and he is falling when the speaking aloud of that name jerks him clear and leaves him sitting upright in his bed.

He listens. He is glad no one has heard. It's a good thing he sleeps in the fold-down bed in the living-room. He can keep his madness private. His family are sanely asleep upstairs.

Mahatma Gandhi? Where did he come from? Almost immediately Tam knows that the small, skinny man in the Indian frock has wandered out of his own most potent obsession: his wondering about ways of how people get it.

'It' – in the darkness of his head he lets that cryptic cipher open out into some of the variations he has heard it given and repeats them to himself like a satanic litany: your hole, sex, rumpy-pumpy, intercourse, making love, houghmagandie, 'you know' (with a smile), a ride, a bit of the other, a shag, hi-diddle-diddle, copulation, sexual union, 'Christ, it was incredible!'

Why were there so many names for it? Were there that many different ways to do it? And if it was so various, springing up everywhere like a genus of weed with a thousand species, how come you'd managed to avoid it so far? You had heard it called about a hundred things. (You could almost bet that any euphemism you heard and didn't understand, that's what it meant.) But you'd never had it. You had read it, thought it, heard it, certainly mimed it, and once been sure you smelled it, but you had never felt it. To judge from what you'd been told, it was running amuck like the bubonic plague and you were boringly, agonisingly immune.

He can't believe it. It winks and nods at him from everywhere but won't come out to play. What is wrong with him?

He remembers having to translate *The Anabasis* in the Greek class. And that's another thing: Latin and Greek at school – what does that have to do with living in Graithnock? He can't remember the woman's name now but it was someone who came to see Cyrus of Persia about something. At least he thinks it was Cyrus. It could have been Xerxes. But he had to translate the passage.

He had looked up the words. When the Greek appeared before him, he said, 'It is said he lay with her.' He got it right. He was good at translation. He could translate one word into another word. But what the hell did it mean? It is said he lay with her? All right, he was in third year at that time but he was fifteen going on five. He *lay* with her?

All Dusty Thomas said was, 'Well done, Docherty.' That was well done? He had translated it from one foreign language into another foreign language. He felt like screaming, 'But what did the bastard *do*?' (He likes swearing in his head.)

He hasn't just read about it in Greek. Being so bookish, he has tracked it down in a lot of places. He has even memorised some of the references. 'His need pistoned into her.' 'She screamed in agonised ecstasy.' He sometimes says the words to himself like a wine-taster with no taste-buds. He follows the spoor of those references round and round without finding any corresponding reality in his own experience until he begins to think that he is tracking a beast which, perhaps only in his private world, has become extinct.

But he continues to brood on ways of how to get it. No medieval alchemist was ever more obsessive in his search for the philosopher's stone. Out there is gold – pure, undiluted sex. He has to discover the formula that will transmute the base metal of cafés and the dancing and brassieres that seem welded to the body and skirts that defy levitation into the transcendental shining of doing it.

He studies much. He will read or hear things that will stop him dead and leave him staring into space, wondering if he has come upon the key that will unlock the golden hoard. Sometimes the revelation will only come in retrospect. He will be lying, as now, in his fold-down bed in the living-room, the house quiet as a mouse's breathing, and the turmoil of his mind will become very still, transfixed. That thing he has read or heard. Of course. Is that what he has been looking for? Has he reached the culmination of his quest?

Yes. That is the news the Mahatma brings him. For he read recently of Gandhi's determined search for physical purity. Apparently he thought that intercourse with women (and, therefore, presumably with men) should be avoided because they took away a man's vital juices. (To judge by that criterion, Tam must be so full of vital juices they are coming out his ears. Purity? He sought physical purity, did he? No problem. Here was the answer in three words: be Tam Docherty.)

The person who was writing about Gandhi was full of praise for the Mahatma's constant need to prove how pure he was, how immune to temptation. In order to do this, he would take different young women to bed with him. They must sleep together without having sex. That way, he could prove his purity was still intact. The writer was in awe of such holy self-denial.

Sitting up in bed, Tam realises that his own reaction is completely different. How could he have read so carelessly as to let the writer's attitude simply become his own, without examining it? He is always doing that. He reads something in a book or a newspaper, or he listens to someone, and it may be two days later when he thinks, 'What a load of shite that was! Why did I accept it?' He feels that now.

The thought that comes to him as he sits upright on his lonely bed, bathed in illumination, is a simple one, stunningly clear. 'Mahatma, you fly, old bastard.' For it was perfect, wasn't it? You had it either way. You couldn't lose. If you didn't manage to perform, your purity had triumphed. If you had sex, it was a sad lapse from your desired standards and you must try again. And again and again and again. Ya beauty. No pressure. The ultimate, self-indulgent con. The man was a genius.

Tam is staring ahead, hardly daring to breathe in case he displaces the brilliant idea that is forming in his mind. He is already calling it The Gandhi Technique. It is a marvellous way to get a woman into bed. He finds himself going through a leisurely selection process. This sustains his exhilarated optimism for fully half an hour until realism intrudes like a burglar into the privacy of his meditation.

To make the technique work, you first of all have to become more or less world-famous. It is dependent on the veneration of others, their preparedness to believe whatever you say is your motivation. That seems to let him out.

When he explains to them the lofty reasons why they must come to bed with him, his eyes brimming with religious sincerity, he can't imagine any of the girls at the dancing saying, 'I hear and obey, o holy one.' No. Such divine lack of scepticism doesn't go along with a woollen sweater to accentuate your tits, a tight cotton skirt and cigarettes and matches held in one hand while you dance forehead to forehead with a plumber's mate. And there must be few people who have ever jitterbugged themselves on to a plane of metaphysical understanding. Perhaps when he is famous and revered throughout the world, the technique may provide him with a pleasant way to pass his seventies. But at the age of seventeen it's about as useful to him as a French letter to a eunuch.

The vision disperses. The embers have died in the fire. The room has lost its magic, gone grey again. This isn't the enchanted land where sex can happen. It's 14 Dawson Street, Graithnock. The drab furniture mocks him with the unchangeable ordinariness of his life. It isn't going to happen, it tells him. Whatever you thought would happen, it won't.

He huddles down in his bed, feeling suddenly cold. What's the betting even his dreams are in black and white?

THAT WOULD BE TOWARDS THE BEGINNING of the summer of the kiln, before the weather warmed. Otherwise, why would the fire have been on? He sat in his flat near the Water of Leith and he could hear a ringing phone. But he knew that it wasn't ringing here. It was ringing in Grenoble, in the darkness. Perhaps he shouldn't have answered it. But what else could you do? And that call he received led to others he must make.

'NE QUITTEZ PAS,' the woman's voice had said.

No, he wouldn't be *quittez*-ing. Fat chance. He was joined to whatever dull information she would give him about flights as compulsively and inexorably as he was joined to the boy thinking of Mahatma Gandhi on his bed.

They might cut the umbilicus but you carried your end of it

in you everywhere, even here in Grenoble. The first place you left followed somewhere behind you always, like a lover who couldn't bear to part, so that you could spend the rest of your life going back to take repeated farewells of it and thinking, 'Why the hell can't you leave me alone? It's over now. That's not who I am any more.'

But it was. It always was. You can't disown your past without becoming no one. He felt that now, holding the phone. He would go back in body now as he had gone back so often in his head. Perhaps he had never really left.

The woman told him some times of flights from Paris to London. He could busk it from there. He thanked her and the '*merci*' sounded ambiguous in his mouth, plea as well as thanks. Forgive me, old places, old times. I may have been untrue. For now he had to go back not just across space but across time, to the summer when, effectively, he left.

HE SHOULD HAVE KNOWN, even as it happened, that he would always think of that summer as one of the definitive seasons of his life, its seemingly dull colours made not less but more vivid with time, and he was someone realising in retrospect that what might have been mistaken for the ordinary was the unique travelling incognito.

He would have been inclined, for example, to think that memory had made the weather impossibly bright, like a crude restorer retouching old scenes with anachronistic new paint, except that he knew the newspapers of that time had been given to stating that this was the hottest Scottish summer since records were kept. That scientific fact was objective confirmation of something he had felt subjectively. This summer wasn't just special to him. It was special of itself.

Maybe he needed that summer to be so lambent, he would think in Edinburgh, so clear in the memory because it mattered so much to him, had become a kind of magnetic north of the mind from which he subsequently took his bearings. Maybe he had made the summer as much as the summer had made him.

But, if so, it was an honest making. Being unable to remember everything, memory is obliged to edit. And even the passion with which we misremember may be a kind of truth, an error which, in pushing aside a surface fact, may admit light to the darker reaches of wish and longing where our natures most intensely live.

Then he would realise that, while all such memories were somehow *about* that summer, they were by no means all memories *of* that summer. That interested him. It was as if that summer were a kind of lodestone of his experience up to that time, drawing all previous memory towards these few warm months and defining its significance in relation to them.

The moments might seem to come back haphazardly. But no matter how aimlessly they drifted into his consciousness, he knew they related somehow to that summer. They led him to that time, pointing him – in their confused and preoccupied ways – towards the direction he had needed to take to search for himself.

The searching would probably never be over while he had breath and the wit to understand what was going on around him. But those wandering memories all seemed to converge for him, as at the cross of a ghost town, in the summer where perhaps the search had seriously begun. Before then he suspected that he had merely happened, like a series of accidents. This was the summer when he started learning to become himself.

THIS WAS 1955. This was a different time and a different place.

This was when he was seventeen and experience was coming at him like flak. Everything seemed to be beginning, perhaps because there was nothing he had managed to finish yet, unless you counted school. He was such a welter of impressions, he never seemed actually to go places. He always found himself in them. Everything was an ambush – a girl's face, the shape of a tree, a film, a book that was going to change his life, a cripple seen in the street, a girl's face.

This was when he was still a virgin and determined not to be one. But he was a secret virgin. Outside, he had some of the mannerisms of a man of the world. He could smoke like Humphrey Bogart.

This wasn't too long after he had given up the compulsion to write on bits of paper: Thomas Mathieson Docherty, 14 Dawson Street, Longpark, Graithnock, Ayrshire, West of Scotland, Scotland, Great Britain, Europe, the Northern Hemisphere, the World, the Solar System, the Universe, the Cosmos, Eternity. Maybe he was trying to work out where he was.

This was the summer of the kiln, a ghetto in time, when rock 'n' roll was just a whispered rumour of new things and divorce was something he thought people did in America and sometimes people visited a house to see a television set and post-war rationing had ended and drugs were pills you bought at the chemist and the town had seven cinemas, each showing a main feature and a supporting feature twice weekly, and sex was a fabulous mystery and radio was a major force in most households and the presence of Cran hung over his life like the coming of the Kraken and cigarettes were stylish and one of his many ambitions was to be a writer and cars were what other people had and Maddie Fitzpatrick was his unattainable ideal of what a woman should be and the world seemed as young as he was and Sammy Clegg would ask him every so often, 'Have ye done it yet?'

This was when, regardless of the weather outside, he lived in a private climate where it was always raining questions. Everything in him and around him seemed to be in doubt.

How could the Christian God be just if the ancient Greeks were born too early to know about Jesus? How can we bear to go on living if we are certain to die? Did Margaret Inglis not know that every time she stooped or leaned over, he could see, like a draped sculpture, her incredible shape, and he wanted to pull up her skirt, ease down her pants and put his hands on those bare mounds of flesh, regardless of what happened afterwards? If she found out, would she tell the police? If Alexander the Great hadn't cut the Gordian knot, would civilisation be different? Is it possible to get syphilis from a lavatory seat? If it is, will he die of a sexual disease before he manages to have sex? If he does, is there reincarnation? Why did Oscar Wilde change his name to Sebastian Melmoth? What's the point of plooks in the great scheme of things? Where is Macao? Why does he keep a secret notebook in which he writes down quotations and one-sentence reviews of books he hasn't written yet (his favourite is 'Makes Tolstoy look like a miniaturist') and thoughts about experience? What experience? Why has he started writing imaginary notes in his head to dead or fictional people? Dead letters, right enough. Is he mad? Will he ever get past being seventeen?

Seventeen – that doesn't feel like a year, it feels like a decade, one of those years you think you'll never get out of. Time doesn't seem to go forward. It seems to go round and round, an endless stationary journey in which he keeps coming back to the same places, has to wrestle with the same insoluble problems. His only chronology seems to be perpetual now, mind-shadowed by the future and the past. Now. And now. And now.

AND NOW HE IS PLAYING FOOTBALL in the Kay Park. It is late June. An empty Sunday has suddenly filled with raucous voices and the thud of foot on leather. The goalposts are discarded jackets. Sweat binds them together into a fierce intensity. Time stops. Everything contracts to reflex and instinct – move left, turn, release the ball, collect the ball. People are shapes that loom and recede, colliding energies. Nothing else matters. There is only the game. They make a small conspiracy there in the pale sunshine, twenty-odd disparate teenagers who have melted the complexity of things down into brute energy, a brief, invented passion whose relevance is consumed in its happening.

'Next goal wins,' somebody shouts.

And they score. His side has won 15–14.

They collapse on the grass and become themselves again. It was only a game of football after all and it has solved nothing for him. He is ejected suddenly out of the almost mystical completeness the game had given him into the tics and worries of his individuality. As if he has just descended from a different planetary sphere, he sees the strangeness of his fellow earthlings. Beef Bowman's attempt to grow a moustache makes his upper lip look like a caterpillar when he talks. Tommy Sutton's glass eye stares at

Tam accusingly. Many years ago he pinned Tommy to the ground and wouldn't let him up until he had explained to him what was different about his eye. The thought of it now is a double scar on his memory: nobody has the right to be as insensitive as he was and no writer should be that dumb. Sammy Clegg is passing his laughter among the group as if it were an alms-cup – like me, like me. Tam does.

They are talking in a desultory way, conversational jazz, a thought thrown out, taken up, developed, moved on from. Two girls pass in the park, fifty yards away. Shouted invitations are issued. They discuss the girls' departing shapes as if they had a right to. He participates but his remarks are not really him. They are the camouflage he wears.

An altogether different conversation is taking place inside his head. It is an endless hubbub of voices in there, a talking multitude who seem to him to have been at it as long as he can remember. Will they ever agree about anything? There are countless suggestions about what he should be. For, although it was decided by someone in him when he was fourteen that he should be a writer, this is a decision which is constantly under review. There are so many other possibilities. He often wonders why that other, distant summer afternoon, when he lay on the grass of the back green, should be allowed to have such a definitive effect upon his life.

He discovered *The Three Musketeers* and the day fused. The sun receded to a night-light. He became D'Artagnan and Ayrshire was Gascony. Called in for a meal that had nothing to do with him, he found it awkward to sit at the table with his sword on.

He has never been the same since. His world has become interwoven with the world of books, to the frequent confusion of himself. Besides reading with manic ferocity, he has been trying to write and his mind has become a literary salon where Hemingway argues with Dickens and Dumas with one book of Jane Austen and Kafka will barely nod to anyone. And his mother keeps butting in too and his father and people he meets in the street and things he reads in the paper and everybody, all talking through one another. It's chaos in here. How is he supposed to sort things out?

Maybe he should just try and become a professional footballer.

That would simplify things. The man who runs the amateur team he has played for has said he thinks Tam could do that and Smudger, the gym teacher at Graithnock Academy, told him more than once he had a natural and exceptional talent for the game. But how do you combine that with writing a masterpiece? It isn't easy.

Besides, what he gets out of playing football has no practical application that he can see. It's not about tactics and wearing down the opposition and hitting on the break. It's a feeling. It's a feeling of belonging, of things being right. He reaches a place where he just loves the sound of feet striking the ball, the hastened breathing, the shared exertion. This will do, he thinks. This will do for the time being. He doesn't want the game to end. He doesn't even care too much what the score is. He doesn't think that would go down too well with a professional team. He can imagine coming into the dressing-room after playing for Graithnock FC.

('What a feeling, eh? That was some feeling. Did you get that feeling? That sense of the rightness of things? I hope I can get that feeling again next week. And maybe we won't lose 10–0 next week as well.'

The dressing-room reverberates with delighted laughter and applause.)

That's a definite problem he has. His sense of purpose is always being waylaid by the moment for its own sake. He remembers once in an examination he was going well when he happened to glance up from the question he was answering. He saw the examination room filled with frozen sunlight. It was beautiful and the bowed heads had the dignity of statues – a boy with his hand on his neck and a girl's dark hair falling, screening her face. He knew in that instant that everybody here was their own purpose and their preoccupation with other things was missing the point. He wanted to get up and share his revelation with everyone, declare a celebration of just being there. He didn't but he must have lost at least twenty minutes in purposeless wonderment. It was lucky he passed.

Maybe that was one of the reasons he hadn't made it all the way with a girl yet. The underground oral Handbook of Machismo they passed among them might have programmed

him for merciless seduction but the way she smiled would render
him idiot with enjoyment or the soft flesh of her upper arm would
delay him indefinitely and he would forget what he was supposed
to do. Why is he like this?

VORFREUDE?

GRETE TAUGHT HIM THE WORD, he would remember in
Edinburgh. Never having learned German, much to his regret
(Ancient Greek had much to answer for in his life), he seized on
the word as if it might somehow help to plug him into German
culture, rather like a day-tripper to Boulogne trying to convince
himself that he has explored France. The Greeks had a word
for it, they said. He would often think, with sorrow for missed
opportunities: no, the Germans did. *Schadenfreude. Doppelgänger.
Zeitgeist. Weltschmerz.*

Vorfreude. 'Pre-joy', she said it meant. He didn't catch any
nuances since they were both naked in a wood near Cramond
at the time, and the picnic basket didn't contain a dictionary and
the wine said school's out and the finer points of connotation
were not their chief concern just then. But the word stayed with
him and acquired in his mind the accretions of private meaning
he quite wilfully gave it. Often when he thought of it, it came
attended by slats of sunlight pushing through thick trees. It was
the least of the gifts she gave him but, as a smoothed stone found
casually on a beach may stand as cipher for a bright and happy
day, it reminded him of them. And just as that stone may become
something it was never intended to be, such as a paperweight, so
he was never to be sure what precise relevance the word had to
the use he made of it.

In his private dictionary it didn't just mean anticipation or
expectation. It was a means of bringing into focus a tendency
which had troubled him since childhood. It was a lens through

which to see more clearly an error of which he was too guilty, an experiential tic he would have liked to cure. His *Vorfreude* meant the imagining of a coming intensity of experience which no actual set of circumstances could quite deliver, a kind of over-rehearsal for life.

Was this the source of his many impressive achievements in the genre of social mayhem? How often had his despondent anger turned a dinner party or a night out with friends or an arranged celebration or a conversation in a pub into the Somme in civvies and left him firing at will at any head that came above the parapet? Did the root cause lie in the fact that the event had yet again failed to live up to his overblown idea of what it should be? That seemed far too simple.

There was, for a start, the booze. When he had enough to drink, he could imagine that somebody who nodded to him was trying to put the head on him. Midges of perception developed messianic delusions. Small, slighting references inflated to amazing proportions until the air was filled with barrage balloons of insult. All you needed to do to cure that was to stop drinking as much.

And yet. Drink might render the form of expression grotesque. But sobriety didn't eradicate the content which the form had obscured with its exaggerations. After such times, he always felt guilty. But there still nearly always flickered within the guilt, a minnow in a murky pond, something of what he had felt which refused to die, refused to succumb completely to the condemnations of others. And he somehow knew that, if it did, if it finally went belly-up with the toxin of other people's idea of him, he would lose a crucial part of his sense of himself and start to imitate who they expected him to be.

It was the extremity of the form, he kept thinking, which had been wrong – not what he saw but the way that he said it. If he thought somebody was full enough of his own shit to start a sewage farm, he could perhaps find a better way to say it. Perhaps. His intellectual and emotional antennae were preposterously sensitive. There was nothing wrong in that. What was wrong was what he did with the effects of that sensitivity. He demanded too much from people and events.

He had always suffered, he decided, from a kind of elephantiasis of the occasion, wanting an event to be bigger than it could be and to bear more weight of human truth than it could possibly bear. When it collapsed under the strain, he was inclined to shoot it (usually without a silencer) to put it out of *his* misery. That was hardly fair.

He must do something about that, about his *Vorfreude*. Maybe that had been part of the problem between Gill and him. Maybe what he had been expecting of marriage had always been unrealisable. Perhaps she just got tired of living with Peter Pan. She certainly got tired of his social tantrums. Eventually, she developed a technique of setting them up in public.

There were two basic methods involved. One way was to initiate a topic in company about which they had both reached agreement in private. Once he had started to expatiate on their shared position in the matter, she would suddenly abandon it, inviting everybody else to join her. His outrage would leave him like a dancing bear, frothing slightly and bumping into the furniture. Such occasions made him think that he could always have behaved more properly towards her in public if only he had never had to meet her in private.

The other way was to introduce a subject, or at least seize on one, about which she knew he was likely to disagree with everyone else. It came to be as if, unable to stop his tendency to go over the top in argument, she decided to stage-manage it. Mrs Barnum. Presenting My Husband, The Man Whose Reactions Overflow Every Context. He Will Now Attempt To Stage An Opera In A Phone Box.

He would laugh to himself when he thought of those occasions. Happy Times. His memory had a library of them, all filed under C for catastrophe. Pluck out any one, it would show the same, recurrent symptoms – like the dinner party before they had gone for that year to Grenoble. By that time, Tam had been reclassified as Tom in the mouths of most of his friends, perhaps in an attempt to confer a status more befitting a teacher. Gill invited his headmaster at that time and his wife, Brian and Elspeth Alderston. Tom had made the mistake of telling Gill that Brian had singled him out as someone he wanted to push for promotion. He had taken Tom into his office twice to say he thought Tom had 'headmaster potential'. He said it as if he were bestowing a knighthood. Tom thought it sounded like a disease for, judging by the deterioration he observed in most teachers who were promoted to headmasterships, he had decided it was a job you didn't get so much as contract.

But Gill was determined to lay the ground for their return from France before they left, which seemed to Tom rather to contradict what was supposed to be the ground-breaking boldness of the move in the first place.

'LET'S DO SOMETHING ADVENTUROUS, DARLING – I'll bring the insurance policies.'

THE MEAL HAD BEEN GOOD. If only they could have eaten it in silence. Brian and Gill were engaged in a very unsubtle conspiracy, like whispering through a tannoy. Brian said things about Tom 'getting it out of his system' and 'career consolidation'. Gill talked about when they had 'done the Bohemian bit'. They dangled the prospect of a dazzling career in teaching before Tom as if it weren't a contradiction in terms, while Elspeth kept chiming in with details of Brian's meteoric rise from assistant teacher to headmaster in twenty-five years.

Tom experienced a feeling that had been becoming more and more familiar since Gill had completed her course in cordon bleu cookery. It was a feeling of being caught in a montage sequence from a film he didn't want to be in, a dinner-time equivalent of the breakfast scene in *Citizen Kane*. He seemed to be for ever at the dinner table arguing with people and every time he looked up from his plate he was arguing with someone different and, while the plates came and went, he knew himself aging remorselessly.

That turned him sullen and his sullenness began to show.

Gill caught the feeling and reciprocated generously. She had been for a long time getting weary of the vagueness of Tom's ambitions. A quarrel of mood was already happening. Any healthy married couple can quarrel about anything. They have so many related resentments all over the place that, once they feel they're going to a quarrel, they jump on any excuse like the first bus that comes along. It doesn't matter where it's going, their anger is sure to find a home there.

Gill had set up this whole evening to convince Brian Alderston of his wisdom in spotting Tom as an heir apparent and he was coming across like a boor. He resented having their house used to tout for professional support. He never entertained the boss. If he didn't come as a friend and no more, he could stay away. Their motives were already there. They were only looking for the pretext. When they found it, it must have seemed to an outsider as daft as the War of Jenkins' Ear.

They were in the lounge when the guns went off. He thought he remembered it pretty well. He had exceptional recall. A critic had once said of him that he was one on whom nothing is lost. A lot of the time he wished it wasn't so. He wouldn't have minded losing a lot of the stuff he remembered.

They were in the lounge. Brian was nursing a Remy Martin. Gill and Elspeth were drinking Cointreau. Tom was on the good old whisky, bottled aggression. They were all boring one another politely to death in the usual way – around the world in eighty clichés.

('Blah,' someone would say.
'Blah?'
'Blah.'
'Surely blah, blah.'
'No. Blah.'
'Blah? What about unblah?'
'Yes, unblah.'
'No. Blah.'
'I think what we all mean is half-blah, half-unblah. Eh?'
'Of course.'
'That's it. Half-blah, half-unblah.'
'Or, if you like, half-unblah, half-blah.'
'Ha, ha, ha, ha, ha.')

It was all slightly less interesting than an Andy Warhol film when Elspeth innocently released the safety-catch. Elspeth would. She had the dangerous innocence of the truly boring.

What makes boring people dangerous is that they keep forgetting that other people are present. They wander through life in a kind of holy idiocy, believing that the rest of the world's population consists entirely of ears. Ears never take offence. Only the entities attached to them do that. Thus, your bore is always amazed at causing trouble. You were only there to listen, after all. Nobody asked you to react.

To be fair to Elspeth, she didn't really say anything wrong. The way Gill and Tom were feeling about each other at that moment, if Elspeth had said, 'I love you both,' they would have been snarling at her to make her choice and stop hedging her bets. What she did say was, 'Sandra Hayes. There's someone I would say is beautiful.'

'I pass,' Tom said.

Gill raised her head slightly and turned it towards him at a quizzical angle. As a veteran combatant, he knew war had been declared.

Sandra Hayes was one of those handy instant quarrels married couples always have in stock in case they haven't time for a three-course barney. She was pre-cooked disagreement. Elspeth wasn't to know it but, between Gill and Tom, Sandra had often stood in for an hour too long in the pub or no clean shirts or a day of small frustrations. Part of her usefulness was that she crystallised differences in their attitudes, the incompatibility of their tastes. She was the painting Gill insisted on hanging up that made Tom puke.

Sandra had been a friend of Gill's for a long time. She was one of those enigmas of the life they were leading he didn't expect ever to understand. She was spectacularly popular. People kept festooning her with words it seemed to Tom she contradicted almost perfectly. 'Beautiful' was one. People kept calling her that. She had, it seemed to Tom, a kind of shallow prettiness. Fair enough. But if we keep breathing reverently that our Sandra Hayes are beautiful, what are we going to say about Greta Garbo? 'Witty' was another. Sandra was trivially facetious. But then, to be fair, so were a lot of people he knew who were given this accolade. True wit is one of the great weapons of the spirit, he thought, a refusal to surrender to experience – not picking your neighbour's pocket. 'Vitality,' they said of Sandra, and appeared to Tom to mean supermarket enthusiasm. Sandra enthused about everything. Show her any top and she would go over it. She created oral poems to wall plaques and new refrigerators. 'Very intelligent,' people said, and he had never heard Sandra utter an original or perceptive remark. If Sandra should ever have an original idea, he pitied it, for it would die a lonely death in search of company in there.

He had to draw back a bit because it wasn't Sandra he resented. What he resented was the burden of false glamour Sandra was made to carry. It was what she represented in the life he found himself living that he resented. For although the quarrel Gill and he had about her that night seemed irrelevant and disproportionate, it wasn't quite as irrelevant or disproportionate as it seemed. They knew in a way what they were talking about, although they couldn't expect anybody else to.

The reason Sandra had been one focus for their quarrels hadn't entirely escaped their comprehension. She was valid battleground. What their friends did with Sandra Hayes was, Tom thought, what they tried to do with life generally and it was something he had been fighting against for a long time. In falsifying Sandra, they were falsifying their sense of their own lives. In elevating her, they were elevating themselves. It was a simple act of cultural appropriation.

One way to avoid the awesomeness of mountains is to live where it is flat as far as the eye can see and never travel. Psychologically, that's what their way of life was doing. If Sandra Hayes was beautiful, then you could find your Naked Majas and Olympias on page three. If she was very intelligent, then so were they, because they could appreciate her intelligence. By an inverted alchemy, they could transmute the rare gold of the world into the ubiquitous base metal of their own lives.

Ah, the polite viciousness of bourgeois life that with false generosity to some bestows mediocrity upon all. The key is language. When words depreciate, our awarenesses go with them. Intensity dilutes and a gantry of potent spirits is replaced by the insipid afternoon tea of complacency. He supposed Sandra was for him some kind of high priestess of that decadent cult.

For a long time he had felt himself a heretic among them, writing his own apocrypha – not just in the books he had published. He had developed such anti-social tendencies that he had started to write a sort of private dictionary, a notebook where he tried to establish his own understandings, his own definitions of honour and pride and tragedy. This notebook was his conspiracy with himself, a linguistic revolutionary caucus of one. He had shown it to no one but that hadn't stopped Gill from finding it. Fortunately, she seemed to have skim-read it, so that her mockery was generalised and felt a bit like being beaten with a loofah.

'Sandra Hayes *is* beautiful,' Gill said.

'I pass,' Tom said again.

Did he hell! But he might as well let Gill start the fight. He liked counter-punching.

'She *is* beautiful.'

He was aware of Elspeth glancing at Brian, baffled by the tension she had created. Brian responded by adopting a jocular interventionist voice.

'Who's this we're talking about, you two?'

'Sandra Hayes,' Gill said as if that explained everything.

'You know her, Brian,' Elspeth said.

'Who?'

'Sandra Hayes!'

There followed a fairly long discussion between Elspeth and Brian about who Sandra Hayes was. It was one of those 'That party where the woman fainted' conversations, getting lost among memories that led to other memories that became a labyrinth where everybody seemed to be wandering except Sandra Hayes. Brian steadfastly didn't know her. You could see the suspicion begin to grow in Elspeth that Brian was being deliberately obtuse. She was becoming querulous, perhaps convinced that he was hiding from his responsibility to take her side. How could he defend her opinion of Sandra Hayes if he couldn't remember her? She was getting so exasperated that she was going in for a little role reversal – the headmaster as dumb primary pupil.

'You're always doing that,' she said. 'Your memory's pathetic.'

It looked as though they might be having a doubles match. It occurred to Tom that Brian might be consciously teasing things out to give Gill and him time to cool down. It was possible.

Like most modern headmasters, he suffered from the Pontius Pilate syndrome, mentally washing his hands a hundred times a day. If that was his ploy, it didn't work. By the time Elspeth had established Brian's immutable stupidity to the satisfaction of the company, Gill was still waiting to impugn Tom's character.

'I hate it when you tell a deliberate lie,' she said.

'It's not a lie. It's what I think.'

'What weird taste you must have!'

'Careful. You're going to walk right into your own insult. Let's leave it, Gill. You send your Valentines, I'll send mine.' Sweet reasonableness, one of the most effective incitements to rage. 'I just don't think Sandra's beautiful. And I'm sure she'll manage fine without my homage.'

Brian laughed. Elspeth didn't.

'That seems a reasonable compromise,' Brian said. Accurate observation wasn't his strong point.

Gill was walking down some private road to confrontation. She took a ladylike gulp of her Cointreau.

'Tell me one thing about her that isn't beautiful,' she said.

Brian laughed. Tom was aware of the depressing familiarity of that laugh, waved about in times of crisis like a flag of truce. He ignored it and concentrated on Gill's question.

'One thing?'

'One thing.'

They might have been two gunmen daring each other to draw.

'I'll tell you two,' he said.

The room was ridiculously tense, as if a great revelation were at hand.

'Tell me.'

'Her eyes.'

'Her eyes?'

'Her eyes.'

'Sandra Hayes' eyes?'

'Sandra Hayes' amazing actual eyes. Those things she's got one on each side of her nose. Only in her case only just.'

Gill looked at Elspeth and Brian and shrugged with a falsely beatific smile and sadly shook her head. That headshake was a small opera. Behold, it sang, my grief. Thou seest me married badly to a man of infinite malice. My tiny heart is broken. But she recovered quickly.

Holding her left hand slightly towards Brian and Elspeth as if making sure they were paying proper attention to Tom's next enormity, Gill said sweetly, 'And what is it that's wrong with her eyes?'

Realising already that in this conversation he had been modified from a bus into a tramcar, he released the brake and started towards his predetermined destination.

'They're too close together.'

'Too close together?'

If it's a crash, he thought vaguely through the whisky, let's make it a good one.

'As if they were planning a merger.'

Gill gave what might have been mistaken for a laugh. It was a high, harsh, sudden sound, as jolly as an axe embedding itself in a skull. Right, he thought. If that's the way you want it.

'Another quarter of an inch and she would have been a Cyclops.'

The displaced cruelty marriage can give rise to appalled him even as he expressed it. You're so determined to get at your partner, you trample over innocent people to do it. Sandra was really quite attractive. Why did he have to scrawl his graffiti all over her face?

'Who the hell do you think you are?' Gill shouted. 'Robert Redford?'

'No. I don't kid myself. I'm not entering any beauty contests. It was you that put Sandra in for one.'

'That takes me to the fair. It really does. Men.' Gill was looking solely at Elspeth now. Brian was being helplessly herded into the same pen as Tom for slaughter. 'They think they've got the right to sit there and pass judgment. It doesn't matter that they look like something the cat brought in.'

'You *asked* my opinion. I don't have any illusions about me.'

'Don't have any illusions? I've seen you shaving.'

'Sorry?'

'I've seen you shaving.'

'Please, darling. Not such intimate secrets in front of our guests.'

'You know what I mean. The way you look at yourself.'

'That's quite a handy thing to do when you're shaving. What do you want me to do? Shave with the light out?'

'The *way* you look at yourself. From this side and that side. Head back, head forward.'

'Jesus Christ!'

Elspeth froze. She hated swearing. He had heard Brian say 'Damn!' once. He thought it was during an earthquake.

'Uh-huh,' Gill was saying. 'For someone who seems to be so ugly, Sandra's done all right for herself.'

Tom's advance observation post went into action, assessing the range. He knew where the next attack was coming from. She was shifting position to hit him where he was weakest, as the successful provider, the man who was all for his family. She was also bringing Brian in behind her (she already had Elspeth) with the heavy artillery. The big guns of 'career consolidation' were trundling behind her.

'Look at the husband *she* has.'

He needed a pre-emptive strike. First obliterate Elspeth – one fewer to worry about. Then a diversionary tactic.

'Oh, Jesus, Jesus Christ!' he said. Elspeth took both barrels and spoke no more. 'Before this conversation finishes up being conducted in Sanskrit. Two things. I didn't *say* Sandra was ugly. And I'd rather not look at Ted Hayes. If I can help it.'

'What? Is there something wrong with Ted Hayes now?'

It had worked. He concealed his success under exasperation.

'Holy bejesus!'

'It's incredible.'

'Hear, hear.'

'It's incredible. According to you, there's something wrong with everybody. God and I both feel . . .' She hit home there. It wasn't that he thought there was something wrong with everybody but he couldn't see the amazing rightness that everybody else seemed to see. He was aware of an awful lot wrong with him – but what exactly? Gill was always ready to help him with that one. 'You're a creep. You don't approve of Ted Hayes either? Is there something wrong with him?'

'Aye! As a matter of fact there is. He would bore the shite out you at a hundred yards. That's what's wrong with him. If they bottled him, they could sell him in Boots the chemist. As a bloody sedative!'

'No, you wouldn't approve of him, would you?'

'He's a uxorious wee turd.'

'Oh, we're on the Eng. Lit. words now, are we? "Uxorious." But the last one let you down a bit, didn't it? Like a birthmark. Uxorious! That just means he's nice to his wife. Doesn't it? Of course, I can see how that would be an insult in your vocabulary.'

'What it means is he runs after her like a wee waiter. He probably bottles her farts for posterity. He needs her round him like an oxygen tent. If she goes out the room for five minutes, poor wee bugger's gaspin' for breath.'

He was cresting the hill of his rage like Alaric the Goth. But suddenly Rome was shut for the night. Gill sat back without warning and sighed and shook her head with something that looked like sad contentment. It seemed she hadn't been taking part in an argument, just a demonstration. He stood fully caparisoned with no enemy in sight, only some bemused tourists thinking: 'Look at that funny man. Why is he so excited?'

Childe Roland had come to the dark tower and set his slug-horn to his lips and the tower had disappeared. Hm. Well. All he could think of to do was give the solitude he found himself in a final defiant blast.

'Anyway,' Gill was saying to Elspeth and Brian. 'They seem happy. *Their* lives are completely unruffled.'

'So they should be,' he said, unnecessarily loudly. 'They're as good as dead. Nothing out of the ordinary's ever going to happen there. Any time life comes near wee Ted, it falls asleep.'

The room went quiet,

AS QUIET AS A ROOM IN EDINBURGH, to which his seem-ingly incurable discontent with things would bring him. He stared at the fading, leafy pattern on the carpet. It might have been an old forest he was lost in. Was there some wrong turning he had taken when he was young? Perhaps seeing so many films in his boyhood and adolescence had helped to confuse him about who he was. Maybe his multiple-identity problem came, in the first place, from growing up in a small town where there were seven cinemas.

There was the Plaza and there was the Empire and the Regal and the Palace and the Savoy and the George and the Forum. He found something appropriate in the grandeur of the names, the way they resonated in his head. For these were embassies of world experience located in his home town. Just by entering their doors he could learn, however haltingly, the foreign inflections of other people's lives, usually translated very wilfully into a broad American idiom that became his second language.

His favourite was the Savoy because, having fallen on hard times and being very run-down, it never showed the new films. It recycled old pictures endlessly and it would be much later that he would realise why that battered building had meant so much to him, why he would always remember with affection the wooden benches for children at the front (where, if a friend arrived late, you could always make a space for him by a group of you sliding along in concert and knocking off whoever was sitting at the end of the bench) and the padded seats that sometimes spilled their wiry guts like a device to keep you awake during the film.

It had been, without his knowing it, his personal art cinema, where he could re-read films the way he could re-read books and develop unselfconsciously his own aesthetic of the movies and confirm what kind of man he was going to be, what kind of woman he would marry. He watched and listened attentively, his face pale as a pupa in the back-glow from the screen while the gigantic figures raged and kissed and taught him passion and style and insouciance and stoicism, before he knew the words for them.

'FRANKLY, MY DEAR, I DON'T GIVE A DAMN,' Clark Gable tells Tam more than once.

'Made it, Ma – top o' the world,' James Cagney seems often to be shouting.

'Do you always think you can handle people like, eh, trained seals?' Lauren Bacall says.

'Where do the noses go?'

'Never's gonna be too much soon for me, Shorty.'

'Does that clarinet player have no soul?'

'We are all involved.'

'By Gad, sir, you're a chap worth knowing. 'Namazing character. Give me your hat.'

'Get yourself a phonograph, jughead. I'm with him.'

And Garbo stares at him and Ava Gardner lounges barefoot. Peter Ustinov preserves his tears in a phial. Charlton Heston fights Jack Palance to the death. Rhonda Fleming makes him wish for a machine by which you can grow up instantly because he is going to be too late. And Cagney shrugs and Bogart's lip curls over his top teeth and Silvana Mangano is standing in a paddy-field and he would die to be standing beside her.

In his head the endless voices are talking like so many crossed transatlantic lines he will sometime unscramble and the endless images move in and out of one another like a phantom selfhood he will one day discover how to make flesh. There in the darkness he is secretly practising himself.

So he has already been in love with many women, though nobody knows it, not even the women. He must have the most promiscuous mind in the world. Their names are a private harem: Greta and Rhonda and Alida and Lilli and Viveca and Lana and Ava and Olivia and Paulette and Vivien and Hedy and Maureen and Silvana and Sophia and Gina and Ingrid and . . . He is a virginal roué, he realises with horror when he discovers the word 'roué'. (He has hoped that Frank Sinatra never learns about him and Ava, for he seems to be an angry wee man.)

If they ever found out about him, he would have a board of censors all to himself. Even Margaret Dumont, the big woman in the Marx Brothers' films, has evoked some stirrings in him. There is something in that statuesque presence that makes him want to climb it.

But it is true that Marjorie Main has so far remained immune to his talent for falling in love. He *likes* Ma Kettle but he doesn't love her. This gives him some hope for himself. Hope that he may survive his own promiscuity (and avoid dying of mental sexual exhaustion before he is twenty) is further confirmed by the fact that, no matter how often his affections stray, he keeps coming back to Greta Garbo. He is not sure why this should be but it has something to do with the way her gaze seems to him like a continent he would love to explore.

He has been more faithful to the screen men in his life. James Cagney was probably the first actor he adopted as his secondary father, then Errol Flynn, then Bogart. But they have turned out only to be surrogates for John Garfield, his man of men. It isn't just that Garfield does look a little, it seems to him, like his real father. It is that Garfield exudes a style that might have come off the streets where Tam is living. Of all his heroes, Garfield translates most easily into his own idiom. Tam feels as if he's seen him at the dancing.

Recently, though, Garfield's pre-eminence has been under threat. When Tam saw *On the Waterfront*, he knew immediately that Marlon Brando was the best actor he had ever seen. In fact, he decided he knew that Marlon Brando was the best actor anybody had ever seen. And when James Dean loped through *East of Eden*, he became instantly iconic in Tam's thoughts.

Still, Garfield may be dead but he lives on, his place not quite usurped, there beside Greta Garbo. This summer is still theirs. When he feels he has been kidding himself about the significance of yet another girl, he thinks of Greta Garbo. When he senses himself threatened by the arrogance of yet another hard-case, John Garfield stands beside him.

—AFTERWARDS, he would be living alone in an attic flat in the Boulevard Haussmann in Paris. It was a bitter winter and lonely as a cabin in the Yukon. He shivered in his eyrie and went out into the cold for coffees and *tartines beurrées* to eke his money out and came back in to the novel he was working on and it sat staring at him silently as if it were a former friend who didn't wish to speak to him any more.

But François, the man who had loaned him the flat, had the French intellectual's passion to make a library of experience.

He had one room full of books and tapes of old films and pornographic magazines. One of the books was a biography of John Garfield. Reading it, he knew he had been right about Jules Garfinkel all those years ago. He still loved this man, his trying to stay true to where he came from, the intensity of his political beliefs, the passionate dishevelment of his life, the dread of betraying his friends that finally burst his heart and left him lying dead in an awkward place before he had time to testify in front of the Un-American Activities Committee.

There were no tapes of Garfield's films, which was maybe just as well, for he feared looking at former magic and finding it had been reduced to a few tricks. But there was the book of John Garfield's life and it talked him through a part of that winter like a friendly ghost. If you're in the shit, it said, I've been there too. Remember the way I was? And he did. How he entered rooms as if he were challenging their contents; the jutting face that prowed bravely into whatever was happening like a ship cleaving unknown waters; the hurt puzzlement of the eyes looking into their own wrongdoing.

He faced a bad time and stared it down. John Garfield helped. But he was still left wondering how far he had travelled towards being whoever he really was.—

MIRROR, MIRROR, ON THE WALL, Who the hell am I at all? He wondered how many times he had looked in a mirror for confirmation of himself. He was doing it again. He saw the reflection of the open suitcase that was behind him on the bed. His attempt at packing was a mess. Not only had he never learned to pack, he suspected he had never learned to unpack.

'What are you staring at, Dad?'

Megan stood in the doorway. She was giving him her own stare, those remorselessly innocent eyes that made him feel he was facing a plenary meeting of the Spanish Inquisition.

'Nothing, Meganio.'

'You were so.'

'No. Ah was just lookin'.'

'You were so. You were staring and staring. Into the mirror.'

'Ah wasn't really staring *and* staring. Ah was just staring. I was just checking I was there.'

That seemed to make sense to her.

'This it, Dad?'

She held up his toilet-bag.

'It is, it is. You are a total cracker.'

She came across and handed him the bag.

'I put things in.'

'Thank you, Princessa.'

He dropped the bag on the bed and, as he turned back, he noticed the self-containment of her standing there. He felt the utter wonder of her presence and he lifted her up and spun her in the air, laughing. She was smiling calmly. He set her down on the floor.

'Is that all?' she said.

'Well. Ah suppose it'll have to do. Where's Gus?'

She shrugged and walked out.

He picked up the toilet-bag. He smiled at how well Megan had done. Then he noticed that she had also included Gill's L'Air du Temps. He laughed to himself and put the perfume on the window-ledge. He looked at the open suitcase. Was that enough? He could never tell. At least he had his one formal suit in it. Just in case. Just in bloody case. He thought of taking the suit back out, for packing it felt like signing the death certificate already. You should never welcome the bad stuff. If it wanted to come in, let it beat the door down. No. The suit stayed. Superstition doesn't change the rules, it just lets you refuse to learn them. You have to learn them. Would he ever learn them?

He crossed to the window and looked out at Grenoble. He fingered the bottle of L'Air du Temps. Perhaps Megan thought his uncertainty about himself extended to gender. Or did she see him as inhabiting the same not quite reachable place of certainty where he had sensed his own father to be? He hoped not. He hoped it was different for girls. He hoped it would be different for Gus, too. He hadn't even been able to tell his father about Cran, though he had wanted to.

Two feelings had held him back, instinctively. The first was that it seemed unmanly. He was seventeen and had left school. He should be able to look after himself – too late to run home from the playground, picking hardened blood from your nostrils, to receive from your mother the sweet solace that the rest of the world is wrong and a plate of tattie soup that warms your insides like ointment for the soul, to receive from your father advice on the politics of fear and kitchen lessons on how to deliver a good left hook. There had to come a time when the womb was shut, owing to the fact of your being too big for effective re-entry. It was a pity, though.

The second was, paradoxically, that his father would have understood Cran and the cavernous brutishness where so much of his nature seemed to reside, littered with the bones of dead compassion. For part of his father, too, lived in those shadows. The very fact that his father would have recognised Cran, though he had never met him, had created in his mind a bond between the two men, one which excluded him. Somehow he must have sensed that you didn't gain admission to that dark brotherhood by invitation. You had to earn it for yourself. Somehow he had come to know it was his father most of all who blocked the entrance, shaking his head, acknowledging his own powerlessness to let Tam pass, implying with every spontaneous gesture of his nature that the only way past him was through him.

(There is a code of rules here I didn't make and don't control, he seemed to be saying, and the core of the code is this: no entry but by the force of your own nature. I will offer help but it will be weirdly codified help and it's down to you to crack the code. Take me on and win your entry. Don't and stay outside.)

IT IS SUNDAY MORNING

HE LIES AWAKE IN MICHAEL AND MARION'S BED, luxuriating. (As usual on a Saturday night, they have been staying at Marion's mother's.) He reflects on his talent for long, deep sleeps. He can do this even in the living-room with noise all around him. ('If sleep wis brains, son,' his father has said, not without a hint of jealousy, 'you'd be a genius.') He thinks of the girl he took home from the dancing last night. Marilyn Miller. It was pleasant – bruised lips and delicate adumbration of firm breasts. He has discovered the word 'adumbration' recently. He likes it. Adumbration. To adumbrate. He had done some adumbrating last night, but nothing more. Only adumbrators need apply was obviously Marilyn Miller's motto. Adumbration. One for the files. He would have to find an excuse for using the word in front of his father.

('Okay, smartarse, so ye've swallied a dictionary. Noo tell us whit ye mean.'

'Look, Feyther, I'm just tryin' to adumbrate this basic idea.')

Marilyn Miller. She has an auntie who lives in Melbourne and it seems that this auntie once lost a baby. The night before the miscarriage, Marilyn's auntie dreamt that a nun stood at the foot of her bed, sneering and shaking her head. That is amazing, isn't it? A prophetic dream, one that's definitely got the edge on Auntie Bella's dreams about nocturnal visits to the shops. Isn't it strange how two dances with a stranger can open doors on to experiences you never imagined? People are amazing.

Marilyn Miller. He likes her but he doesn't think they'll be trying it again. He's pretty sure Marilyn would prefer it that way. Everything was fine between them but nothing was more than fine. Nothing really happened, no thunderbolts, no tidal waves in the blood. It was more like a school trip to the seaside where the water remained too cold to do more than paddle and there was shared conversation like stale sandwiches. He is glad she introduced him to her auntie but he and she parted without having really met. Sorry, I thought you were someone else. He doesn't know who she mistook him for. But he suspects that he knows who she wasn't. Margaret Inglis. He sighs and thinks about getting up.

And Sir Alexander Fleming died this year. Penicillin. It must be wonderful to have discovered something that benefits the whole world. You could really say that Fleming changed the terms of human life. It's enough to make God get fidgety. And Fleming was born just a few miles from here, up the road in Darvel. An Ayrshireman did that. There's hope, there's hope. Tam remembers a newsreel where you saw Fleming in his laboratory. He was pottering about with a cigarette hanging from his mouth, like a man mending a fuse or something. He's seen his father like that when he was fixing a wireless or, in the case of Bryce the Grocer, blowing one up. He loves that image of Fleming. For him it's a symbol of the democracy of achievement. You don't need to have been born in a big estate or talk as if your mouth had piles or act pompously to achieve great things. Maybe it would be good to be a doctor. But would medical science ever discover an antidote to Margaret Inglis?

He gets up and pulls on a sweater and the trousers he was wearing to the dancing. He pads on bare feet downstairs and into the kitchen, where his mother makes him a cooked breakfast.

'Let 'im fend for himself! Breakfast's like a Jew's weddin' in here,' his father is shouting through from the living-room.

'Thank you, Pater,' Tam calls back. 'May I have the Bentley today?'

'A kick in the arse. That's what ye can have.'

Ah, the sweet, domestic sounds of a peaceful Sabbath. He is flicking through the *Sunday Post*.

He finishes his breakfast and decides that what he'll do is get the packet of ten Paymaster from his raincoat pocket in the lobby, go upstairs with the paper and have a quiet smoke, like a gentleman in his club. He never smokes in the house. He hardly ever smokes anywhere, mainly just at the dancing and even then only a few. Cigarettes are for him essentially a prop, only appropriate to certain social scenes. You really have to smoke at the dancing, he has decided. It's hard enough trying to camouflage yourself as a tough guy as it is. Go in there without cigarettes and it would be like wearing a blouse.

He has never smoked at the brickwork, it occurs to him. Would that help? Cran might have to take him seriously then. What could be more manly than giving yourself lung cancer? Anyway, Michael smokes and nobody will notice the difference of a little more smoke in the bedroom. And Tam has only recently begun to realise how good a cigarette tastes after food.

He rises and rinses his crockery and cutlery at the sink, laying them on the draining-board.

'Here,' his mother says. 'You've got yer good trousers on. Who d'ye think ye are? Beau Brummell? Change them.'

'Aye, Mither,' he says abstractedly.

He hardly hears her. The thought of smoking at the brickwork has brought the image of Cran from the edges of his mind, where he constantly loiters, until he is looming darkly in the forefront. He is thinking that perhaps he *should* mention Cran to his father, as he goes to fetch the Paymaster from his coat pocket. He reaches absent-mindedly into his left-hand pocket, then into the right-hand one. He pauses. He thinks back through last night. He only smoked three. The insult of it jars him into action before he has time to think. He is standing in the living-room.

'Here,' he says.

The aggression in his own voice takes him by surprise. His father looks up from his newspaper, observes him over the top of his glasses.

'Somebody's nicked ma fags.'

His father takes off his glasses. The newspaper settles, rustling across his knees. Tam is embarrassedly aware of the silliness of the 'somebody'. There is only his father in the room. Marion is out for the day with her friends. His father's eyes haven't left Tam's face.

'Ah wonder who it could be?' his father says. 'D'ye think yer mammy's started smokin'?'

'No, but,' Tam says, and he feels the lameness of his remark even before he makes it. 'Ah bought them.'

'D'ye want the money?'

'Naw, it's no' that.'

'"Nicked" yer fags? Strangers nick, son. Families share.'

They stare at each other. Tam is cringing at the way he has created a crisis out of nothing. Suddenly, it's Cigarette Fight at Sunday Creek. Tam continues to return his father's stare because he doesn't know what else to do. But he has become sickeningly aware that his gun's empty. His father leans towards the hearth and picks up the Paymaster packet.

'Here,' he says. 'Little Lord Fauntleroy. Ah believe this is your property.'

He throws the packet to Tam and, in having to crouch in order to catch it, Tam has the involuntary sensation of bowing, as before a superior force. He straightens up quickly but he still doesn't feel much taller than a bug. He despises himself for having been so stupidly mean as to grudge his own father a few cigarettes. Was he supposed to waken Tam up and ask permission? Seventeen years of providing for him hasn't earned his father the assumptive right to take a couple of fags when he feels like it? Oh, Jesus. Tam can't believe who he is, what a crummy person he can be. Will he ever get it right?

He stands uncertainly in the middle of the living-room. He struggles to find something to say.

'It's okay, Feyther,' he says. 'You can have them.'

'Naw, it's all right, son. Ah'll smoke the pipe.'

Anger would have been easier to take. The gentleness of his father's voice is very painful, kindness as whiplash. His father is reading the paper again, repeatedly pushing up his glasses with his forefinger as they repeatedly slide down his nose. Tam is still standing. His father glances up again.

'It's okay, Tam. Ah've got the pipe here.'

'Aye.'

The border is closed. He feels again that sense of his parents' dismay with him. What's their problem? 'Where did we go wrong, Betsy?' his father will say. 'What did we do to deserve this?' his mother will say. Come on. He's not an axe murderer – though if they keep this up, who knows? Tommy Borden with an axe . . . If they only knew some of the things he wants to do, fantasises doing. They should count themselves lucky, he has often thought. They should think about how some parents must really wonder how their children turned out the way they did.

He turns away and comes upstairs and shuts the door of Michael and Marion's room.

(Dear Parents of Attila the Hun,
Where do you think you went wrong?)

BRIGHT SUNLIGHT INFUSES THE ROOM. It says in the papers that this July could have the highest sunshine figure for any month of any year since they started keeping records in 1921. It certainly makes things look better. Seen in this light, the place looks like an advert for domestic life. The permanently set-up card table with its chequered cover, where Marion and Michael take their meals, resonates with sharp colours of red and white. The floral easy chairs with wooden arm-rests sit on each side of the fire. Michael and Marion have the only bedroom with a fireplace, because this is their living-room as well as where they sleep. The fire is cleared and set with firelighters and rolled-up newspaper and a few sticks and small pieces of coal, waiting for the first match of autumn. This looks like a good place to be.

He comes here every Sunday, when Marion and Michael stay overnight at her mother's, to replenish his purposes at the beginning of each week. This is one of the essential places of the summer, along with the kitchen, the Grand Hall, the Queen's Café, the brickwork, the countryside round Bringan, the pictures, the inside of a book. These are landmarks for the wild wanderings of his mind. Here Sunday merges with Sunday – different occasions, same troubled and unresolved time.

Sometimes the scene excludes him. He doesn't belong. This is a place for people who seem to know who they are, what their lives are about. They seem to have things worked out. He tries to fit in.

He takes Michael's ashtray and places it on the tiled hearth beside Michael's chair. He sits down and lights a cigarette. He begins to read the paper. He smokes. He has seen his father do this. He has seen Michael do this.

But it doesn't work. He feels like a bad actor. He is imitating the attitudes of others without personal conviction. Self-doubts invade him. He thinks of The Chair. Even when it sits empty at the piece-break, it is more full of Cran than this chair is full of him at the moment. He is simultaneously smoking suavely and brimming with panic, the terror of having to be who he doesn't know how to be.

He leaves his cigarette burning in the ashtray and crosses towards Marion's dressing-table. He kneels down in front of it, as if it were an altar. He does this every Sunday and every

Sunday his image floats back at him like a ghost. He stares at himself in the mirror. Who *is* that? It could be anybody. What is the secret people like his father and Cran and Michael have? Michael is only eight years older than he is but he seems like an awfully big brother. He's married now and working in the creamery and Marion is pregnant. He has done his National Service. He served in Berlin at the time of the Berlin Airlift. He seems so relaxed about everything. How do you get like that?

Tam watches his own jumpy eyes in the mirror. He has no substance as a person, he realises with panic. The mirror is composed of one centrepiece and two side flaps, which move on hinges. He pulls the flaps in towards him so that by looking in one flap he can see the back of his head in the other. That is what people coming behind him see. It looks solid and masculine. Maybe he should practise walking backwards so that people won't see the nervousness in his eyes.

('There's a real man. He walks funny, right enough. But he looks like a real man.')

He studies himself frontally again. The nose is all right.

('Where d' ye get that nose, our Tam?' Michael once said. 'It's the only straight wan in the family. It's about half the size o' ma feyther's.'

'When God wis givin' them out,' his father said, 'Ah thought they were for eatin'. So Ah took the biggest one Ah could find.'

'Naw, it's odd, though,' Michael said. 'You didny have a wee thing wi' a passin' gypsy, Mammy?'

'Aye,' his mother said. 'But that wis you. Dark-haired and shiftless. Except that you're blond. It was a blond gypsy.')

The hair could be better. There is plenty of it but it's much too fine. He insisted on getting a crew-cut last year, against the advice of Mr Guthrie, the barber who is also a phrenologist. ('You're an intellectual, son. I can tell by the bumps.') The result was an unqualified disaster. Separate strands of hair kept waving in all directions. He went about for a fortnight like a porcupine. That was his first experience of being a recluse.

He stares in the mirror and wishes he were John Garfield. He is not. He is Thomas Mathieson Docherty, who still hasn't come near to fulfilling any of the five ambitions he set for himself this summer: to have sex (preferably with a human being but let's not be too choosy); to face up to Cran; to read as many books as possible; to come to terms with his partial estrangement from his family and friends; to begin his life's work as a writer.

He has told John Benchley about wanting to start what John calls 'the magnum opus' before the end of the summer. It seems a reasonable enough idea. His example is Thomas Chatterton, 'the marvellous boy'. But he feels he should make a few modifications to the model. The fact that Chatterton committed suicide at seventeen doesn't seem to him an example he should necessarily follow, especially since he hasn't really written anything he likes yet and this doesn't give him much time. He will be eighteen in November. What does appeal to him about Chatterton was his hunger for fame while he was more or less young enough to enjoy it. For anything beyond about twenty-five seems to him to be bordering on the twilight world.

(Dear Thomas Chatterton,
           Could you not have given it another week or two?)

But that project isn't going well. He has just abandoned his second attempt to find the form for what he wants to say.

> The clock striking another nail into my tomb,
> The creak of darkness closing in the rain—
> This painted night locks up her hired room,
> Straightens her clothes and takes to the streets again.
>
> My mind like a miser huddled on his hams
> Counts his beliefs like pennies in his palms,
> The loose change of my father's prodigal ease,
> A vast inheritance of verdigris.
>
> The future flutters fiercely for release,
> Caged in the rusty past.
> The present's fingers bleed on the rusted bolts.
> The key is lost.
>
> Each man who lives must live towards a grief
> And while he lives must bear mutation out.

> The world turns not on faith but disbelief
> And here the final certainty is doubt.
>
> We meet no god in names that we create.
> We meet our own refusal to continue.
> God waits for us in loving and in hate,
> In action's arm and in endeavour's sinew.
> Himself he gave us in the things we are
> And bade us worship him with every scar.
> He named himself in everything we do.
> And shall we dare to christen him anew?

This isn't any good, he feels now. He can't believe that, when he finished it maybe eight weeks ago, he thought it was worth memorising. It is part of a 800-line poem he wrote in a fortnight called 'Reflections in a Broken Mirror'. It was meant to be more or less his philosophy of the world. But then what does he know about the world? It's embarrassing. After he had finished it, he wrote a letter to T.S. Eliot, offering to let him see it. For three weeks afterwards, he suspected the postal service of incompetence or T.S. Eliot of having died. But when no news arrived of the death of a major poet he got his sister Allison to make a typescript surreptitiously at her work and he sent it off to Chatto and Windus. A nice letter came back, talking of 'great intellectual vigour' and the impossibility of publication. He keeps the letter in his notebook, regarding it as his first review.

But now he wishes he could forget those lines he memorised. They keep coming back into his mind and suffusing it with the intellectual equivalent of a blush. They have become especially embarrassing because they led him into yet another misjudgment with a girl.

He was sitting in the Queen's Café with her and she discovered that he was trying to write. She asked him what he was writing. Suddenly, he was quoting the lines. Once he had started, he couldn't manage to stop. It was as if he had taken a mental emetic. He looked on in dismay as his mouth careered on and she looked as if she was going to fall asleep. When the words ran out, there was an awkward pause, rather as though someone had farted and they were waiting for the smell to dissipate.

'But that's not poetry,' she said at last.

She was voicing something he had himself been suspecting. Those words seemed somehow like an anteroom to writing, not the thing itself. For a start, he thought forlornly, you don't put nails in a tomb. You put them in a coffin.

How could he have written anything so self-absorbedly inaccurate? Writing, he has already decided, is making love. It's not masturbation. (Is that why he can't do it yet, since his only experience so far lies in the second of these areas?) Whatever it is you're trying to relate to must be justly learned, not pre-decided or merely imagined. Lose the details, you lose the lot. One compass he has given himself in his uncharted creative ambition is to distinguish between details and trivia. A detail becomes a detail by acquiring specific separate relevance to the whole. It achieves identity in conjunction. A triviality is interchangeable with other trivialities. It remains functionally anonymous. In that one line he has turned a detail into a triviality.

The clock striking another nail into my tomb. Crap. In that imprecision he sees the loss of the whole poem, as if one careless compass reading has multiplied the error of direction in the whole thing until it finds itself not in the New World he had imagined but standing in Antarctica in tee-shirt and jeans and doomed to instant death. That bastard nail had made a tomb of the poem, or a coffin.

He was aware of her watching his gloom – Hamlet in the Queen's Café. She was not unkind, May Walkinshaw. She might have a sense of poetry as all-inclusive as that of Miss Stevens, his English teacher in third year, who taught the class 'Daffodils' for two weeks solid, as if it were the aesthetic Ten Commandments, beating its rhythms relentlessly into their heads with a ruler on her desk. And she might treat her tits as if they were the crown jewels, to be filed past and admired but never touched. But she wasn't unkind.

'I'm sorry,' she said. 'I hope I haven't hurt you.'

'Naw,' he said. 'It's all right.'

But it wasn't. He knew he would never write again. And he thought of Greta Garbo. It was several days before he started his blank-verse play about working-class life. He decided he wouldn't mention it to any of the girls at the dancing.

WHY DOES THE DANCING MEAN SO MUCH TO HIM? He stares in the mirror and wonders. The dancing is the most important place in his life, he thinks. This mirror is in Allison's room. It is Saturday morning. Allison works on a Saturday morning at the office where she is a typist. He can come in here and use it as a dressing-room.

Only when Allison is out can he come into her room. The rest of the time she protects her space with the ferocity of a guard-dog. He feels pissed off about the living arrangements in the house. Where is his space here? On Saturday mornings he may enter the sanctum of Allison's room as long as he leaves no telltale signs of his having been here. Sundays he has access to Michael and Marion's room. Saturday nights he can kip in Michael and Marion's in a real bed. His clothes are kept in his parents' wardrobe. Six nights a week he sleeps in the fold-down bed in the living-room. It's like sleeping in the middle of the road. You have to learn to ignore the traffic. He feels like a refugee living on the edges of other people's lives. How are you supposed to find out who you are when you have to borrow yourself from the leftovers of others like second-hand clothes? No wonder he needs the dancing. At least there he can feel part of a community of nomadic hunters with the same rights as anybody else.

He tries to find a hunter's expression in the mirror. He hopes the dancing will be good tonight. He'll probably go to the pictures as he does every Saturday afternoon, now that the football season's over. Then it will be the dancing.

At least he has no obvious plooks at the moment. The skin of his face is more or less clear. Sammy Clegg's in a bit of a state just now. Plooks. That's a really Scottish word, much more expressive than 'pimples'. Plooks: the sound of illusions bursting. Why are all things in Scots designated by the least romantic sound the mouth can encompass? Scottish vocabulary is like a fifth column operating within the sonorous pomposity of English, full of renegade plosives and gutturals that love to dismantle pretensions. It's English in its underwear.

He has some plooks on his shoulders but that's no problem. Your shirt conceals them. Just don't go to the swimming-baths. Forehead plooks are bad but things can be done with the hair. He has a theory that the Tony Curtis hairstyle owes its amazing popularity to its effectiveness as a plook-concealer. Plooks on the cheeks are much more difficult. It would take a hairstyle of insane exoticism to cover them. The best you can do is to become elaborately thoughtful for a few days, developing a style of resting the face meditatively on the appropriate hand, or on both hands in time of extreme crisis.

The ultimate cosmetic nightmare is a plook on the nose. You can do nothing with them except suffer. Valderma seems to feed a plook like that instead of curing it.

> (Dear Inventor of Valderma,
> Don't give up your day job.)

None of the theories current for dealing with them seems to work very well in practice. 'Squeeze early' is one school of thought: better a red lump than an angry hill crowned with a white cairn. But he always finds that he is sculpting it to an even greater grandeur, feels he is assisting in the perfecting of his own ugliness. And those ones always seem to come at exactly the wrong time.

Does the adult world realise the significance of plooks? One nose-plook may have affected his chances of happiness for ever. It was so huge, so embarrassingly bright, that he believed it was flashing like a Belisha beacon. It reached maturity on the very evening he was to go out with Margaret Inglis. It was after he had taken her home from the school dance this year.

That was some dance. He knew he was leaving school and he appeared in his new, tight-trousered suit, casual shoes and Michael's maroon waistcoat. ('That tie,' his father had said. 'Like an explosion in a flooer-shop.') Some of the teachers looked at him askance and Miss Hetherington said in a loud voice as he was passing once, 'I didn't know they were inviting hooligans this year.' But Mrs White had stopped him to say, 'I thought you were staff there, Tom. Then I realised you were dressed too maturely to be staff.' That had left him wondering.

He had a great night. All his experience at the dancing seemed to pay off. It was like his coming-out ball. He was picked early at every ladies' choice. By the end of the dance there were at least four girls he thought he could ask to take home. But there was only one he really wanted to. Margaret was just finishing fourth year but she didn't look like it. She looked as if she had modelled for the Jane cartoon in the *Daily Mirror*. And she had given him two ladies' choices.

On the way home it started to rain and they took shelter in a phone box in which someone had broken the light. It became the most erotic experience of his life so far. He does not know why it should have been so intense. Maybe it was the excitement of being simultaneously so public and so private. There was glass round them on three sides and yet they were invisible, at least from a distance. The rain came down like a defensive wall. Maybe it was the inescapable closeness, as if just by entering the phone box they had gone past each other's inhibitions. There were no gestures of distancing they could make in this confined space. Every movement became an involvement with the other.

They became impassioned before they knew it was happening. She had her hands inside his shirt, kneading him roughly, and his right hand was inside her pants, feeling the awesomeness of that bristly, secret hair, when she suddenly said, 'Wait, there's someone coming.' They pulled apart. She adjusted her skirt. He buttoned his raincoat over his open shirt. They stood casually with their backs to the street, as if they were innocently talking. 'You're too dangerous for me,' Margaret said mysteriously. The glass of the phone box was opaque with their breathing. He heard footsteps coming nearer. They stopped. There was a long moment while he wondered if it was a policeman. The door opened. He couldn't believe it. He turned round slowly and saw a man with a soft hat looking in.

'This is an offence, you know,' the man said, and let the door close and waited.

'Oh my God,' Margaret said. 'That's my dad.'

He was a very big dad. They had no time to synchronise reactions. Margaret stepped out of the phone box immediately and Tam followed her, having buttoned up his coat.

The three of them stood in sheeting rain. Margaret put up

her umbrella. Tam envied her possession of a prop. It gave her something to do. All Tam could do was stand there swaying slightly with nerves, like a potted plant, being battered by the rain. He felt disadvantaged by her father's hat. He felt as if he had wandered into a scene from *The Maltese Falcon* by mistake, one in which he had no lines.

'You,' Margaret's father pointed at her. 'Home, lady. You,' he pointed at Tam. 'I've a good mind to take you over the park and give you a hiding.'

'And what will Ah be doin' while you're doin' it?' Whose voice was that? It wasn't him speaking. It was some instinct he hadn't known was there, expressing itself through him. 'Ah wouldn't let ma father do that? Why should Ah let you?'

That sounded good. It sounded really good. His voice had somehow transformed his fragile timorousness into something strong and threatening, a chihuahua barking through a megaphone. It had worked. But it had worked too well.

'Right. Come on. Let's see.'

Suddenly, they were walking towards Piersland Park. This was ridiculous but Tam couldn't think of anything else to do except walk beside the stranger. With his shirt unbuttoned to the waist inside his closed raincoat, he was freezing, but he didn't think it would be a good idea to button it up just now. That wouldn't be an action calculated to calm this big man down. Tam was wondering if he could turn embarrassing partial nudity to advantage by stripping off coat, jacket and shirt as one when they reached the park. That might look impressive. Come ahead. You're dealing with somebody here that's keen for action. That might give him a head start. 'Half of fightin's psychology,' his father had told him once. 'Most losers lose of a fractured heart.' But what about the other half? He remembered Michael clapping him on the shoulder once, withdrawing his hand in mock pain and saying, 'Christ, Ah've cut maself. Tam, you've got shoulders like razor-blades.' Tam Docherty stripped was not going to be the most intimidating sight. He was probably going to get hammered.

How did he get from the warmth of Margaret's body to this? The prospect of rolling about in the rain getting his head punched in? And Margaret was clicking along behind them. What was she going to do? Referee? Life was ridiculous.

'This is ridiculous,' her father said.

He had stopped. Tam stopped. Margaret stopped.

'Just leave my daughter alone. Okay? Come on, Margaret.'

The two of them walked away. Tam stood alone in the rain. He was both relieved and cheated. He knew this was just postponement of the inevitable. For he would have to find out some time what it would have been like in that darkened park – and it might have been better to find out from Mr Inglis than some of the Teddy-boys at the dancing.

'Remember. Leave her alone,' Mr Inglis shouted back.

But he hadn't. There were still those anarchic schooldays just before the summer holidays, when senior pupils lounged in the prefects' room and played shove-ha'penny and chess and briefly acted as if they owned the school. He talked to Margaret a lot and eventually she agreed to meet him outside Boots on Friday night. She agreed on the day he was leaving to look for a job. He didn't go back to school.

Meanwhile, came the plook – a record-breaking mound of white right on the tip of his nose.

'That's not a plook you've got there, Tam,' Michael said. 'Ah think it's a Siamese twin.'

Everything he did to hurry it on only made it last longer. It seemed to have the gestation period of an elephant, which was appropriate to its dimensions. Early Friday evening, he moped in front of Marion's mirror, feeling like a Quasimodo whose hump has transmigrated to his nose. He applied some of Marion's face powder but that only seemed to make it more conspicuous, seeming to him as vivid as the gentian violet that had shamed some of his classmates in primary school. Wiping the powder off, he saw his nose glow blindingly again, a light-bulb with the shade removed.

He stood Margaret up. He stood her up. It was the only time in his life he had done that. He thought if she saw him like that she might not want to see him again. He keeps hoping she will turn up at the dancing. But she never does.

He stares at his plookless face in the mirror and thinks that he looks not bad today. Margaret, where are you now?

'Tom!'

His mother is calling him down for his dinner. If he had been born into a wealthy family, she would be calling him down for lunch. Or maybe a servant would be striking a gong. (His mother's voice sounds a bit like a gong – To-o-o-o-m.)

Either way, it would still be a pain in the bloody arse – the knight's quest for himself constantly interrupted by trivial irrelevancies.

AT LEAST HUNGER IS A CONSTANT, he would think. No matter what pretensions you had about yourself, your stomach was always waiting to bring them down to the ordinary. It was like the man who stood behind the triumphant Roman general on his chariot, while he took the plaudits of the crowd, and said, 'Remember thou art but mortal.' Is that what he said? Something like that. Anyway, what your stomach said was, 'You better eat.' In the tracklessness of thought, that was some kind of basic compass. In the confusion of selfhood, it was some kind of crude badge of identity. Even in the ecstasies of the mystics, there must have been a lot of bellies rumbling. Maybe that was what they mistook for the music of the spheres. You better eat.

Jesus, look at that fridge. It was like the laboratory of Sir Alexander Fleming. Get your home-made penicillin here. He would soon be frightened to open the door because, when he did, behold – a small abandoned universe of determined life. Cheese where lichen grows. Fruit that nurtures a dark, internal being. All around, small clumps of fungi continue their furious and meaningless existence and, when the god who carelessly created them absent-mindedly shuts the door, are plunged again into cold darkness.

He could forget about something to eat. Suicide by Roquefort. Stick to the liquid nutrition. He'd better clean it out in the morning. Before they all came out to get him like the invasion of the body-snatchers. The bastards.

He filled out another whisky, watered it and went back through to the living-room. Lit only by the light from the gas fire and the reading lamp that made a small bell of brightness on the table by the window, the darkened room seemed mysterious beyond the purpose to which he was putting it. He crossed it as if it was a walk-through painting of someone else's place.

Shit, he thought as he sat back down at the table, I'll have to stop thinking like this. It's just a room in a rented flat. Why see it in any other way? Was that tendency what had been wrong with his life all along? He hoped not. He distrusted romanticism.

But he wondered about that fixation with Margaret Inglis. Was it not partly about his sense of her as being not quite attainable? And Maddie Fitzpatrick. What chance could he ever have imagined he would have with her? And he remembered the girl on the bus, who had haunted him all that summer.

Something Jack Laidlaw had said some years ago came back to him. Four of them – Vic Vernon, Ray Harrison, Jack and himself – had been drinking in the Admiral in Glasgow. Ray had been teasing Jack about not having settled with a woman after his divorce. 'Philanderer' was mentioned.

'I'm not a philanderer,' Jack said. 'Several hundred women will testify to that.'

They had all laughed. But the joke bothered him. He didn't believe it was true of Jack. And he knew it wasn't true of himself. He could only remember about a couple of one-night stands. Otherwise he had only made love within a relationship, even if it was a brief one.

But then why was he sitting here alone? It wasn't because he wanted the freedom to be promiscuous. If it had been, why was he living like a hermit? And he had always suspected sexual romanticism in relationships as being for some a means of justifying promiscuity. He had known people like that, both women and men, but mainly men.

They made such demands on the other that she must disappoint. The disappointment recreated a romantic vulnerability that made the man attractive to and attracted by a new woman. She thought she would be the one to give his restlessness a home. But in order to do so she would have to kill the very dynamic of his nature – his searching romanticism. His instinctive realisation of this danger made him dissatisfied with her and critical of her and the only mode of survival was by renewal of the quest. The cycle could begin again. Romanticism could only be in the search. To accept that you had found the object of the search was to commit a kind of suicide of the romantic self.

Also, he thought, sexual romanticism often had a very pragmatic method which it could contrive to conceal from itself in order to maintain its faith in its own romanticism – for example, by keeping many apparently innocent social contacts with women, like lines trawling in the sea. If nothing happened, nothing happened. But if the woman gave a hint of romantic interest the romantic was ready to take advantage of it – the bait had been taken. But the romantic could still convince himself that he had been surprised by coincidence, did not contrive his own ambush. Isn't romance wonderfully, undeniably spontaneous? The machinery of seduction had been kept concealed, was ostensibly separate from the seemingly spontaneous result.

Thus, those who profess the purity of their romanticism, their removal from baser motives of self-seeking and pleasure profiteering, are often street traders in emotion, barrow-boys of the affections – magpies pretending to be lovebirds.

He didn't believe he had done that. But then why was he sitting here alone? He couldn't exactly claim that he hadn't met any terrific women. Why wasn't he with one of them now? Or was it that good creates the appetite for best and baffles choice? At least in some people. To seek the impossible ideal was a perfect way of never connecting finally with anyone.

But that wasn't him, he thought. Surely not. Let us pray. Surely not.

But

TE AMO DEL UNO AL NUEVE

IN A CAFÉ IN BUENOS AIRES, near the Plaza de Mayo, he would sit with Cristina Esposito and she would be explaining to him the meaning of that sentence. I love you from one to nine.

Without zero. *Sin cero. Sincero.* She had a torn-off piece of grey napkin paper and a biro pen and she was breaking down the words for him as if they were an equation. She was speaking with the preoccupied pedantry of a schoolmistress. She looked as if she were trying to explicate some impractical science of the passions. In the space between her fussy manner and her luxuriance of chestnut hair, the black eyes where tapers of intensity came and went and the astonishingly mobile lips speaking a silent sub-text that sometimes made him forget to hear the real words, he sensed the impossible place where, though he could not remember the moment of choosing, he had perhaps chosen to live, where passionate compulsion could find no way to cohabit with necessary pragmatism.

Across the café, a middle-aged man looked up from his thoughts towards them. He smiled and winked, seeming to understand where he and Cristina were. In that generous Latin way of joining in other people's parades, he made an elaborate sidelong glance towards Cristina's intensity.

'*Esta noche,*' he said. He pointed at him threateningly. Tonight. You. He made a throat-cutting gesture.

'*No hay problema,*' he had replied. '*Viva la muerte,*' grateful for having read Robert Lowell. Manifold were the uses of literacy.

He felt in that moment the strangeness of his being here, simultaneously the joy of Cristina's presence and the anguish of its fleetingness. It was as if the poignancy of this time lay in their inability to sustain it. Maybe if you make what is wild captive, you destroy its nature. He had that familiar, haunting sense that his emotions and his practical experience lived in separate but parallel universes and he wondered if he would ever manage to make them live permanently together. It was a feeling less of déjà vu than *déjà senti*, a sense of the impossibility of what is happening. Was it that very impossibility that attracted him, like a brief escape from the cage of time and circumstance?

Within the café, like a box within a box, occurred a car. He was driving with Gill in Ireland. It was the kind of day he associated with Ireland, bright and windy, the weather good enough to let you see the greenery but not good enough to let you luxuriate in it – a beautiful virago. He was rounding a corner when the image of a woman hit the windscreen like a hand grenade, blinding him.

She was tall and her hair was threshing in the wind. She was barefoot and her shoes, the laces tied together, hung around her neck. She seemed to ride the wind like a witch, her simple dress blown along the contours of her rich body. The stunning face, in the second that she looked at him, was smiling – sardonically, it seemed to him, as if she knew that he was seeing the best place there was to be. And she was gone. Two children walked behind her. They were laughing. No wonder they were laughing.

'D'you see that?' he said involuntarily.

'What?' Gill said.

She was checking Megan, who would be two years old at that time and strapped into the child's seat in the back, and he felt the wantonness of the betrayal and compounded it with deceit.

'Barefoot in this weather,' he said, and stored in his head that image, innocent enough in itself but also like a talisman betokening the continuing possibility of an unforeseen and chance future which would not grow naturally out of his present.

And within the car within the café, like a box within a box within a box, he remembered sitting in a bus in Graithnock on a day of intense heat, and he would know again the feelings of that summer, that they were not dead but boarded in him somewhere still, lonely and gibbering and dissatisfied, like Mrs Rochester in her attic, denied by practical circumstance and the pretences of society but denying them in return, haunting them with longings they could not meet.

A GIRL COMES ON TO THE BUS who is a woman walking naked with clothes on. She wears a blue cotton dress. She has black hair, so carelessly abundant that he feels he could make his home there. Her face is broad and sensuous, with lips that seem poised for the next bite. The eyes, ah well, the eyes. He suspects they are the sort of eyes the passionless would describe as 'come-to-bed' eyes. They aren't come-to-bed eyes. Who needs a bed? All Tam knows is that when he looks in her eyes he thinks he can see all the way down to the dark place.

Her body isn't describable by him any more than he could inventory the happening of a thunderstorm. It drenches him in its presence, that is all. When the dusty bus, which on this hot day is like a decrepit sauna on wheels, rattles to a halt, she comes on, looks at him, takes him in and turns away, yanking his heart out of his body as if it were attached to a string.

It no longer matters where he is going. Where can he be going that is more important than where she is? He experiences instantaneously the awesome sensation that he could forget he has relatives, abandon friendships, live anywhere, wrap his past up in the one small parcel and put a match to it, just to be with her.

She has noticed him. She has three friends with her and they all sit down across the passageway, taking up two double seats. She is at the window of the further forward of the two seats and, as she sits with her back against the glass, turning towards her friends, he and she can see each other. She will take a smile that she is giving to one of her friends and pass it on to him. Her eyes keep coming back to his, resting on them thoughtfully, and he seems hardly capable of looking away from her at all. They are having a brief affair of the eyes, optical copulation in public. There is no self-conscious regality about her but you can see that her friends are her ladies-in-waiting. She's the one, dispensing a shower of light in which they bathe.

The longer she sits, the more intimately interlocked their eyes become. But she and her friends rise to go several stops before he is due to get off. She pauses briefly in passing and looks down at him. The proximity of her vivid face and body blots out the rest of the day. She smiles at him and then her lips form an infinitesimal 'ooh' sound and she is gone.

As he sits stunned in his seat while the bus pulls away, he looks out of the window. She has been walking off, chatting to her friends, when she suddenly, and obviously without warning to them, turns away from them and back towards the bus. She stands quite openly on the kerb and stares at him and smiles and waves. Her face seems to him to be expressing a kind of wistfulness that nothing more has happened between them.

He is breathless with longing. He feels a panic that makes him unable to sit still. He has never seen her before. Some phrases of conversation he has caught tell him that she isn't Scottish. Maybe she is visiting relatives and will leave for ever tomorrow, or today. The way she looks, maybe she is the Lady of Shalott just out on a day-trip to the twentieth century. This could be his only chance.

He gets off the bus at the next stop. He runs all the way back to where she had stood on the kerb. Obviously, she isn't there. He starts to wander the streets around the area. He looks in shops. He checks a couple of cafés. Nothing else matters. He has become a mad seeker for lost love. For more than two hours he scours the day, drenched in sweat that comes partly from the heat but partly from the imagined possibilities that hold him in a fever. As each compulsive, desperate step seems to bring him relentlessly nearer to the final and irrevocable admission that she is no longer there and may never be again, he curses himself as a weakling, a bloody robot so programmed into habit that when experience suddenly opens up before him and says, 'Turn here for El Dorado,' he is likely to reply, 'Sorry, that would be great. But it's not on my itinerary for today. I've arranged to go to the shops.'

He cannot believe it. For several long, luxurious minutes, an amazing possibility has shimmered before him. Five minutes later, it is gone – for good, he fears. He stands breathing heavily on the corner of a street that is busy with everyone in the world, it seems, except her. He knows, he just knows, that if only he could meet her again, something wonderful and important and maybe life-changing would happen between them. And he goes on looking.

And he never sees her again.

IDEALS, he would sometimes fear, were like items you packed in your luggage and took with you everywhere and then never got to wear. For they never really fitted anyone. But you kept looking at them lovingly in private and trying them on secretly from time to time. They were the you you longed to appear as but couldn't quite find the occasion for.

Perhaps that was why he sometimes felt that everything he did was just a substitute for what he should really be doing, whatever that was. There was often the sense of being a surrogate of himself, an impostor in his own life, the servant of his circumstances and not their master. He supposed the feeling might be related to his attempts to write, that compulsion that precluded him from merely accepting who he was and sharing it with others. He must always be trying to use his own experience to project imaginatively into experience he had never had. The other self that was the writing could ghost through the most ordinary actions, haunting them with dissatisfaction, some vague demand for more.

Such talent to create as he had, he thought once, was like having an elephant on a leash. It complicated your entire life. It forbade the using of itself merely for enjoyment. It seemed to invite you to a banquet of life and then you found that you couldn't get through the door to where the revelry was without leaving it behind. And if you did leave it behind, you couldn't be sure it would be there when you came back.

These self-doubts left him vulnerable daily to a host of practical questions most other people dealt with automatically.

'SO WHAT'S HAPPENING?' Gill said.

The remark was innocent as an ambush. He thought of the talk between husbands and wives, the tripwires of hurt that could be hidden in a phrase, how casual conversation became mined with the resentments of the past and needed careful stepping, a delicate evasiveness, zig-zagging answers. What's happening? We're losing ourselves down endless quarrels. We're discovering that betrayal may be buried but doesn't die and that no place can be as lonely as a bed. What's happening?

'Ah have to go back tae Scotland obviously,' he said. 'Come on, Gill. We've talked about this.'

'You're definitely doing it?'

'Ye think Ah've got an option?'

'Yes, I do.'

'Ah suppose ye're right. Ah could always be a bastard.'

'What do you mean "could be"?'

'Oh, aye.'

He recognised this bleak terrain. He should do. He had helped to make it. This was where rusted hopes lay abandoned and the ground was trafficked into mud where nothing grew. This was no-man's land. Across it they observed each other, sniping casually and sporadically.

She was unpacking the things she had bought. Hopelessness goes on shopping. Even futility has to be fed. He noticed hurtingly how attractive she was, someone he could have fallen for in another situation, rather like a soldier realising that he might have been best mates with one of the enemy if there hadn't been a war on. She put the three baguettes on the table. Bread-shells.

'Have you phoned already?' she said.

'Ah phoned Michel. I go from Grenoble to Paris by train. He's going to meet me at the station. We go to the Café de Flore. Colette'll pick me up there. She'll drive me to Charles de Gaulle. I get the plane to Heathrow. Heathrow to Glasgow.'

'It's well organised, isn't it?'

'That's what you do when you're travelling. It's got the edge on hitching.'

She put the melon in the fridge. He was trying to choose a book to take with him from the four he was holding.

'You're all packed, I notice,' she said.

'You're the one who wanted to bring us to Grenoble,' she said.

'What about your students?' she said.

'So what about Megan and Gus and me?' she said.

'We're your family, too,' she said. 'Or is family only where you come from?'

She had seen the suitcase in the hall. To call his vague gathering of chance clothing 'packing' was a misuse of a word. At least he had put in his one formal suit, just in case. Just in bloody case.

They had discussed coming to Grenoble and they had both agreed on it.

He had phoned Joe and postponed his classes. It was just a matter of tying up the loose ends of the semester. Anyway, did she think that was a major issue in the scale of what was happening?

She reminded him of the first inspector who had assessed him at the end of his first year of teaching in a secondary school. He sat in on several lessons and then told Tom that he was a competent teacher. But there was one serious problem. Tom's record of work was not up to date. Any teacher taking over from him would be confused as to exactly what stage the classes had reached on the course. The inspector stared solemnly at Tom, as if he had terminal cancer. Had he realised the gravity of this?

'Imagine it,' the inspector said. 'What would happen if you were knocked down by a bus? What do we do then?'

(Tom had a sudden, dislocated image of himself lying under the wheels of a bus. A solicitous crowd has gathered. As they bend over him, straining to catch his last words, they eventually realise that he is gasping, 'My . . . record . . . of . . . work. Is. In my desk in Room Two. It's . . . under the register. It's not' – tears course down his cheeks – 'up to date.' He dies unfulfilled.)

Tom stared solemnly at the inspector, as if he had terminal cancer. *What do we do then?* 'Shove your record of work as far up your arse as you can get it,' he wanted to say. 'I'll have more to worry me.' Instead he looked away in embarrassment, hoping his expression was conveying an adequately chastened awareness of what was important in life, as indeed it was.

Gill and Megan and Gus would probably survive for a little while without him. Did love of the family you came from diminish your love for the family you made? He would have thought it would augment it. I could not love ye, kids, so well loved I not others, too. The best gift I can give you is the truth of myself, as benignly and as honestly as I can give it, and that includes a passionate concern for people living beyond the enchanted circle of us four.

He heard Megan and Gus playing in another part of the house. May his and Gill's damaged lives never quite reach them. Forgive us for the gifts we give our children.

He chose the poems of Catullus, translated by Frederic Raphael and Kenneth McLeish – immortal trivia, living disrobed of false ideals, the scurrility of unacknowledged individual experience within social pretence. The randomness of the choice didn't help his state of mind. Did anything form a coherent pattern? He watched while Gill moved about the same room as he sat

in but a different one. He couldn't quite believe that this was
Grenoble or that he was going back to Graithnock.

He remembered a feeling that had often come upon him
in his teens. He would be reading and suddenly a perfectly
ordinary word – it might be 'doorway' or 'bus' – would turn
into a weird hieroglyph. He couldn't imagine where the word
came from or what it was supposed to mean. The continuity
of the text fused and only that single word palpitated and
glowed in the surrounding darkness, as if a flying saucer had
arrived from another universe and he was the only one to see
it. And through that fissure in assumed normality poured the
overwhelming mystery of things.

Or he was in a room with which he was familiar, perhaps in
John Benchley's house. He knew every piece of furniture and
an armchair suddenly disjointed from the coherence of the room
and was an incomprehensible extrusion, an alien in an ordinary
day. The pattern of the cloth which covered it seemed impossibly
intricate and bizarre. He wondered who could have made it and
how it came to be in this place. It was as if he became immediately
aware that all the contexts of his life, among which he moved
so confidently and assumptively, were as fragile and as wilfully
invented and as unreal as a backcloth in a theatre, and the cloth
had just ripped and he glimpsed beyond it the real, ubiquitous,
breathing and impenetrable dark.

Why did that feeling happen to him?

'YOU'RE REALLY A MYSTIC,' John Benchley replies. 'But then
a lot of teenagers are.'

He is in the sitting-room of his manse where he lives with his
very elderly housekeeper, Mrs Malone, whose smile is a wince in
disguise. The manse is on a hill beside the church and evening is
gathering slowly in the room. Through the wide window a long
low bank of cloud is reddening like a hillfire. The books that line
the walls are receding into darkness, as if rejoining the past from
which they emerged. The coal fire is hypnotic with blue flame.

'All young people are expatriates, I suppose. They come from another country and they haven't quite settled in this one. They don't quite know the customs here. Some learn more slowly than others.'

'I just wish I would hurry up.'

'Maybe you shouldn't. Your self hasn't formed yet. Your social identity is still intermittent. Fragmentary. And nature keeps coming through the gaps. What's wrong with that?'

'It can be embarrassing for a start.'

'Embarrassment's all right. Never confuse embarrassment with shame. Embarrassment's when you can't bear others to see your secret self. That's a healthy instinct. Shame's when *you* can't bear to see your secret self. One's maintaining an honourable contract with yourself. The other means you've broken that contract. So be embarrassed.'

'That's easy to say.'

'Come on, Tom. A red face isn't fatal.'

'Not so far.'

John laughs his thin laugh. Tam likes him so much, he always wishes he could laugh better. It's too small, that laugh, as if he knows he has restricted rights in this area. Tam thinks of his Uncle Charlie laughing like a chaotic symphony. If laughter's an orchestra, John Benchley is playing the triangle in it. Maybe that's what happens living with Mrs Malone.

'There's an essay by Harold Nicolson. 'In Defence of Shyness'. '*A* Defence of Shyness'? Anyway. He makes the point that shy people often have further to grow up to. I think there's something in that. If you know how to conform too quickly, you lose your originality. You can start to mimic other people instead of finding out who you are. Don't undervalue awkwardness. It's often just the truth clumsily refusing to be denied.'

'I must be full of the truth, then.'

'Like those times you were talking about. When you lose touch with the practicalities of what's going on. You see things out of context. That's you catching experience raw. Not dressed up in the purposes to which we insist on putting it. That really is a low-grade mystical experience. You're in touch with something beyond other people's preconceptions. You're seeing things fresh.'

He certainly seemed to be doing that all right. He is even

doing it while John is talking. He doesn't want this moment to shift. He fears that John will rise and put on the light. He wants the darkness and the gathering sunset and the murmur of their voices in the stillness. It doesn't matter so much what they say. It is that they are talking, making their small human communion in the dusk.

He wants to say something to keep John talking, to maintain his concentration. But he is baulked by two feelings. The first is petulance that John has referred to his having 'low-grade' mystical experiences. It is as if he has failed some kind of exam. The second is the very embarrassment he has been talking about.

He has thought of an example of what John called 'nature coming through the gaps' and 'the truth clumsily refusing to be denied'. It is a fairly crass example but nevertheless relevant, he feels. He thinks of his erections. They can happen anywhere – on buses, at the dancing, standing in a shop. One had even come upon him at his brother Michael's wedding.

HE IS DANCING with his Auntie Bella. They are doing a slow foxtrot among the circling relatives, smiling sweetly at each other, when one movement out of rhythm make their bodies come together. He is caught instantly in one of the frames of the American comics he used to read: Bam! Pow! Zowie! Hector is between them.

('Touch of flaccid tit on the port bow, Cap'n. Reporting for duty.'

'Piss off, you dead head. It's ma auntie. She's ma mother's sister-in-law. She's the auntie of the groom, for God's sake.')

But he remains adamantly there, nosing blindly about, trying to find out where he is required. Tam is too horrified to notice if she's noticed. He thinks of feigning illness. But if he collapsed, that would only advertise the situation. And if he walks off the dance-floor with a small baton in his trousers, he might get lynched for mental incest.

He starts to dance like Quasimodo. Observing his new,

crouched style of dancing, Auntie Bella probably thinks he has gone insane. But that is better than her realising the terrible truth. Then he has the inspiration of becoming suddenly drunk. That would be convincing. He is a boy who has been playing at being a man in the relaxed atmosphere of the wedding. As he mugs outrageously, he hopes nobody notices that his face is really screaming, 'Don't look at my trousers.' When the dance ends, he completes his performance by jocularly leaving the floor in the manner of Groucho Marx walking. He subsides on a chair, puts his legs under the table and waits for the rest of him to subside.

He can't cope with this. When he has settled down, he goes to hide in the bar in case another woman asks him to dance. His Uncle Charlie buys him a half of shandy and looks at him.

'Anythin' wrong, son?' he says.

He has always been able to talk to his Uncle Charlie and he is so guilty he has to find a confessor.

'Something terrible happened there,' he says. 'Ah was dancin' with ma Auntie Bella. And Ah got a hard-on.'

He waits for his uncle's reaction to establish a scale of horror for what he has done.

'Ah hope she noticed.'

'Uncle Charlie!'

'Naw, Ah hope so. She'd be tickled pink. Ah bet she doesn't have that effect too often on yer Uncle Davie these days. She's probably in the toilet puttin' on her make-up. Singin' "Oh, how we danced on the night *they* were wed".'

Then he sang the next bit: 'We vowed our true love though a word wasn't said.'

'It was terrible. Ah'm frightened to dance with anybody. In case it happens again.'

'If it does, give us a shout. Ye can pass it over.'

'Ah'm that embarrassed.'

'No. Ye just think ye are. See when it doesn't happen? That's when ye'll be embarrassed. Come on, kid. Relax. A limited number of boners in any man's life. Enjoy them while they're there.'

Uncle Charlie has always had a rough ability to put things in perspective for him. But he also has a strain of gentle wickedness.

Later, when the singing has started and Auntie Bella is innocently belting out 'Lay that pistol down, babe', Uncle Charlie taps him on the shoulder.

'Ye think she's tryin' to tell you something, Tam?' he says.

BUT IF HE HAD BEEN ABLE TO TELL HIS UNCLE CHARLIE about the problem, he cannot tell John Benchley. He is a minister of the church. He has told Tam to call him John but that isn't the same thing as saying, 'Use my carpet for disgorging the sewer of your mind any time.' Yet he is tempted.

Fortunately, he delays so long that John stands up and crosses to put on the light. The dark crystal of the room is shattered and his memories of the wedding dissolve. Magic has again dissipated into mundanity. The harsh brightness makes this just a bleak, modern room, its coldness thawed somewhat by ageless fire and the books that lag its walls. John goes over to the sherry decanter, comes to the small table beside him and fills him out another glass.

And that's another thing. In that simple action he is conscious yet again of the contradictory cross-references in his life. How will he ever reconcile them? Sherry? Every time during these talks John gives him two sherries. He has wondered if John is trying subtly to civilise him beyond his working-class habits while, by restricting his intake to two glasses only, ensuring that he doesn't corrupt him in the process. He is a very measured man.

This is the only place Tam has tasted sherry. Holding the stemmed glass in his hand with its hoard of yellow light, he feels its strangeness. It glows mysteriously, a prism of contradictions in which he sees himself. He drinks sherry and talks about mysticism and has an erection at his brother's wedding and talks rough with his friends and is supposed to be going to university and wants to be a writer and lusts after strange girls and wonders what he is doing here. He starts to talk again, donning the camouflage of normalcy.

'What about church attendance?' he asks. 'Numbers okay?'

'Well, we're under no pressure to build an extension.'

'Maybe television affects it. I thought Billy Graham would have helped.'

'The crusade had a big enough impact while he was here. But I certainly don't notice any lasting effect on my congregation. Maybe Graithnock's particularly stony ground. Though I don't like to think so. Perhaps that's just making excuses for myself.'

'You've done well. The congregation must be bigger now than before you came.'

'I don't know that I've done so well. I've managed to reduce the congregation by at least one.'

He looks at Tam sadly.

'That wasn't you. I just became an agnostic.'

'You make it sound so positive.'

'I think it is. I think it's the only thing to be.'

'You trying to convert me?'

He looks so forlorn, Tam feels guilty. He is almost sorry to have become an agnostic. John Benchley has mattered to him over the past couple of years. His gentle wiseness has saved Tam, during his frenetically religious phase, from going quietly mad with impossible holiness. When he was fifteen, he had wanted to become either a minister or a priest – a priest for preference, because that was harder and more demanding and seemed to him to reduce the complexity of life to one massive, final gesture. Attending his church and talking to him, Tam had realised how ill equipped he was to become the apprentice saint he had hoped to be. He finds rectitude boring. Girls fascinate him. How could he forswear life before he has tasted it?

No, he can't regret having become an agnostic. In a way, John has helped him to become one. Much as Tam likes him, he has to admit that he is glad to have forsworn the religious life if John is an example of what it does to you. He seems to Tam like someone who endures life as if it were influenza and hopes to get over it soon. Maybe his generosity to others relates to his belief that we are all ill with living and in need of psychological medication. Maybe it's not so much a careless gift of largesse as a measured bartering of mutual inadequacy. Can even kindness have dark and twisted roots? Does everything have dark and twisted roots?

His confusion is more or less total. He might as well be back in primary school, faced with one of those forms on which the unanswerable question has appeared.

FATHER'S OCCUPATION:

MAYBE THE PROBLEM IS GENETIC, he would think. He looked at himself with some of the soap still on his chin. The small round mirror he was using for shaving looked like a porthole through which, as he kept moving to get the angles right, he seemed to see a version of himself who was drowning. Maybe that was why he didn't bother to shave every day, to avoid having to see the drowning man he didn't seem able to save. Or maybe it was just another expression of his social isolation at the moment, a rehearsal for being a down-and-out. Or maybe it was because he was more and more aware of the resemblance to his father.

As the shaving soap was removed, there kept looming out at him a past he wasn't sure he could move beyond. Was there a Docherty gene, or maybe a Mathieson one, that condemned him to perpetual failure to fulfil himself, an inability to decide what he ought to do or what he ought to be? Was he sentenced to be like his father in that respect? Or like his Uncle Charlie?

His mother used to talk more than once of a recurring moment she had learnt to dread. It was when she would go upstairs to get ready for bed and his father was already there, lying with his head cupped in his hands.

'Betsy,' he would say, his eyes gazing at the ceiling as if it were the promised land. 'Ye know what Ah've a helluva notion o' tryin'.'

And she would scream silently. Another money-making project was threatening their lives.

No wonder the uncertainty of what his father was had troubled him. It must have been like living with X the unknown. After leaving the pits he seemed determined to try everything. When Uncle Josey challenged him for being a working-class entrepreneur, he said, 'Negative capitalism, Josey. Ah'm tryin' to get the wealth intae the hands of the workers. Then we can share it out more fairly.'

The most intense expression of his confusion with his father always came at primary school. Every so often they were given forms to fill in. He hated forms, always would. But he could always handle these questions easily enough, except for one. He always checked the form over first before writing anything down, to see if that one dreaded question was there, and it seemed it always was. The question simply said 'Father's occupation' and then a colon and a space to put your answer in. That was an insoluble space for him. He hated that space.

He used to steal glances at his neighbours' forms. It seemed to be for them the easiest question in the paper. Storeman, they'd write. Joiner. Plumber. Fitter at Mason's factory. What the bloody hell is ma feyther? He took venomous delight in swearing in his head towards him. Why did everybody else know what their father was and he hadn't a clue? The bastard. What was he trying to do to him? He made him feel like a dunce.

He would go out to the teacher's desk and begin an elaborate, apologetic mumble. At four o'clock he'd be out of the school like a sprinter – there were no devious routes home taken on those days. He was confronting his mother at five past four, his teeth bared in an imitation of his father. 'What,' he once said, feeling as he said it how clever the expression was, 'is he this week?' He could be bitter about his father.

Sometimes his mother could answer the question and sometimes she couldn't. Sometimes his father didn't seem too sure himself. He would ponder, picking his way round unimaginable obstacles, and he would say something like, 'Tell ye what, son. Jist say Ah'm on for maself.'

'The boay canny say that,' his mother would say. 'He needs to say something specific.'

'Unemployed,' his father would say.

Eventually, he found his own way round the problem. He knew his father had been a miner. But that was very specific. Panic can make you understand context in an exact way. (He picked up a lot of words from his mother. She once told him words were power and he took the thought into himself like a secret weapon.) You're either a miner or you aren't. His father was obviously not a miner any longer. He didn't have a lamp for his bunnet and he didn't come home black. Anybody could see him and find that lie out easily.

But he had also been a van driver and a labourer and tried to be a scrap dealer and had been a street bookie. He knew that being a street bookie was illegal because his mother had told him not to mention it to anyone or the police might get to hear of it. That was out. He decided to make his father a general labourer.

It was a genuine inspiration, he felt. No teacher ever questioned it and he came to feel that he had made a contribution to the security of his family, shut out the prying eyes of strangers, given his mother one less worry and protected his father's strangeness.

But it certainly didn't change anything except the ease with which he could fill in forms at the school, he had to admit as he washed the residual soap off his face and dried it. His father had continued to dream incorrigibly about the big breakthrough into wealth.

It seemed his father and his Uncle Charlie had once made a handsome standard lamp at a time when standard lamps were coming into vogue. They made it out of a brush shaft from the brush factory in Graithnock and some pieces of wood they found. Everybody who saw it admired it and, within the praise, his father and his Uncle Charlie fancied they saw the glint of gold. They went round the houses with the varnished standard lamp and a small notebook, taking orders. They came back with a lot of names and addresses. They calculated how much money they would make and were amazed. Then they discovered that they couldn't make another standard lamp. After a week, the back green was littered with misshapen and broken brush shafts. They went back round the houses and cancelled all the orders. The reason they gave was that they 'couldn't get the right parts'.

The summer of the kiln was also the summer of the Collaro. Collaro was the name of one of the latest kind of record-players. His father bought one. The family realised that it was more than a form of domestic entertainment when his father invited Uncle

Charlie round to listen to a batch of new records neither of them liked. While they grimaced at the sounds they heard, Uncle Charlie made a list of the titles and seemed to be working out some kind of running order.

That week they hired a hall in Stewarton, a nearby small town. They were organising dances there two nights a week. For a fortnight, things went well. A lot of teenagers turned up to dance to the music. But the venture collapsed when a bunch of nosey teenagers pulled back the curtain that had been rigged up at one end of the hall. The vision of Uncle Charlie in shirt sleeves and bunnet, changing records and telling the boys to fuck off before they got their arses kicked, seemed to destroy the mystique of the evenings. There was a mass walk-out. They tried once more but word had got around and the last evening was a boycott.

Looking for what Kristofferson called his 'cleanest dirty shirt', he stopped with the black denim shirt in his hand. He saw his father's fortnight in Stewarton in a new light. Like Edison or Logie Baird, he was simply a man ahead of his time. He had arrived at something which would, when the time was right, make vast fortunes for many people. Putting on the shirt and clicking shut its buttons, he understood with sudden and open-mouthed awe the amazing truth. His father was the man who invented the disco.

But maybe his father's most dangerous enterprise had been his attempt to be a fruit-and-vegetable man. Who would have thought that potatoes and apples could turn so nasty? For him, that adventure had reached its dark conclusion the night his father said, 'Oh ho.' Those two syllables would sound always in his mind like the double turn of a key to unlock a special chamber in his memory vaults.

'OH HO,' his father has said.

His blue eyes widen. Sitting in his armchair, he slowly takes from his mouth the cigarette he has just lit. He purses his lips as if interpreting the meaning of the sound they have all just heard. It was a triple knocking at the door and very loud.

They have been listening to the wireless. Almost half an hour beforehand, there had been the familiar tolling bell, the plangent chord of menacing music, and Valentine Dyall, in a voice as dark as a subterranean passageway, had intoned, '*Appointment with Fear*. This is your story-teller, the Man in Black . . .'

Tam loves that voice. He has often practised being Valentine Dyall in the bath until the water went cold – with fear, it seemed to him – around his body. Sometimes the family has put out the light and listened by fireglow, Michael making terrifying faces at Tam any time he dares to look over. ('Stop that, you,' Tam's mother says. 'Ye'll give the boay nightmares. A face like yours. Worse than any horror story.')

They haven't done that this evening. Only his mother and father and Tam are in the house. But this story is frightening enough in the light. It is about a very self-confident man who claims to have no superstitions. To prove his contempt for such nonsense as the existence of ghosts, he makes a bet with another man that he will spend the night locked in a funeral parlour surrounded by dead bodies. He is given a tape-recorder to record his reactions throughout the night, so that he cannot come out in the morning and deny what he really felt. He tapes a few bland and relaxed comments at first. All is going well, it seems, until in the course of recording another message, he says how boring all this is and that he wouldn't even be afraid if that corpse in the glass-topped coffin were to tap three times on the glass.

Just at that moment there is the sound of a fingernail tapping three times on glass. There is almost simultaneously the sound of a hand knocking three times on a door. Tam is nearly out of his chair before he realises why he is so frightened. The door that someone is beating on isn't inside the radio. It is in his house. It is as if the story has come out of the wireless to get him personally. In embarrassment at his own obvious fear, he starts to laugh. He is taking relief from the fact that the knocking is real. But the relief doesn't last long.

His father's widening eyes are looking at Tam's mother. His mother's eyes look back nervously. Dawson Street isn't exactly the wild frontier but it can be rough. When you open that door, nobody is going to shoot you. But this can be an angry place, friendly but angry. You learn to know the different knocks on the door. This knock is too brisk. It is at least impertinent. It isn't the way you knock at people's doors. It means trouble.

'Ah'll get it, Conn,' Tam's mother says.

Tam's father nods slowly.

'All right, Betsy,' he says.

While she goes to the door, his father's eyes stay on the fire as Tam watches him. Neither of them can hear what is being said but Tam understands that his father is not listening for words. He is listening for sounds, a signal of what is happening out there. His body has become tense in the chair. His eyes are seeing nothing, as if he has erased sight instinctively in order to achieve what Tam has heard is true of the blind – intensified hearing through the absence of vision.

With the heightened intuition of fear, Tam suddenly realises why his mother has gone to the door. It is to defuse a dangerous situation with a woman's presence. If she can speak to whoever is there first, things may be calmed down. When she comes back in, she doesn't look too calm. Her face is flushed.

'Conn,' she says nervously. 'It's the Burleys. The van's broken down. There's three o' them. They're awfu angry.'

This is bad. Tam's father is unlikely to die. But he is likely to be very severely dealt with. There is a reason for this, as there usually is, if you can find it.

Tam's awareness knows the reason. His father had tried recently to run a fruit-and-vegetable business. It was the latest of his dreams of instant wealth, negative capitalism in practice. He bought a van. He converted its interior into shelves that could accommodate various fruits and vegetables. Michael was involved. He had come out of National Service with a driver's licence. He would drive for his father. The Dochertys have suddenly achieved the status, it would seem, of having a family business. It is not a status they are destined to enjoy for long.

Michael has told Allison and Tam, out of earshot of their father, about the first sale achieved by the family business. Michael drives the van into Shortlees housing scheme. Their father gets out, dressed in a leather apron and with a leather satchel slung over his shoulders. ('Like a wee-boy that got a tattie-man's outfit for his Christmas?' Allison says.)

'Tattees! Vegetables!' their father begins to shout. Michael is instantly helpless with laughter. He is stretched full length along the double seat in the cabin of the van, moaning for mercy. The image of his father, transformed in seconds from sardonic fireside philosopher into town crier, is too much for him. ('It was so corny,' Michael says. 'Like he'd been to RADA and not passed the course.')

'Behave yerself, ya daft bastard!' their father is hissing at Michael between public announcements. 'They'll think we're amateurs at the game. Tattees! Vegetables!'

The first customer is a small woman 'with a face like a vinegar sponge'. (Michael describes her through the tears of his renewed laughter.)

'Yes, ma bonny lass,' their father says. 'What can Ah do for you this fine day?'

'Ah'll take half a stone of potatoes.'

'Yes, you will. That is what you will have.'

Michael hears him working with the metal weights which he bought in a second-hand shop and of which he is so proud. He has spent an hour or so practising with them in the living-room.

'There we are, ma dear. And many, many thanks.'

Michael climbs down from the cabin and comes round to the back of the van. Their father is smiling.

'First sale for the old firm,' their father says. 'Off and running at Ascot.'

Michael looks at the scales, where the small metal block that has been used to measure the weight of the potatoes is still in place.

'What did that woman ask for, Feyther?' he says.

'Tatties. Half a stone. Not much but a beginnin'.'

'Even less than ye think. The scales say a quarter of a stane.'

'Eh?'

Their father looks at the scales.

'Ah naw,' he says. 'Those fuckin' daft weights. Ah can never get them right.'

Michael describes the long moment of indecision on their father's face. Allison and Tam can see it as if it were a close-up in a film. He isn't sure which house the woman has gone into. He looks at the scales. He would like to give the woman the extra potatoes. But he is too embarrassed to start making enquiries.

'Fuck it,' he says. 'Let's get our arses outa here.'

And they rattle off like the James gang on wheels.

The first sale was an omen. In five weeks the business had folded and someone had reported Tam's father to the Inland Revenue, who were claiming tax on mysterious sums of money he had never seen. The business has run at a loss.

The threat of financial ruin and roup hung over the family until Tam's mother went down to the tax office and spoke to a man there. She explained that, far from being a tax-dodger, her husband had rendered the family a hardship case. She told the man how little she had received for housekeeping during the five weeks of what the family would afterwards call 'the great potato famine'.

She cited some of the other ventures her husband had engaged in. She mentioned the ton or more of gasmasks he had bought. John Grant, who had a lock-up near Tam's father's had tipped him off that each gas mask contained a small disc of copper. She told how he and Uncle Charlie, for a fortnight, turned up at 8 a.m every weekday at the lock-up where the gas masks were stored. They treated it as a full-time job. They brought a piece with them and took only a half-hour lunch-break. They worked until 5.30 p.m. each day, chatting as they worked about the riches they were accumulating. At the end of two weeks they went, with hands scarred and chapped from stripping each gas mask down to that small particle of precious metal, and delivered their hoarded wealth to Piebald Lundy, a local scrap dealer. He gave them two pounds ten shillings to split between them.

She told him about the standard lamp fiasco. She was going to tell him about—

'Mrs Docherty,' the man said. 'Let's stop there. Tell me any more and I'll feel obliged to lend you a pound from my own pocket.'

He took a letter he had on his desk and tore it up and put it in a waste basket. When she came home and told them what had happened, there was general relief and laughter. Only their father was quiet, brooding by the fire.

'One thing, Betsy,' he said darkly. 'He didny give ye the name o' the bastard that shopped me?'

Next day he sold the van to the Burleys for thirty pounds. That was maybe ten days before.

Now he stands up and nicks his cigarette into the fire. He puts the stub on the mantelpiece.

'Be careful, Conn,' Tam's mother says.

His father shrugs to her. John Garfield couldn't have done it better. Tam is impressed by that shrug, for the Burleys are a known family in the town, violent and fierce and sudden, offering the rule of force. Anyone who tries to take them to a law beyond their own is liable to appear in court with a bandaged head and an imperfect set of teeth with which to state his case. Tam's father goes to the front door. Tam and his mother wait tensely in the living-room. He watches her. Her eyes are scouting the room nervously. Perhaps she is looking for a suitable object, should things turn physical.

The living-room has been redefined for Tam. He sits in a cave of warmth and brightness. Beyond its entrance bad things can happen, dark creatures roam. His father guards that entrance. The sounds that come from there rumble and threaten. The voices of all three Burleys are deep and indistinct. They all seem to be making noises at the same time. His father's voice is light by comparison. His mother and Tam are statues. The exchange that is taking place out there is only sometimes meaningful.

'No' good enough' growls towards them.

'Sold in good faith.'

'Some kinna refund.'

'Ye'd have tae take that out the brig.'

It's an expression Tam has heard his father use before. The brig, Tam realises with panic, is the bridge of the nose.

'Ah don't have a copper tae spare.'

'It's no' gonny do.'

The grumbling continues, ebbing and flowing.

'Look, boays. Decide what ye want tae dae. It's cauld oot here.'

The voices growl on but slowly, Tam realises with relief, the growling is receding. He hears the door being closed.

On the wireless, Valentine has completed his story about

the man in the funeral parlour, unaware that he has been broadcasting to Madame Tussaud's for the last few minutes. It seems the other man, who put the bet on with him, persuaded a friend to lie in one of the coffins. He had tapped on the glass three times when he heard the recording being made.

When the funeral parlour is opened in the morning, only one man survives from the two who were alive the night before. At first, they can't tell which it is, for he is transformed, lined with age and grey-haired and raving. Eventually, they understand that he is the man who bet he could stay in the place overnight. He had thought the man in the coffin was a ghost and had strangled him and had lived the rest of the night in dread that another ghost would come. Unusually, Tam hasn't been able to give in to the horror the man is supposed to have felt. He thought ghosts were frightening? Had he met the Burleys?

Tam's father comes back in and takes the butt of his cigarette off the mantelpiece. He sits down, finds a match and holds its head against the hot grate till it flares. He lights his cigarette and throws the match in the fire. He looks across at Tam's mother and, beginning to smoke, he winks.

THAT WINK STANDS LIKE A MONOLITH IN HIS MEMORY.

—ATERWARDS, he would be talking to his aged mother and she would mention his dead father. He would see her dimming eyes go suddenly and preternaturally bright, as they did in those days when an image of the past renewed itself without warning in her and her eyes grew momentarily younger to meet the memory. He loved that brightness but it gave him a pang as well. Out of the deepening darkness, another moth of memory had collided with the dying flame of her life. How many more would come? And she would say:

'If he was back just now, Ah would change that many things. Wouldn't everybody? There's a lot Ah wouldn't put up with. That man could be an awful trial. But Ah'll tell ye one thing, son. When he was here, Ah could leave the front door wide tae the wall an' sleep like a wean. Nobody and nothing was goin' tae come in that door an' hurt me. He was always problems but he was always man. An' the problems were the careless daftness of his nature. They were never malice. As a financial provider, he was a disaster. An' Ah blame him for that. But in other ways, in a livin' way, he was a true protector.'

And he decided he knew at last the answer to that space on those forms.—

FATHER'S OCCUPATION: MAN. Maybe that would be as much as his children would be able to say about him. Or maybe it would be more than they could say. He wasn't too sure he qualified even in that category. When he thought of the stable lives his friends seemed to have made for themselves, he wondered how he came to be here, staring across the road at Warriston Cemetery. Waiting in the anteroom.

Why did he sometimes feel betrayed? When he was young – at university, for example – they had seemed to be so many, setting out together towards the identified enemies of materialism and selfishness and careerism and denial of the community of being human. You became fewer. Then suddenly it was dark and it was cold and you were tired and you could see those enemies no longer as abstractions but real and immediate as skinheads closing in and, as you moved towards them, you felt you were on your own. You looked around and thought, 'We used to be a crowd.' What lighted houses had they ducked into, what private comforts? And there seemed nowhere to go but on. You had narrowed your choices to this.

How had he managed to do that? Did the answer lie in some uncertain responses to the experiences of that summer, how they precipitated him into who he was to be?

HE SITS IN A CHAIR and he can see himself sitting in a chair. It is one of those moments when the self-consciousness of what we are doing makes us audience as well as actor. He watches himself with not a little amazement. This is an important thing he is going to do. Is he really going to do it? The hero makes a life-affecting decision.

The chair is outside the Rector's office. As he sits here, he can listen to the sounds of the school all around him. The building is a three-storeyed square tower with a central well. Noise carries. On C Flat above, someone is getting a row outside a room.

'How dare you! Are you insane? Well. Are you?'

It seems a curious question to Tam. According to something he heard, if you think you are, you aren't. So if you say no, presumably the question remains open. No way to answer.

'I asked you a question.'

Not really, Tam thinks. The voice belongs to Mr Fenwick, Principal Teacher of Modern Languages. As the only male in the department, he affects a kind of hysterical masculinity as if to compensate for the feminine gentleness all around him. This takes the form of cosmic rages about anything from a dropped participle to an unlocated fart.

'I'm waiting!'

The indecipherable answer seems non-committal.

'Well, if you aren't, there's no excuse. Only a plea of insanity would suffice. A shitty? A shitty? How do you do a shitty?'

For a moment Tam thinks it is Mr Fenwick who is insane. He has finally cracked. Maybe all those rages were just practice for the big one. His interest quickens. He may be overhearing a historic moment.

'The verb is *acheter*. And well you know it.'

Tam understands. Someone has been trying to be subversive and get away with it. Under the pretext of enquiring about the conjugation of *acheter*, a bad word has been introduced, like someone smuggling a mouse into the classroom and then disclaiming it. It has to be a first-year class Mr Fenwick has.

Only in first year could a question about *acheter* pretend to be real.

'Up, up. I'll show you how *not* to do *acheter*.'

There is the thwack of leather on flesh. Tam's memory winces. He counts. Only two. A door opens and closes with a bang. There is comparative silence. Just an average day at the two-way trauma factory.

From his lofty position as a fifth-year pupil he finds the apprentice rebel pretty pathetic. Apart from mistaking cheek for protest, his technique is crass. If he really wanted to be a bampot, he should have taken lessons from Gorman, who had been in Tam's year.

Gorman came out of the part of Graithnock that was nicknamed Tintown, from which stories emerged of coal kept in the bath and skirting-boards ripped up for firewood. Gorman hated the Academy from the beginning. He had done quite well in his qualifying exam and must have been bright enough. But whatever intelligence he had was steadily converted to negative cunning. His ultimate educational achievement was to devise a method of swearing in class with impunity.

What he did was develop a stammer. It happened when he came back from the Easter holidays in the third year. It may have seemed to the more sympathetic teachers that the pressure of academic failure had reduced him to an exaggerated inarticulacy, as if he were acting out his inner feelings of inadequacy. But the pupils noticed that he stammered only in the class. It soon became clear to them why. It was his last defiant gesture before he left in the summer.

It allowed him to look for the first syllables of words which would have been, in isolation, swear-words. He could then say them several times before adding the rest of the word, thus claiming innocence. His greatest triumph was probably a question he put to Miss Stevens in the English class.

'Please, miss. Arse-cunt – arse-cunt – arse-cunt – are Scunthorpians people who come from Scunthorpe?'

Miss Stevens's eyes widened fearfully, as if she were standing on an edge so high that she couldn't see all the way down. She blinked and stepped back from the brink.

'I believe so, Gorman,' she said.

Gorman smiled a bitterly happy smile.

Isn't education wonderful, Tam thinks. Sitting here, he realises how important this old building has been for him. He feels nostalgic for a lot of people, though not quite Gorman. That would be like feeling nostalgic for a dose of the pox you once had. Thinking of which, here comes Dusty Thomas. He stops in front of Tam, looking down on him. He would be, wouldn't he?

'Well, Docherty. What have you done now?'

'Nothin', sir.'

'I find that hard to believe.'

'No. Ah haven't done anything, sir.'

'So why are you here?'

'An interview with Mr MacGregor.'

'About what?'

'It's personal, sir.'

Dusty stares at him.

'Huh. I'll bet.'

What the hell does that mean? But old Dusty smiles in a self-satisfied way and walks off. Why do teachers, when they're stuck for a riposte, say the most banal crap with clipped and meaningful delivery, as if it is an aphorism they've only just invented?

Why does Dusty Thomas hate him so much? It must be because he gave up Greek in favour of French. But what kind of reason is that? He used to think Tam was somebody special. When he scored ninety-eight and a half in first-year Latin, Dusty said he had never given a mark as high as that before. So he seemed to decide that Tam belonged to him. Then, as soon as Tam gave up Greek, he was disowned. He changed overnight from being a classical scholar to a hooligan. Out of my sight. You have pissed upon the tomb of Agamemnon. Okay, Dusty. Who was it that got the mark in the first place?

The door of the main office opens and Mrs Ainslie, the school secretary, comes out. She is a stern woman who looks as if her idea of a good time would be knitting, preferably under the guillotine.

'Mr MacGregor will see you now,' she says.

She knocks at the Rector's door and opens it.

'Docherty's here, Mr MacGregor. Shall I show him in?'

'All right.'

She gestures Tam into the room and closes the door. This is the ritual – no unauthorised knocking at the Rector's door. Maybe the chapped hands of the plebs would defile the sanctum. Tam wants to think it's ridiculous but he has to admit it works. The few times he has been in this room have not seen him at his most self-confident. This time is no exception. He stands awkwardly inside the door.

Mr MacGregor sits behind his large desk, preoccupied. He looks impressive enough like that but, standing, he must measure six feet two. He has a large, carved face and rich, silver hair. He looks positively biblical. He stares over his glasses and points Tam to the seat in front of his desk. Tam sits down. Mr MacGregor goes on looking at the papers on his desk and writing things on them. Whatever he is doing, he makes it look very important. Perhaps he's rejigging the Ten Commandments.

The room doesn't help, Tam decides. It looks as if it has more books in it than the Bodleian Library which Boris told them about. The bookcases look like antiques. The air is pungently heavy, a mixture of musty volumes and dispersed pipe-smoke and furniture polish. It's as if only grave business may enter here. This is the opposite of what Auden said about Macao: And nothing serious can happen here. And nothing trivial can happen here. (Where *is* Macao, anyway?) You feel that, if a fly came in here, it would apologise on its way back out the window. He feels maybe he rates about even-steven with the fly.

'Well, Docherty?'

The glasses are off. Tam looks into the deep-set, self-assured eyes and tries not to let his own self-assurance founder there.

'Yes, sir?'

'What is it this time?'

'I'm applying for university. I just wanted to tell you, sir.'

'Of course you are. Next year.'

'No, sir. This year. Ah'm leaving at the end of fifth.'

Mr MacGregor lifts his ready-filled pipe and a box of Swan Vestas. He lights up carefully, ceremoniously, and puffs out smoke. He now looks even more Old Testament. For burning bush, read burning bowl.

'Oh, Docherty. You've had the fidgets all this year, haven't you? What is it with you, boy?'

(Have you got a spare week? How many answers do you want? Like, my imagination's a harem and my reality's a eunuch. I'm seventeen and I might as well be ten. Would you not be fidgety if you'd never had it? I'm fed up trying to walk about like John Garfield when I feel like Peter Pan. If it goes on like this, I'm liable to jump Mrs Ainslie. And neither of us would like that. In fact, now that I think about it, do you mind if I go to the toilet? Back in two shakes. Well, maybe more than two. Aaaaaaaaaaagh. Does that answer your question?)

'What was it last time? Before Christmas. Dropping Greek, wasn't it?'

'That's right.'

'And now this. This would mean you couldn't sit the Bursary Competition.'

'That's right.'

The Bursary Competition is a big deal in the school. It is a series of subject exams taken by pupils all over Scotland. The results are published in the *Glasgow Herald* and a high placing is supposed to bring honour to the school.

'I have high hopes for you in that.'

'I'm sorry, sir.'

'You've thought about this?'

(No, I just made it up sitting outside your door.)

'Yes, a lot.'

'Do your parents know?'

In the innocence of the question Tam sees the different set of assumptions from which he and Mr MacGregor come, making it difficult for them to meet. Tam regards both his parents as seriously intelligent people but that intelligence has never been allowed access, due to their time and circumstances, to such esoteric issues as whether it is better or not to do a sixth year at school. They will be guided by whatever Tam thinks. They haven't the information to do anything else.

'Yes,' Tam says simply. 'We've discussed it.'

'Ah, well,' Mr MacGregor says. 'I suspect economy is involved in this somewhere. And it is hard to argue against the economic circumstances by which other people are obliged to make their choices.'

Tam is reminded of why he likes this man as well as respects him. It is perhaps a surprising liking for him to have. Mr MacGregor's style is patrician and authoritarian. He always seems to Tam like someone out of *Tom Brown's School days*, which is not his favourite book. In Tam's mind he occupies approximately the same position as one of those Victorian statues you sometimes see at the centre of a town, striking a heroic pose and staring into some lost horizon of idealism, while the present throws chip-pokes around its feet and chalks graffiti on its plinth. But within the stony rigidity, he knows that there lives a perceptive and humane man.

When he announced the new prefects at the beginning of fifth year and made Tam one of them, an appointment not universally approved of by the staff, he made it very clear to the assembled pupils that being a prefect didn't necessitate the wearing of a blazer. As the only casually dressed person in a roomful of blazers, Tam appreciated the public declaration that he was not a pariah.

'Your reason for dropping Greek,' Mr MacGregor says. 'I seem to recall it was not unconnected with your ambition to be a writer. Is that right?'

'Yes.'

'Yes. I remember your saying that it was interfering with your reading. The Greek was. I suggested that perhaps your reading was interfering with your Greek. I think you replied that if you weren't going to be a writer you weren't going to be anything.' Mr MacGregor smiled briefly to himself. 'Does this present decision relate to the same . . . compulsion?'

'I suppose so, sir.'

'I sometimes think, Docherty, that winning the Rector's Essay Prize has not been good for you. It seems to have given you delusions of grandeur.'

Tam doesn't mention that he has always had them.

'And now you're going to be a writer. Just like that?'

'No. I realise it might take a few weeks, sir.'

Tam could have bitten his tongue. He hasn't meant to be smart-arsed. This was meant to be more like a joke between friends. But they aren't friends. Why is he always confusing conversational styles, mixing social genres?

'I don't think it's a laughing matter, Docherty.'

'No. It's just that I've been trying to write for years, sir.'

'You think you'll have more time at university?'

'Well, at least I can concentrate on things that don't interfere with my writing.'

The pomposity of it seems to make Mr MacGregor realise that he is dealing with someone who is more or less certifiable.

'Good luck, Docherty,' he says. 'You'll need it.'

He returns to his papers. Tam turns at the door. Mr MacGregor has replaced his glasses.

'Mr MacGregor. Thanks for your understanding.'

Mr MacGregor looks over his glasses.

'No, Docherty,' he says. 'Not understanding. Bafflement. Thank me for that. It has made me accommodating.'

And as soon as Tam comes out of the room, he begins to doubt his decision. He spends the rest of the day feeling nostalgic for the future he has given up, realising in each of the classes he visits that he will not be here next year. He can no longer understand why he is leaving school until he is stopped by Dusty Thomas in a corridor. Dusty has heard the news.

'Docherty.' The way he says the name makes it sound synonymous with dung beetle. 'You're a disgrace. After all this school has done for you, you're preparing to scurry off rather than show your gratitude in the only way you could. By doing well in the Bursary Comp. I've watched you for five years, Docherty. You know what you are? You're an iconoclast. Do you know what an iconoclast is, Docherty?'

'I think so. Isn't it—'

'I'll tell you what it is in your case, Docherty. It means someone who can't say yes. You've done well in the highers. You've got the possibility of a year's more intensive study ahead of you. Culminating in the Bursary Comp. A lot of people have contributed to give you a chance. And you reject it. Go back to your housing scheme.'

'Ah never left it, sir.'

'Oh, how true. You know something? I've a good mind to bounce you off that wall.'

It must be something about the way he looks. Beef Bowman. Mr Inglis. Now even Dusty, who looks as if walking fast would give him a seizure.

'I wouldn't do that, sir.'

'What?'

'I might bounce back.'

'Are you threatening me?'

'Ah thought you were threatening me, sir.'

'I was in the Second World War, sonny.'

'Are ye sure ye didn't start it, sir?'

Dusty's long stare decides to congeal into distant contempt.

'Leave today, Docherty,' he says. 'You have no place in this school. Leave today.'

In spirit, he does. Dusty has made sure of that by telling him that, after five years, the school only knows him as an adjunct of itself. He feels doubly alienated. The school rejects who he is now but only after educating him into the rejection of who he was before he came here.

'HAVE YE DONE IT YET?'

This time they are standing in Bank Street. The bright summer has been suspended for the moment. A dim Scottish sun is out, less day realised than day potential, as if God has left on the pilot light. People move above the street in mezzotint. He has bumped into Sammy Clegg and they stop to talk.

Gentle, stubborn, lost Sammy – one of those to whom life has dealt a yarborough: thirteen cards in his hand and not one above a nine. (Tam had thought up that image for Sammy and was pleased with it. It was the main reason he was grateful to his Uncle Josey for having taught him how to play bridge, however inexpertly.) He knew Sammy from primary school where he had early on shown promise of being a loser with a streak of defiance in him, as if he knew his role in life and refused all assistance. A definitive moment in Tam's sense of him had occurred while they were still in infant class.

A group of them are filing into school at the end of playtime

– little, regimented, clockwork creatures. The infant mistress is walking beside them, clapping her hands in time to their marching feet. Tam is near the end of the line and, as those at the front turn a corner of the corridor, the infant mistress stops clapping. Confused noises are heard off. Whatever is happening up there feeds itself back through the line unevenly as a refusal to go on. The children bringing up the rear are bumping into those in front. Unexplained sounds are occurring, gasps of shock and muffled cries of amazement and the hysterical voice of Mrs MacPherson, the other infants' teacher. Always eager for experience, Tam breaks ranks and, under cover of the confusion, turns the corner of the corridor to see what's going on.

Sammy is standing in the corridor. (Presumably he had slipped into school before the end of the interval, a heinous offence in itself but not half as heinous as what he has done once he got in.) Mrs MacPherson is doing what looks like the rain dance she told them about the previous month. The infant mistress, Miss Stevely, is screaming. She is terrifying when she screams. She is terrifying when she doesn't scream. She has rimless glasses and a chest as bumpy as an ironing-board. On Tam's first day at school, when she peremptorily asked who would be wanting milk, he didn't put his hand up for fear of her rage when she found out he couldn't pay for it.

'Go home, Samuel Clegg!' she is screaming. 'Go home this instant.'

'Naw,' Sammy is saying.

This basic exchange is repeated several times without either of the teachers daring to lay hands on Sammy. The reason for this reluctance is simple. Sammy has been caught short in the corridor and a leg, a stocking and one of his boots are liberally encrusted.

Eventually, perhaps because the flaunting of authority is an unhealthy spectacle for the young or perhaps because of the risk of death by smell, they are marshalled again into obedience and marched past Sammy in a wide detour, while he stands there like a Hun surrounded by Rome.

Sammy has improved since then, it has to be said. He has also outgrown his unbrushed teeth phase, when his smile had been like the Hanging Gardens of Babylon. By the time they are talking in the street he is, like Tam, seventeen and very conscious of his appearance. He is scrupulously clean and his hair is carefully groomed into a pendulous quiff at the front and what is called a 'D.A.' at the back. He is wearing a Teddy-boy suit, blue in colour, long of jacket, short and drainpipe of leg, with brothel-creeper shoes, the soles of which are thick crêpe.

Yet in spite of his sartorial elegance, the appearance of being a sophisticate, Sammy is still a loser and internally a mess. He must be one of the few people who know less about practical sex than Tam does. He is the *Encyclopaedia Britannica* of sexual ignorance. Tam suspects that's the main reason he doesn't want the conversation to stop this day.

Since they have left primary school – Sammy to go to Junior Secondary and Tam to go to Graithnock Academy, the Senior Secondary – they have met each other occasionally and casually. Their intermittent exchanges have acquired the guardedness of sentries talking across the borders of separate countries. Education can do that to you, Tam thinks. Your head emigrates and you're a full citizen neither of where you were nor of where you are.

Even this accidental meeting with Sammy Clegg in a Graithnock street holds something of the strangeness of this summer – a small tableau of one of the many confusions of Tam's life. He is partly a stranger in his own town. Sammy is where he has come from. Sammy's potential life is a chart Tam feels himself abandoning and he envies Sammy his sense of direction. For what does Tam have to put in its place?

Sammy is an apprentice joiner. Tam is supposed to be going to university at the end of the summer. He has been accepted for an arts course but, being the first of his family ever to have seriously contemplated university, he doesn't honestly believe it will happen. It isn't what his family does. Sammy wears his Teddy-boy gear like a uniform. Tam is more eclectically dressed, with a jacket that doesn't match the trousers, one of his brother Michael's old shirts and slip-on shoes. Sammy reads the sports pages. Tam is wrestling with the *Journals* of Kierkegaard and has written a long poem about the nature of life. Sammy will marry soon and have children and fight occasionally and get drunk and do his work. What the hell will Tam do? The familiar shape of

Sammy's life seems to Tam like a lost Eden and him living east of it, wondering if it is already too late to get back in. Maybe he should just keep working in the night-shift job he has taken at Avondale Brickwork for the summer holidays and forget about university. That way, his life could be as uncomplicated as Sammy's.

But how uncomplicated is that? It certainly doesn't look too uncomplicated. Even in his self-absorption, Tam at least manages to see the mirror image of his own searching for self in Sammy. Sammy hasn't a clue who he is either. Tam is wondering if anybody has. They stand there and have one of those slightly desperate conversations by which the lonely and the lost refurbish their image of themselves in each other's eyes. Sammy tells him about his apprenticeship, spitting a lot and swearing more and more as he talks himself towards the tradesman he will be. Tam makes a lot of jokes about Graithnock Academy, beginning to be amazed at how funny his school life has been.

'Tam,' Sammy suddenly says.

Tam knows the pretence of shared identities they have been maintaining is about to collapse. Sammy's tone has a shy suspiciousness. Tam waits.

'Tam,' Sammy says again. He looks down Bank Street and then furtively back at Tam. 'Talk French.'

'Come on, Sammy.'

'No. On ye go. Talk French.'

'What would Ah say?'

'Anythin'.'

'Come on, Sammy.'

'They learned ye it at the school, didn't they?'

'Aye.'

'Well. On ye go. Ah just want to hear what it sounds like. To hear you sayin' it.'

Tam's not sure why he is so embarrassed. He thinks it is perhaps because it feels like being invited to pick someone's pocket. Sammy's wonder is there before any reason for it. Whatever Tam says is going to impress him. But what is the point of words that aren't your own, unearned experience? Language without dynamic content is meaningless, just an oral conjuring trick. It is said he lay with her.

'*Le livre est sur la table,*' he says quietly.

'Sorry?'
'Le livre est sur la table.'
Sammy might be looking at someone from the Amazon basin. He stares at him for some time. He shakes his head.
'Whoo,' he says, awestruck. 'So?'
'So what?'
'So what does it mean?'
'The book is on the table.'
'The book is on the table,' he repeats slowly. 'That's what it's sayin'? The book is on the table.'

His reverence could not be more if the book had been *War and Peace* and Tam had written it. He is still shaking his head and it is as if, unknown to himself, he is refusing Tam re-entry to the past they have shared. Tam has become something different. Like someone remembering an old password, Tam comments on a passing girl.

'Ah know what Ah would like to do to her.'

This is less than entirely accurate. The liking is there but the knowledge is sadly absent. Still, it has the desired effect on Sammy. The wonders of language are forgotten.

'What a body,' Sammy says. 'Have ye done it yet?'

He manages to flannel his way out of a direct answer but, thinking of going to the brickwork tonight, he reflects that there are some situations you can't fake yourself out of.

'DON'T SIT THERE.'

The voice comes out like marsh mist, so obscure with hoarseness that words appear as blurs in it. Your ears have to peer to catch the meaning. The face from which the voice emerges is battered and stamped with varied experience, an old suitcase with a lot of labels on it. The labels are no longer legible.

'Ho no,' a sing-song echoes.

This time the speaker's face seems to float on his lumpy, awkward body, as if his head is loosely anchored to his being. The face has the indeterminate age of the simpleton, lives in a limbo of features where, if maturity can't properly take hold, neither can aging. When he looks at you, his eyes gley over your shoulders, seeming to communicate with someone you can't see and usually suggestive of mysterious mirth. It is as if the rest of the world is a joke only he has rumbled.

'Ho no.'

'That's the King of Avondale's seat,' a small man says.

He doesn't seem to belong here, as if he might just be taking shelter while waiting for a bus.

'Might as well sit in the electric chair,' a big, fresh-faced young man says.

He is wearing a long, Teddy-boy jacket, drainpipes and working boots.

Tam is relieved he isn't the one who tried to sit in the chair. It was Jack Laidlaw who did that. Tam makes a sympathetic face as Jack comes over to sit beside him. They are glad that they know each other. Jack is still at Graithnock Academy, a year behind Tam. They have been no more than acquaintances but they feel as close as conspirators here in the strangeness of their first night at the brickwork. They feel like migrants arrived together in a foreign country.

They have strange customs here, strange people. Tam has been mystified by everything. Time, for example, is divided into one-hour units. For an hour you sit at the machine and pick up the unbaked black bricks that spew out at you relentlessly and stack them on a hutch. While your head screams with boredom, the machine keeps throwing the bricks at you until you think its action is a deliberate and personal insult to the mind. For an hour, while someone else becomes an extension of the machine, you push the loaded hutches out of the lighted shed into the darkness and along the rails that lead to the kiln. One of the two men in the kiln accepts the full hutch and you bring the empty one back to the shed to be reloaded. For an hour you sweep the shed and try to remember that you're not a robot. Then you return to unloading the bricks.

Tam hates it already. It is raining tonight and he has turned up wearing casual shoes. Fred Astaire visits the brickwork. His feet are soaking and he is up to his kneecaps in mud. Twice he has pushed the heavy bogey off the rails and has almost wept with the strain of having to lift it back on. Only the shame of asking for help has given him the strength to realign the hutch single-handed. But he doesn't know how much longer he can go on.

Yet now, as he sits at the tea-break, he finds an unexpected compensation. The sandwiches his mother made him taste wonderful. He remembers his father telling him something his grandfather once said about being a miner: 'Pit-breid is the only guid reason for goin' doon a mine.' The sense of being part of a family tradition sustains him a little. He has found a direct connection, however tenuous, with the legendary grandfather he has never known personally. That dead man of reputedly awesome hardness gives him some sort of credentials here, tells him, 'This isn't so strange.' No matter how strange it may seem.

'So this army wallah is comin' tae teach the Home Guard about hand grenades,' the man with the lived-in face is saying.

'Ye didny use hand grenades in the Home Guard?'

'Only as ornaments. But ye had tae be prepared. An' we're all lined up in front of him. An' he's holdin' up a hand grenade. An' he shows us how ye pull the pin. Without actually pullin' it, mind ye. An' he says, "Once you've done that, you count." An' he counts. "One. Two. Three. Four. Five. Six. Seven." An' he kids on he's throwin' the grenade. An' a long time after, when he's goin' away. Sandy Lamont. Ye know Sandy? Helluva stammer. Well, Sandy's got a question. "H-h-h-h-how m-m-m-many d'ye c-c-count up tae again?" An' the man stares at him for a while. "Just you fuckin' throw it," he says. "Never mind the counting."'

The gaffer, who is an Englishman, comes in.

'Right, you lot,' he says. 'Holidays over.'

As Tam rises, he feels the pains in his arms and legs and he thinks he won't make it through his first night. But he does and the first night becomes the second and the second becomes the third and the third becomes habit. He is wearing Michael's old boots now and an old boilersuit of his father's with the hems on the legs let down. He has become better at keeping the bogey on the rails. The trick is to apply the weight only forwards as you push, never downwards.

The gargoyle faces of the first night have resolved themselves into recognisably human forms. They have developed names and identifying attitudes. The man with the marsh-mist voice is Hilly Brown. (Hilly? He doesn't look like a Hilton. Hilliard? Hillman?)

Hilly is the talker of the company. His beat-up face releases wry words and arresting thoughts into the stillness of the tea-break when the silence of the machines sounds like freedom to be yourself. His use of language interests Tam.

'Farquhar, ya bastard!' Hilly says at the beginning of a break.

'What's up, Hilly?' James Morrison asks.

'What's up? Ah've just had the first bite o' ma piece here an' this balloon hawks a thing on to the ground like a jaur o' tadpoles.'

A jar of tadpoles. That's a terrific description of a certain kind of spittle. Hilly uses some amazing images. He is telling them of going through a wood one night and coming upon a couple making love on the ground. 'His arse,' he says, 'was openin' and shuttin' like a sea-anemone.'

He is the one who gives Tam his apprentice's initiation. He has discovered that Tam did classics at school.

'So ye're a classical scholar?' he says. 'Tam, is it? Okay, Tam. What's Latin for aeroplane?'

Tam has been searching his mind for about fifteen seconds before he twigs.

'Aw naw,' he says. 'Thanks a lot.'

He realises he has been subjected to a variant of being sent for a left-handed brush or a tin of tartan paint. The feeling of stupidity is minimised by the fact that the others have been waiting quite seriously for the answer. As the laughter subsides, Dunky Semple, who has joined in, speaks.

'Can ye no' think of it, Tam?' he says.

Dunky's brains, as Hilly says, 'are still in the box. He's waitin' for instructions comin' through the post about what to do wi' them.' Dunky gazes vaguely past their conversations, constantly nicking and relighting a Capstan Full Strength cigarette and passing weirdly tangential comments that seem to come, as Hilly has suggested, from 'Radio Mars'. They are discussing women, as they often are, and Dunky chooses a thoughtful pause in the conversation to interject.

'At the pictures one time,' Dunky says. 'A lassie took ma hand. She just sat and held it, so she did. For ages it was. Her hand was warm. An' it was that soft. The softest thing Ah ever felt. She went out before the lights went up.'

Nobody laughs, not even Billy Farquhar. They sit staring ahead.

'Ye shoulda got her address, Dunky,' Hilly says.

—AFTERWARDS, he would be talking to an old woman who lived alone in sheltered housing. She suddenly began to talk about a Wallace Arnold's bus holiday she took to Brighton many years ago. The thing she remembered most vividly was an afternoon tea-dance. The same man had asked her to dance twice. She could describe the man very clearly. Listening to her recall that luminous moment, he would think of Dunky and wonder about the varieties of quiet lonelinesses there were, a one-handed love-affair, a two-dance life.—

BILLY FARQUHAR IS THE TEDDY-BOY'S NAME. He is nineteen, huge and with his thick red hair done in a quiff and a D.A. at the back. (Duck's arse is translated by the papers into duck's anatomy.) It's surprising that he didn't laugh at Dunky's confession of lost love for he seems as sensitive as one of the bricks that come red from the kiln. He doesn't take much part in the conversations, preferring to stare round about while Hilly and James Morrison talk, using a large knife to cut up the turnips he steals from a neighbouring farmer's field for his piece. If something they touch on catches his attention as being noteworthy or surprising, he tends to say 'Fuck!' as his contribution to the discussion, or, if he's feeling expansive, 'Holy fuck!' He only really animates if he is invited to report on his latest experiences of getting a ride or having a fight. He is reputed, by Hilly Brown at least, to have 'a dong like an anaconda'.

James Morrison doesn't welcome such information. Both Tam and Jack Laidlaw have been separately informed by him on the first night that he doesn't really belong here. He has been a builder with his own firm until 'the drink got the better of me'. He still has his bungalow and he is off the drink and he is only working here to keep the house going 'till the trade picks up'.

All the strange talk that swirls around Tam at the piece-break seems wild and uncontrolled and yet it is hobbled by something. That something is, he comes to realise, The Chair. Even when it sits empty during the break, which is most of the time, it still manages to dominate.

'DON'T SIT THERE.' No. Nobody ever does. Except the one.

THE CHAIR. It would often come back to him. He would smile to himself at how it had always expressed itself to him with capital letters at the time. But it hadn't seemed funny then.

It came again into his mind as he stood at the bar in the Stag's Head. It was the pub nearest to the flat in Warriston. But it wasn't just the nearness that appealed to him. Ever since Michael had taken him for his first official drink at seventeen to the Akimbo Arms in Graithnock, he had had a weakness for rough talking-shops. That first time, the abrasive noise had unnerved him a little and he had been glad of Michael's knowledge of what to do. Not knowing what to drink, he had accepted Michael's advice and he took a Double Century. The taste was a faint echo of those sips of stout he had sometimes stolen from his grandmother's glass when she was out of the room.

Just as the tartness of the drink passed from being something that made him wonder how anybody could voluntarily drink this stuff into being an experience he enjoyed, so the crass earthiness of the pub became an intermittent release from introspection, the nearest thing to animated Brueghel he would find. The pub was the social convention he had missed most any time he was living in France. French people tended to drink in psychological alcoves. Among them, he had sometimes longed for the communal atmosphere of a Scottish bar, the shouted long-range conversations, the jocularly insulting comments that were thrown around the place like spears, the impromptu seminars on football or politics or the nature of relationships between men and women, the man or woman who suddenly decided a song was necessary.

He had once written a short poem he called 'The Young Man's Song'. He didn't like it but it had caught for him something of what he had felt about pubs when he was younger, how they could form a kind of interesting crossroads for an evening (which road will we go from here?), could ambush routine, could catalyse dull habits into an event.

> I want to go to some strange pub
> Where women's eyes are dark with risk,
> Their bodies unknown continents,
> And talk is sharp and laughter loud
> And there are flaring hands whose quick
> Intensities light up our selves
> And there are threat and noise and song.
> Whatever happens shall be sheer—
> My stillness has been overlong—
> Passion or hurt or kiss or tear,
> Remorseless spinning of the hub.
> I want to go to some strange pub.

That wasn't exactly how he felt these days, he had to admit. But a diluted form of that feeling had always stayed with him. It had survived long enough to follow him to Edinburgh, no longer a song perhaps but at least a hoarse whisper that could be heard from time to time in the stillness of the flat at Warriston. Living alone there, the nearest thing he had to a social life was wandering occasionally into a down-market pub of an evening. You took your chance of stumbling across Walter Mitty on an off night, assuring you he was an eccentric millionaire or an unpublished genius, or of getting into an argument with a man who seemed only marginally sane or of meeting someone who was deeply interesting and whom you would otherwise never have met.

And if you were becoming just boredly stoned, you could always shift your pitch.

And there are threat and noise and song. The threat had always provoked in him both fascination and fear, like a child wanting to climb a height from which there is a possibility of falling. He remembered the way some of them always used to walk across the parapet of the railway bridge at Bonnyton on the way home from the pitch-and-putt. The parapet sloped downwards towards a thirty-foot drop to the railway line. Presumably, it had been designed that way deliberately to discourage tightrope walkers and it was exactly that which made them want to walk it.

There was something of that repellent fascination in his sense of Cran. It had started with The Chair. In the two nights before he saw it filled, it had managed to acquire a mysterious authority. Cran Craig only visited the tea-break intermittently, appearing without warning among them, steaming from the heat of the kiln like Vulcan from his forge. But on the first two nights, as the small man called Frank, who worked with Cran, took each bogey that was delivered, Tam had caught a few striking images of a big figure, stripped to the waist inside the kiln and glowing red. He had stared out steadily at Tam a couple of times, like a beast wondering what careless creature had dared to approach its lair.

Those shocking glimpses were developed into dread by the way the others talked about Cran. They didn't talk loudly, as if prepared for his arrival at any moment. They said he had been a merchant seaman. They said he had been in fights all over the world. Hilly, the philosopher of the group, wondered if he had ever lost a fight. He thought he must have but he didn't think anybody should suggest that to him.

Billy Farquhar warned Jack and Tam that Cran didn't like anyone looking at him unless he was talking to them and sometimes not even then. Sitting on their wooden benches, they tended to glance at The Chair when they mentioned him.

It was an ordinary wooden chair, high-backed and scuffed, a floral cushion fixed to the outer rings of its back with two tie-cords. But plain as it was, Tam dreamt about it after his second night's work. The Chair seemed to palpitate in the dark and he somehow knew that he was moving towards it, although he couldn't see himself in the dream, and he couldn't reach it. The sensation was reminiscent of those other times in dreams when he was trying to punch someone and his fists felt liquid, could achieve no impact. The Chair in the dream haunted him like a throne he aspired to ascend but was afraid to.

When on the third night Cran came, Tam thought his subconscious wasn't a bad judge.

It wasn't just his bulk or the face like a stone mask. It was the aura of dangerous stillness he gave off. His nature was fat on a low heat. It could look bland and still as long as it was left to itself. But introduce any alien substance to it, an unacceptable opinion or attitude, and it flared and seethed and you risked scalding.

The one who risked scalding most became Tam. Cran had discovered he was a Docherty. He had heard of his grandfather's reputation as a street fighter and had obviously decided that the Docherty blood-line was running a bit thin. His contempt for Tam was not expressed directly. It manifested mainly in talking across him until he was silenced. Cran's philosophy, such as it was, was stark and harsh.

'The kiln,' he said more than once, 'is where cley either hardens intae brick or breaks down intae rubbish.'

He had obviously decided which Tam would do. Each time he appeared at the tea-break he was pushing Tam further to the edge of the group, leaving him no place for his pride to stand. No matter what sense of himself Tam might have achieved during the day, Cran would unravel it at night. He seemed to enjoy doing that, a steady forbidding of Tam to be himself.

'I SUPPOSE YOU'RE SOMETHING OF A CURIO to them,' John Benchley says.

Not just to them. He's something of a curio to himself, he thinks, as he goes on responding mechanically to John's remarks. Taking the night-shift job in the brickwork for the summer has produced another split in his sense of himself. He feels he is subdividing into such a crowd of multiple personalities he'll never be able to unify them into any kind of order. He can imagine how Cran and the others would react if they knew he tried to write poetry. Ritual stoning with reject bricks. But at the same time as he doesn't really fit in there, he cannot honestly believe that his acceptance for university is real and that he will be starting there at the end of the summer. This is not what anyone in his family has ever done. A part of him is waiting for the inevitable day when an official-looking envelope will land on the doormat addressed to him. He knows roughly what its contents will be.

(Dear Mr Docherty,
   We regret to inform you that there has, of course, been a mistake in the matter of your being given a place at this university. We trust that this error has not inconvenienced you too much by, for example, giving you absurd fantasies concerning the possibility that learned men will waste their time on a working-class toerag from Graithnock. We do, however, hope that you will find in the future some activity more suited to your abilities, such as shovelling shit.
Yours faithfully,
                    An Amazingly Clever Man)

His sense of being outside any social norm hones in on him with fresh intensity now and distances him even further from conversation with John Benchley. He sees his lips moving and he realises that it is not what he is saying that matters but his need to say it, the compelled persistence of his nature. He has often persuaded Tam of the necessary existence of God but, Tam realises now, while he was doing so, he had a mole on his cheek, about an inch from his left nostril. That mole becomes more and more significant as Tam looks. It appears to him now as one reason why, after going through his devoutly Christian phase, he decided to become an agnostic.

For what is the point of the mole on John Benchley's left cheek? If the universe has one coherent divine purpose, that purpose should include everything. In his omniscient wisdom, what could God possibly have meant by putting a mole on John Benchley's left cheek? Come on, God, check your books. What was it you meant by that again?

He remembers a poem he wrote in his secret notebook, where he often stores little cosmic anomalies he thinks he has found because, if he ever reaches the Golden Gates, never mind the questions St Peter may put to him, he has a few he'd like to ask St Peter. And if Peter can't answer them, he doesn't even want in, because if heaven is as ramshackle a conception as earth is, they can keep it. The harps are probably not even in tune and the milk and honey's guaranteed to be sour. And what about the company? All those bland do-gooders sitting around, unable to remember one really bad thing they did. An eternity of boredom. Not one spicy story among them.

('Let me tell you about another sin I never committed.')

Oh boy. It will be enough to make you ask for a transfer.

('Excuse me. I think there's been a mistake here. You think you could go through your records again? Just check it out? I think you must have missed the time I stole two biros and a Dinky toy from Woolworth's. Should be listed somewhere. It was a Rolls-Royce Silver Wraith. One of the dearest models. I've been a right bad bastard. Where do you get the lift that takes you downstairs?')

The company's bound to be better in hell. They must have some stories to tell.

('How did you finish up down here?'

'How did I finish up here? Wait till you hear this one . . .')

He wrote the poem after he had heard about Mrs McAfferty's new baby. She lived near them in Dawson Street at the time, though she moved later to one of the prefabs in Altonhill. The child was a boy and soon after the birth Tam overheard his mother tell his father, in the quiet reverential voice she always used when referring to the inexplicable oddities an inscrutable fate visits upon the unsuspecting innocent, that wee John McAfferty had been born with one toe missing from each foot. His father, with typical pragmatism, observed that it would only be noticeable if he went swimming at Barassie shore and then – the Scottish climate being what it is – most people would probably just think it was frostbite. But the small pointless cruelty of it stayed with Tam for days and eventually crystallised in a poem that for no reason he could understand made the child both English and the son of a man travelling on a train.

(The Englishman opposite coming from Crewe
Speaks of his son, who is John Edward Frew.
John Edward, it seems, has hazel-brown eyes
And a talent for drawing beyond all dispute.
But, strangest of all, and to mankind's surprise
John Edward has only four toes on each foot.

And this is a fact which has troubled my dreams.
And, taking my bath when the water is hot,
I look at myself and my toes say, 'It seems
That we number ten and John Edward's do not.'

It's a question which, dying, I leave to the wise
To settle the wherefors and find out the whys.
If I get to heaven, I'll straighten my tie
And ask a policeman the way to God's seat.
Introducing myself, I'll say, 'Dear God, why
Does John Edward Frew have eight toes on his feet?')

And he'll have other questions. What part of the divine plan is
it which demands that some children be born spina bifida? Or
decrees that there should be such a thing as congenital syphilis?
Or arranges a world in which there can happen the casual horror
that befell a man he heard of recently? The man was in his thirties
and having a holiday with his family.

(Yea, and it came to pass that he did an thing of great evil and
that was as an abomination in the sight of the Lord.)

At least it must have been, if we are to believe that what
happens to us has any connection with divine justice. What
he did was, he went hill-walking on his own, only in safe
and well-frequented places. But he stumbled and scraped his
leg on a rock and later he was dead. The abrasion of the stone
had burst the skin and there had been rat's urine on the rock
and it entered his bloodstream. Hey presto. We have a widow
and two fatherless children. And why not?

(And God writ upon stone other commandments. And one of
them did read: thou shalt not scrape thy leg against the rock that
hath upon it the pish of the rodent. For thou shalt die thereof
and the name of thy dying shall be called among men Weil's
disease.)

Uh-huh. Back to the drawing-board, God.

'How goes the writing?' John Benchley is saying.

It is a moment or two before Tam can focus on who John is. It takes all your concentration, giving God a row.

'Well. It goes.'

'Have you finally started the masterpiece yet?'

Tam takes the question seriously. There it is again. One part of him suspects that he doesn't have the ability to deserve a university place and another part of him has the gall to believe he can become a writer. Why can't he introduce the two parts to each other?

'I think maybe,' he says to John.

He is being cagey. He has started to write something which he thinks may be his final statement on the nature of human experience but he knows that writers don't like to talk about these things. It would be like letting air into the womb. ('You don't want to talk it all away.' Or something like that. Ernest Hemingway, *The Short Happy Life of Francis Macomber*.)

'So what form will it take?'

He hesitates. He is trying to shape a statement that will satisfy John's probing curiosity without damaging the foetus he thinks he is carrying.

'It will,' he says carefully, 'be a blank verse play about working-class experience, Ah suppose. But just a play for reading. Not for performance.'

'Sounds like Goethe's *Faust*,' John says, smiling into his sherry.

'In a way.' He is smiling still. 'Sort of. Kind of.'

Who is Goethe again? Tam has heard of him. But why does the name jar some tender place in his mind? Then he remembers he went into Fulton's bookshop when he was fifteen, sweaty and dishevelled from two successive games of pitch-and-putt, and asked Mr Fulton if he had any of the works of Go-eth in stock. Mr Fulton stared at his muddy, grass-stained hands for so long that Tam could feel them enlarging to a grotesque size.

'I suppose you're referring to Goethe,' he said condescendingly. 'And please don't touch any one of these books. Why don't you come back when you've had a bath?'

Go-eth. His mind cringes all over again. Maybe his literary aspirations will never survive his background. He often pronounces big words and foreign names in a strange way because he has only ever read them. Where he comes from, he has never heard anybody say them. He supposes he has been suppressing the name of Goethe ever since and he certainly has never tried to read him, as if some rule has banished him from the privilege. Maybe he will always be – the joke gives him a certain masochistic pleasure – a Visigoeth.

'You have a title?' John asks.

'A working title,' Tam says, very professional.

'What is it?'

'"Actions in Generic Tense."'

That leaves John thoughtful.

'Hm,' he says. 'Probably better not to offer it for performance. Not a title calculated to have them queuing round the block.'

Tam knows John is trying to understate his sense of how ludicrous Tam is. He is a kind man. He is trying not to laugh. Faced with that not unfamiliar feeling of adult disdain (some of his teachers were expert at that), Tam feels a familiar response. It is a desire not to back off from his pretensions but to come ahead with them. He knows they can be ridiculous but he also knows they're who he may be in embryonic form. He feels the colossal energy they give him – a desire to test himself and discover who he is, more powerful than any intimidation that can come against it. (Maybe that's what Bernard Shaw means by the life-force?)

He watches John sipping his sherry and can see the wisdom of his attitude, as he could see the wisdom of the Latin teacher who, when he had a full page of poetry in this year's school magazine, said to him sneeringly in front of the class, 'Don't worry, Docherty. It's a phase we all go through. You'll get over it.' Tam hopes not. He has always found that teacher pathetic. Who would want to be like him? An expert in desiccation who might be able to conjugate *amare* but don't ask him to feel it. Did you have to kill your dreams to be wise? He remembers a line of Yeats he has rewritten to suit himself in his notebook: 'Imaginative decrepitude is wisdom.' He is in no hurry to get there.

'Anyway, it would seem to be an improvement on your last venture. "The Fourteen Stations". Remember them?'

Unfortunately, he does. He told John about six months ago that he had found the form for what he wanted to say. His idea was the fourteen stations of the Cross as a symbol of any individual life. He would follow one character's life, dividing it into fourteen phases. John had glanced away, slightly embarrassed.

'It sounds,' he said so quietly Tam could hardly hear him, 'like the sort of idea you might get late on a Saturday night when you're stuck for the subject of a sermon.'

It wasn't long afterwards that Tam had abandoned the project and started on 'Reflections in a Broken Mirror'.

'Verse?' John says. 'Is it set in contemporary times? Just now?'

'Aye. It's about the people around me, Ah suppose. The way they live. I want to try and catch some kind of essence of my life so far. Before it goes.'

'You've probably got time. Do you think blank verse is an ideal medium for expressing working-class life?'

'It's very flexible. It lets you move from the particular to the general. The universal.'

'Hm. But you don't think it's a less than natural medium for writing about working-class life?'

'You could put Hamlet in jeans,' Tam says.

John's thin laugh puts on weight. It is almost beefy. It must be relief. Tam laughs as well. Perhaps they are both relieved, John at having been released from having to humour Tam's grandiose ambitions, Tam at not having to expose them any more. He decides not to reveal his secret writing life to anybody else ever again. Silence is strength. It is not that other people's tendency to pour very cold water on his enthusiasm is going to quench it. He may not know his Goethe from his Go-eth but it will take a lot of fire brigades to douse the energy that burns in him. It is just that he finds himself getting angry at the complacency of the people who do that to him and he has enough talent for anger without unnecessary reasons for it. It is better to change the subject. He does it successfully while he finishes his second sherry and it is time to go.

'Good night, Young Werther,' John says at the door.

Tam doesn't understand the reference.

'Young Werther in the Grand Hall, eh?' John calls after him.

IT WOULD BE A LONG TIME BEFORE HE KNEW WHO WERTHER WAS. But at least the reference to the Grand Hall had been clear enough. Why had the dancing meant so much to him? Saturday nights weren't just a social experience, they were a religious observance. He couldn't imagine not going to the dancing every Saturday. Some undeniable impulse turned him towards that place at the same time each week, like Moslems towards Mecca. (Maybe it wasn't surprising that a chain of dance-halls had been given that name.) The compulsion could perhaps be traced to that night when he was fifteen and his mother asked him to go to the dancing.

HE IS WORKING FROM NORTH AND HILLIARD, that text-book which has begun to oppress him with how little he knows, how much he will never know, no matter how hard he studies. Those two names have assumed a vaguely menacing significance for him, like strangers who have been given authority over his life. North and Hilliard: who are they? What do they look like? North is fat and Hilliard is thin. They live in Oxford. They meet nearly every evening in a room overlooking a quadrangle. As the sun slowly sets over a spired and castellated skyline, they do not notice outside their window the kingdom of golden towers and purple clouds they have casually fallen heir to. They are too busy unsmilingly devising tortures for the minds of pupils all over Britain. Like religious fanatics, they know that all the apparent wonders of the world are just dross concealing the true meaning of life, which is Greek syntax. One day they will come for him, sadly shaking their heads, and lead him away to the place where failed Greek scholars are condemned to decline meaningless nouns and parse incomprehensible sentences for ever.

Meanwhile, he wrestles for salvation. Jacky, the incredible thinking dog, lies at his feet, whimpering peacefully in a dream.

Tam envies him. It's a dog's life? It doesn't seem too bad to Tam. Jacky doesn't have to remember how to conjugate γνωθειν. His mother comes into the kitchen. He is dimly aware that she has come in and then aware that nothing appears to have happened since she came in. He looks up. She is standing with her hand on the door-jamb, smiling at him.

'You fancy goin' to the dancin', Tam?'

She puts her hand on her hip, elbow out, and lowers her head, looking at him through fluttering eyelashes.

'What?'

'Ah'm invitin' ye to the dancin'. What's the problem? Ye think Ah'm too old for ye?'

'What?'

He is still wandering in a labyrinth of Greek syntax, unable to find his way out.

'Anybody in? Yer father an me's goin' to spectate at the Grand Hall. Ah think he just wants to check up on Allison and Michael. Ye want tae come?'

'Ah've got this exam on Monday, Mither.'

'So. This is Saturday. Ye've all day Sunday.'

'Ah don't know. It's a lotta work. It's Greek.'

She comes towards him, takes the textbook in her hand and closes it. North and Hilliard are demystified into a plain, closed book. Their power over him will be neutralised until he opens the book again.

'Come on,' she says. 'Let's go. Ye can overdo it, son. Ye can work again the morra. If ye're havin' trouble, Ah'll help ye. Ah'm an expert in Greek. Everything's Greek tae me.'

With that casual exchange his mother pushes him out into another stage of his life, as she has done so often before, as if she were rebirthing him. She was the one who, when he was still quite small, had kept putting books in his way, unobtrusively and with apparent cunning indifference, until he fell hopelessly in love with them. Now she has closed one of these books with instinctive timing and is his guide beyond its covers. The message coded into the ordinary moment she has made might read: 'There's more to life than this, son.'

And there is. The evening is transformed. Perhaps it is the spontaneity that gives what happens such impact on him. (He has always loved unforeseeable events: the older cousin who arrived without warning, his new girlfriend with him, and suddenly there was a blonde stranger in the house, telling them unimagined facts about her family and exuding a ravishing scent that made him find excuses for going near her.) Perhaps it is the unexpectedness with which he is volleyed out of the arid recesses of the mind into a night that jostles with rude life. Perhaps it is just that he will never lose his addiction to contrast and paradox.

—AFTERWARDS, he would write:
  The heartbreaking complex of paradoxes at the centre of Gerard Manley Hopkins's nature: so ascetic that a crumb of bread could ravish his palate; so dedicated to poverty that his senses reminted the world every day into uncountable wealth; so physically chaste that his sensuousness became an orgy.—

SOMETHING LIKE THAT HAS HAPPENED TO HIM NOW. From studying the skeletal past stretched out in diagrammatic form upon the page, he is thrust into the pungently fleshy present and the shock of the transition brings him startlingly alive.

It is winter. (Of course it is. He had forgotten.) Becoated and scarved and with his mother wearing her headsquare, the three of them hurry through a darkness that crinkles with frost. His father is inexpertly singing 'Teddy O'Neill'. The night invades Tam, every pore of his senses open. Stars shine as if they have been lit for the first time tonight. He cannot stop staring at them.

At the bus-stop Mrs Tomlinson is standing with a sheepish-looking younger man quite near her. Her concave, scythe-like face (of which his father once said, 'It would do for yeuckin' corn') has its customary expression of displeasure with the world. The younger man is standing slightly out of her range, as if he doesn't want to be mistaken for the corn.

'Jeanie,' Tam's mother says. 'A cold night to be out.'

'Colder for some nor for others,' Mrs Tomlinson says.

'Something wrong, Jeanie?'

'Ye could say that. Oh, ye could say that. Oor Sadie. Rushed intae Graithnock Infirmary. Suspected miscarriage. Her fifth. Her fifth she's carryin'. Who needs five weans? Fower boys. Noo this.' She speaks like a telegram, urgent news the world should get as fast as possible. 'It's no' a family her man wants, Ah think. It's a football team. This is him here.'

'Hullo, son,' Tam's father says.

The man nods over his shoulder. Tam's mother smiles at him but he doesn't notice. Tam's mother and Mrs Tomlinson go on talking but Tam isn't hearing them. He is awed by the fact that, if he hadn't come out, he wouldn't have known this. A baby may be dying. Greek verbs seem not very important. It is amazing. You could sit in your house and not realise that all over the world people were doing things, loving each other, dying, laughing, having fights, thinking new thoughts, travelling on trains, crying alone.

'It's always at somebody's door,' he hears his mother saying.

Her remark seems to him to be profound. It *is* always at somebody's door, isn't it? The variety of living overwhelms him, its endless and relentless happening. And every time it happens, it is new. For the people it happens to, it is new. This is all new. When the bus pulls up at this bus-stop, it will be new. This bus will never before have pulled up at this bus-stop with these five people waiting here and one of them with a daughter maybe having a miscarriage. It is very mysterious.

(About two years later, he tried to write a poem about that remembered moment. He called it 'A Prayer for Bus-Stops'. The poem was lost and all he was ever able to remember were the last four lines:

> Oh, God or what it is that understands,
> Accept this prayer from our ten cold hands.
> Have mercy on the waiting five of us
> And send us meaning and a Fourteen Bus.)

When the bus arrives, his awareness of how mysterious things are continues. It is brightly lit and it has an exact collection of people who have never shared its brightness until now and it is driving through the dark. The driver sits unknown in his cabin, his back towards everybody. He will never know who have been in his bus. The conductress takes the fares without realising that what she is doing is not what she always does. It is different every time. It is different tonight. His mother sits beside Mrs Tomlinson. His father sits beside him. Mrs Tomlinson's son-in-law sits alone, staring out of the window, where Tam can see his sad reflection in the glass.

At the next stop a man comes on. He lurches towards a seat and falls into it. The conductress comes up to him.

'A day return tae Afghanistan, please,' he says.

The conductress stares at him.

'Via the Cross,' he says.

She takes his money, gives him his ticket and goes away.

And the strangeness of everything becomes just a prelude to the great revelation.

HE SAW THE DANCING. Carter saw the tomb of Tutankhamen. Livingstone saw the Victoria Falls. Cortés saw the Pacific. He saw the dancing.

He sat on the balcony upstairs with his mother and father and looked down on a wondrous scene – so many people and each one different, a seethe of shifting colours, a cauldron of fiercely attractive energy creating in him a kind of seductive vertigo that made him want to plunge into it. He could pick out from time to time Michael and Allison but they looked different. They weren't just who he had thought they were. They were like strangers who lived in the same house as he did.

He would often wonder later what it was he had experienced that night. Maybe it was a bit like someone who has always lived landlocked seeing his first ocean. Maybe he sensed for the first time the amazing possibilities before him. He could remember glancing at his mother's face and seeing a strange expression there, which he would later identify as wistful serenity. He would feel he had seen surfacing for a moment the face of the girl she had been before it went under again, long drowned in drudgery.

That night he knew he would soon be part of this scene. By the time he was sixteen, he was going every week to the dancing. The compulsion that took him there was a strange compound of opposites. A part of it had the vague intensity of a religious faith, as if he believed he would some night find the Eucharist on the lips of a girl. A part of it was as worldly as the rhythms of the music, a need to work out the practicalities of seduction. Even the gates of heaven, he had heard, are opened with a key.

HE COMES UPON THE CASANOVA METHOD.

THE LIBRARY IS A PLACE HE IS FREQUENTING THIS SUMMER, as regularly as a commuter frequents a railway station, and perhaps his purposes are not dissimilar. He, too, is there to make short journeys. By dipping into a random book, he can transport his head to different places, different times. His mind being as full of multicoloured pieces as a kaleidoscope, an odd paragraph can take hold of it and, with a flick of the word, make the pieces assume a new and interesting shape. Many an afternoon, before reporting like a modern Spartacus to the brickwork, he loiters in the Dick Institute, replenishing his imagination against the mental privations that lie ahead.

This particular afternoon, sunlight is pouring in rays from the high window, widening out into the room like the beams of muted searchlights. The effect is reminiscent of one of the covers of *The Watchtower*. Sun-motes drift, making galaxies in the vivid air. In this atmosphere as mysterious as how he fancies catacombs must be, there move among the serried imaginings of the dead a few people whose banality seems to him transformed into something strange. The woman with the leather message-bag isn't just looking for another Barbara Cartland romance. She is probably trying to find the book which, when she pulls it from the shelf, will – as in some Gothic castle – activate the secret doorway to admit her to a life richer and more dramatic than her own. The ancient man who looks as if it wouldn't be worth his while picking a book of more than two hundred pages is looking for the words that will finally give meaning to who he is before he isn't.

It is an appropriate atmosphere for a small revelation. He has picked up a book without even noticing the title. As he flicks through the pages, a name draws his attention. Casanova. He should know about getting it, if anybody does. It says here that one of his ploys had been to give out to everybody that he was impotent. Ah hah. The idea seemed to be that nobody would give out such humiliating information unless it were true. Therefore, a lot of women's husbands would treat him as a joke and they wouldn't mind if he spent time with their wives. Tam sees the possibilities immediately.

But for his purposes the method would require some modification. Jealous husbands aren't exactly his problem. Unattached girls are, and the defence mechanisms they have acquired from parents and the social attitudes of the time as difficult to unlock as any medieval chastity belt. He needs to find a way past those formidable psychological barriers. Casanova had used the idea of impotence as a weapon of social duplicity, a devious ploy. But what if you used it frontally? Compassion is a great disarmer of people. How many people will remain defensive if they are feeling compassion? He runs a rehearsal through his head.

One of the dance-hall jokes at the time is the one about the man whose chat-up technique is very direct. He takes a girl up to dance for the first time.

'Do you come here often?' he says.

'Yes. Quite often.'

'Do you fuck?'

'You must get a lot of slaps on the face,' someone hearing his method tells him.

'I do,' he says. 'But I also get a lot of fucks.'

He could never be as bold as that. But what about a variation?

('Do you come here often?'

'Yes.'
'I'm impotent.')

He tries to imagine the girl's eyes welling up with sorrow for him, her slowly growing determination to save him from his despair. He tries to imagine them leaving the dancing early so that she can restore to him his sense of his own manhood. It isn't easy.

There were two things wrong here. The first was the abruptness of the heartbreaking confession. A thing like that needed a context of mood conducive to the appreciation of its tragic resonances. A dance-hall bristling with libido, with 'Take the "A" Train' in the background, was hardly the place. Also, impotence is too clinical, too impersonal.

What about the fear that you are homosexual? That isn't an entirely alien role to play. He has had thoughts about that. Why has he not managed to do it with a girl yet? Is he subconsciously arranging it that way? There have been so many times when he could have pushed it harder, been harsher. Were his attempts at seduction all a pretence, a way of concealing from himself what he really wanted? Was his constant failure a coded message to himself? Is he really a homosexual? After all, given his experience, how would he know? Certainly, he has written a mental note to Oscar Wilde.

(*Dear Oscar Wilde,*
   Just a brief note about something which has always puzzled me. See when you got lifted for being a homosexual and put in Reading Gaol? See when you got back out and went into exile in France? Why did you pick Sebastian Melmoth as an alias? Is that not a bit like trying to disguise yourself by going about nude? I can just imagine the first Frenchman you introduced yourself to when you got off the boat.
   '*Sebastian Melmoth? Quel nom! Ah, you must be ze English pouff who was in ze jail, n'est-ce pas?*'
   Liked the Ballad and bits of the plays.)

He remembers a group of them playing football once in Bonnyton Park when Bobby Braithwaite cycles past. He dyes his hair blond and has soft eyes that he lowers often and walks like an imitation of a girl. He manages to cycle that way, too.

The response from the footballers appals Tam. One of them has spotted Bobby on the road about thirty yards away. He is wearing a yellow polo-neck sweater and green slacks. He is cycling with that special style he has, as if his legs are so much in love with each other they don't want to part company. His blond, wavy hair is blowing theatrically the wind. It is the second time he has passed this way.

'There he's again!' Beef Bowman shouts.

The ball bounces unattended out of play. They seem to have more primal things to attend to. A group of bored teenagers becomes an instant mini-mob. Some deep, atavistic impulse welds them into unity minus one. It is awesome how all the shouting voices appear to have one mind. It isn't the mind of Albert Einstein.

'Bobina!'

'Yoo-hoo! Bobina!'

'Bobina! Bobina! Bobina!'

'Bring yer arse over hee-errr!'

'Watch ye don't have a puncture! Your tyre'll go Poooooof!'

Amazing hilarity. Isn't true wit a killer? Strafed by voices, Bobby is hit. His bike wobbles and he falls off. There is dancing on the park. It is then Tam speaks.

'Shut your fucking faces.'

Where did that come from? He could only suppose it related to the feeling that remained from the only time he had been in Bobby's company. A group of them had been standing outside the Queen's Café, talking. Bobby happened to be there. He had seemed to Tam then and ever since a kind and nervous person, so uncertain of who he was that even statements came out like questions. He agreed with everybody, seeing his identity perhaps in the reflection from other people's attitudes. To aggress on him is like shooting a man with his hands up. It can only mean you are a bastard. He doesn't want his friends to be that.

But he is sorry he has spoken. Why does his mouth declare independence from his brain so often? As Bobby gathers himself up and cycles off, Tam becomes his stand-in for the others. They are looking at him as if he somehow doesn't belong in their group. Some of them look embarrassed for him. In their eyes he has committed a social gaffe. Others are feeling contempt. Beef Bowman is sneering.

'Oh-ho,' he says. 'What's this we've got? You wan o' them as well? Maybe we'll have tae start callin' ye Thomasina. Do ye want to do it wi' boys, son?'

And John Garfield stands beside him.

'Well,' he says. 'It won't matter who you want to do it with, will it? You make the Phantom of the Opera look like Errol Flynn. The only thing that could make love to you's yer right hand.'

There is a tense pause during which he remembers something his father once said to him: 'You're too smart for yer ain good, son. Wan o' these days ye're gonny dig yer grave with yer mouth.' This could be the day.

Beef charges at him. His six months at the Old Mill Road Boxing Club, during the phase when he had decided that his future lay in becoming a world champion, stand him in good stead. Beef is as strong as an elephant but he has the same nimbleness of foot. As Tam side-steps him easily, he can see exactly where to hook him. Fortunately, he decides not to. For if he hits him the fight is real and it will only take Beef to fall on him for the future of literature to be impoverished. Taking his customary minute or two to turn, Beef charges back. Tam waits, matador-style, until he can see up Beef's flaring nostrils. Then he side-steps again and trips him as he passes. The ensuing laughter relieves the tension of the situation. Someone goes to retrieve the ball and the rest of them come between Beef and him and jostle the situation into mockery and tell them to behave themselves. He is glad to agree. The game restarts. Luckily enough, he is playing on the same side as Beef.

But, standing in the library, he plucks from the thorns of the past the rose of potential. Homosexuality. How about that? He ponders.

(The scene is the Dean Park in summer. Margaret Inglis and he are sitting on the grass and talking. Her floral skirt has ridden gently up to reveal a band of firm, white thigh. Her body strains against her blouse. They are talking of things they hope the future may bring.

A young man and woman cross their vision a few yards away. The man swings his child down from his shoulders. She is giggling.

He sets her on the ground and, about one year old, she begins to stagger happily back and forth between them, as if every footstep hovers on the edge of a precipice. They are all laughing. Margaret and he are smiling in that transfixed, slightly idiot way people do with children.

'What about children?' Margaret asks softly.

His smile freezes on his face and she notices.

'Tom?'

He stares at his hands.

'I don't know that that could ever happen.'

'What do you mean?'

'I don't know how to tell you this, Margaret.'

She is staring at him tenderly. He forces himself to look at her. His eyes are wounded. Their pain is being reflected in her own.

'I think I may be homosexual.'

'How do you know?'

'I just know.' No. That's too definite. How can you influence what has already happened? 'It's not how do I know. It's how do I not know.'

She looks puzzled.

'I mean, I've never experienced sex. I may be homosexual for all I know.'

'You're not, Tom. You're not.'

'Maybe.'

'Don't say maybe. You're not.'

'But I don't know.'

'Well, I know.'

'I wish *I* did.'

There is a long pause in which he can feel that wonderful feminine compassion gather and focus itself on him. She must save him from his darkening despair.

'You will,' she says. 'You will know.'

She takes his hand. And suddenly that marvellous, rich body is stretching itself erect and pulling him up after it. She walks him boldly towards the wood at the edge of the park. As they come under the foliage, shadows claim them and leaves whisper conspiratorially around. As they walk, the shadows deepen and her smile is a glimmering promise in the gloom.)

And his imagination walks into a real tree.

It wouldn't work. Well, it might work but, if it didn't, you would be in worse bother than you had been trying to get out of. Where he lived, there were a lot of girls just as severe on what they considered deviant behaviour as the boys were. They wouldn't be slow to pass the word around. By the time it took you to find the compassionate one, you could be a social outcast, living in a cave on Craigie Hill with passing children chucking stones at you for sport. No, it was too dicey.

He puts Casanova back and wanders round the library. All this experience, and when will he get his share of it? He suddenly remembers a book they used to have in the house. He wonders what happened to it. It was called, intriguingly, *Fifty Greatest Rogues, Tyrants and Criminals*. Or was it *One Hundred* . . .? There were a lot of them, anyway. How had that book come to be in the house? He suspects the source may have been his father's preference for fact over fiction. It was a big book, bound in red leather with an embossed cover. There was an illustrative scene for each rogue, tyrant and criminal – a black-and-white line drawing. They were all pretty interesting. But there was one chapter which had fascinated him utterly. He was maybe thirteen when he read it, or rather when he started to read it. For it became a compulsion with him to read it again and again. He used to read it as an almost daily ritual until the book disappeared. Maybe the book disappeared because someone had noticed how often he was reading it and had checked which part he was reading. It was easy to tell. If you held the book shut, a line of grime betrayed which few pages his grubby fingers had been nervously fretting for weeks.

The chapter was called 'Messalina, The Illustrious Harlot'. Once he had looked up 'illustrious' and 'harlot' ('the' was no problem), he knew he was on to something. Messalina had been the wife of a Roman emperor. He was certainly sorry for her husband, Claudius. But mainly, he had to admit, he just wished he had been there at the time. It seemed Messalina would do it with anybody, so even he must have had a chance. The illustration showed her reclining voluptuously. (He knew that was how she was reclining because it said it in the text.) Her face looked attractively mad and the rest of her just looked amazing, and hardly dressed for a

Scottish winter. Around her what appeared to be dying men lay abandoned.

For a time after the book disappeared, it didn't really matter for he had memorised whole sentences and moments. He especially liked the part where she pushed an exhausted wreck off her couch on to the floor and shouted to wake old so-and-so, he would do next. In his mind he was stepping between her and old so-and-so and waving hopefully. But as his memory of her exploits began to fade, he missed being able to revisit Messalina.

In the library, he reflects that he had the right idea at thirteen.

Back to plan A. Invent a time machine. And he thinks of Greta Garbo.

Will he ever learn to live outside of books and films?

> (Dear Messalina,
>   Why did you leave no forwarding address?)

'ET LE ROMAN?' Michel said.

'Ça ne marche pas en ce moment.'

'Ah, Thomass, Thomass. Monsieur Angst.'

'Oui, c'est ça.'

'Ce que tu peux être écossais. J'aime discuter avec toi. Mais des fois ça pèse un peu lourd. Toujours à la recherche du sens de la vie. Tom Docherty ou le livre vivant.'

'Tu exagères pas un peu?'

'Pas vraiment, non.'

'Shit.'

'Maintenant on parle anglais? I see.'

'Well, at the moment I don't feel like trying to feed the rawness of my feelings through the gracious formalities of la belle fucking langue. Ye know?'

'Okay. Entendu.'

In the bistro a man was reading Le Figaro. Tom took a boiled egg from the middle of the table, peeled it, salted it and began to eat. He wondered why he was doing this. He wasn't hungry.

Maybe he was eating Scotland to remind him of who he was. Boiled eggs were an Esperanto food, something he had been familiar with all his life. He felt the need for things familiar. Even the smells here were in a foreign language.

He remembered coming back from a dinner party at Michel and Colette's place near the Pont Neuf. It was early morning and he was wandering beside the Louvre, looking for a taxi. The quiet darkness erupted suddenly into violent voices and, drawn to the sounds, he watched mesmerised as a man began to kick a taxi. It was a passionate performance. His rage exorcised, the man wandered off, still shouting at the dark. Tom thought he understood the man's frustration. It was presumably occasioned by the tendency of Parisian taxi drivers at certain times not to accept your fare if you were heading somewhere that was off their route for going home. It worked to Tom's advantage that night. The driver was prepared to go to Boulevard Haussmann. But as he sat in the cab, the scene of assault on a taxi and the memories of the dinner party (that sense of intellectual chic, of ideas being worn rather than inhabited) made him feel terribly alien. He had a sensation of urban panic, of being adrift in a vast strangeness.

He felt something like that now. He thought of some of the other dinner parties to which Colette had taken him, to be joined later by Michel. She had a small notebook in which she kept the combination numbers to her friends' apartments. Standing beside her at a locked door while she found the numbers she would have to press to open it, he had sometimes thought that Paris for Colette and Michel and their friends was like a series of private chambers with interconnecting secret passageways. Maybe he hadn't been living in Paris at all, just a mental village within it. Maybe the continuing strangeness of the place had made it more difficult to finish the novel, since its contents seemed hardly relevant to the alien life here. Michel echoed his thoughts, as if he were reading them.

'Perhaps because you are trying to think in French, you will be finding it difficult to write in English. To finish the book.'

('What are you doing these days?'
    'Trying to finish a book.'

Since he had been about twenty, that had been his standard answer to the question. It made his life sound as interesting as the sex life of a stick insect. He would have to think of something else to say.

'Designing an eighteenth-century garden.'

'Sleeping rough.'

'Planning the revolution.'

'Having an affair with three lesbians.')

'Maybe you're right, Michel,' he said eventually. 'I've been thinking about that. It's bound to have some kind of effect, I suppose. An occupational hazard of living in a foreign country. You know what I was thinking? Hemingway. I sometimes wonder if his style had something to do with how stilted his French and Spanish may have been. That maybe he learned to break down the problems of vocabulary into simple circumlocutions. You do that when you're struggling with a language. Find the most basic way to say things. Reduce it all to prepositions and simple nouns and verbs. Mind you, I suppose the theory depends on how good he was with French or Spanish or Italian. Maybe I'm just talking about myself. Lumbering him with my own linguistic incompetence.'

'I vote for the latter theory,' Michel said.

'Thanks.'

Tom abraded the salt from his fingers into the ashtray.

'I am sorry to have heard about your troubles,' Michel said.

'Yes. I'm not too pleased myself, I have to say.'

'You are close?'

'At one time, very. One of the compasses of my life.'

'At least it will not be long now till you are home. *Colette arrive*.'

Tom watched her walk. She was still unaware of them and Tom saw her as if she were a stranger, preoccupied in crossing the wide intersection outside the Café de Flore, just another Parisienne. He noticed how attractive she looked. It wasn't that she was conventionally pretty. It was that she rendered conventional prettiness irrelevant. She was so effortlessly and self-confidently herself. She looked womanly and strong, with that chic that seems to be genetic in some French women. He liked that in her.

He understood so many women's current dismissal of the need to look determinedly feminine, perhaps having been prepared by his awareness of the penal clothes Garbo had taken to in her retirement, as if serving a life sentence to atone for her earlier submission to the demands of her own beauty. And he would allow that the fifties might not have provided him with the ideal conditioning for seeing gender clearly. But then neither, as far as he could see, did the seventies. The distortions of conditioning were an inevitable part of growing up, he thought. No time's nurture was without its impurities.

What mattered, he supposed, was the justness of the tension you maintained between conditioning and the rational analysis of that conditioning. In that tension was developed honest selfhood. The conditioning remained a valid part of yourself. How could it be otherwise? To claim to have abandoned it entirely was to become an identikit of attitudes, not a person. A lot of people were guilty of that these days, he felt, preferring to stand on the stilts of a cause rather than wait to grow up into the impure complexity of being an individual.

You can't disown your past without becoming no one.

To challenge conditioning without trying to eradicate it, to modify it honestly in the light of individual thought, was to become yourself. The rest was an act of psychic self-deceit. He wouldn't be pretending to be who he wasn't.

ONE THING HE HAD TO ADMIT. If he died dreaming of a woman, she wouldn't be wearing Doc Martens.

MADDIE FITZPATRICK'S SHOES THAT DAY.

HE SEES HER IN THE LOCAL LIBRARY in the Dick Institute. Can we create what we want to happen by imagining it intensely enough? Do we project events, precipitate them out of thoughts and wishes as well as having them simply occur to us? He has sometimes thought mistakenly that he has seen someone in the street only minutes before he sees that person in fact. Has he wished her into the library?

He sees Maddie Fitzpatrick. The very name, incanted like a silent charm in his mind, creates an aureole in which she stands. She is at the end of a corridor of books. Sunlight glistens the black, drooping hair that makes her face a secret between her and the book she is holding open. He shouldn't be able to tell that it is her but he can tell. The awkwardness of his breathing is instant recognition. Nobody else could make a yellow linen skirt, a yellow blouse and fawn high-heeled shoes seem to him as exotic as a yashmak. Her stockingless legs are unbelievable, light brown with summer. They keep making his mind follow them to where it shouldn't. Where she is the air looks clearer, a pellucid patch. Somehow she seems to consolidate the space about her, make it her own and distinct from the rest of the room, as if she creates a composition from whatever is around her and she is its centre, like the subject of a painting. This one is by Vermeer, whose work he has seen in an art book he found in this library. It was through the eyes of Vermeer he first saw the kind of light she stands in.

He doesn't approach. You cannot enter a painting. She stands there surrounded by the unimaginable difference of her experience and he is afraid. How can he ever come near her? How would he know what to say? The different, isolated space in which she stands leads from a past he will never know and towards a future he cannot imagine. He is a stranger in both places. Also, he associates her with his Uncle Josey. It was from him that Tam first heard her name and it was at his uncle's funeral that he first saw her and was spoken to by her.

She came up to him while he stood around aimlessly in his grandmother's house after the funeral. It had been a weird day. There was a service in the house without any ministers – just Alf Hanley, his Uncle Josey's best friend, speaking for several minutes. Then some of the men spoke at the graveside while they all listened in a whipping wind – two dozen empty suits, Tam thought, his own included, flapping round a hole. Back at his grandmother's house, his social behaviour stalled on him completely. He couldn't participate. People were talking and drinking tea and eating sandwiches and some women were crying with his grandmother. He couldn't do anything. He didn't want to talk. He certainly couldn't cry.

Yet he thought he had loved his Uncle Josey. What was wrong? It was as if he felt resentment of his uncle. It was as if he needed to change his sense of him now that he was dead. He found himself remembering against his will things which he regarded as failings in his uncle. He hated himself for doing it but he couldn't stop doing it. Why?

—AFTERWARDS, he was to be several times in the company of an old man after the man's wife had died suddenly. The old man's grief began by iconising his dead wife. Her perfection was untarnished. Then, as time slowly and painfully passed, he began to desecrate the icon he had himself made. There was a story he was inclined to repeat about something which had happened over forty years ago.

The story was this: during the war, when fruit is a luxury, the man's mother comes to visit at his and his wife's house. The man is out at his work and, therefore, doesn't meet his mother but his wife tells him of her visit. A week later, the man visits his mother and she asks him how he enjoyed the bananas. He doesn't know what she is talking about but says they were fine. When he returns to his own house, he asks his wife what this means. His mother left him two bananas but his wife and her father ate them without mentioning them to him.

When he thought of the old man's story, as he sometimes did, he would wonder what it was exactly the old man had been doing in burnishing this story like an ornament he didn't like and giving it, however briefly, pride of place in his mind. How could something so minute give rise to such long pain? Then he would imagine that an untreated hurt might last for over forty years. He would wonder if we need, somewhere in us, secretly to hoard the hurts those we love give us, to store them even against our conscious will, so that we may protect ourselves with them against the agony of an impossibly continuing love after those loved have left us. And he would wonder if that was what the old man had been doing and if that was what his teenage self had been doing when his Uncle Josey died.—

BUT that day of the funeral he was simply standing, loathing himself, when Maddie Fitzpatrick came up to him.

'Hullo. You're Tom, aren't you?' she said.

He just about managed to realise that he was. He had noticed her as soon as she came in. He couldn't imagine doing anything else. He had been trying not to watch her all the time as she moved around the room, talking easily with whoever was beside her. Once she leant and kissed his grandmother. The demure black costume that she wore was defeated by her body, became, in spite of its plainness, a strikingly sensuous outfit. He had been frightened that, if he kept thinking about her, he would get an erection. That would be the final expression of his inability to feel what he should feel – an erection at a funeral.

Now, her beautiful face looking straight at him with its flecks of delicate brown in the eyes, the guilt of what he had been thinking surfaced in a blush. She smiled at him. Would she still be smiling if she could see inside his head?

'I'm Maddie Fitzpatrick,' she said. 'We were friends of your Uncle Joe's. My husband and I.'

Naming his uncle as 'Joe' was like hearing her mention someone other than the man he had known. He wondered what they had talked about, although it was probably politics, he thought. He knew that she and her husband were members of the Communist Party, too. About all the Communist Party had meant to him so far was going to charity dances in the Bethany Hall and sliding up and down the floor with the other children while the grown-ups danced.

To the guilt of not being able to mourn for his uncle and the guilt of thinking lustful thoughts about a woman at a funeral was added the guilt of being jealous of the time his uncle had spent with Maddie Fitzpatrick. He was a guilt machine today. Behold the evil one. He had to try and say something before he grew horns and cloven feet. Or before she decided he hadn't learned to talk yet.

'He said,' he said.

He blushed again.

'He said about you.'

He felt like an Indian, talking in the basic way they talked in Hollywood films. How! Maybe that's what she liked about him. For she smiled again.

'Your uncle talked about you a lot. He expected great things of you. I can see what he meant.'

He couldn't see what *she* meant. He tried to smile and his upper lip froze above his teeth. But it wasn't like Humphrey Bogart. Humphrey Bogart wouldn't have been blushing again.

'It's the eyes,' she said. 'You have sensitive eyes.'

Where he came from people didn't *say* things like that. He could find no way to react. He thought the redness of his face must be as bright as a poster colour. She took pity on him. She squeezed his arm gently.

'Try not to get *too* hurt,' she said, and moved on.

That was it, one moment when a shining presence had paused, like a film star, and autographed his life – 'with best wishes'. He had never forgotten that occasion and sometimes – perhaps when he wasn't feeling good about himself, which was often enough – he would take it out again and hold it in his mind as if it were a talisman.

He had seen her again several times over the last couple of years. Once, in the street, they had stood and spoken for about an hour. She was always open and friendly to him, without a trace of that patronising distance some adults seemed to need to put between them and younger people. Yet he somehow managed to put that distance there himself, measured in awe. Why couldn't he be as open towards her as she was to him? He suspected it was because he thought of her in a way she didn't realise. He had a guilty secret about her, one he couldn't share with her. That guilt had grown as he grew up a little more. It was because he wanted to be *so* close to her, like inside her pants, that he couldn't come close at all, in case he betrayed himself and her horrified shock spread to his family and everyone he knew.

Now, in the library, he stares at her secretly and longingly. He gets so excited that he has to walk away. If he goes up to speak to her, he is liable to start touching her curiously, like that Indian in the Western seeing his first white woman. He tries to lose himself in the labyrinth of books. He is picking books at random and opening them. He isn't seeing the words. Each page might as well be blank, a screen on which he is projecting his thoughts. The thoughts are wildly improbable.

('Hullo, Tom. My car's outside. Let's go to my house.'
The background music is Nellie Lucher:

> Comeona my house, my housa come on,
> Comeona my house, my housa come on.
> Comeona my house, to my house,
> I'm gonna give you candy.
> Comeona my house, to my house,
> I'm gonna give you apple ana plum
> Ana pomegranate, too.)

('Hullo, Tom. I've had enough of this pretence. I want you. What I want, I get. There's a park near here. It won't be busy just now.'
Ah, the delicious martyrdom of being an object of compulsive desire. Depravity without guilt. Who could blame a naïve boy for being led like a lamb to the slaughter of his innocence? You could have it both ways. You get the pleasure, you don't pay the bill.)

('Hullo, Tom. I don't know how to say this. It's not the kind of thing you say in Graithnock library. I love you. I can't help it. Whatever you want to happen is what will happen. I'm in your hands.')

('Tom?')

The word is real. Maddie Fitzpatrick is standing beside him. He couldn't be more embarrassed if she had recognised him coming out of a brothel.

'I thought it was you.'

But is it really him? She hasn't a clue about the rabid imaginings of the person standing in front of her. She mustn't know.

'Hullo, Mrs Fitzpatrick,' he says and, under the circumstances, that phrase, which is spoken in a steady voice, feels to him like an act of brilliant and elaborate duplicity.

'I wasn't sure at first. You seem to be growing up more by the week these days. Like something in a hothouse.' Maybe that's what happens when your foetid thoughts seem permanently to inhabit the tropics of desire. 'You're quite the young man now. I heard you did very well in your highers. One more year at school then university, eh?'

'No. Ah go in October.'

'Oh. You really are in a hurry to grow up, aren't you?'

He almost wants to tell her that there's one crucial element missing for him in the process of growing up, and maybe she could help him there. But his mind puts a grille across the dungeon where such dark and misshapen wishes scream and gibber for release, while he tries to starve them to death. She reaches across and turns the book in his hand towards her, so that she can see the title on the spine. She bursts out laughing. She is laughing. She is looking at him wide-eyed. He realises with surprise what the book is. He is mortified. The hypocrisy of his pin-stripe behaviour is revealed. He might as well be a bank manager carrying around a placard reading: Head Full of Dirty Thoughts.

'*Dangerous Liaisons?*' she says. 'Tom. What are you up to? Are you using this as a manual?'

He tries to laugh. It sounds like a clogged sink trying to drain.

'Ah just picked it up there.'

'Uh-huh. I assumed it hadn't jumped into your hand right enough.'

'The French teacher's mentioned it. She told the class about it. Laclos.'

The mention of the author's name is an attempt to legitimise his prurience. He is a scholar with a rather clinical interest in the classics of French literature. One has a duty to read such things in the quest for erudition. He doesn't add that when Miss Kimberley told them the name in French, the words almost gave him an orgasm. *Les Liaisons Dangereuses.* He couldn't have explained the effect those syllables had on him. But they went straight to his groin. God, did he want some sort of liaison that was amazingly *dangereuse.* The words connoted for him mad passion, sudden and cataclysmic, happening just out of sight of people going on with their routine lives. And afterwards, somehow, he and some mysterious woman reappearing, dressed in the pretence of nothing-has-happened, like a mask behind which they are smiling secretly at each other.

He also doesn't add that, since he has heard of the book, he picks it up almost every time he comes into the library and flicks through it, looking for the dirty bits. He has not been hugely successful. He has never quite recovered from his initial disappointment in discovering that the book is a bunch of letters. You wouldn't expect too many lurid details in a letter, at least not in any he has seen. ('The weather hasn't been too great here lately but maybe it'll pick up.') But he keeps trying. One day he is going to get up enough nerve to brass out the disapproval of the woman at the counter, the one with the grey hair and glasses and the big mole on her cheek. She's the one who threw him out for having dirty hands the first time he came in.

Now she seems to want him to wash his mind. When he took out *The Man Who Died,* he thought she was going to phone the police. (How did she know what it was like anyway? The title told you nothing. Has she read everything in the library? Or was it just because the author was D.H. Lawrence?) He's going to take *Dangerous Liaisons* up to the counter and get it stamped and bring it home so that he can conduct a proper search. But, obviously, it won't be today.

'She told you about it, did she?'

'Sorry?'

'The French teacher. She told you about it, did she? What's her name? Brigitte Bardot?'

He laughs for real this time. Miss Kimberley as a sex kitten is a gloriously incongruous image, he thinks, like imagining

Auntie Bella in her underwear. Miss Kimberley, whom he has always liked, is short and dumpy. Her torso looks as blandly undifferentiated as a pumpkin inside the big costume jackets that she wears and the proximity of any male teacher makes her fluttery. But she has, he remembers, beautifully shapely legs. He suddenly feels guilty for laughing. Maybe she is quite sexy at that. Does this mean that he is able to see beyond sexual clichés or just that he is a sexual maniac, aroused by anybody female?

'She was called Miss Kimberley.'

'Nice name. So what are you doing these days? Apart from reading up on how to have a dangerous liaison.'

'Ah'm workin' night-shift in Avondale brickwork.'

'Really? How do you find that?'

'All right, Ah suppose.'

Except that I wish somebody would transport Cran Craig to Botany Bay. (He had looked up 'cran' in the dictionary yesterday: a measure of capacity for herrings just landed in port – 37½ gallons. How the hell did that come to be his nickname? Maybe it was the amount of blood circulating in his prodigious body.)

'Hardly seems the ideal setting for an intellectual like yourself. Don't you feel out of place?'

'Only when Ah push the bogey off the rails.'

She smiles thoughtfully at that. She is looking at him assessingly.

'Listen,' she says, serious now. 'We're having a party soon. I'd like you to come. We'd like you to come. The others might seem like old fogeys to you. But I'm sure you can handle it. Will you come?'

'Yes.'

He can't imagine why she would ask him and he isn't very sure what he is agreeing to but he can't think of anything else to say. Then he does.

'Only thing is. As Ah say, Ah'm workin' night-shift.'

'Not at the weekend, though.'

'Ah get Friday and Saturday off.'

'Good. There will be *some* younger people there. It's 14, isn't it? Dawson Street?'

'That's right.'

How did she know that?

'All right. I'll drop you a card. Time and detailed directions and things. Time you came out into society, Thomas.'

She leans over and runs her hand gently along the side of his head.

'Bye.'

She walks away, apparently oblivious to the effect she has had, like some kind of Superwoman who casually touches a building in the passing and doesn't realise that she has demolished it. Her touch judders through him like his small personal earthquake. It's all he can do to keep standing upright.

HE WOULD ALWAYS HAVE A WEAKNESS FOR PARTIES. The sight of the living-room at Warriston made the thought ironic. This was some one-man party he was having.

This place is going to drive me even crazier than I already am, he thought. The dust on the ledges was beginning to make them look like indoor window-boxes. The fluff on the carpet drifted back and forth when he moved about, like tumbleweed. There was a cup on the mantelpiece that he couldn't remember not being there. If he looked inside, the coffee dregs would have hardened into porcelain. Like an archaeological site.

And he was its only archaeologist. Gently unearth the broken pieces of the past. Breathe on them softly, brush them delicately with thought. Let's see if we can make out any pattern.

Parties. Definitely parties. There had been some significant parties in his life. There was the one at Caroline Mather's house that summer. She met him in the street and invited him and he found Margaret Inglis again and was able to confront her with a plookless nose. But before that there had been the party at Maddie Fitzpatrick's. He had wandered around, awkwardly trying to talk to older people and feeling he had come to the wrong planet, until Maddie Fitzpatrick took him into a small room and read to him some of the poems of William Morris, of whom he had never heard. That was when he *knew* he had come to the wrong planet. He managed to escape eventually, clutching a very slim book of poetry she said he could return in the free week he had decided to have between packing up at the brickwork and going to university.

There was the party Gill and he had not long before they separated. It had for him one moment definitive of how his life was going at that time. He had gone upstairs to see how Gus was doing. He would be fifteen then. He had his bed-light on and he was reading.

'Hullo, Dad.'

'Aye, kid. The noise bothering you?'

'No. What's it like?'

'It's like a party, I suppose.'

He sat on the edge of the bed. He noticed how big and raw-boned Gus was, his face two fiercely interested eyes around which a bundle of features hadn't yet set properly. His spiky punk hairstyle helped to make him look as if he had always just wakened into the world and was wondering where he was. The colour was pink this week. Tom loved those remorselessly questioning eyes. Sometimes he would tell Gus a fact that had become banal with familiarity for him and he would shoot him a look that seemed to be probing Tom for signs of insanity. Gus had a history of asking interesting questions. One of Tom's favourites was one he had asked him when he was two and a half years old: 'Does God wear a tie?' He had gone through a particularly long phase of calling Tom by his first name. In his first primary class the teacher had asked him who his best friend was and he had replied, 'Tom.' When she had asked if Tom was a little boy who lived near him, Gus had said, 'No. He lives in the house with us.' He was no longer on first-name terms with him but some of the friendship remained.

These days he was even more disconcerting in the way he switched roles on you. Just when you had him comfortably cast as an awkwardly immature teenager, his Doc Marten boots scuffed from playing football in the street, he would suddenly appear garbed in thoughtful solemnity and wanting to discuss the USA's role in Central America. That night he was in philosophical vein. The eyes assessed Tom compassionately.

'You not enjoyin' it, Dad?'

'No' much, Gus. No' much.'

He nodded. They talked. It didn't matter what they talked

about. Having taken both of them by surprise by coming upstairs like that on impulse, he saw Gus somehow fresh, his eyes not fully returned from the imaginative distances his reading had taken him to. He didn't see just his son or a recurring worry. He saw an emergent young man, sensitive and thoughtful. He admired him. He was reminded of one night more than a year before when Gill and Megan and Gus and he had driven back from having Christmas dinner at Gill's brother's house more than ten miles away. The roads were snowbound and the driving had been slow and a strain, an unpleasant end to an evening he hadn't enjoyed. But when they got back, Megan and Gus and Tom had created spontaneously one of those meaninglessly happy times you will never forget. Sitting with Gus in his bedroom he remembered the poem he had written about it and misplaced somewhere. ('He is one on whom nothing is lost' – not even unpublishable poems.) It was called 'Snowball Fight'. As they talked, the words of it played under their conversation in his mind like a descant:

> The accidental manna, how we find
> Things as themselves by coming on them blind.
> A bad drive home, each road a precipice
> Of horizontal falling, garage ground.
> With purpose done, the night became. My son
> Fashioned a snowball, found he'd made a world.
> We dervished in the darkened street an hour,
> Discovering us, my daughter, son and me—
> Snowballs like presents of us. And to see
> Each in a different place, a different time,
> Receding from me helplessly, was good.
> Laughing a lot, we made love to strange life—
> Brief, separate stays in undiscovered land,
> A melting gift, sweet wetness in the hand.

Perhaps a part of Tom had already taken its leave of him, or at least of the way of life they had shared until then. But he gave no explicit sign of it, probably because he didn't know himself what had happened. He simply felt an undertow of sadness in the pleasure of talking to him.

When he said goodnight and come out on to the landing he didn't want to go downstairs just then. He went into Megan's room and put on the light and sat on her empty bed. She was in her first year at Edinburgh University and she came back through to Graithnock only on occasional weekends.

Megan was a keeper of the past, which meant that her room preserved the recessive layers of her experience, like an archaeological site. You could still see the evidence of her babyhood in the first teddy bear she had ever had, sitting propped against the head board, badly beaten up by her affection but retaining those bright, idiot eyes that didn't seem to know that time had passed. Along one wall, where pop stars and film stars stared back at him, he could check the roll of her dream lovers. There was a mobile her first boyfriend had given her. There were old cards. There were books that went from *Black Beauty* to *Père Goriot*. There was the mirror that had absorbed her growing's many faces and stayed as bland as water.

He tried to think of her in Edinburgh. She might be in a bar now or with a boy or reading a book. The risks for her appalled him. But she was strong and properly determined to work out everything for herself, including her mother and him. He trusted her. That didn't mean he trusted her to do what her parents wanted. He trusted her not to do that. He trusted her to live with what she did.

Feeling slightly elegiac about her and Gus as he sensed them growing away from Gill and him and into themselves, he wondered what they had given them. More specifically, he wondered what he had given them. The thought depressed him, for he could think of nothing definite to attach it to.

WAS THAT HIS AND GILL'S FAREWELL PARTY TO THEIR MARRIAGE? How could you tell precisely when successive mutual disenchantments congealed into hopelessness? It was such a gradual process. It had probably begun many years earlier, as early as the party they gave the week after the dinner party with Elspeth and Brian Alderston, just before going to Grenoble. His dubiety about that one was probably an omen in itself.

IN SPITE OF HIS LACK OF ENTHUSIASM when Gill had mentioned the party, he found himself caught up in the preparations. He made several trips to an off-licence to buy the booze, remembering piecemeal particular drinks that certain people liked. Gill had an impressive buffet set out in the sitting-room. The downstairs bedroom was the bar. The lounge was to be the orgiastic centre of the party, ringing with epigrams, awash with warmth and wit and muted sexuality.

It was a nice thought. He almost believed it for a while. Even when Brian and Elspeth Alderston arrived first, he didn't give up hope. It was true that they were to parties what a pail of cold water in the face is to euphoria. But he was already feeling the primitive thrill in the blood that comes from the presence of men and women mixing in a bright room, a muted tomtom. So his goodwill repaired perhaps a little of the damage he had done the week before. And as the other guests began to come, he started to enjoy himself.

He wasn't aware at the time that the party might be a kind of terminal experience for him, the end of something, the writing on the wall of the mind, although it might take him many more years to decipher it. He took pleasure in the early stages because he was so busy. He was welcoming the people and giving them drinks and making sure they knew where the bar was so that they could help themselves. His sense of the party was by pleasant proxy, like the smell of good food which other people are eating.

Once the preliminaries were over and he was able to be not merely a waiter but a participant, he found it harder to maintain a sense of enjoyment. Familiarity made of his eyes an X-ray plate in which he was aware of distressing symptoms in some of their guests. He tried not to see such things but it wasn't easy. There were depressing phenomena present which he couldn't avoid.

For example, Clive Cunningham was telling his jokes. Tom had heard two before he could get out of earshot. He regarded even two as a dangerous level. Fortunately he couldn't remember them, which might mean he had escaped permanent brain damage.

Clive had decided that his role in life was to tell jokes. Tom hated set jokes, which were to humour what masturbation was to sex. Especially, he hated Clive's set jokes. They were all about girls doing it and ways of getting it and cuckolded husbands. He suspected that in Clive. The jokes were always accompanied by this big, deep, masculine laugh he had been practising for years. Laughter seemed to Tom one of the least effectively fakeable things in the world. But nobody had told Clive that.

Perhaps nobody had told him because he was six feet two and an ex-rugby player. He was standing like a barn door with a suit on, a whisky glass like a thimble in his hand. Two women and a man were his audience. They were laughing at the right time. The right time to laugh at Clive's jokes was when he laughed. Sandra Hayes, she of the remorseless intelligence, was laughing louder than anyone. Why do women accept such crap from men? Why didn't Sandra get a step-ladder and spit in his eye?

'Have *you* heard this one, Tom?' Clive said to him.

'Aye, when I was ten.'

Clive laughed the laugh he probably wrote away to Charles Atlas for. He and Tom had an understanding: he couldn't stand Tom and Tom couldn't stand him. But at least he didn't attempt his overwhelming physicality bit with Tom. No doubt he could beat Tom's head in but no doubt he also knew that, even caved in, it would still work better than his.

Probably Clive's standing off from Tom related to their time at school together. Since that time, he knew that Tom knew that he knew (complicated are the rules of macho head-wrestling) that Tom was better at playing rugby than he was. Yet Tom gave it up. He suspected this had troubled Clive in some dark recess of himself. What fulfilment in life could Tom have found that was better than rolling about the ground on a bitterly cold Scottish Saturday, up to the arsehole in muck and with a fourteen-stone troglodyte trying to stand on your face?

He played rugby for only one season at school and scored a lot of tries. But he could never quite see the point of all that bodily contact. He was a fast runner and his keenness not to be groped by a lot of boys made him a very fleet wing three-quarter. But if he could shake off tackles, he couldn't do the same with his sense that it was fundamentally ludicrous for thirty boys to spend eighty minutes in sweaty pursuit of what is, after all, a symbolic testicle. It was a manhood test he didn't believe in, a degenerate modern equivalent of knights trying to win their spurs – boys trying to win their balls. It was a good game, though, but not as good as football.

Aileen, Clive's wife, was talking to Alice and Frank Spiers. He had known Aileen at school as well. She had been very attractive then, seemed to him in his awestruck innocence somehow what girlness was, quick and usually a little breathless, as if she were hurrying to somewhere the rest of them were plodding towards. Her laughter evoked barely understood stirrings in the boys around her. She had been a pleasantly disturbing presence.

She was still attractive but in a slightly caricatured way now. Breasts and bum had exaggerated themselves to the point where she was beginning to look like a seaside postcard. She had acquired a coarsening of nature to match the physical change. The Cunningham effect? Tom wondered. He had a moment he didn't like of pondering what things might be like between them in bed. Did Clive turn towards her in the darkness and murmur, by way of subtle foreplay, 'Darling, have you heard the one about . . .?'

Contemplating Alice Spiers didn't help to lighten his mood. That way guilt lay. Frank was Alice's second husband. They were only recently married. During the time that Alice had been separated from her first husband something had happened between them.

It was one night during a previous incarnation of marital disillusionment. He no longer recalled which great issue sundered their marriage that night. It could have been Sandra Hayes' beauty. Or it could have been the fact that Gill insisted on pronouncing 'liqueur' as a French word, the phoniness of which drove him crazy. He thought it probably dated from the cordon bleu cookery course, an event he might cite as a co-respondent in the divorce, since it was also there that she met Aileen Cunningham – an ill meeting by gaslight, as it had brought Clive, whom Tom had thought safely stored in the past, back into his life.

Whatever cosmic issue had reminded them that they were,

each of them, engaged in a psychic struggle to what might be the death, they finished by withdrawing behind their favourite separate modes for such occasions. He started to rant, a meaningless convoy of obscure rage within which any rational significance had as much chance of occurring as a daisy has of taking root on a motorway. Gill told him that she would be sleeping downstairs from now on, rather in the manner of God banishing Cain to the east of Eden. He thought the news was supposed to have made him a broken man but he felt at the time that he'd rather cuddle up to a buzz-saw. Anyway, he was used to this tactic and the accompanying threats of testes lopped off when he was sleeping if he dared to force his way into her bed. One time she had kept this isolationist policy up for six full weeks, presumably waiting for his exploding sperm to bring him to her, screaming for mercy. What killed Tom was what she said when, at the end of that time, she came back into their bed. She felt safe in doing so, she said, because obviously he was homosexual. Who else but a raging queen could have avoided sexual contact with her for six weeks? He succumbed to the cold logic of it. Sweet is woman: sometimes he thought she was a question which, no matter how you answered, you must get wrong.

He had brought their quarrel to a close with fine masculine originality. He went to the Akimbo Arms, a pub he had used to refresh his sense of himself and where he came from. The public bar there was a time-lock of the fifties. But it didn't help much. Harry was on duty that night, the only barman he knew who insisted on telling you *his* troubles.

Tom drank too much and stumbled out at shutting time, bearing the woes of the world on his innocent shoulders. The scene outside didn't lessen his self-pity. There were girls in twos and threes everywhere, done up like circus performers. There was a group of them queuing at an autobank. He realised they were heading for the discos that had proliferated recently in Graithnock, like cake shops where bread was scarce. He seemed to be travelling through a forest of walking women and he was alone and aging, listening to the circus leaving town. Poor Tom. What had he ever done to deserve this?

He needed to share the amazing injustice of his life with

someone. He couldn't go home. Gill was waiting there like a computer in which were stored all the inadequacies of his past. On impulse he went into a phone box and looked up Alice's address (her name was Johnson at that time). The phone book had been dismembered by some happy vandal but he must have become bored before he completed the job, because one of the few intact pieces contained Alice's number.

He rang. That seemed simple. But given how drunk he was, it was an achievement on a par with inventing the wheel. He spoke to two puzzled voices, one of them a man who threatened to come through the phone to him, before he reached the haven of Alice's breathy tones.

'Hello?'

'Allah? Tom hee. Yew alrih? Howsa go?'

'I'm sorry. Who is this?'

'Allah. Smee. Howsa go? Eh?'

'Listen. Who *are* you?'

His last few surviving brain cells caught a faint glimmer of what was happening. Alice thought she had a heavy breather on the line. He knew that somehow he had to say something sharp to set her mind at rest, something really intelligent. His mind made a supreme effort.

'Tom,' he said. 'Tom Docherty.'

'Tom! Where are you?'

'Box. Box on street. King Stree.'

'God, what's happened?'

'Huh! Watsappen.'

It was at this point that three young men took up their positions outside the box and started to tap on the glass. One of them pressed his lips against the glass derisively. Tom gave them all the fingers and continued to converse in his mysterious way with Alice.

'Watsappen, Alice? Eh? Watsnotappen? Don belee this. Dew?'

Various oaths were coming from outside and the three young men were trying to force their way into the box. He tried to wedge himself against the door and dropped the phone. Dangling there, it must have given Alice the impression she was plugged into a riot.

'Pissaw.'

'Get the bastard.'

'Shove, shove, shove.'

'Get los, ya buncha turs.'

'He's goin', boys, he's goin'.'

'Heave ho, me hearties!'

Tom was knocked against the phone and his elbow came down, cutting the connection. It was his good fortune to have picked a fight in a phone box. The young men were fighting with each other rather than Tom in their desperation to get in a telling hit, be the one who could claim Tom's scalp. They heaved uselessly around one another like armless boxers. They would probably all have died of asphyxiation without an effective blow being struck if the police hadn't arrived. One of the young men saw the car rounding the corner and shouted a warning. The phone box suddenly felt very roomy. By the time the police car had pulled up, the young men were gone.

'Are you all right, sir?'

Does the corpse feel well?

'What was all that about?'

He had come out of the phone box. Sweat dried on his forehead as if it were ice being held there. He'd always found one policeman equivalent to about four cups of black coffee. There were two of them. They didn't seem particulary friendly.

'A loada nothin',' Tom said.

'That's not what I would call it. It looked like a disturbance of the peace.'

'Not disturbin' any peace, me. Trying to make a phone call there. Three mugs. Forced their way into the box.'

'You sure that's what happened?' the other one said.

Tom nodded.

'You feeling all right, sir?'

'Fine.'

'You look under the weather to me.'

They really develop their powers of observation in the police. Finger-counting would have been higher mathematics for him at that moment. They decided to give him a bit of the treatment.

'What do you think?' one said to the other.

'It might be for his own good to take him in,' the other said.

'Hm.'

'Aye.'

Tom couldn't resist it. Just as the alcohol had assured him that he could insult three young men with impunity, it now convinced him that he was witty and could take the mickey out of the police.

'What's the charge?' he asked. 'Molesting a phone box?'

'Listen, you—'

And another car pulled up at the kerb. Providence seemed to be running a taxi service for Tom that night. Things sometimes happen that way when you're drunk. Out of the car stepped Alice and the talking policeman lost his train of thought. She was tall and willowy, with very long black hair you felt you could get lost in. She was wearing an astrakhan-type coat with the high collar up, and long black boots.

'Tom!' she called as she got out of the car. 'Where have you been?'

She shook her head in a long-suffering way at the policemen.

'Celebrations,' she said to them. 'This is him supposed to be enjoying himself. I'm sorry, Officers, has there been some trouble?'

She had neatly created the assumption that she was his wife. His status had risen in the eyes of the two policemen. He might be a drunken nyaff but he had quite a woman to drive him home.

'There could have been,' one of them said.

'We just got here in time,' said the other.

'Is it all right if I get him home now?'

They enjoyed taking their time about the decision and watching her.

'Well, all right, madam. But just make sure he's not back out on the streets tonight. He could be a danger to himself.'

'Thank you. And thanks for helping. Goodnight.'

It was as easy as that, provided you could wear an astrakhan coat and boots the way she could and live under a waterfall of black hair. When they got into the car and she put in the clutch, her coat fell open and she was bare-thighed to the hem of her shorty nightie. He was being driven along in one of his adolescent dreams, the one where the car pulls up and the woman tells you to get in and you go off to the land where sex actually happens and isn't just talked about.

'My God!' she said. 'You look as if you've been in an air raid. What happened?'

He gave her his version of the phone-box war.

'We better get you sorted out before you go back to Gill.'

He felt that might take a year or two.

'You ever tell anybody I came out of the house like this to get you and you're a dead man.'

She turned the car into the runway and they got out with almost the whole of the street in darkness except for her light. They came into the house quietly. She told him the children were asleep upstairs.

The strange rituals and expressions with which we patrol the edges of our bodies, the sentries of the sanctum, are interesting. Perhaps often when they profess to be most adamant about keeping us out, they are already suborned and inviting us to come in. Are our bodies busy sending each other subversive signals while our minds fondly think they are in control of the situation?

That night with Alice occasioned such thoughts. When they came into her house, she left him sitting in the lounge while she put on a dressing-gown and made them coffee. He found the furniture of other people's lives slightly awesome. The carriage clock sounded disapproving, tut-tutting with its brass tongue as if it knew it belonged and he didn't. He wondered where the ornaments had come from, who had chosen which prints. One was Monet's garden at Argenteuil, which seemed to him at the time like a distillation of all the summers he had lost.

He thought of Harry, the departed husband. He had had a drink with him not long after Harry had left Alice. Harry had been raw at the time, flayed with self-pity, his eyes looking out with painful disbelief on what had happened. It wasn't easy to equate his garbled tale of agonies endured with this nice room. Visiting the scene of the crimes, Tom found no thumb-screws, no iron maidens, no instruments of primitive torture. Had Harry been raving? Or should he flee before the subject of Harry's dark hintings reappeared, perhaps dressed in a black evening dress and carrying a rhino-whip?

Alice came in wearing the same floral housecoat and mules. She was carrying a tray with cups and a china coffee-pot and a small plate of biscuits. She left the tray on the table beside him, crossed to the music centre and put on a tape. Vivaldi came on quietly in two different parts of the room like ornamental fountains playing there.

There took place then a civilising ceremony: Monet, Vivaldi, coffee and biscuits – a small brightness in the emptiness of the night. The street was quiet, most people in bed. Upstairs, Alice's two children slept safely. They sat opposite each other and talked, Alice demure in her housecoat, Tom rather red-eyed from his sojourn on the streets. He sensed rationality slowly return, felt the gentling effect men and women can sometimes have on each other. The bruises on his mind faded to mild discolorations.

He didn't remember much of what they talked about at first – probably the ridiculousness of the incident at the phone box, Alice's dramatic intervention, how the children were getting on at school, the feints and side-steps by which we draw nearer to each other. But they moved on to more confessional matters, the problems of living alone, the problems of not living alone, inspection of the corpses of small dreams, the griefs of marriage. The propriety of it was marvellous. There were no innuendos, no phoney looks of longing passion. He enjoyed the complete innocence of Alice sitting in her housecoat and him with not even his jacket off, taking coffee and biscuits and talking. They were outside any assumed role they should be playing. Then it happened.

Alice had moved the table away from between them so that she could go round and turn the tape. When she came back she didn't return to the chair she had been sitting in. She sat down on the settee, a little along from him. They were still just talking interestedly. He made a remark about the sadness of the way couples become indifferent to each other's secret fears and thoughts and delicate aspirations, the very things that generated intimacy in the first place.

The comment was one of those accidentally stimulating contacts, a touch in exactly the right place at the right time. Alice became very animated, flicking her long black hair away from her face. She told him about an apparently irrelevant incident that had meant a lot to her at the time. He could see why.

She had been out for a night with some girlfriends. Her marriage to Harry wasn't going well at the time. The night had affected her with an awareness of what other women were doing and therefore with an alternative sense of what her own life might be like. She had been propositioned at least three times and had turned them all down. When she came home, Harry was in bed. He had asked a couple of perfunctory questions about her evening. Alice had wanted to talk to him, somehow to earth her restlessness in his reassurance, to neutralise her mood by sharing it with him. But she didn't want to tell him explicitly about her evening. Harry was the kind of man who sifted her glances and put her smiles under the microscope. If she had mentioned being propositioned, Harry would have wanted to know immediately what she had been doing that anybody would think he could approach her. Some men use their own cultivated casualness of response as if it were a charm against their wife's attractiveness.

Alice started to tell Harry about something that had happened when she was a child. Like a lot of the things we say, it was only in the telling of it that she realised how important it was to her. She was sitting at her dressing-table mirror, brushing her hair as she told him. She was transported into the past. Details she had long forgotten came back to mind and she supplied them excitedly. When she finished, she was almost breathless with wonder at what the incident meant or what effect it might have had on her. She asked Harry what he thought. Harry was sleeping.

An echo of that moment's hurt appeared on Alice's face. Tom remembered Harry's own almost incoherent indignation about his relationship with Alice and, without warning, a caption came to mind to go with that blissfully unconscious figure, whose marriage was perhaps finally disintegrating at that very moment. It was a caption a lot of men could adopt as their marital epitaph: 'I don't know what went wrong with my marriage. I was asleep at the time.'

What happened next began innocently. Alice looked so sore that he couldn't just leave her sitting there alone. He reached across and touched her cheek with his palm. The gesture, light as it was, sprang her. She closed on him, starved of touch. They held each other.

They cuddled. But comfort was just a staging-post to passion. When they kissed, their intellects abdicated, abandoning the premises to a riot of instincts. Alice, adept housewife, peeled him of his jacket and slipped his tie and undid his shirt buttons with a couple of mystic passes as easily as if they had been a zip. Her hands on his nipples had them aspiring to be obelisks. Confused movements were taking place in his trousers. He managed to pull Alice's housecoat off her shoulders and down her arms and with it her low-cut nightie and, having started on that route, was too excited to rethink the logistics of dismantling her social defences. He pulled both garments down to her feet and beyond, knocking off her slippers as he went, and she lay, long and small-breasted, with only her silk knickers on, from which some black hair curled. She had his belt unbuckled, and unveiled what he had to offer and stripped him naked as he wrestled off her pants.

So much for civilisation. Perhaps those people in the garden at Argenteuil were protecting their eyes from more than the sun. Vivaldi seemed to become more frenetic, as if demanding to be heard. The carriage clock said nothing Tom could hear. They intimidated time into pausing briefly. They rolled across the floor, two naked searchers rooting in the crevices of self, trying to snuffle each other out, wedding saliva, hunting the spoor of sensation along the pores, until the final meeting was achieved in a deep and dark exchange of their hot juices, a shivering mutual surrender of the innermost place.

They emerged from their private storm drenched in disbelief. What had they been doing? They looked at each other and kissed gently and cuddled, staring past each other's shoulders at what this was going to mean. He felt mugged by the experience. Had it really happened as suddenly as that? Or, when he stood drunkenly in the phone box, was there already a demonic brain cell planning what might happen? Had they really been talking so innocently? Or had they simply been making love to each other's heads before they came to bodies?

They nursed each other back from the shock of where they had been. Alice was very friendly with Gill, and he assumed it was a reference to that fact when she said, 'Oh my God,' several times. His head was like a computer which had taken in a piece of information the implications of which couldn't be foreseen. He would have to wait and see how it would affect the confusion already stored there. Neither of them knew what to do next.

What they did was become cold and put on their clothes, trying to reassemble normalcy. Dressed, they became again less familiar. The event that had fused them had, by releasing them into separation, become something different for each of them. He suspected in Alice a desire to go off alone with what had happened and work it out for herself.

'You better not be too late back,' she said. And at the door, 'Goodbye.'

Her mode of farewell struck him like a charm, a spell against their moment ever being able to mean more than itself. It felt at the time very hurtful. It was as if she were aborting an embryo they had made together. He wasn't sure what he felt himself but he resented her unseemly haste in refusing to find out. She had her reasons, no doubt. The complications of going on from there terrified him as well.

But, coming up the road slowly and by a roundabout way, he saw her as belonging in one of those darkened houses, the private temples to an orderly conformity. She was probably even now rinsing out her dark place in case what had happened might take root in her. Fair enough. But he wondered how far Harry had been right. Her elegant coolness began to look more sinister. He could see one of the reasons why she was a friend of Gill. They both took lust with their eyes closed, as it were, perhaps for fear of recognising themselves in it.

It was something you disposed of quickly, whereas he had always seen lust as an honoured guest, a visiting divinity that imparts a compulsive truth, making us gifts on which to build, not throw away. Lust should be invoked with ceremony, not rendered outcast. To deny his rites was to make his power malignant, resulting sometimes in the ultimate obscenities of rape and murder.

He formed no plans to see Alice again. She had phoned once since then when Gill was out. She indicated she was alone but they left it at that. None of them ever referred explicitly to that night. Seeing her at the party with her new husband, he felt that there might never have been anything between them except for one moment when her lips, not showing her teeth, gave him a slow secret smile, like a pressed rose. As far as he was concerned, it had a canker in it.

That canker began to infect the whole party for him. What he saw as being Alice's hypocrisy to herself, to the reality of our natures, seemed to spread wherever he looked. He wondered how many betrayals, backslidings, lies, equivocations, strangled hopes lay buried in the jollity of this event, what obsequies were represented by that laughter. He wasn't merely being fanciful. He knew a lot of things about a lot of people here, some of whom didn't know he knew.

People tended to confide in him. He'd sometimes wondered if it had something to do with being a writer. But it had been happening to him since long before he published anything. At school he ran his own teenage agony service. He was giving advice about things he had never experienced. It had continued. A year or two ago, a big man he had known for about an hour in a pub suggested they 'go outside'. He was very large, with a nose that had obviously been manually readjusted, and Tom declined. But he was very insistent. Finally, thinking that perhaps his end had come and wondering what he had done to offend him, he accepted. When they were outside, the big man started to cry quietly and told Tom he was having trouble with his marriage. He'd never been more relieved at someone else's misery.

This kind of thing had made him wonder what stigmata he carried that signalled to the unloader of private griefs that he was their man. Perhaps it was just that he found it hard to walk away. Like the wedding guest in 'The Rime of The Ancient Mariner', he could hear the music playing in the distance but it would take too harsh a reaction to get there. He had missed some good times that way, so many that he once made up, in a moment of exasperation while listening to a sadness about which he couldn't possibly do anything, his own plaintive wedding-guest poem:

> It is an ancient mariner
> And he stoppeth one of three.
> 'By thy long grey beard and glittering eye—
> Christ, why is it always me?'

So when he looked round the room, he was seeing, at least partly, what he knew to be there. His vision was informed by a lot of conversations, phone calls when Gill had not been in, meetings in the street, occasional coffees, pub chat – those moments of benign conspiracy when people meet like spies against themselves and confess therapeutically some of the things their lives are determinedly hiding. No doubt they often regretted those times but there were those of them who were doomed to keep repeating them. He was with them. Who wanted to live without being known as fully as possible? It was only by confessing ourselves honestly to one another that we could find out who we were and what life might be.

Moving among their guests, he knew – provided the confessions were the truth – that one of the couples here hadn't had sex for the last eight years, at least not with each other, that one marriage had never been effectively consummated at all. He knew which woman was 'only there for the children' – that strangely obscene moral stance (and one he had often adopted towards his own situation) by which we piss upon life and claim to be consecrating it. He knew there was a woman who had aborted her lover's baby. He knew there was a woman whose husband was having an affair with her sister. The woman was so preoccupied with her own thoughts that, perhaps blessedly, she didn't seem to know what Tom had meant when he said, having been drinking at the time, 'He has to sleep some time and you must have a small axe somewhere.'

It was just any average respectable gathering, he supposed. Had they known his thoughts, they would probably have felt, like Brian Alderston, that he was taking things too seriously. Perhaps he was. Maybe it was all a question of style. Maybe the difference he felt between the background he had come from and the foreground he stood in was one of style. Certainly, the essential substance of their lives didn't vary much: thoughts and feelings and love and work and children. There were people in the room who would have found Greek tragedy elaborately nonsensical and yet lived calmly among the material for one, given the sole missing ingredient of passion. At the entrance to some primitive, dark doorway of the heart, they remembered to say 'So what?' and turned away, like Ali Babas who have found a formula for closing off admittance to riches that have no place in their lives. Their wealth was wholly practical. It was cars and houses and possessions and a good education for their children. They made sure nothing in them, no experience, supplanted those priorities.

Tom sensed himself part of a different tradition. He had imbibed other values in the housing scheme he came from, in those continuing arguments his family had into the early hours of the morning. They discussed everything, regardless of whether the facts were able to attend or not. But he never remembered them discussing the importance of possessions. Their search was for themselves. The future he learned like an imperfect map throughout those long exchanges of thought and dream and belief had no imaginary mines of wealth or success located there. It was all forests of sensation to come, cities of shared experience. Money and career and security were luggage you couldn't depend on in that terrain. He had always vaguely believed that he would give up every penny he had rather than settle for being less than the person he could be.

That belief embarrassed him when he remembered it there at the party. For he was part of the hypocrisy of the event. He, too, was full of unacknowledged areas, longings stashed away inside him that he only took out to look at when he was lying awake at night, large ambitions that shamed him when his thoughts bumped into them, beliefs that his living denied. He felt a traitor to himself.

Tom's knowledge of those others was also knowledge of himself. The canker in Alice's smile had its source partly in his guilt, towards Gill and towards himself. Perhaps the unease from being among them came from seeing too clearly what he had become.

He left his drink on a bookcase and started upstairs. Mavis Kerr was coming out of the lavatory. She kissed him lightly on the cheek and said, 'It sounds like the fall of Sodom down there, eh?' He went to check that Gus and Megan were asleep. They were. He sat on the edge of Megan's bed, watching her.

We're in the shit. That was the deep thought that came to him sitting on Megan's bed. Who can choose the moment when our great revelations will come to us? Feeling doubts about the quality of his own parenthood, he generously extended his doubts to everyone else.

He listened to the whirling merriment downstairs. It sounded so confident, so fulfilled, an orchestral celebration of the conquest of happiness. But, practised listener to the frequently disguised woes of man and woman, he knew the score. Heard from a distance, listened to casually, it swamped you in its own apparent conviction. But he could break that music into its contradictory component parts. Part of the laughter was at Clive Cunningham's jokes – like thinking into a condom. Ted Hayes was there, no doubt telling them the same story he had already heard him tell three times that night. The Epic of Gilgamesh it wasn't. It seemed that Ted had been driving home on the motorway that night and he was overtaking a car when an articulated lorry pulled out right in front of him. Right in front. Three times that happened before Ted managed to overtake, with his life miraculously intact. But that was a shabby summary of Ted's tale. Tom lacked the story-teller's art to convey it in all its human drama, unlike Ted. His listeners were not to know immediately that the horror of his experience had happened three times in succession. They had to wait till the third occasion was actually there, by which time they may have been wondering if the incident was destined to repeat itself twenty-three times. And on the way, what slammings of brakes, what hearts in mouths, what proximities to death, what wrenching of steering wheels would have to be undergone. Down there a woman quaffed and talked and wondered when next her man would screw her sister. There were at least two fairly young couples who enacted a marriage that stopped at the bedroom door. He listened to the sounds downstairs and compassionately translated them into his mood.

(Ah, Docherty on Olympus. Ye poor mortals, I condemn ye to being as screwed up as I am.)

And he supposed most of them were or, if they weren't, perhaps that's what their problem was. How could they accept the way we lived?

All this pseudo-sophistication, playing musical chairs with our bodies, never-mind-the-quality-feel-the variety, trying to purchase meaning like real estate. What were we trying to do with our lives – build a cut-price Babylon?

'Tom! Tom!'

The voice belonged to Gill, but it was an echo of other voices that had been attempting to locate him all his life. Ghostly within it were the lost, plaintive callings of boyhood, his friends looking for him in forever darkened streets. There was in it the remembered exasperation of his mother, sadly baffled by the strangeness of his doings.

'Tom! Tom!'

Who was it that the name was looking for? Which of his split personalities would answer? Dr Heckle or Mr Jibe? The endless internal argument with his own life, the self-appointed seeker after truth? Or the dark joker, prepared to settle for turning the moment into laughter? Or maybe someone else altogether. For in him the highly developed Scottish propensity for duality of nature divided like an amoeba into a small riot of confused identities. He probably *was* having a nervous breakdown, a part of him reflected calmly, like a doctor observing a patient through a spyhole.

It was certainly Tom Docherty who rose from Megan's bed, the father reborn confusedly from the child, but which one of him? The prophet of gloom. He came down like Jeremiah from his private mountain to behold the vanity of human pleasures.

He was also required to help in dishing out the buffet. There was cold ham, cold turkey, chilli con carne and a large bowl of pâté, as well as gateau and fresh fruit salad. He opened the wine and left it on the sideboard beside the glasses. He distributed food for maybe twenty minutes, aware that, behind the veneer of suavity he was wearing, there still lurked the ghost of the passionately confused boy, looking for more substantial flesh than this. He was hoping that for Megan and Gus the finding of themselves would prove easier than it seemed to have been for him, especially in the matter of sexual relationships.

ENTRY FOR THE LOVE-FILES OF THOMAS MATHIESON DOCHERTY: Attempted seduction No. 2,412. (It feels like that anyway.) Name: McMurtrie, Senga. Occupation: brickworker.

Distinguishing features: everything. Location of attempted seduction: entrance to disused stables off Soulis Street. Result of attempted seduction: miserable and abject failure. Observations: not so much a one-night stand as a one-night collapse.

He still can't believe it. Saturday night may be the trauma from which he will never recover. If Sigmund Freud were still alive, it would be Vienna next stop. How could it happen? That's more than twenty-four hours ago but the images still flare in his mind. They flare like cressets. (Cressets is a good word.) Senga jitterbugging like a maenad under the lights of the Grand Hall, her athletic legs defying the tightness of her skirt, while he tries self-consciously to mime a similar abandon, finding it difficult to lose his self-consciousness because dancing with Senga is like dancing under a spotlight; Senga's delicate laughter going off in the street like a maroon, advertising their intimacy; Senga's bared and lamplit breasts, mocking him with their availability.

The images and the self-disgust weave in and out of his working. He sweats not just with labour but with the dread that Senga will be appearing with the day-shift. He's glad, for two reasons, that Big Billy Farquhar didn't turn up for work tonight. He won't be a witness to Tam's humiliation in front of Senga. And his absence has meant that there's no spare hour for brushing up and thinking relaxedly about things. What Hilly calls 'the philosopher's hour' he can do without tonight. It's just alternate tasks: one hour unloading the black bricks from the machine on to the bogey, one hour pushing the loaded bogeys up to the kiln and bringing them back empty. The less room he has for thought the better.

But thought is the thing you can't turn off. Every step he takes, pushing the heavy bogey along the rails, Saturday night's failure is added to the weight progressively, until he begins to feel as if he's humping a house. Every time Cran appears at the mouth of the kiln, his face carved in contempt, Tam is more inclined to agree with him. What will Cran think when he hears?

At least at the piece-break Cran doesn't turn up. But The Chair exudes disdain for Tam. As he listens to the others talking, including him occasionally, he thinks how that disdain will spread to them by the morning. Faced with the prospect of losing such limited acceptance as he has among them, of being an object of laughter with them ever after, he realises with surprise how much he will miss the rough texture of their company. They are part of where he comes from and even if it is a small part and one which he may be leaving behind by going to university, he would prefer to leave it with their respect for him intact. He wouldn't wish to shame his relatives by seeming less of the man than he should be. But that shame is coming, he's afraid.

He remembers a poem Boris taught them in fifth year – by somebody called Brecht, he seems to remember, who Boris said was a German. It wasn't in a book. They were given separate sheets with the poem typed on it. Where did Boris get that poem? Does he speak German? Or did he have someone in the Modern Languages Department translate it for him? Either way, he appreciates belatedly the creative eccentricity of Boris in wanting to introduce them to influences beyond Tennyson and Wordsworth. 'Questions of a worker who reads', the poem was called. It has given Tam a working title for his piece-break: 'Elegy for the reputation of a worker who reads.' Everything that happens has a special poignancy for him, a feeling that this may be the last time he will be able to be, however marginally, a part of this.

When he is rinsing out his cup at the end of the break, having spoken only a few words, and Jack Laidlaw says, 'You all right, Tam?', he thinks how embarrassed Jack will be for him a few hours from now.

'Is it Cran?' Jack asks.

Tam shakes his head.

'If it is,' Jack says, 'Maybe Ah could help ye tae hold him down while we both run away.'

The smile freezes on Tam's lips. Working again, he wonders how he came to get involved with Senga. He blames last Friday morning.

That morning, she came in as usual for her day-shift as they came off the night-shift. For her work, she affects dungarees, a variety of checked shirts and neat little hobnailed boots. Those are the busiest dungarees Tam has ever seen. The seat of them records every wiggle and their apron front is a jostle of unseen delights. Her shirt, always three buttons down, shows half an inch of the narrow gap between her breasts, like the start of a road he would love to travel. But it would be a dangerous journey, he has decided. For the voice of Senga, breath of the dragon that guards the maiden, comes out at all-comers like a blow-torch.

'Fuck off, you arsehole. You couldny get a ride in a brothel wi' fifty quid an' a doctor's line.'

This remark, which Tam takes to be a rejection, has greeted Big Billy's deliberately clumsy attempt to help her off with her black tailored jacket, an oddly stylish part of her ensemble, presumably a remnant of an outfit she formerly wore for places other than the brickwork. Big Billy laughs uproariously. He seems to have decided, with a subtlety of interpretation which eludes Tam, that this is some kind of verbal foreplay.

'Ye want me to help you off wi' somethin' else?' he asks, smiling rakishly.

'Ye couldny help yerself tae a wank.'

'Ye want tae bet? You can watch.'

'Ah'd rather watch the Interlude.'

Senga's reference, to those fill-in moments on television when they show you things like a potter's wheel or a kitten playing with a ball of wool, may have been lost on some of the others, many of whom don't yet have television. But not much else is being lost. The people on the changing shifts are standing around, whooping and cheering. Such merry sexual banter fairly relieves the gloom of the working day.

Senga, surrounded by so many masculine presences, is completely unintimidated. She tosses her dyed blonde hair and hangs up her jacket. She turns her boldly attractive face towards the company and the blue eyes, which look as if they could stare into the brightest sun and never flinch, scan them. When she gets to Tam, she winks.

'Ah-ha!'

'It's young Tam she fancies.'

'Hard luck, Billy. Go tae the end o' the queue.'

Of such casual moments is disaster made, Tam thinks as he pushes the bogey towards the kiln. If only he hadn't seen her last night at the dancing.

He had seen her in the Grand Hall often enough before, discreet as a carnival, seeming to bounce off the edges of the place, as if the biggest public hall in Graithnock was too small to contain her sexual energy. Unlike some of the other girls, who would dance with each other in a lean hour, Senga was always partnered by a male. She was in great demand. In the stag line, where boys stood around exchanging worldly wisdom that was as foetid as a boxer's pants, the word was that she was a certainty. Tam had heard one plooky man of the world brag that she had given him a gam, which Tam had recently discovered meant that the woman did it to you with her mouth. Standing with a face like a plook factory, the suave one explained that that was him finished with her. The hypocrisy of it had made Tam want to vomit. How could you share something like that with a woman and then accuse her of it? Gratitude was more in order.

Watching her leave with yet another boy in tow, he had more than once wished it was him. But he was afraid of what being with Senga might involve. Woman at work. Ego-crushing in progress. She seemed so frontal about sex, he wondered if she carried a measuring-tape.

But this night is different. It is one of those nights of rhythmic melancholy which only the dancing can provide. He watches the gently rotating bodies on the floor, a shifting organism of dreams and longings, and he feels a kind of prospective nostalgia for these times. He won't always be doing this. Going to university seems a complete irrelevance. This is where he belongs, among these people.

Even Margaret Inglis feels like a mirage he has been pursuing. She comes from a different place from him. And Maddie Fitzpatrick's address might as well be the moon. Who is he trying to kid? University? Writing? He should keep working in the brickwork and learn just to enjoy the life around him. He sees Senga. Tonight she is wearing a tight black skirt and a white mohair sweater. He remembers the way she winked at him. He asks her to dance.

The night goes into the fourth dimension. Something magical happens. Moving into the energy field that is Senga transforms the Grand Hall. It becomes an exotic place. The yellow, distempered walls have the sheen of muslin in the bright lights. The ordinariness of going to the dancing breaks up into weird fragments. The overweight female singer, who is reputed to do more for the band than sing (an allegation Tam knows from Michael to be nonsense), looks to him tonight like someone out of a Hollywood film, a bit like a Rita Hayworth who's been overeating. Seen through the vitality Senga imparts to him, the other girls' faces are more exciting than any make-up could make them.

In a whirl of vivid impressions the rest of the evening happens. Senga's inhabiting of the moment is infectious. The moments pass in a dizzying blur until they find themselves outside in a lamplit street. A man he has seen come into the brickwork in the morning with Senga's shift shouts across the road at them, something Tam can't make out but knows is suggestive.

'Fuck off,' Senga calls merrily.

She wants a poke of chips and a bottle of Irn Bru. Senga comes from outside Graithnock and he is pleased to be able to tell her that he knows of a chip shop which will still be open. It makes him seem like a man of the world. He feels like Cary Grant.

('I know a little Italian place.')

Eating as they walk, they come to the arches at Soulis Street, where there used to be stables. They toast each other with some Irn Bru drunk from the bottle, which Tam lays on the ground at their feet. And, in the shadows, they begin.

Senga does not go in for preliminaries. As he kisses her, he feels her open coat slide off her shoulders. The mohair sweater rises softly under his knuckles. Senga's right hand moves away from his neck and her brassiere pops. The dim lamplight from the street makes a holy picture of her tits. As he gasps for breath, touching them, she unbuttons his trousers deftly and takes out his cock, which has been trying to butt its way out for the last ten minutes. It is big and hard. He hopes it's big, anyway. At least Senga didn't have to search for it. 'Oh,' she says. She tugs at it with her right hand while her left hand expertly rolls her skirt up her thighs to her waist and he is stunned to realise that she isn't wearing any knickers. Whether it is the exciting shock of the realisation that causes the disaster or the impatient wait his cock has had, chafing in the darkness of his trousers, or the way Senga's hand is kneading it like dough, he can't be sure. But he knows that disaster is imminent. He knows it's on its way. He is going to co-o-o-o-ome.

He tries to jerk himself away from Senga to save face, if that's what you call it. But Senga's hand follows him wherever he tries to go and a disobedient part of him doesn't want to leave her palm. It likes it there. And, as her hand guides him towards that bush between her legs by some instinctive radar, like a bird towards its nest, it happens. He is coming.

He can't believe it. But he's coming all right. And how do you persuade spunk to turn back? He comes like a small hosepipe somebody is dancing on. Here a spurt, there a spurt, everywhere a spurt-spurt. He looks on aghast as his cock takes on a life of its own. It is as if his sperm, having spent years of pent-up frustration, come rushing out like lemmings, not caring that their instinct is an expression of futility. Little kamikaze bastards. They've watched so many of their mates entombed in toilet paper, you would've thought they might learn sense. But no.

('Fuck it, boys. It's a chance, isn't it? We're almost in range of an actual human pussy. Let's go for it.')

They do, fatally. All they achieve is to litter the inside of Senga's new, tight, black skirt with their corpses, like an assault force that didn't get beyond the foreshore. They lie bleaching there.

'Ya silly bastard, Tam,' Senga says. 'What'll Ah tell ma feyther?'

She discusses these things with her father?

('Hopeless again the night, Dad. Another premature ejaculation.'

'Never mind, love. There's more pricks in the sea than ever came out of it. Ye'll meet a good screw one of these days. Never fear.')

As he pushes another bogey into the dawn, the sun comes up on him like his personal searchlight. His shame at the moment is just hidden memories, sores in the mind – Senga taking her knickers (appropriately white as far as he is concerned) from her handbag and covering her unmolested crotch – her niceness to him at the station where he takes her to catch her train – the forgotten bottle of Irn Bru which must still be lying there, marking the spot like a plaque for which he knows the inscription: Tam Docherty was here and might as well not have been – traces of mohair on his jacket in the morning. But his shame will soon be as visible to everyone as facial scabs.

His plan to get out at the end of the night before the day-shift gathers doesn't succeed. Most of them are there before he reaches the rest area to collect his jacket and satchel. The man who shouted at them in the street has obviously been telling the others what he saw.

'Ah-ha!' somebody shouts as he comes in.

'It's Errol Flynn.'

'Saturday night with Senga.'

'There's a reporter fae the *News o' the World* here.'

'Gonny give us the blow-by-blow, Tam?'

Senga is among them, unruffled as ever. What has *she* been telling them? Discretion has never been her conspicuous talent. She waits for the noise to settle.

'Ah'll tell ye somethin',' she says, and his stomach develops a chill. The others are statues of prurience. 'He's mair of a man than any of you lot'll ever be. And that's the truth.'

'Whoo!'

'Show us yer credentials, big yin.'

'Senga should know.'

She does but she isn't telling. She winks theatrically at him for everyone to see and a legend without substance is fully formed. He can't pretend it's him but at least it gives him camouflage till he tries to work out who he is.

He smiles at her and the smile is misconstrued by the others. But he knows what it means. Senga may have a tongue as rough as a scrubbing-brush. She may treat sex like fast food. But, as far as he is concerned, she's class.

IF HE HAD BEEN CAPTAIN COOK, he would have named a small island after her – preferably one with a turbulent stretch of water to the north, to be called McMurtrie Sound.

COLETTE WAS DRIVING with her usual expertise. She effort-lessly overtook a man in a Peugeot and Tom caught a glimpse of his distraught face, incredulous that a woman had passed him. He would probably have to see his analyst.

'You will be returning to Grenoble by the way of Paris?' she said.

'No other way, is there?'

'It is the only reason?'

'Sorry?'

'You speak as if it is not done by choice. I thought you loved Paris.'

'I do. I could eat it with a teaspoon.'

'Maybe we can see you then. Shortly.'

'That would be good. Then you and I could do more joint work in murdering each other's language.'

'You're not thus bad.'

'*So* bad. I'm worse. I'm like the English shop where they had the sign in the window saying "*Ici on parle français*" and when the French tourist went in and asked, "*Qui c'est qui parle français?*" the man behind the counter said, "*Je*".'

'Yes. That sound like you.'

'And that definitely sound like you.'

'Anyways. When you and Gill come to Paris next time. *Nous pouvons aller encore au cinoche avec Michel. Quelle joie pour toi! Tu aimerais bien ça, n'est-ce pas?*'

She looked across at him and winked and began to enjoy the driving. He laughed. They never let him forget that one. Michel had arranged a special treat for the four of them at a cinema near Deux Magots. He kept refusing to tell them what they would see, just that they had to be there at half past midnight. When he and Gill caught up with them, Michel spirited them into the cinema, still secretive. Tom couldn't believe it when the credits rolled. It was a Sonja Henie film made in 1942. It was crap on ice. The only alleviation of the misery was Tyrone Power. He was young and starting out and trying things. His energy crackled. But even he wasn't enough to dull the pain. When the lights went up, Tom made to go. Michel leaned across Colette to restrain him.

'There is more,' he said.

'More what?'

'More of this.'

'Sonja Henie pictures?'

'Two.'

'Three Sonja Henie films at a sitting? What is this, Michel? Suicide by Sonja Henie? Come on.'

'You will enjoy,' Michel said. 'Observe the motifs. One film is as good as another when you do that. Just observe.'

'It's shite.'

'Tom,' Gill was saying. 'Behave and watch the film.'

'He is right,' Colette was saying. 'I tell Michel all the time. Films like this are just *merde*.'

Sensing support, Tom pressed on.

'Listen, Michel. Don't gimme all this structuralist stuff. It comes down to a simple fact. If the pictures were combat, Sonja Henie would be a war criminal.'

He liked that but nobody else did.

'Sh!'

'Pssst!'

He looked round at the people who were mouthing at him.

'What's your problem? You want tae shoot the doctor? Ah'm tryin' tae save you lot from brain death.'

'*Monsieur! S'il vous plaît. Nous voulons voir le film. Si vous ne voulez pas le voir, vous n'avez qu'à partir. Nous voulons voir le film.*'

'What fuckin' film?' Tom was muttering on his way out.

Twenty minutes later, Gill joined him in the bistro. She ordered a coffee and shook her head at him. He apologised.

'Not to me,' Gill said.

'To Michel?'

'He paid for the tickets.'

'Bought the tickets? But that's like apologising to the Marquis de Sade for leaving in the middle of a whipping.'

She sipped her coffee.

'Is he still watching them?'

'Yes. Colette isn't too happy to watch.'

'She's a good judge. Look. Let's go back to Haussmann. You're only here for a week, you know. I'll apologise in the morning. Honest.'

She seemed to be pondering.

'Well. There are certain things that will have to be done at

Haussmann. I'll decide what they are. How is it said in French? *Pour expier?'*

He smiled.

'Some of that penance can be great,' he said.

But when he phoned Michel later that day to apologise, he realised that he had been set up. Besides wanting to see the films, Michel had wanted the entertainment of Tom's reactions to them. He regarded the experience as some kind of triumph of Gallic culture over Scottish lack of subtlety. You mean effeteness, Tom suggested.

It became a continuing wrangle between them. Michel said Tom didn't know how to look at films. Tom said Michel didn't know how *not* to look at them and, if they put Warhol's eight hours of the Empire State Building in front of him, he would watch it as avidly as *Le jour se lève*. Michel said Tom didn't understand filmic form. Tom said Michel appeared never to have heard of content. Tom hated the way films were edited these days in defiance of any feasible credibility. Michel said that was structuralism. Tom said it was self-indulgent lack of talent.

Michel eventually developed a theory, as he would, to explain what he called Tom's 'neurotic response to the performing arts'. He developed the theory from 'two cultural traumas in your experience'. Unfortunately, Tom had told him about one of them.

He had explained that the first opera he ever attended was in English. He had heard snippets of other operas before that and enjoyed the music. But when he discovered the banality of what they were singing, he couldn't believe it. There was a moment in the opera where a man and woman were singing about closing a door. 'Close the door.' 'No, I will not close the door.' 'Will you please close the door?' 'No. The door stays open.' That sort of thing. Tom said he had wanted to shout, 'Shut the fuckin' door an' let's get on with it,' as if he were at a football match. To hear what those supposedly impressive people were actually singing to each other, he said, was like eavesdropping on the conversation of yuppies: all that opulent style fuelled by an articulacy out of a shopping catalogue – off-the-peg emotions, interchangeable clichés of response, style without individual content.

Michel pounced. Tom didn't believe in art for art's sake. No,

Tom said, he believed in art for fuck's sake, because it was so necessary it shouldn't be squandered as mere fodder for critics. Yes, but that made him miss the point of art, which could only function effectively within its own parameters. Tom kept demanding that it relate to 'real' life. Every time art invited him to come out of his working-class prejudices and enjoy it on its own self-referential terms, Tom panicked and retreated back into those prejudices, found an excuse for denying the self-containment of the art, invaded it with disbelief. Anyway, Tom said, he would stick to listening to Mozart on tape rather than buy tickets for *Cosi fan tutte*.

(Dear W.A. Mozart,
What does it feel like to take down God's dictation?)

The second experience Michel used against him was something Tom had told Colette and Colette had passed on to Michel. Colette and he had been talking about great moments in cinema and he had said, only half jokingly, that one of his most memorable cinematic moments had happened in the Forum Picture House when he was a boy. He couldn't even remember the title of the film or the name of anybody who was in it. But it was a film about people travelling in the jungle and lost in an amazing density of foliage, the sort of film where someone says, 'It's *too* quiet,' or a native bearer mutters, 'Drums say no go on, Bwana.' The camera was tracking slowly through the foliage. The silence was utter, when there was the most sudden and chilling scream Tom had ever heard. It lifted him clean out of his seat, along with many others. The cinema was in panic, nobody more so than Tom. Then he realised why. The scream was real. It came from a local man who was well known for taking fits at the pictures. That moment of an imaginary scene peopled by a real living scream had haunted his sense of what art was ever since.

'Of course,' Michel had said. 'Art is not enough for you. You must be always disrupting it with the real.'

'No,' Tom said. 'It's just that, if you're alive, it always *is* being disrupted by the real.'

Tom had pretended outrage at Colette for giving away his secrets to the enemy. Looking at her now as she drove, he smiled and decided he was glad he hadn't told her about some of his early experiences of the theatre. That would really have given Michel evidence for the prosecution. Those occasions had sometimes felt like a play within a play, or maybe part-play, part-unrehearsed happening, distorting the original into a hybrid.

'What do you think about?' Colette said.

The Merchant of Menace

THE SCENE IS THE HALL OF A JUNIOR SECONDARY SCHOOL IN GRAITHNOCK. It is a wet Tuesday afternoon. On the stage a play is in progress. The audience is a motley throng of junior pupils from various schools in Graithnock. The actors are contending with an atmosphere which might be described as seething. Not all the dialogue is restricted to the stage.

BASSANIO: In Belmont is a lady richly left.

FIRST ARSEHOLE IN THE THRONG: Ah'm for a feel at that yin on the road oot.

BASSANIO: And she is fair and fairer than that word.

SECOND ARSEHOLE IN THE THRONG: Tell'er to show us her tits.

BASSANIO: Of wondrous virtues. Sometimes from her eyes.

FIRST ARSEHOLE IN THE THRONG: Show us yer tits.

BASSANIO: I did receive fair speechless messages.

FIRST ARSEHOLE IN THE THRONG: See when we're filin' oot, Ah'm for a grab at your tits.

BASSANIO: And many Jasons come in quest of her.

SECOND ARSEHOLE IN THE THRONG: Hey, you. Skinny bastard. We're gonny cut your heid aff.

FIRST ARSEHOLE IN THE THRONG: An' play at fitba wi' it.

FIRST AND SECOND ARSEHOLES IN THE THRONG: Ooh, ooh, ooh. Oooh, ooh, ooh. Big skinny bastard's heid cut aff.

PORTIA: By my troth, Nerissa, my little body is aweary of this great world.

She's not the only one. Tam Docherty sits in a crossfire of

contradictory awarenesses that are exhausting his concentration. He isn't sure but he thinks he may be the big skinny bastard due for beheading. It is not a reassuring thought. But at least he can safely assume he isn't the one whose tits are going to be grabbed. They would need tweezers for that. He is trying desperately to focus on the play but the guttural whispers are going off all around him like sniper fire and Shakespeare's words stagger across his devastated attention, tattered and bleeding, grandeur in retreat from the assaults of his own guerrilla culture.

He has read the play in school this year, his second year at Graithnock Academy, and the bits he understood have fascinated him. When he was told they were being marched to one of the local junior secondary schools to see their first performance of a Shakespeare play, he had been excited. But the reality of the experience has no resemblance to his expectations of it. He has not imagined that watching his first play would be a dangerous experience or that so much of his time would be taken up by planning his escape at the end of it. For they will simply be dismissed into the playground when this is over. The two mad whisperers sound like part of a gang. If it's him they're after, he'd better find handers or make a quick exit.

Also, the performance of the play has thrown him completely. He cannot understand at first what is wrong. Then he realises that all the actors are women. The jackets and shirts couldn't fool anybody and the voices are a dead give-away. He cannot imagine why this is the case. As the play progresses, it isn't only the haranguing voices around him that destroy the pleasure. One simple fact keeps intruding on his thoughts, defying his belief in the play. Bassanio has bigger tits than Portia.

A Streetcar Named Backfire

THE SCENE IS THE PALACE THEATRE IN GRAITHNOCK. The time is evening on a Friday in 1955. Tam Docherty is one of a very sparse audience. A summer repertory company is in residence at the Palace. He has been coming most Fridays with dutiful aestheticism and mixed feelings. He has seen *Night Must Fall*, *Dangerous Corner*, *The Admirable Crichton* and *Music at Night*. Tonight is more interesting but the audience remains intimately small. He feels he knows most of them by now. He sits in the same almost empty row as usual and the same middle-aged woman sits along from him. She always brings a bag of boilings with her. During the first few scenes, the sound of crunching sweeties accompanies the action like static on a radio. Then the play begins to come over loud and clear, for the woman is asleep, the poke of sweeties resting on her lap. Tam thinks that this is probably the only place she can find peace and quiet from the weans. He has developed an almost filial affection for her. Asleep, she looks like a vernacular version of an earth-mother, heavy body filling the seat comfortably, slightly tousled head gently askew on her neck. Awake, she has a face like a well-stoked fire. You feel warmed by its presence. Over the past few weeks they have been exchanging facial reactions at the end of each play – raised eyebrows, noddings. Her usual comment is, 'That wis good, son. Eh?' Presumably her critical criteria relate to the quality of sleep induced. Given some of the performances, Tam can see the validity of her terms. Tonight she has taken longer than usual to get to sleep and he wonders if that means a good review or a bad one. Does that mean that she is enjoying it so much that she is prepared to postpone sleep for a little or that the play is annoying her so much she can't *get* to sleep? The question is rendered irrelevant by her gentle silence. Tom is relieved, for a part of his mind, against his will, has been concerned about her critical insomnia. He has almost been tempted to tell the actors to keep their voices down. Now he can relax and enjoy the progress of the action. It holds him for scene after scene until—

BLANCHE: What do you want?

MITCH: What I been missing all summer.

BLANCHE: Then marry me, Mitch!

MITCH: I don't think I want to marry you any more.

BLANCHE: No?

MITCH: You're not clean enough to bring in the house with my mother.

BLANCHE: Go away, then. Get out of here before I start screaming fire! Get out of here quick before I start screaming fire. Fire! Fire! Fire!

MIDDLE-AGED WOMAN: Holy Christ!

She lurches to her feet. There is the deafening sound of scattered boilings crashing on the uncarpeted floor under the seats in front of her. They rattle ominously for seconds, like departing thunder. Combined with the electric tension on the stage, it is a genuinely heart-stopping moment. For Tam it has an almost supernatural feel to it, like being caught in a science-fiction film called *The Invasion of the Ball-Bearings*. His startled eyes catch sight of the woman already out into the passageway and heading for the exit. She freezes suddenly and blinks around, locating reality. The curtain has come down on that scene and is now going up on the next one. Tam observes the woman standing in the half-light and staring at the stage. She is checking things out.

BLANCHE: How about taking a swim. A moonlight swim at the old rock quarry? If anyone's sober enough to drive a car! Ha-ha!

The Ha-Ha seems to do it. Not many people say Ha-ha when they're caught in a conflagration. The woman tiptoes back to her place and begins to scrabble under the empty seats in front for her boilings. She manages to salvage a few. She seems calm now. She glances along at Tam, who has found her behaviour more riveting than the play, and hisses, 'Christ, son. Ah thought the place was on fire there.'

Before the play ends, she manages another short nap. Tam tries to focus on the stage again. But the play is gone. He likes this play. He will always like this play. But tonight, for the last two scenes, he is seized by a prolonged paroxysm of the giggles. It reminds him of the time his Auntie Bella announced to the family that his Uncle Davie had broken his leg in two places trying to change a light-bulb and Tam thought he would die of laughter. He couldn't stop laughing even while his father skelped his head. He was sent outside until he could learn to behave like a human being. He went out the back and rolled around silently on the doorstep like an evil spirit unfit for human company. Later that evening, he heard his mother and father laughing between themselves and his father was saying, 'Wee bugger. Ah thought he was gonny set me off. Ah had tae send him out. Bella was that serious.'

Now he is again experiencing that worrying tendency in him to laugh at serious matters. It's like a neurotic reaction. Solemnity provokes hilarity. While Stanley Kowalski rapes Blanche Dubois and Blanche is led away to the nuthouse, he is crouched down behind the seat in front, heaving in an agony of suppressed laughter. Tears are running from his eyes. He is whimpering and moaning for mercy, praying for the play to end. He doesn't care if they all rape one another. Just so long as they let him out.

When the curtain finally comes down and rises again and the scattered onlookers are erect to applaud the cast, he cannot stand up. He is rocking in his seat in helpless laughter. A man and a woman a few rows ahead turn round and stare at him disgustedly. This makes him worse. He cannot explain to them that, much as he respects the actors' performances, they remain mere supporting players to his unofficial star of the evening, the woman who had performed so convincingly her own small drama – *Behaviour in a Theatre which is on Fire*. He notices that she hasn't wakened up yet. He manages to calm himself with deep breathing and moves along the row and touches her respectfully on the shoulder.

'Excuse me, missus. That's it finished.'

The eyes click open brightly. That lovely warm face looks up at him.

'Oh, thanks, son.'

He waits for her to get up and move out into the passageway. As he is passing her in the aisle, she speaks again.

'No' quite as good the night, son. Eh?'

He makes a muffled noise and keeps his head averted and stumbles out, starting to laugh again and finding it impossible to agree with her.

Buchanan

HE WOULD GO TO THE TRAVERSE THEATRE and see the play. Like almost any impulse to act which he felt at the moment, no matter how simple, it became not so much a decision as the blueprint for a decision. The paralysis of the will he had been experiencing for some time meant that he found himself submitting anything he thought he might do to a kind of committee of motivations. His spontaneity had gone into coma. Just to keep alive the justification for doing anything, he seemed to need to have reasons beyond mere instinct, since his instincts were largely in suspension. The making of a cup of tea might be preceded by a complicated inner debate concerning whether he really wanted tea, how long it would take to make it, whether in the process he would lose the spoor of the past he was hunting in his head. The more reasons he could find, like tubes attached to a patient in intensive care, the better the chance he had of keeping himself functioning as more than a mind.

So, as he got ready to go out, he tried to work out why he was going out. He shaved with the last of his disposable blades and the soft flesh under his chin told him he had better buy a new pack. Grimacing in the mirror, he told himself that going to the play would be an act of homage to the fighting career of Ken Buchanan.

He had always admired Buchanan. He regarded him as the greatest professional boxer Scotland had ever produced, a man who had what only the great fighters have, the ability to enlarge in crisis, to ignite the reflexes under pressure, not to fold. Then, as he searched for the sweater that looked least in need of washing, he felt returning to feed on his small purpose the self-doubts his love of boxing had always had to deal with.

When he was twelve or thirteen, his father had taken him to Firhill in Glasgow to watch Peter Keenan win the European bantamweight title against Luis Romero of Spain. Something which he would often wish to disown had surfaced in him and was never quite to go away, a domesticated darkness, a barking black dog no logic could ever quite muzzle. That day encapsulated a continuing ambivalence in his nature.

Keenan had been brilliant. Romero was reputed to hit like a kicking horse and Keenan had no great power of punch. Yet for fifteen three-minute rounds he neutralised Romero, displaying a stirring array of skills, like a man ballet-dancing among bombs without once losing his nerve or the grace of his line. There was something he had found too moving in that to be denied.

But the next fight had horrified him. It was between a blond man from the North of England and a black man from Nigeria. In the first round the black man had threatened to overwhelm the blond one, with the crowd shouting him on. From the second round onwards, until it was stopped in the fourth, the black man had been mercilessly beaten and the crowd bayed like an amphitheatre. Crouched far up in the stand and often staring at his feet, he didn't want to be there. Ever since then, his fascination with boxing had lived queasily between visceral thrill and a desire to distance himself from a part of himself.

He put on the black leather jacket to go with the black jeans. Clothes might not make the man but maybe they could hold him together. Still unsure about going out, he decided maybe he was testing himself against Michel's accusation of philistinism in relation to the performing arts.

Once in the theatre, he had to admit that he wasn't answering the accusation too effectively. The play seemed to him fair enough and the acting all right, although three people had walked out noisily, as if their departure were a significant comment. He could never do that. It seemed so hurtful to the actors. His method was simply not to come back in after the interval. (He was glad it was novels he had been ambitious to write and not plays. Authors didn't hear their books being slammed shut all over the country.)

While he could bear the play, he couldn't get excited about it. Maybe that was merely the way he was just now but he didn't think so. Very few plays had nailed him to his seat. He could remember a few at random – the original London production of *Who's Afraid of Virginia Woolf?*, productions of *The Crucible* and *The Caucasian Chalk Circle*, and an amateur production of *Oh What a Lovely War!* Their impact stayed with him.

And Stratford-upon-Avon was one of his favourite places. He had stood a lot of times at the interval on the outside balcony, overlooking the river. It had always been a soft summer evening. He would have a drink in his hand, talking with someone he wanted to be with and there would be ducks and swans on the river and people boating. And they would be halfway through seeing *King Lear* or *Hamlet* or *Much ado About Nothing*. Perhaps happiness is only realised in retrospect, for those moments seemed to him suffused with a rich and quiet joy. He was in a good place with a good person, taking a long, slow drink, and he had just been enjoying the company of the writer who meant most to him in the world and in a few minutes there was more to come. He was poised between two great pleasures and the interim was a pleasure in itself. Perhaps he would go back to Stratford soon. Whatever the production was like, you couldn't miss with Shakespeare. You were bound to come out with countless arrows of perception lodged in the mind, to be pulled out at your leisure. Great theatre was a wonderful experience.

Bad theatre was as bad as bad art gets. You couldn't turn away from it like a painting or turn the volume down on the music centre or switch it off like the television or throw it across the room like a book. And on celluloid the actors couldn't be embarrassed. A bad play was a double torture. It trapped both the actors and the audience in it, to their mutual excruciation. He should know. He had once written a play which was put on at the Edinburgh Festival and which was so bad they should probably have issued a razor-blade with every ticket, so that the audience had a form of silent protest. He winced in the darkness. They always went out like corpses anyway.

('Author! Author! Right, there he is now. Let's get the bastard.')

Sitting there, he knew why he had come out. The play was an excuse to be with people. It didn't matter too much in itself. Michel was probably right. He saw 'art', if you wanted to call it that, not as some purist abstraction but as an extension of companionship, a way to share the company of people you would never meet. Even a book was a special kind of social event. That must be why he had always enjoyed the moments that interrupted creative preconceptions with the unforeseen, the man from Porlock who had come to the door when Coleridge was writing 'Kubla Khan' and left him unable to finish it. He was always knocking at the door of every attempted poem or play or novel, demanding admission. Over the shoulder of every writer, some aspect of reality that was being excluded was leaning perpetually, saying, 'What about me?'

He remembered a night in Malta, when Gill and he were living for the summer with Don and Jennifer. That was before Megan was born. They all went one evening to an open-air production of *The Merchant of Venice*. It was performed in countryside outside Sliema, set among trees in the ruins of an old house, part of which provided a natural stage at the top of crumbling steps. Moths and cockroaches thronged the lighted air like unpaid extras. Animal sounds barracked the text constantly.

It was an unexpectedly exhilarating experience, as if he were watching creativity struggle for survival in a hostile environment. The animal life didn't care about reputations, Arts Council grants, who was in or out, how they were wearing talent this year. They just got on with their own serious business, copulating and eating one another. Only the force of the creation could make it survive. It had no life-support machines of textual commentary or precious aesthetics or fashionable theory or hype. It happened like a human force in the chaos of nature and took its chances that the strength of the imagined actions and, most of all, the truth and perceptiveness of the words could withstand the erosions of chance and the infinite denial of alternative circumstance, and hold.

They did, through a haze of insect life and above the preoccupied scutterings of animals and past the pleasure he and Gill were taking in each other. They were luxuriating in touching thighs and exchanging glances that could see far into the future of a few hours from now and he was being continuously roused by the smell of her. The fires of orgasm were already being quietly stoked. But Shakespeare could still make himself heard.

The voice, accented as it was by the prejudices of its time, distilled an essence which survived those prejudices and helped to explain Tom's own time to him. The resonant humanity of the voice was inescapable. It did not overwhelm the distractions of the night but it was not overwhelmed by them. It took its place coherently and undeniably among them. Prospero had found another island.

Experiencing that, Tom would reaffirm one aspect of his own problematical aesthetic. You cannot talk beyond your own time by denying its specificity. You must try to inhabit it so intensely that you may, with luck and honesty and talent, say some words that relate to any time, to the nature of times.

That night in Malta clarified for him an afternoon in James Hamilton Junior School, Graithnock, and an evening in the Palace Theatre. Those happy Philistines wanting just to grope a girl in the shadow of Shakespeare and the woman who saw a theatre as a dormitory had been telling him something. Even them he owed.

Like them, nature was undercutting the self-importance of humanity's sense of itself as they sat there in the dark. It wasn't life, he thought (much as he loved Camus), that was absurd. What was absurd was people's attempt to conceptualise it whole, reduce it to a philosophical order. It was the human demand to understand comprehensively that created absurdity.

Only people had that absurd need to understand. He remembered a poem by Edmund Blunden in which the poet was embroiled in the question of who wrote Shakespeare and went out for a walk and saw a flower fulfilling itself just in growing and 'Beheaded it for blooming insolence'. Auden in 'Fish in the unruffled lakes' expressed how no other creature had any problem with knowing how to be. Auden was right. Fish didn't find themselves agonising over whether they should swim left or right. They just swam, became part of their element. No Hamlets in the fishy world. 'To swim or not to swim: that is the question'? Naw.

The Maltese summer had been one of those times when Gill and he had found an almost complete, animal naturalness in being with each other. That was before the questions came, like assayers born of hurt, to start analysing every gesture and check out instinctive responses for dubious content. Then their interpretations of each other's actions had seemed assumptively and automatically benign.

Why was it, he wondered, that the things which attracted couples in the first place so often become the things about each other they would want to change? The social vulnerability, the unpredictable spontaneity, the tendency to laugh without inhibition. Was it that they were conscious that what had attracted them might also attract others and, therefore, had to be camouflaged? Or was it just the irritation of another's habits which had been outgrown and which now abraded where they had once fitted comfortably?

Why did the niceties and romantic gestures, like flowers or familiar expressions of affection, have such a positive effect at the beginning of a relationship and such counter-productive results near the end of one? Maybe then, he thought, they had been tokens of what would happen, promising potential. Later, they would be measurements of what hadn't happened, simply defined failure.

He felt again in the darkness of the Traverse Theatre the sadness of a failed relationship, not dulled by time but sharpened by the greater understanding that time had given him. The deepest grief wasn't in the mourning for what would no longer be but, given the changed perception of your own experience, in the fear that it perhaps had never been at all and you had dreamed it. For, if she had really been who you thought she was, how was it possible for her to be who she later became? In that despair could drown all hope, all belief in the value of your personal experience. You might suspect that you would always live in a hallucination, had been doing that all your life.

Perhaps who you thought you were was a fiction of your own devising, a stranger neither you nor anyone else could ever quite know.

'EXCUSE ME,' THE VOICE SAID. 'You Tom Docherty?'

It took Tom a moment or two to come back in and land again at Heathrow. He realised how busy the airport was around him. He checked automatically that the plastic bag containing the two books was still on the ground between his legs, in front of his plastic seat.

The man would be about fifty. He had a direct, aggressive stare, as if he wouldn't like Tom to deny it.

'Sorry?'

'Tom Docherty. You him?'

'That's right.'

'Ah thought that. Seen ye on the telly. Back up in Scotland. Go up an' see the mother every so often. She won't come down here to live. Ah thought it was you.'

'Aye.'

'Ah thought it was.'

'Aye.'

'Aye.'

It didn't sound as if this was going to be Oscar Wilde meets Bernard Shaw.

The man started to make a come-here gesture with his right hand. Sensing danger, Tom tried to see who was being invited over. All he noticed was an undifferentiated crowd on the concourse. The man seemed to be summoning Heathrow.

'Janice! Janice!'

The man must have established contact, for he turned back to Tom.

'It's the wife. She's the reader in the family. Haven't read any of your books maself. Don't have the time. But she seems to like them.'

A businessman, Tom thought. It was probably an unwarranted assumption but he couldn't stop himself. Too often he had spoken at Burns suppers and found himself introduced afterwards to some local businessman, encased in self-esteem like ormolu, who made an act of condescension out of an ignorance of literature. 'The wife's got a couple of your books. Don't have the time to read myself.' The implication was that the world of commerce was where men lived. Books, like knitting patterns, were for women. Unless his book was a bestseller, and therefore became a commercial phenomenon, a male author was not clearly gendered, a psychological transvestite.

'It *is* him,' the man said.

At least he gave Tom the benefit of the pronoun.

Janice was an attractive, dark-haired woman, probably in her late forties. She was casually but expensively dressed and conspicuous with jewellery. Tom stood up awkwardly. The man, himself dressed in a style Tom thought might have been described as Armani Scruffy, seemed to be looking from one to the other expectantly. Tom had an impression that the man was looking at him and almost nodding towards the woman. It was as if he were being asked to appreciate her. He did.

'It was Eddie recognised you,' the woman said. 'Are you really Tom Docherty?'

'Guilty as charged.'

Instinctively, she leaned forward and kissed his cheek.

'I love your stuff,' she said.

And then she compared his work with that of an author whom he quite liked but who, he thought, was doing something entirely different. He had heard the comparison made before and had eventually decided that people who could make that comparison would probably have linked Attila the Hun with General William Booth. They both led an army. Now he erased that thought guiltily, as if he were removing an embarrassing phrase from a manuscript. He must stop judging people so hard. He liked Eddie and Janice. Why shouldn't he? They were two strangers who had gone out of their way to give him a present.

They talked. Eddie and Janice were on their way to Magaluf. Eddie was from Partick in Glasgow. Janice was from Newcastle. They now lived in Richmond. Eddie had made his money in the building trade. They were still endearingly nonplussed at how much the money was. Their children were away from home now.

As they talked, Tom discovered yet again how the self-regarding purity of ideology will always be called in question, if the ideologue is honest (though an honest ideologue might well be a contradiction in terms), when confronted with the complex reality of being a person. He had always had contempt for the idea of devoting your life to the making of money. Eddie had certainly done that to a fairly large extent, it would seem. Tom ought to have disliked him, according to his own rules.

But he couldn't. It was the principle of the mole on John Benchley's left cheek. That mole had compromised his ability to believe in God. Now Eddie's slightly bulbous nose humanised a concept into doubt. These direct eyes were staring out of a man, not an idea. He had severe limitations (though maybe not as many as Tom) and those limitations were some kind of absolution, because he had so patently not acted malignly out of them. He had made his money because he thought that's what you had to do. Tom heard that in what he said and, with an unspoken apology, he removed his name from the role of philistine materialists, where he had put it.

One conversational moment clinched it. Janice and Eddie were saying how they had considered selling up and living in Spain.

'But we decided the ex-pat thing wasn't for us.'

'We met some of them,' Janice said. 'Nice enough people. But.'

'Bore ye tae death,' Eddie said. 'It would be like livin' in sheltered housing.'

'So we take more holidays than we used to, instead.'

'An' we can still feel we're part of the livin',' Eddie said. 'Ah mean, that way tae live. That's not retirin' from work. That's retirin' from life. An' tae think that the money sent by selfish bastards like that can affect the government of Scotland.'

'Eddie! We don't need the swearing.'

'Ah would think not,' Tom said. 'Eddie. Mind yer fuckin' language.'

They had to go. Eddie and Tom shook hands and Eddie gave Tom his card. Tom explained that he didn't have a card.

'If ye're ever in London. Seeing publishers or that. Give us a phone. Ye're an hour away from Richmond, in London. Ye can come and stay. Plenty of room.'

'Stacks,' Janice said. 'We're rattling about in that house now like peas in a drum.'

'Or if ye're short of time,' Eddie said. 'We can come into town. We'll have a right night.'

Tom understood suddenly another reason why he liked Eddie. It was the quality of Janice. You couldn't not like *her*. She wore diminishing attractiveness with careless style. She didn't try to tart it up. That was why the attractiveness stayed. She wore it as if it had merely become an accessory to the character which had grown out of it. The jewellery was there, Tom imagined, just because she liked jewellery. And there wasn't a trace of that portcullis in the eyes he had noticed in some of the well-off, as if the world couldn't quite get to them any more. She had the eyes of a younger woman, wondering still what it was about. Her money hadn't sealed her off. It had just given her an altered vantage-point, from which she continued to see how interesting things were. If someone like her could get such obvious pleasure out of being with Eddie, Eddie was doing something right, don't worry.

She and Tom embraced briefly.

'I know what I'll do,' she said. 'We've just got time, Eddie. I saw a copy of *The Stone Dream* in the bookstall. I've read it. But I'll buy another one. Read it again in Magaluf.'

'Boost yer royalties, eh?' Eddie said. 'Ye can sign it when ye're down at our place.'

They all agreed that's what would happen. It seemed at the time a certainty, as if the improbability of their meeting again was too remote to imagine.

Left to his thoughts, he reflected on how lucky he had been with such chance encounters with someone who had read something he had written. They had almost all been positive. Perhaps that was just the kindness of not wanting to embarrass him. He supposed most people who took the trouble to come up and talk to you wouldn't do it to say bad things.

('Excuse me. Ah saw ye from the bus there and Ah got off specially to tell you. Yer stuff's a crocka shite.'

'Ah don't suppose ye want ma autograph?')

But any popularity he might have certainly didn't seem to manifest in sales. Were they all library users? His publisher had almost closed a deal once with a book club and then it fell through. That had seemed to him a significant omen at the time and he wondered about it now. He suspected it was the swear-words that had put the book club off. Was that what had doomed him to marginal sales? Had he sworn himself out of the market?

(*Dear Mark Antony,*
I suspect my literary earnings and your career have something in common – both brought to ruin by a few fucks in the wrong place.)

He would never make serious money with writing, and surely wouldn't make it with anything else now. Why did you have to wait till you were dead before posterity got the message?

BUT POSTERITY ITSELF IS DEAD, he would think, insofar as it can be seen as any kind of final arbiter. After all, this was posterity for the writers no longer alive and contemporary criteria seemed to be re invented by the week. The modern trend was criticism by aerosol can, the present convincing itself of its revolutionary credentials by spraying the monuments of the past with simplistic slogans. In that climate he could no longer pretend to himself that the swear-words he had used were any hindrance to acceptance. These days there were books around which had more fucks than a year in a brothel and they were doing fine. No. Don't wait for posterity. It doesn't stop here any more.

The only motivation he could find for writing was the one with which he had started, a compulsion to try and understand the strangeness of things, a fascination with our hardly known selves.

'I'M LYING ON MY BED,' she says. 'I've got no clothes on. I'm completely naked. I'm lying on top of the covers.'

The lamplight filtered through the curtains is giving her skin an eerie, translucent sheen. Colour me strange. Her rumpled hair makes her look wild, a woodland creature. Her eyes seem almost phosphorescent in the semi-dark. She doesn't look as if she belongs in Graithnock but in some fable of the female. Maybe 'La Belle Dame Sans Merci'.

'Across the room,' she says. 'It's not my room. It's a room I don't know. Across the room there's a wardrobe. Hanging on the wardrobe door is my favourite dress. It's a dress I had when I was small. I mean, I did really have this dress. When I was about nine, I think. Blue with white roses.'

She shudders infinitesimally, faintest ripple on the surface of still water. As she remembers, the hunching of her shoulders is barely perceptible, a small and heart-touching gesture of self-protection.

'All round about me. On the bed. There's these huge, fat rats. I'm afraid to move. My head's over to one side. There's a wound on my neck. Blood's running out on to the bed. One of the rats is feeding on the blood. Its nose is next to my neck but it's not touching it. Another rat is resting against my leg. At the top of my calf. I can sense other ones round about me.'

Sitting on the bed, she looks terribly bereft. Her beautiful legs, revealed by the rucked skirt as far as her suspenders, seem contradicted by her mood. They are a come-on she can't help but does not mean.

'I know,' she says. 'I know that if I move. The smallest movement, and somehow the rats will attack me. I know that if I can stay absolutely still, until the blood stops flowing, I'll be all right. The way my head is lying. It's turned away from the window and towards the wardrobe. I'm watching the dress. It's the original size it was when it fitted me as a small girl. And I know it'll never fit me again. I'm crying. Very quietly, so that it doesn't make my head move. The tears are running across my nose and face and on to the bed. I want to really sob. To let my body shake with it. But I can't. Because, if I do, the rats will get me.'

She looks at him sitting on the bed beside her. She has remembered he is here. His left hand is resting on her thigh. She lays her own right hand on top. He takes his hand out from under and covers her hand with his. Downstairs, the other party goers are rocking around the clock. Put your glad rags on and join me, hon.

'It's a strange dream, isn't it?' she says.

He softly strokes the back of her hand with his thumb, as if it were an answer.

'It ends there?' he asks.

'Yes. That's when I woke up. What do you think it means?'

He doesn't know. But he knows that, if he's anywhere in there, he's one of the rats. It's not a happy feeling.

'Maybe,' he says, unable to resist bringing the weight of his considerable experience to bear upon the question, 'It could be that you're frightened by your own sexualness. It could be saying that. The frock. You want to go back. That was safer. What ye are now. People might abuse it.'

He feels as if he's bearing witness against himself. He had been busy only with her body. He had had her skirt far enough up to show the white triangular shimmer of her pants as she lay back. He had her blouse unbuttoned and her brassiere loosened. He had been frustrated and annoyed when she suddenly sat up and seemed upset and wanted to tell him about her dream. Jesus, had he resented that bloody dream. Nobody invited dreams to the party. He had known what would happen. And it had. Listening to that dream was a good way to lose an erection.

But that resentment has somehow evaporated in the listening. He looks at the taut, protuberant breasts with the brassiere rumpled above them. He sees the helplessly attractive legs. But now he is also seeing past the parts. He sees her. She is as insecure and vulnerable as he is. Just because she looks so perfectly complete, it doesn't mean she is. This isn't someone just to make fantasies from. This is someone to care for.

He puts his arms around her and they hold each other. She is clasping tight.

'You okay?' he asks.

'Yes. Thanks.'

He's not sure what the thanks are for. For understanding? For not making love? Then he realises that this *is* making love. It comes as a mind-opening revelation to him. This *is* making love. You don't have to be dismantling a girl to nakedness to be making love to her.

He thinks about the endless talk about girls between his friends and him over the last few years. Which of those less-than-trustworthy reporters back from the front line of experience ever bragged about how good it had been to hold each other? Which of the eager inquisitors ever asked, mouth open in anticipation, 'What was the cuddling like?' They had been programmed to assess their sexual experience by a method as mechanical as that of a school examination: breasts covered but touched (elementary) – 25 per cent; breast naked (secondary) – 50 per cent; pudendum naked (advanced) – 75 per cent; intercourse total (graduation) – 100 per cent. (Pleasure experienced by the woman will not be taken into account in any of these sections.)

This is good. It is good just to hold her close and feel the soft warmth of her body and know the gentle rise and falling of her breathing. An amazing awareness arrives. He feels like a man. More than at any of the not very numerous times he's managed to stand up to a would-be hard-case at the dancing, more than at any of the times he's managed to coerce a girl to let her breasts out of her brassiere in the shadows of the Burns Monument in the Kay Park, he feels like a man. He may not know what a man is but he knows it has something to do with moments like this. It's a good feeling.

This is one way of making love. He's certainly not giving up the attempt to do it in at least one other way he can think of but he will postpone it for just now. Don Juan is off duty for the night. He just wants to nurse her through the memory of her dream. He just wants to be a shell for her hurt.

They hold and kiss each other softly.

'It'll be all right,' he says.

How he can tell, he wouldn't know. But the certainty arrives from somewhere and he voices it.

'You feeling all right?' he asks

'I'm all right,' and she kisses him.

He eases her brassiere down over her breasts. He reaches his arms round her and hooks her brassiere at the back. He buttons her blouse for her. Reverse seduction. Is that 'The Last Post' he hears being played for the death of his machismo? They smile at each other.

'You want to go down?'

She nods.

'We've been a while,' she says. 'I hope they don't know what we've been up to.'

'Discussin' dreams? Ah won't tell them if you don't.'

PUT YOUR GLAD RAGS ON and join me, hon.
We'll have some fun when the clock strikes one.

THE MUSIC IS THE PULSE OF THE EVENING. The record has been playing continuously. No other song is allowed. If someone tries to put something else on the record-player, the murmuring threats of riot are heard in the room. Bill Haley and the Comets rule.

Something has happened here, something new. Tam can feel it. This is the night rock 'n' rôll came to town. A group of motley teenagers who came here as vague and uncertain individuals have become a sect. Faces shine with Pentecostal fervour. The dancing has turned wildly experimental. People gyrate and gesture with laughing awkwardness, sometimes falling delightedly in their attempts to meet the music. New postures are constructed out of sound, form like blueprints in the air, and the young bodies contort desperately in their efforts to fit themselves into the shapes they hear coming at them from the music. It's open day at the zoo of the imagination. Let all those caged-up creatures out to play.

Coming downstairs with Margaret, Tam feels as if they have gone upstairs for half an hour and missed a revolution. They pass instantly from the self-conscious personal worries of their intimacy into a communal frenzy of unthinking abandon, without a decompression chamber. Tam starts to dance jerkily, as if he has the bends. Margaret joins him. The room goes into orbit. They are travelling to a new place. As they part and dance with others and as the evening spins further and further away from the assumptions they all brought to it, Tam talks and dances and goes into amazed reveries and stands in the kitchen and walks in the garden and sits on the stairs and keeps meeting people he knows who look and talk like strangers, suddenly interestingly unknown.

He finds Jack Laidlaw drinking with the cat. He is sitting on the steps outside the back door. He is drinking a bottle of Newcastle Brown Ale. He has found a saucer into which he is pouring beer for the cat.

'Come on,' Jack is saying. 'Drink up, Cuddles.'

The cat seems to be more interested in the elaborate stroking Jack is giving it than in the beer, although it does go back to the saucer from time to time.

'That's the stuff, Cuddles. You wire in. Ye're gettin' the hang of it.'

Tam brings out a kitchen chair and puts it in the pathway beside the door and sits facing Jack. It seems like the most natural thing in the world to do. He thinks, with some surprise, that Jack doesn't look sixteen. He doesn't look like any age particularly. His handsome face appears both wise and naïve. Maybe the beer does that. The amount he has had surfaces in his eyes when he looks up at his new visitor, smudging their blueness.

'Tom. Hullo. Tom, this is Cuddles. Cuddles, Tom. What a name for a cat, eh? Cuddles. Cuddles, the tom cat. Like puttin' a frock on a tiger . . . That's why Ah'm givin' it the beer,' he adds mysteriously.

They talk. They agree that this has the edge on Avondale Brickwork. A girl Tam doesn't know appears in the doorway behind Jack and puts her hands over his eyes.

'Guess who,' she says.

Jack sits without saying anything long enough for them to think he has fallen asleep.

'Come on,' the girl says.

'Rhonda Fleming,' Jack says.

'No.'

'Well, sorry. Ah'm waitin' for Rhonda.'

'Ah'll tell Jennifer you said that,' the girl says, and goes away.

'Rhonda Fleming?' he says.

'What?' Jack says.

'Rhonda Fleming? You fancy big Rhonda as well?'

He means as well as he does. But, given his heightened state of mind in which he is catching the ambiguities of his remarks even as he makes them, he realises that, in his own case, it could mean as well as every other woman in the world.

'Dream woman,' Jack says simply.

Immediately they are improvising a duet in praise of Rhonda Fleming. Her tits are perfect, imagine looking at that face across the table in the morning, and do you remember that time in *Build My Gallows High* when . . .

'That's amazin,' Jack says.

They stare at each other as if they have only just discovered they have the same parentage. Jack's beer is finished and they share Tam's bottle.

'Ah've got to practise,' Jack says. 'This is the first time Ah've been guttered. But Ah think Ah'll get better at it.'

They go on to discuss Tam's going to university in a couple of weeks. Jack sits his highers next year. He's not sure about university. He'll see how he does in the highers. They talk about what they might eventually do. Jack wants to travel. Tam admits that he wants to write. It seems all right to say it here, where they sit out of range of the sniping pragmatism of common sense. The possibilities seem endless. From the house, Bill Haley and the Comets are still evoking wild vistas.

'Tom,' Jack says seriously. 'Ah like you. Come and we'll be friends for life?'

He agrees. No problem, deal done. They shake hands solemnly. The handshake is appropriate not just as a gesture of a compact made. It is like meeting each other for the first time. Tam has known Jack slightly at school and then at the brickwork but he had never imagined how much they had in common. He leaves the rest of the beer with Jack and goes for a walk in the garden.

'Come back an' see me any time,' Jack says. 'Now that ye know where Ah live. But bring somethin' for ma cat. Ah always like visitors to bring somethin' for Cuddles.'

Vegetation is wonderful, isn't it? Thirty yards from the house the music whispers and the smell of grass and leaves makes him feel different and alone and distant. He inhales a dark and other sense of himself. Finding a new awareness, he draws the scent up through his nostrils, nature's cocaine. Some day he may try the chemical stuff, when he's living in America maybe. But for now just breathing is a big enough turn-on.

He looks back towards the house. This is a long garden. The house looks impressive from here. He wonders what Caroline's parents will think when they get back. Maybe they should all help her to clear up at the end of the night. In the kitchen of the house next door the figure of a man is walking up and down past the window, the sentry of the suburbs.

He thinks of the party, all those people looking as if they are finding a new expression of themselves. He compares it with other parties he has been to. He thinks of the ones he used to go to when he was in the last year of primary school. There were a lot of them then, a rush of them, perhaps because the class would be splitting up to go to different schools. The parents would go out for several hours in the evening and kissing games were played, Postman's Knock and Torchy and Forfeits.

He remembers one in particular. May Clarke invited him to it. Late in the evening, a game of Forfeits began. It came the turn of a girl he had been watching compulsively since he came in. Her face had simply filled the room for him, striking and dark-eyed. Those eyes made him want to jump into them. Her mouth was the first time he had really noticed mouths. He had kept his distance, intimidated by her age. He was twelve and he had learned that she was fourteen. But her breasts, he thinks now, appeared to have been sent on ahead of her. They must have been seventeen at least.

The boy who was giving the forfeits was sitting, blindfold, on a chair. The boy who was standing beside him, stating the sex of the person who was to make the forfeit, was his friend. They were both about fifteen. As the girl stepped up to be told what she had to do, Tam noticed that the standing boy squeezed his friend's shoulder. He realised that they were working a ploy between them. One of them expected to be chosen by her to carry out the forfeit. Tam couldn't tell which, because both of them had been round her all evening like muzzled dogs round their dinner. His joy was unlimited (early stirrings of the latent machismo) when she picked him. The forfeit was to choose her favourite boy in the room and kiss him according to the number of stars in the sky.

The joy was short-lived. When they stepped outside into the darkness, the sky was starless. Tam shrugged helplessly and they waited a little while, cuddling coldly, and went back inside, where he discovered that May Clarke wouldn't speak to him again.

Standing in the garden, he can't believe how stupid he was then, what an unimaginative little bore. He never saw the girl again after that night. No wonder the girl cuddled him coldly. That mouth he might have kissed haunts him still, like the girl on the bus he allowed to wave him goodbye before he had met her.

He makes a decision there among the leaves. If he misses life, it won't be for the want of trying. May the guilt that comes to plague him when he is dying have its source all in sins of commission, never in sins of omission. He would rather die of overload than inertia.

He should have invented the stars. The thought arrests him. But not invent – discover. See them where no one else can. You must discover your own stars. He decides that he will.

You must discover your own stars. That cryptic statement, created by himself, makes him feel philosophical. He ponders the end of this summer. It is officially over now. He has been prolonging his personal version of it falsely, to give him more time, reluctant to abandon his adolescence because he has found no ceremonial moments to mark its closure. For which of the markers he set himself on leaving school has he managed to reach? None.

He is still terrified of going to university. The plan he had developed was to try and read more or less everything before he went, no matter how skimpily. That way, he reasoned, it would be a lot harder for them to find him out. But it had failed on two counts: he couldn't read enough and what he did read so quickly was like skating on a frozen loch. What was going on in the depths below the surface?

The *Journals* of Kierkegaard was the book of this summer that represented his failure to him most dramatically. His persistence with the journals had not been entirely for dubious reasons. There may have been an element of the flash in it, like someone contriving to have his passport stamped with an exotic location to which he has never been. But a deeper truth was that he did find the journals fascinating. The references could be bewildering, so assumptive, as if this man had a private map of the world which he thought everybody must share. The ferocity of the thinking sometimes knotted like a migraine in his head. The details of the enterprise might sometimes baffle him but what had sustained him was the almost mythic grandeur of the whole. The book had slowly taught him something he had never realised before: that it is possible to live ideas through to the death. He wasn't sure whether this was noble or merely mad or both. But he was sure that he might have to spend the rest of his life reading Kierkegaard in order to come honestly to terms with him. This meant his summer plan was a fiasco. He would still arrive at university as an ignoramus.

He is still a virgin. The nearest he has come to having sex is the Great Senga Débâcle, when he came into the air, touching no one, and he wonders if he is condemned to live in his own hallucination, able to make love only to the idea of making love.

He still dreads Cran, stripped and sweating in the infernal glow of his kiln, where things harden into what they really are or break down in the heat. He still doesn't know if he would harden or break down.

He still sometimes feels sadly distant from his family, a foster child who doesn't quite fit in. He still hasn't written anything that could be put to better use than kindling for a fire. 'Actions in Generic Tense' has been abandoned. This summer has been a fair old disaster.

But something – maybe it's the insistent promise in the music coming from the lighted house like a hoarse voice that reaches him in the darkness where he stands – is forbidding him to lose heart. There's still two weeks. It occurs to him that whatever happens in the next two weeks cannot constitute a bigger failure than he has achieved so far. There's a kind of perverse hope in that.

This philosophical stuff's all right. You must discover your own stars. Where the hell were they, though? Still, he feels at the moment a kind of defiance of his own past. Maybe that was a philosophy in its own right. He suddenly thinks of a motto earned from the shambles of this summer. He likes mottos. He remembers two classical ones he picked up from *The Oxford Companion to Classical Literature*, which he won as a prize in third year for 'Distinction in Classics'. One was from Epictetus, a stoic philosopher – 'ανεχου και απεχου,' he said. Endure and abstain. The other was in Latin, source unknown to him – '*nosce teipsum*'. Know thyself. Was that the Delphic oracle? Thomas Mathieson

Docherty, philosopher (1937–), has just added his own epigram to the store of Western thought. It's not original to him, he has to admit. As he mutters it into the night, he knows that all he is really doing is rearticulating the contribution of the Scottish working classes to the history of philosophy: 'Fuck it.' Perhaps he's not that far alienated from his background after all. Fuck it. Let the battle recommence.

He notices, as he arrives back at the house, the saucer with some of the beer still in it and the empty chair sitting facing the open door of the kitchen. He finds a surprising poignancy in those two objects resting in conjunction, rather like looking at a house where he has had good times but from which the friend who owned it has long since moved. He takes the chair back into the kitchen. When he has managed to work his way through the bodies back into the living-room, he sees two images which will fix the specialness of this party always in his mind.

MARGARET INGLIS, standing in a corner by the window, leaning against the wall. She is listening to someone. Her head turns slowly towards him. She flicks her blonde hair in the direction of outside and smiles a wide, slow smile and stares at him.

MATT GLOVER standing beside the door as they go out. He has a girl hanging onto his arm, a glass of beer in his hand and, preposterously, a cigar in his mouth. He winks at Tam.

—AFTERWARDS, he would hear news of Big Matt's death in Australia at the age of forty-two. He would remember an afternoon in the reading room at the Dick Institute. They both happened to have gone there to study for exams. They didn't do much studying. They played shove-ha'penny and talked. That was when he understood the anguish Matt was going through. He was asking Tam for advice. His family were Close Brethren and every natural impulse Matt followed crippled him with guilt. He masturbated compulsively while thinking it would drive him straight to hell. He must have been one of the glummest self-pleasurers on the planet. He was forbidden to go to the pictures and the first film he went to see was *The Seven Deadly Sins*, not to further his religious education. He was wracked with self-doubts while they talked. It was like seeing Gulliver bound by a million threads. For Matt was big in body and big in spirit. When he was sixteen and working on a building-site during the summer, he had fought one of the labourers for taking the Lord's name in vain. That was presumably worse than wanking. They had talked for hours but the resolution of the problem remained down to Matt. When told he had died of a heart attack, he would feel sorry but take solace from the fact that he had seen him on the night he started to live as he wanted.—

GET YOUR GLAD RAGS OFF AND JOIN ME, HON.

THE PARK IS MOONLIT and they are walking in it. There are clouds, the torn clouds that sometimes blow about the sky at night like refuse. The clouded moonlight makes the distance smudgy. He is briefly a connoisseur of moonlight. Nervousness scrapes the scum off your eyeballs. It's maybe a false perspective, like a microscope, but it makes you notice things. He is noticing moonlight.

He is walking with Margaret, at last. Walking is an interesting thing. He has his left arm round her shoulder and her right arm is round his waist inside his jacket, her thumb hooked on his belt, giving him nervous spasms. His right hand is vaguely around her left breast. Her left hand is touching his stomach. Their heads are leaning together. Every step, they jar each other's heads, grind hips, bump arms. This is no way to walk. They move like a malformation through the park. But he is afraid to disentangle himself in case something is irrevocably lost, some door to some sanctum that he senses inching open slammed shut.

In the middle of that bodily discomfort, in the gabble of expectations and fears and thoughts of dire diseases and flashes of half-remembered teenage advice that make his mind and nervous system like a telephone exchange where all the wires are crossed, his nose, maybe deciding that central government is lunatic, declares independence. It makes a putsch for total power. He can smell *everything*.

His nose is the Tower of Babel. Messages pour into it out of the darkness, most of them incomprehensible. He knows the grass all right, not long cut and remorselessly calling him back, like the smell of childhood. He never loses the pungency – from a nearby farm or from the nursery above the park? – an occasional whiff of acrid, as if the wind were burping and had dung on its breath. But mostly he smells mystery. The world is a foreign language he wonders if he is ever going to learn.

They are moving towards the lake. He has a plan. It is a plan the way a straw may be a plan for a drowning man. Something abjectly determined in him, which is perhaps manhood, is insisting that he go through with it. He is going, he is going. The blind man's stick in his trousers is feeling the way. None of the names in which he has learned to dress it to make it sociable or anti social, none of the roles, from the comic to the mythic, in which he has learned to cast it, fits. He feels that now. It shucks them off like its foreskin. It is itself. It is his and he is its.

The plan is the wooden building beside the lake. This is a plan? Somewhere in him an incubus has its face in its hands and is groaning. And the almost mystical power he has been ascribing to the building seems to move further away the closer they get. It won't work. It's not exactly dinner at the Ritz.

He doesn't know what they use it for, perhaps for storing tools. It is a small hut, its slatted wood weathered grey and mossed with age in the crevices, set back about twenty yards from the lake in the shelter of trees. They move clumsily towards it until her back is against the wood and he is facing her.

They cuddle without talking, almost as if they are wishing each other luck. It seems they both want more to happen and don't know how, nor what it will feel like if it does. This is a tricky moment, he knows, one of those when, if you don't get your timing right, your ardour will frost on you like cooling sweat. But from previous scufflings, he has evolved a kind of technique. It is not a sophisticated technique. You grope and mouth around until something happens.

He applies it or rather lets it apply him. He hopes it is not as silly a technique as he feels it to be at the moment. It is dimly meant to be a patient way of trying to let honesty happen. They kiss each other, testing for what is there. Their hands are moving uncertainly about each other. What she is thinking he doesn't know, although he suspects her thoughts may be less taken up with nonsense than his are, since even his fragmentary experience – for example, with Senga – makes him believe that women tend to be more honest to their bodies than men are.

His own thoughts are like a picket line against his instincts. They jostle in his mind, blocking his responses. There are various of them, all dressed in borrowed clothes. They are a formidable bunch, muscular with prejudice and with all the certainty of those who don't have to think any more. They are shouting slogans at him.

Fragments are penetrating his preoccupation. 'Show them who's boss.' 'Say anythin' ye need tae say tae get it.' 'Once ye've got them goin', no retreat.'

But none of them relates to what he feels. He's nobody's boss. He is trembiing beyond speech. He knows no conflict with Margaret, only an overwhelming need to meld. As the years of foetid and stale advice withdraw from him, something happens. He senses himself being moved past thought, into self-governing feeling.

The thighs do it. He has the beauty of female thighs naked before him, not in imagination, not in a book, not in a cracked and thumb-marked picture – but there, offered and waiting in the cool night air. They are awesomely moving, smooth and overwhelmingly powerful, the columns of the temple. Idiot with awe, he touches them and goes into a kind of motionless paroxysm.

He touches them again and again. He is overjoyed just to touch them. The prolonged, still seizure he experiences is the emotional equivalent of what he imagines Indians must be expressing in a Hollywood film, dancing round whatever they happen to be dancing round. It has often struck him how they seem to forget the object of their ecstasy in their celebration of its presence. They go off on their own, as it were. 'Ho, ha, hum, ha, hum,' they chant as they dance, or words to that effect. Their noises translate in his West of Scotland demotic into something like, 'How aboot this then? This'll do me.' 'Ho, ha, hum, ha, hum.' And his mind dances round and round the beauty of her thighs.

How long he might have continued his joyous celebrations, he wouldn't know. Perhaps until heart failure claimed him at his post or World War III broke out. But one thought thaws the moment into moving time again. This is a private party he is having. That isn't fair. Margaret is there as well as him, however distantly in his mind she has become connected to those formidable thighs. She is waiting for something to happen. He'd better try to make it happen.

Instincts move of their own volition. Margaret's skirt is round her waist. She steps out of her pants and he puts them in his pocket. He moves to push into her and the hair abrades the tender skin. It's like trying to ride a hedgehog. Not that he's tried that yet but if things keep on as they are . . . But suddenly the hair parts wetly and he is entering her slowly.

'Tom,' she says urgently. 'Wait.'

'I'VE GOT THE CURSE.'

The sentence would stay with him, would feel for a time like a statement he could apply to himself. As she pulled away, it was immediately as if all the hope of that summer moved away with her. Initially, he hadn't known what she meant. The term was strange to him. She sounded like someone speaking from inside a fable.

Once he realised what she meant, he couldn't believe his bad luck. 'O bloody period!' (William Shakespeare). 'I second that'

(Tom Docherty). She explained that she had just realised her period was coming. It could happen as suddenly as that? The expression of panic on her face made him wonder if it was about to take place with a sudden rush on the spot.

In retrospect he would decide that the worst times of the summer dated from that moment. It was in the following week that his grandmother died. He had known how ill she was but the sadness of her death was compounded by guilt. His self-absorption appalled him. He had been so busy agonising over Margaret that he had let his grandmother die in the wings, as it were. Listening to his gathered relatives talk of her, while her body stiffened in the bedroom, he understood for the first time the remarkable endurance of her living. Her courage and resourcefulness and decency were preserved in anecdote and passed round among them. He remembered a vivid moment from the past—

HIS GRANDMOTHER IS SAYING, 'Ah've been readin' some mair o' that book.'

She sits at the fireside in her pinny with her grey hair coiled into a bun. Released, that hair still reaches to her waist. He takes a bite of the dry madeira cake and melts it with a mouthful of tea.

'What book is that, Granny?'

'Ye ken the one Ah mean. The one Ah told ye about the last time ye were here.'

'Ah don't remember that.'

'Ye've a memory like a sieve, boay. Whit's his name?'

He takes some more tea.

'That McGorkey. That's it,' she says.

'McGorkey?'

'The one yer Uncle Josey gave me tae read. McGorkey.'

He remains puzzled.

'It's on the sideboard there. Get it and bring it over here.'

He gets up and crosses to the sideboard. As he lifts the plain brown hardcovered book and turns its spine towards him, he sees the title and the author's name: M. Gorky – *Childhood*. And as he buckles slightly, clamping his laughter in, the book he holds in his hand, seen in proximity to the porcelain clock that refuses to keep the right time any more, becomes an enduring cipher of his grandmother.

—and he felt the wanton carelessness of failing to appreciate her more. He came out of the house and went for a long walk alone. Leaning on the gate of a field, he found that, in mourning his grandmother, he was able for the first time properly to mourn his Uncle Josey.

—AFTERWARDS, he would write:

I came across an old book the other day, one of those working-class equivalents of an heirloom; something that is kept and passed on, not because it is supposed to have any intrinsic value but because it evokes a labyrinth of memory to which it acts as a clue. I don't think I'll take it to the *Antiques Roadshow* in case I am led from the room in a net. But, holding it in my hands, I felt its worth beyond doubt. Like ashes, it doesn't look much. Like ashes, it testifies to an old fire – a passion for social justice that burned undiminished to the point of death in a man in whom I, as an admittedly naïve boy, found hardly anything that wasn't worthy of love and admiration.

The book is *Childhood* by Maxim Gorky. With the passage of time, the title has acquired an extended significance for me. In writing about his childhood, Gorky incidentally created an object that has become for me a cipher of my own. Handling the book, I found summoned up in me, through the necromancy of touch, reminders of where I come from and why I think as I think and believe as I believe.

In accordance with the saying, it is not a book to be judged by its cover. It was, as far as I am aware, sent naked into the world without benefit of a coloured jacket. The covers are of a dull, dark brown and rough in texture. It was a publication for people who believed that a book is a collection of words held together in the most convenient and least flamboyant form. I sympathise. The only lettering on the outside is on the spine. It gives the title and the author's name: M. Gorky.

It is that name which brought back the first memory. I remembered my grandmother referring, in her late sixties, to the fact that she was reading a book by 'that McGorkey'. Whether that interesting linguistic conflation was the result of her fading eyesight or of her determined tendency to see Scotland as the paradigm of all experience, I'm not sure. But it has a certain aptness for me. She made Gorky a naturalised Scot in the same way that her son, who had given her the book to read, translated the ideological rigidity of the Russian political experience into a much more Scottish humanism.

My Uncle Josey was an unlikely manner of the social barricades. He had either been born with or acquired a chronically weak heart, a nice irony given the passion of his convictions. The condition wasn't accurately diagnosed until late in his life. But its effects plagued him from childhood. He was frequently housebound. He missed much of his schooling. He could work only intermittently and then usually only at manual work, to which he was desperately unsuited and which, presumably, helped to hurry on his death.

The death happened in hospital where he was undergoing treatment. It was during the visiting-hour. He had asked to be made more comfortable on his propped-up pillows and, as the members of his family who were there reached forward to help, he said 'It doesny matter' and died quietly. He was thirty-four.

That day in the hospital I had been in another ward, seeing a schoolfriend. As I entered the ward where my uncle was – having come down towards the end of visiting-time – I saw his raised body relax and his head droop, discreet as a closing flower.

Tragedy can be so quiet and casual and ordinary that some-times it is gone before we know that it has been. We are left painstakingly to measure its enormity in retrospect. What I glimpsed that day in my first sight of a human death has stayed with me, not in any dramatic way. It was a quiet occurrence and it has stayed quiet. But sometimes without warning he will come again into my mind and I think not of what is lost, but of the privilege I had in being his nephew.

At first, with the innocence of boyhood, I had thought that my experience of him was who he was. He was tall and pale and thin and shy, with bottle-bottom glasses and a great rampart of crinkly hair. He cared about people with a passionate intensity, too much to let them off with less than the best of what they were. He did the same with me, young as I was.

Never having been married, he lived with my grandmother until he died and I used to like being around their house. My reasons for that liking were curiously ambivalent. Like most children I had worked out early that the climate around a grandparent is often more tolerant of unbuttoned behaviour than the presence of parents is. Your ego can go barefoot there without catching too many chills of disapproval. But I also liked the fact that my uncle would be around to provide some kind of guidelines for my experiential wanderings, for children like freedom benignly picketed by adults. My uncle provided the limits all right, but he established them not with automatic authority but through reason and discussion. The only rank he ever pulled was logic. But he always did it by trying to understand your terms as well as his own.

For that reason I'm glad he was the one who often discovered my misdemeanours first. I'm glad, for example, it was down to him to find out I had been stealing cigarettes, cunningly and stealthily abstracted one at a time from his current packet of Senior Service, as if silence in an empty room were a talisman against the fates. I'm glad he was the one informed by an all-seeing neighbour that a girl of nine and I (by this time a worldly, cigarette-smoking ten-year-old who should have known better) had been seen partially naked, conducting a somewhat puzzled investigation of each other in a rockery. (The choice of venue suggests that even then I had an instinctive sense that the course of true love never would run smooth.) I don't think I would have minded too much if he had been the one to discover that I had been sampling – in the stoical manner of a boy accepting his punishment of manhood – my granny's sweet stout, thus tasting the meaning of misnomer before I knew it. But nobody ever did discover that one.

I don't want to give the wrong impression here. I wasn't so much a primary-school reprobate as an eager investigator of taboos. I never have believed in hand-me-down experience. If something was forbidden, I wanted to know why the Establishment was keeping it to itself. Somehow my uncle seemed to understand that and, taking me aside after my latest transgression of a set of rules I couldn't see the sense in, he would talk to me.

I don't remember exactly what we said, but I remember the feeling those conversations have always given me. It is a feeling of arrival at a place of clarity and warmth, a free border of selves where nothing is contraband because whatever you declare will carry no hidden charge against you. Guilt was not the question. Why you had done it was, and how it had felt, and what you thought about it now that you had done it, and where did you go from here. The dynamic of what your experience meant was always given back to you.

It was only after his death I realised slowly that the gift was one he had made to others as well as myself. My increased awareness began in that extended conversational wake that follows a working-class death, the hoarded anecdotes brought out and passed around, the quiet shared wonder at what had been among us. I learned of the heroism of his self-education, of his mute suffering, of how he might, with Alexander Pope, have referred to 'that long disease, my life'. I was reminded of his skill in drawing, of the peace posters he made alone at night when my grandmother was in bed.

I learned of the time some chancer put the head on him at a charity dance because my uncle was on the door and wouldn't let the man brass his way in free. The man still didn't get in, but there were no recriminations. My father, five feet four but with a PhD in outrage, spent a long time trying to get the details so that he could trace the man and exact summary retribution. But my uncle wouldn't help. He was my mother's brother and like her he lived his principles to the limit, pain or pleasure. Pacifism was one.

I was reminded as well of what an awkward bugger he could be. He couldn't be intimidated, only convinced, and that was one difficult trick. He liked to argue the way Gargantua liked to eat. I remember once, during my Vaughan Monroe period, when I was trying to bring my voice from the soles of my feet and sing 'Ghost Riders in the Sky', he took me to task for singing such an ideologically unsound song. I knew even than that his attitude was ridiculous, like quarrelling with a vacuum. But I took him seriously anyway. I still do. He remains one of the small but bright and unnamed stars by which I steer.

Holding his copy of *Childhood*, I sense him as being like the book, unflashy but substantial – and out of date. The human stock he believed in so sincerely has crashed, probably beyond the point of recovery. For my Uncle Josey was a deeply committed Communist.

I didn't believe in his political philosophy then, I never did since, and I don't now. I am happy to see the present apparent liberalisation of Eastern Europe. But I hope I retain enough intellectual precision and emotional honesty not to be bullied by the aggressive rant of contemporary British and American politics into confusing Eastern Bloc Communism with the humane and pragmatic form the same ideology found for itself in Scotland.

Since John MacLean, Scottish Communism has remained its own animal, less Russian bear than beast of social burden, helping hurt lives in the small ways that it could, given its continuously enfeebled state. It has remained almost entirely free from the theoretical rabies to which its English counterpart has sometimes succumbed.

Besides my uncle, I have met many Scottish Communists. Sometimes they were boringly dogmatic. But then so have been many Catholics and Presbyterians and those of other faiths. More often they have been generous of spirit and deep in their concern for others. Disagreeing with their theory, I have found myself time and again replenished by their practice and renewed in my belief in a more habitable vision of the future. They have long been a benignly crucial part of our awareness of ourselves.

But these are meretricious times, in which slogan passes for thought and the intellectual scatter-gun is the favoured weapon of political precision. You may say with the mood of the moment that if one form goes, all should go. You may say, if you wish, that there was no distinctive baby in Scottish Communism, only the same old bath-water.

You may say it. I won't. I owe these people. I pay my debts of gratitude.—

WE OWE GRATITUDE IN SOME UNLIKELY PLACES, he would think, and we usually only realise it in retrospect. He was sitting at the table by the window, using the last of the sunlight to read an old letter from Grete. Her intelligence came luminous off the page, reminding him of her witty intensity clothed in a broad, sensuous face and a body of marvellous amplitude. The reasons for being grateful to Grete were obvious, of course, and he had always known them.

But he sometimes wondered what would have happened if Margaret Inglis hadn't rejected him that summer. He was so naïvely besotted with her he might never have seen past her. The fifties were not exactly a historical moment of free love, at least not in his experience, and your first fixation could swiftly be socially engineered into the probability of being your last.

This reflection held no bitterness. Margaret had been right to reject him, although he couldn't help thinking she should have done it either a little earlier or a little later. He had to admit he remained somewhat critical of her timing. She was, he supposed later, one of those girls of the time who seemed to have been born with a blueprint of life like DNA. Obviously, screwing in the Kay Park wasn't included in that blueprint.

He had learned to be grateful for that. If they had consummated the moment there in the Kay Park, his tendency to see sex as a kind of beautiful and bestial form of Holy Communion would have made it impossible for him to leave it there. And that would not have been good for either of them. Maybe it never had been good for him. (A woman had once told him, 'You're the man who sets most store by the importance of physical love – as being more than just physical – that I've ever met.') But, if so, he didn't regret it.

But for Margaret that would have been an alien attitude. For her, communion belonged in church, where her father was an elder and she attended regularly. He wondered if, somewhere in the DNA, she had always known that all they had in common was physical attraction, when he had thought they might be kindred spirits. Perhaps she already saw in him the potential to be one of life's dishevelled vagrants, even though that vagrancy was still far in the future. Certainly, he suspected later, she had probably decided to close the door on random callers in her teens. She wanted her life consolidated, not disturbed.

The last thing she said to him that summer tended to confirm him in this feeling. She repeated to him what she had said in the phone box: 'You're too dangerous.' He had briefly taken the remark away like a consolation prize, seeing himself through it as some kind of Heathcliff figure. But it wasn't long before he was talking to himself bitterly. Dangerous? The dangerous virgin? What is it Boris called that? Oxymoron? Still, maybe Senga told her about what happened to her skirt.

The impression of Margaret as someone who would make life sign a contract hardened into conviction after he met her at a party when they were both in their late thirties. She was there with her husband. (Her late husband, as Tom found himself referring to him in his mind. Some wounds heal slow.)

The man was a Clive Cunningham talk-alike, a bank manager with an ego as big as his vault. Margaret's conversation, when Tom talked to her, had become loud and long and phoney-hard. A presence which had seemed to him like a gulp of spring water appeared to have already reached the muddied flats of middle age and had a brackish taste. She complained about her husband while waving affectionately towards him. Tom had the suspicion that her marriage wasn't much of a job but the pay was good.

The meeting depressed him and left him regretting what they had all become. The promise he believed she had once expressed just by being herself continued to haunt him for so long that he exorcised it in a poem, which was perhaps part-homage, part-revenge.

Your talk a loud parade,
Yourself a widow in a house it passes.

Forgive me tenacious affections
That worry the flesh of old times into bone.
And it's maybe something like love
To see that sheer girl
In your blunted postures.

My memory will be standing through cold nights,
A lonely nuisance that police can't shift,
Staring in moonlight at the window where
Your head aches in its curlers and your man,
Tupping and snoring, drowns in his own fat.

Tipping its hat as you take in the milk,
Its expression won't be utterly ironic.

I shall remember who you might have been.

But such retrospective gratitude to Margaret for rejecting him didn't mean he had forgotten the initial effects of that rejection, especially since it had been effected by remote control.

After they had left the Kay Park, the imminence of Margaret's period had mysteriously lessened. She seemed to want the two of them to stay together for a while. They wandered the centre of the town through the early hours of morning. They looked in shop windows. They compared their tastes in furniture. They kissed and cuddled in doorways. They looked at the magazines in a newsagent's window and discussed their favourite film stars. He walked her home slowly and they stopped many times. At her house they arranged to meet again.

She didn't turn up. His attempts to phone her house were always dealt with by her mother or father. Her mother always dropped the same phrase like a little piece of ice into his ear: 'Not in.' The rest was silence. Her father's responses were somewhat more extended and definitely more tropical. He breathed fire, threatening at different times visitations from someone he described darkly as 'a very large friend', the minister of his church and the police. He claimed to know an inspector in the force. Tam gave up before he gave the local fire brigade his address.

But he haunted the streets, looking for Margaret. His mind was in turmoil. He needed to talk to her. He needed to know why she no longer wanted to see him. In his dementia he began to believe that the entire evening of the party at Caroline Mather's was an elaborate set-up, a conspiracy to get revenge on him for standing Margaret up that time. Had Caroline invited him at Margaret's suggestion? Has Margaret's dream been a ploy by which to turn him off after leading him on? Had that look she had given him, nodding towards outside, been a contrivance? Certainly, he didn't any longer believe she'd had her period that night. But this was ridiculous. He had explained to her about the plook and they had laughed about it together. He'd had an enormous plook on his nose. How could having a plook on your nose deserve all this? It was like bombing a butterfly. He'd heard of revenge tragedies. Could you get a revenge comedy? This was ridiculous. He was in love with her, for God's sake. Did that mean nothing? He had to talk to her.

When he did, it was a very brief conversation. He saw Margaret and Margaret saw him as she was following her mother into a shop.

'Margaret,' he said.

'You're too dangerous,' Margaret hissed.

'Margaret!' her mother shouted. 'If you don't come in here at once, I'll call the police.'

People were looking at them. He walked on. He kept looking for her for days after that. But he felt ill-fated from that moment. He felt vulnerably abandoned. He didn't expect to be lucky. He was right.

In his last week at the brickwork, Frank, who worked with Cran in the kiln, went off ill. The gaffer decided to replace him with Tam. It was the thing he dreaded most in his life, being trapped in the kiln with Cran. It was a prospect so frightening, he wished he could go in without being who he was, find a neutral identity for the night.

IN THE KILN, he would think, you will find the very way you breathe threatened. The heat is too intense, as if you have entered an alien atmosphere and must wonder if you can survive in it. Soon you will have to peel off some of the clothes you have worn like social assumptions. This is a place for stripping to the skin. The heat is too intense. You will want out. But to do that you will have to leave your self-respect behind. You will have been judged and found wanting by others and, more importantly, by yourself, if you are honest. For this is a test. What is being tested is you. You will have no time for learning how to pass the test. It will always be new to you. You take it as it comes. The test is not simply to be there. The test is to be there and not lose yourself. No matter the pressure you feel, you must hold on to who you are or a part of you may be gone and may be difficult to get back. But it is not enough to hold on to who you are. You must at the same time try to do whatever else is required of you. There is always something else to be done besides the saving of yourself.

AND CRAN IS THERE, guardian of his little *bolgia*. Cran is always there. For every thumbscrew there must be someone to turn it. This is his terrain, not yours. You may have studied Latin and Greek. He may have studied nothing more enlightening than the racing pages. You may know many big words from the dictionary but his grunts will outrank you here.

This is not a place for poetry readings. Here it's all down to bodies and sweat and strength and manual skill. You live on his terms here. Those are hard terms.

First, he refuses to help. You each bring your hutch of bricks into the kiln on the rails. You must then unload them and stack them in ranks one on top of the other like a lattice-work wall so that the hot air can pass among them. This must be done with speed and skill, so that the empty hutch can be outside the kiln in time for you to receive the next load of bricks.

He does it effortlessly, making a wall so firm the spaces might as well have mortar in them, and stands watching. You cannot do it. The speedy precision required eludes you. Bricks fall off and you have to begin again. You start to imagine a line of loaded hutches stretching from the kiln to the brickwork by the end of the evening. Perhaps he is imagining the same, for he laughs.

'Fucking students,' he says.

This will be his second rule for the shift. While you pour with sweat and struggle to keep pace with the arriving hutches, you will be obliged to listen to his comments. When you decide you have to take off your shirt, you are embarrassed by your frailness compared to his vast, overweight torso. He seems to have grown bigger. And the comments keep coming.

'This isn't fucking theory. This is fact.'

'This is where it really happens.'

'Pathetic. Totally pathetic.'

'Seen mair strength in an Abdine.'

'Ye'll not find how to do this in a fucking book.'

Certainly not in any you've read. Why does he hate you so much, you think self-pityingly. You hope your failure to respond to him isn't just fear. You try to persuade yourself it's because you need so much concentration to stay not too far behind the pace that there's nothing left with which to think up answers. But you're not convinced. If you could think of an answer, you'd swallow it. If that's how belligerent he is when you say nothing, what would he be like if you talked back to him? Why does there always have to be one bastard in any work you go to who decides it's part of his job to give you a hard time?

You are sweating unbelievably. If you were thin enough to start with, you might disappear at this rate. You struggle on. You don't see how you can make it through the night.

But by the time the tea-break comes, you're not as far behind as you had thought. Cran stands outside the door of the kiln, eating a sandwich the size of a Welma loaf and drinking a screwtop of beer. (He doesn't even sit down to eat?) You keep on working until you've emptied the two remaining hutches. You've just got time to put on your shirt, deliver the empty hutches and collect your piece. A mocking round of applause greets you as you collect your mug of tea.

'Better goin' to work on Senga than this, Tam, eh?'

They don't know that your rating is about the same in both cases.

'You okay?' Jack Laidlaw asks quietly.

'Okay? You gonny arrange to deliver the body to ma mother?'

You're not sure that you're joking, given the fierceness of
Cran's antagonism. Will it increase during the second half of
the shift? You're tempted to eat your piece and drink your tea
here. But you decide to go back to the kiln. You don't know if
this is courage or cowardice. Are you going in order to show
him that you're not afraid of his presence or because you might
annoy him with your absence?

He has finished his break and is leaning against the doorway
of the kiln, smoking and staring at you. You swallow the bread in
doughy lumps, washed down with the tea. The second temptation
is to return the cup when you're finished, collect your jacket and
satchel and leg it home. That is maybe what you would do except
that the first bogeys are already arriving.

You slop out the remains of the tea, lay the cup against the
wall of the kiln and, still chewing, collect the second hutch. Cran
has claimed the first. You're dreading this.

But something happens. Your pace has definitely quickened.
It's not nearly as fast as Cran's, nowhere near, but by now this
only means that Cran has leisure time and you don't. You
are actually beginning to stay level with the hutches as they
arrive. This is a good feeling. Your shirt is off again and you
are still running with sweat but it doesn't feel so bad now.
You are a workman who can do his job. This goes on for
some time. You have found a rhythm. You think that the
silence there has been for a while may mean that at last
you have earned a little respect from Cran. This is a serious
mistake.

'Don't get carried away,' Cran says. 'Ye're still a useless
bastard.'

You know then that nothing you do or say is going to divert
the enmity he has for you.

'Useless bastard.'

'But then ye're a Docherty.'

You feel a chill beneath your sweat. You know that he is going
to say anything he can either to call you out or make rubble
of your sense of yourself. Why does he need to do this? But
he does. He breaks the silence in which you are working by

interjecting every so often with another insult to the Dochertys. You can almost hear the cracking of your own nerve. You hate the bastard for doing this to you, for making you ashamed of your own fear. You think of going to the foreman. You think of just walking out. But where will you walk to? How could you go into your own house carrying the shame of these unanswered insults? You hate the bastard. He isn't going to stop. You have to do something.

'Not a fucking man among them.'

You fucking bastard.

'Your family are shite.'

You fucking bastard.

'Useless cunts, the Dochertys.'

'You fucking bastard.'

You have said it. The two of you are standing in the doorway of the kiln. The sound of your voice in the air pulls the rest of your rage out through your mouth.

'Put your mouth on my family one more time and I'll kill you, you bastard.'

He is amazed at your foolhardiness. So are you. He swings a punch. You dodge. But he hits you on the shoulder. You fall beside the jagged pile of broken, discarded bricks. He is coming towards you again. You lift a broken brick. You stagger up. He throws another punch. The punch misses. You swing past him and turn. You hit him on the side of the forehead with the half-brick. He stumbles back and his heels hit the bottom of the pile of broken bricks. His arms flail for balance and he sits down with thunderous heaviness. You can hear the sound of the ragged brick ripping into his trousers. The effect is amazing. He is screaming. You move towards him to do more. Something in you is baying for blood. Cran is helpless.

'Tam!' someone shouts.

THE OTHERS ARE HERE. It is Hilly Brown who has shouted. Tam feels suddenly very cold in the early morning air. He looks down at the brick in his hand, wondering where it came from. It is as if someone has planted it on him.

'Keep that daft bastard away from me,' Cran is shouting.

And something answers from somewhere in Tam.

'That's a good idea,' it shouts. 'Or Ah'll kill the bastard. This is a catchweights fucking contest. Ah mean it more than he does.'

Hilly Brown is there. Billy Farquhar is there. James Morrison is there. Jack Laidlaw is there. They don't know what to do.

'Mention ma family one more time,' Tam says, still holding the brick, 'an' you're dead.'

'Keep back, ya daft bastard,' Cran says.

He is obviously in pain and not offering to move.

'What is it, Cran?' Hilly says.

Two of them go to help Cran up.

'Naw, naw,' Cran says. 'Get back.'

He takes about a minute to extricate himself from the pile of bricks. He cannot seem to straighten up. The seat of his trousers is saturated with blood. He is almost weeping with pain.

'What is it?' Hilly Brown says.

'He's burst every pile in ma arse,' Cran says.

THE TAXI WAS PASSING THE PLACE WHERE AVONDALE BRICKWORK USED TO BE. Tom smiled to himself. An idol with an arse of clay. Cran had gone home and was off work the next night and, when he came back, he let it be known, through Frank, that he wouldn't be in for the tea-break till that loony bastard left. Tam had felt a particular pride when he heard Cran quoted as having said, 'The Dochertys were always mad bastards.' He had kept the family honour intact.

It was only in thinking about it afterwards that he had realised the ironic significance of the chair. What had become for all of them a symbol of power had been in reality a sign of frailty. Cran had needed his special, separate place because he couldn't sit on a bench like the rest of them. It was a lesson that had stayed with him: never take authority at its own estimate.

His own status for the last few nights he was in the brickwork was a fair example. He wasn't asked to go back into the kiln, presumably in case the heat reactivated the demons in him. The others obviously regarded him as someone to be reckoned with, both with women and with men. Yet all it had taken to create this sense of him was an accidental brick up the arse and a girl who was kind enough to lie for him.

At the tea-break on the last night, Hilly Brown moved the chair towards him.

'Ye no' gonny sit on yer seat, Tam?' he said.

He almost did. Then he had a better idea. He gestured Dunky Semple towards the chair. Dunky sat in it throughout the break, eating his piece and rubbing the wooden arms and looking down at the cushion every so often. He had as much right to it as any of them and he certainly enjoyed it more than anybody else would have done.

'Not long now,' the driver said.

'No.'

The driver couldn't know the irony of what he was saying. Time might be so short that Tom was too late. Arriving in Graithnock, he discovered that Michael had been moved from Graithnock Infirmary to a hospital outside of town. The cerebral haemorrhage he had taken this morning was massive. He had failed so far to recover consciousness and they had moved him to a specialist unit.

The headlights of the taxi suddenly showed the entrance of the driveway to the hospital. All his attempts to avoid the likely outcome of what had happened through refusing to contemplate it had come to this, just as the primitive magic of trying to ignore Cran hadn't prevented confrontation. Here came another kiln or rather, he feared, the icy variant of one, where they took you to extremities of cold.

THE ROOM was not somewhere people could stay long, was a place for passing through, like a province of Antarctica. Its clinical sterility didn't accommodate the living comfortably. His mother and Allison and Marion and her three sons, Joe and Don and young Michael, looked awkward there, like misplaced furniture. Only Michael fitted. He lay very still on the bed, his face fixed in an expression that seemed concentrated on a problem none of the others could understand. Tom sensed immediately that he was walking into one of death's anterooms. At least he had arrived in time.

They all embraced clumsily. His mother and Marion were crying. His arrival stirred the stillness into murmured conversation. They asked about his journey. He asked about Michael. The doctors had pronounced no hope. The only time Michael had shown any response was one of the times Marion had tried to take his hand. He had brushed it away gently and they thought he had muttered, 'Don't, darlin'.' That seemed like a long time ago, in Graithnock.

Hearing that, Tom had a memory of watching his father die. Something astonishing had struck him then, at eighteen. A slow death isn't just something you do. It is something you find out how to do. The spirit seems trapped in something it can't get out of. It comes up against death like the final conundrum. Tom thought he understood the concentration on Michael's face. He was looking for the way out. He was already far out of reach of their helpless grief. The best they could do was to be there and wish him success, for anything else would have been a selfish prolonging of his pain.

That pain intensified quite suddenly. He became restless and uncomfortable and breathing seemed something he had forgotten how to do. His lower face took on blue like a shadow of cloud. His distress transmitted itself to the others.

Tom left the room and in the corridor met the sister who had spoken to him when he arrived.

'Excuse me,' he said. 'My brother's breathing is getting very laboured. He's in a lot of distress. Is there something you can do to help him?'

'Of course, of course.'

She came to the door of the room and looked in at Michael.

'Im afraid you'll have to leave,' she said.

Marion started to cry and was refusing to go. Nobody wanted to leave.

'We want to stay,' Tom said. 'We want to be with him.'

'I'm sorry, sir. We cannot possibly set up the equipment unless the room is cleared. You can wait in another room. It's the only way we can do it. It won't take long. And I'll let you back in as soon as we've set things up.'

'We want to be with him at the end.'

'You will be, sir. Of course. It's just a few minutes. The longer you delay, the longer it's taking to help your brother.'

With Tom's help, she led them into an empty room along the corridor. The waiting seemed endless. They wandered around dementedly. Tom went outside and waited in the corridor. As he saw the sister approaching, he opened the door of the room.

'All right,' he said. 'We can go in now.'

As the others came out into the corridor, the sister reached them. Her eyes found Marion among them.

'I'm sorry, my dear,' she said. 'Your husband's dead.'

The sound that broke from Marion and his mother and Allison both grieved and enraged Tom. As the others crowded back into the room where Michael lay, he stared at the sister.

'Was that done for your convenience or supposedly for ours?' he said.

'I beg your pardon?'

'You may beg it but you're not getting it.'

He went past her into the room. He saw Michael dead. No touch, no sight, no sound, no words allowed. The family stood beside his bed. They were huddled together as if trying to merge, become again amoeba. They looked like castaways on a shore of the ocean of silence Michael was lost in.

He stared at Michael. He was embittered beyond bearing that he had not been able to speak to him. Without any warning there occurred to him something he had once rather grandiosely said, that he would have made a pact with the devil for thirty minutes' conversation in a Parisian bistro with Albert Camus. Or now for ten minutes anywhere with Michael. But there was no devil to make any pacts with. Death, you bastard. You're so sterile you don't even accommodate the possibility of evil. Abandon sin all ye who enter here. Hell is simply the worst of the truth. Hell is no human choices. Hell is nothing. What more could heaven have been?

He went over to them and stretched his arms as far around the group as they would reach and wept with them.

AT LEAST WITH HIS FATHER THERE HAD BEEN SOME WARNING.

HE WOULD REALISE INTERMITTENTLY, and with renewable surprise, that he was now older than his father had been when he died. That was a strange feeling, a kind of role reversal. He was now talking in his head to someone who was younger than he was. He would pause in Edinburgh, holding in his hand the plate he was drying or with the kettle poised above the cup where the teabag was being saturated with milk, and he would wonder about that.

Did the extra years and the difference of his experience mean that his relationship to his father was much changed? Would what he had learned have had any power to salve the baffled outrage his father had contrived to distil into astringent comment?

His mother liked to say how proud his father would have been of all his grandchildren, in teaching and in the business world and in social service and in academia, all comparatively successful in their various ways, but most of all as people. 'No' bad for an auld ex-miner,' she would say, and smile. And once, when she was talking about Megan and Gus both doing postgraduate degrees at Oxford, she even roped in Tam Docherty, the grandfather he had been named for and never known except through family story and local legend. He had died down the pit, saving another man's life, and in her sense of him it was as if that brave, compassionate and angry man had been travelling towards a light he never reached but in which his grandchildren would live. 'Ah wish yer feyther had just lived tae see it, though,' she would say.

He appreciated that. But what engaged him more about the idea of his father still being alive was whether they would have understood each other better, if they could have cracked that cryptic masculine code in which they had tended to communicate, as they had failed to that Sunday morning when he had wanted to tell his father about Cran. Would they have been able to move further into that place of openly exchanged love they had at last found just before his father died?

As he stood at the window of the living-room, remembering his father's death, he looked across the road in the early light to Warriston Cemetery. It was no longer in use and was dilapidated and vandalised in many places. It was as though even the dead had deserted it, or at least the lasting sense of them their relatives had tried to establish. For cemeteries were for the living, weren't they? And when the griefs of the mourners went, nothing was left but ruined monuments of feeling. Old cemeteries were ghost towns, haunted not by the ghosts of the buried dead but by the ghosts of all the sadnesses, once felt to be immortal, that had failed to survive. The sorrow they expressed was not that we die but that even the grief for our dying dies.

That summer his father went, he was eighteen and had completed his first year at university and was working as a railway porter during the holidays. He liked the cap they gave him.

He was no longer afraid of university. He had discovered that he was unintimidated by any of the intelligences he had so far come across. He had discovered that he wasn't unattractive to some women. He felt physically stronger than he had ever felt in his life before. It was a good time.

Then, one sunny afternoon when he was lounging on a mail-barrow on Platform 2 and clowning with Matt Bailey, another student, he saw his father walking across the station towards him. It was perhaps the unusualness of the context that first of all made him see his father fresh. But it was also more than that. He looked so small and vulnerable, as if he had lost his way in the town where he had always lived. He came up to the wooden barrier, which his face just managed to reach over.

'Aye, son,' he said. 'How's it goin'?'

'Fine, Feyther. What ye doin' up here?'

'Up at the Infirmary there. Gettin' the X-ray. Told me tae come back in an hour or so. Get the result. Just passin' the time. Thought Ah'd come up an' see ye.'

Just that. (How casual death can be.) A few words like a sealed telegram from a distant place, one he was instantly wary about opening up to see what it was saying. Thinking back on that day, he was convinced he had known already that the news was bad. He knew because he knew his father knew, or at any rate had started to believe. It was as if, even as they stood and talked and included Matt in the conversation (how polite death can be), something in his father had begun to walk away alone. And a patch of sunlight was highlighting an area of oil-stained wood on the mail-barrow, fixing it in Tam's memory.

The guilt about having forgotten for a few hours that today was the day for having the X-ray was sharpened when he looked in his father's eyes. He could see in them a small wincing of the spirit which he had never seen before.

The result of the X-ray was lung cancer. His father was dead in three months. In that time he went from physically formidable man to apprentice cadaver. He was fifty-one.

In those last months, with his father mainly in bed, they had more one-to-one conversations than they had ever had before. At first his father had been able to move around the house and once – in that brief Indian summer the dying are sometimes allowed – he went for a last walk round Bringan, wheeling his first grandchild in the pram. The pram was a prop as well as a pleasure. The walk was slow and he took a lot of rests but it was important to him to see for a last time the places of his boyhood and maybe to be introducing a new generation to them in his mind. (I leave you this legacy, having nothing else to leave you.)

Confined to bed, he lingered on through October, his mind staying clear in spite of the drugs, but his body eroding. Once, in the middle of a conversation with Tam and his mother when they were talking about the doings of some people they knew locally, he glanced down at the skeletal forearms which had once been huge and he said, 'Look at these. Ah'll never get that back, Betsy.' And he smiled absently and went on talking about the things they had been talking about.

It was like that, a man absently acknowledging but being polite and gentle about his dying. What else to do? He had other people to think about.

'So the university, son? How's that goin'?'

'No' bad.'

'Must be a kinda unusual experience for ye. Very strange still?'

'No' so strange now.'

'That's good.'

It wasn't that what they said to each other was of any particular significance in itself. It was that the context in which they said it made everything reverberate with significance, as if they sat in an echo chamber where even talk of the weather would resonate.

Their talk was small ordinarinesses that seemed as monumental as standing stones because of the empty horizon against which they stood. The most casual reference could throw long shadows. A mention of Joseph, no matter how lightly made, inevitably brought with it the realisation that all his father would ever really know about his grandson was that he was there.

Once when he had opened the door to check if it was raining, his father called out his name urgently from upstairs. He had thought he was leaving without having their morning conversation. He never did. And by the time his father died, he felt he had had the chance to understand a little more the simple humanity of his father, its instinctive sources, lying beyond any comprehensive philosophy of life.

WAS IT THE PASCALIAN WAGER OR THE CARTESIAN? He always mixed the two of them up. He knew that Pascal had been born in Clermont-Ferrand and that Descartes had been to Amsterdam. But what help was that to him? Who the fuck was it who made the choice between atheism and Christianity? He had no idea.

He took another sip of his whisky and water and toasted Warriston Cemetery outside the window. He was pissed. He knew that. Was that why he couldn't remember? But sometimes the bevvy was an aid to memory. Sometimes it created weird synapses between memory cells that seemed to have lost touch with each other for years and there, as if in sheet lightning, there was something long forgotten. Not this time, though. What it was, maybe, was that whisky memory was primitive memory, pre-rational. Eh? When you were pissed, you couldn't look up your memory as if it were a reference book. The thoughts didn't exactly come in alphabetical order, did they?

He glanced across at the pile of unopened letters on the table. They were mostly bills which left him baffled as to how the senders had managed to track him down. Soon he would open the two or three which appeared to be personal, but not tonight. He could respond to them when he felt a little closer to answering to the name on the envelope. Meanwhile, more important matters were afoot. Let mental safari continue.

No, not exactly in alphabetical order. They jumped intae yer heid like bellydancers, writhed aboot there for a wee while an' shot the crow. Then another wan skited in. Hullo, it's ma turn. Another drink, methinks. You've had enough. Aye, but sometimes what's enough? Sometimes you need a friend. *Au secours, la bouteille.*

One of them said something like: either there is a God or there isn't. Let's place the bet. The obvious thing is to bet on God – because if He is there, you win. If He isn't there, what do you lose? Nothing. He would drink to that.

Yes. Right enough, Blaise or René, whichever of you said it. But wait a minute. There's a humanist version of this bet. Let's bet that there is nothing there. This is the most human bet that you can make. Firstly, because to be human is to admit that there is no way you can *know* that anything is there. Secondly, because, if there is nothing there, it makes your moral behaviour all the more real, all the more an expression of *you*. It has no basis but yourself. You replace religious cynicism with human idealism. You exist dramatically as you in an empty universe. The God, who is or is not there, becomes powerless. You render Him irrelevant. The question of His existence no longer matters. You will create your own goodness, regardless of Him. Thus, agnosticism becomes the only true faith.

He took another sip of communion whisky. Ya beauty. Sometimes the bevvy worked. If He isn't there, you won't feel cheated.

You *chose* to be moral in his absence, for your own humanist reasons. And if He *is* there, you must be in with a shout of getting into heaven, even if it's just by the tradesman's entrance, for you've at least tried to live a moral life. In fact, maybe it should be by the main door. Your attempt at goodness will have none of the impurities in it of fear or that's-what-they-tóld-me-to-do or Ah'll-swap-ye-a-good-life-for-a-seat-in-heaven. It exists sheer. The only basis for morality becomes love of your kind.

Imagine a prison, he would think. The huge communal cell is crowded with people of every race. None of them is sure what crime has been committed, unless it is that of being human. They don't know what system of law has sentenced them nor the basis of authority for the power which has passed the sentence. But they know they are condemned without appeal. One by one, at a time not to be appointed, they are taken out. Why they are taken out at that time, why they are taken out at all, what happens after they are taken out, nobody knows. They only know that the cell is replenished with prisoners and depleted of prisoners continuously.

What should the prisoners do? Should they fight one another to establish a hierarchy of authority within the cell? They could do that but to what purpose? Such power is patently illusory, since it is a pretence of power within powerlessness. Isn't it dishonest to the reality of their experience for one to claim dominion over another? If you can't finally control the terms of your own life, how can you honestly pretend to control the terms of someone else's? Isn't that claiming not to be the same as someone who is the same as you?

What should the prisoners do? Should one of them claim to know what happens beyond the cell and seek to control the behaviour of the other prisoners with that knowledge? But nobody knows, for they are all trapped in the same cell and share the limitations of that entrapment. Nothing anybody does, says or thinks will alter the unity of helplessness they have in common. The possession neither of knowledge nor of things will change finally the terms on which they all have to live.

Imagine, for example, that the master jailer appears, not to remove someone this time, but to throw a watch into the middle of the cell. The prisoners could fight for possession of the watch.

The individual or group gaining possession of the watch might feel they have an advantage over the others. But they have no such advantage in any real sense. They may have disadvantaged further the other prisoners, who will have less ability than they have to make coherence of the passing time, but they will have gained no greater control over the ultimate meaning of that time, the meaning of which is controlled by the power that imprisons. Thus, if they share the watch with everyone, they lose nothing, since the time within which they live is not under their control anyway. But they might gain, for among the others there may be some whose imagination and inventiveness, given the chance to use the watch, can devise more fruitful ways in which to deploy the time.

He decided that this was the tradition he came from – a long line of logically instinctive Socialists who lived by principle above materialism because it was the only existentially sane thing to do. His father was right. So was his Uncle Josey. Before he passed out in the chair, he drank to his relatives, all his relatives.

'UNCLE CHARLIE. HOW'S IT GOIN'?'

'How's it goin', Tam? Ah used tae unbutton two buttons and it popped out at me, ready for action. Now Ah unzip all the way down an' send in a search party. That's about exactly how it's goin', son.'

As they talked, Tom was still trying to realise that this was the funeral of Michael, his brother. But he couldn't retain the idea for very long at a time. He found himself more than once almost expecting to see Michael. It wasn't all that long ago that Joe, Michael and Marion's first son, had been married here. Many of the relatives and friends who had been at the wedding had returned today. Tom watched his nephews and nieces stunned at being brought back so soon to the Ossington Hotel, as if life was telling them it had made a mistake. Sorry: don't celebrate. Mourn. That's what I meant to say. What were Joe and Fiona thinking, now that their wedding dinner had turned so quickly in their mouths into the funeral spread, like biting fish and tasting sausage-roll.

'Ah suppose he was about as good as it gets, eh, Tam?' his Uncle Charlie said.

If only the minister at the cremation had been able to say something as authoritatively simple as that, Tom was thinking. But, through no fault of his own, the man could say nothing that mattered. All he had were the abstract articles of his faith with which to memorialise the day. As far as the man being cremated was concerned, the minister was a non-believer. If only he had known enough to believe in the way Uncle Charlie did, he might have brought to the event more than a shroud of words in which there was no corpse.

His Uncle Charlie surely believed. Sitting beside him, Tom was grateful for Uncle Charlie's effortless appreciation of other people's qualities. There came to him suddenly an incident at school which he now realised was probably prompted by his Uncle Charlie.

When Sinatra was being regarded as a has-been, in the early fifties, Tam had taken four of his 78s to school. In the playground the day before, he had been trying unsuccessfully to convince Harry Walker that Sinatra was a genius. He had brought the records in to lend to Harry so that he could learn how stupid his lack of appreciation was. The records were lying on his desk in the maths class when Dozey Davidson, the teacher, lifted them up and examined each as if it were a long-dead fish. He replaced them sadly.

'I'm sorry for you,' he said.

'If you don't like him,' Tam said before he could stop himself, 'I'm sorry for you.'

It was maybe the first time he had been so cheeky to a teacher and he was glad. What gives people the right to make fun of your family? Would Dozey like trying to tell his Uncle Charlie that he's sorry for him? As Tam's mother once said, 'Charlie's ma brother. An' Ah love him. But Ah have to admit he could pick a fight if he was on his own in Madame Tussaud's.'

Uncle Charlie had told Tam on several occasions of the time he went to hear Frank Sinatra at the Pavilion in Ayr. About forty people turned up, scattered throughout the hall. Who wants to listen to a clapped-out singer? Uncle Charlie always smiles at this point, the smile of a man who was in the right place at the right time, when nearly everybody else has taken a wrong turning.

'Well,' Uncle Charlie says. 'Ye know what happened, Tam?'

This is the moment Tam loves. Uncle Charlie's eyes are looking towards magical realms, like the old man in *The Boyhood of Raleigh*. Uncle Charlie talks slowly, carefully. Summoning up an historic moment is a delicate business.

'This wee thin man walks out. Right? He's tired-lookin'. He looks kinna beat up. He looks round the audience an' he gives a wee laugh to himself. An' he goes . . .'

Uncle Charlie always pauses here. Tam knows he is rehearsing in his head how to talk American. Uncle Charlie likes to talk American. So does Tam. Tam knows that Uncle Charlie's version of what Sinatra says will vary from what Sinatra said the last time. Sometimes Sinatra begins by saying, 'Hi, folks,' and sometimes by saying, 'Hello, you guys.' Sometimes it's just 'Good evening, ladies and gentlemen.' Tam doesn't mind. The words may vary but the experience they are capturing is the same. Listening to Uncle Charlie's repeated anecdote has become an impromptu lesson in story-telling. What matters is not so much what Sinatra said as the feeling it generated in Uncle Charlie. In trying yet again to renew that feeling, it's almost as if he has to renew the words as well. That way the experience comes back fresh, re-energised by the search for words to match it.

'Hi, ladies and gentlemen,' Sinatra says this time. 'Hey. Let's not be strangers. Forget the ticket price. Why don't we get together? We're not enough to make a crowd. Let's just be company for each other.'

He brings everybody down to the front rows. He sits on the edge of the stage. And he sings. How he sings.

'That wisny for money,' Uncle Charlie says. 'That was a gift tae the people who came out on a dark, wet night tae say they loved him. He made us just a bunch o' friends. That was a night, Tam. That was a night.'

Tom thought, sitting at the funeral with his Uncle Charlie, that maybe his anger at Dozey had been a tribute not just to what Sinatra had achieved but to the sincere joy of Uncle Charlie and to the remembered pleasure of a teenage boy. It occurred to him that many of our carefully articulated and supposedly rational opinions are perhaps just attempts to justify the way we can't help feeling, a helpless innocence trying to assume a sophistication that doesn't really fit, the way that children like to dress up in adult clothes. Maybe he hadn't been defending Sinatra so much as defending that time in the living-room when the reflected wonder of his Uncle Charlie's experience had taught him that this is what talent can do, be a secular Jesus with the loaves and fishes, take a handful of banal ingredients (a dark night in Ayrshire, a few appreciative people, a dingy hall) and make a miracle of shared pleasure.

When he thought of it, that was what these people he came from had had – a talent for living that could feed on scraps, make an event out of a pot of tea and a couple of relatives who dropped in uninvited, memorialise small moments in anecdote, construct a family legend out of somebody falling off a bike, develop a poetry reading from a remembered book someone had accidentally come across, find a sense of community in some shabby council houses and a few bleak streets. Would Gill and he ever be able to give their own children that talent, even if they stayed together?

'That's ma two best pals away now,' Uncle Charlie was saying. 'No offence, Tam. But after ye went to the Uni, we were never quite as close again. You were always a bit of a maverick, son.'

'That's for sure.'

'When yer father died, Michael took his place for me. Know what he did, Tam? When Ah took ma heart attack that time. Must be what? Twelve year ago now. He was still workin' then for Smith Brothers. In the van. When Ah was confined to bed. He came in early every mornin' an' shaved me before goin' to his work. Left me fresh as a daisy to begin ma day. Every day. Until Ah could do for maself. Fairly helped me that, son. When Ah wis down. Gave me a daily sense of maself Ah could try tae get back to. An' nobody ever asked him. He just decided. An' Ah bet he never told anybody. Did *you* know that?'

'Naw. Ah didn't.'

But he was glad to know now. He was reminded of lines he had memorised for himself at school. He had done that a lot in Boris's class, leafing surreptitiously through poetry books while Boris talked one of his strange, meandering monologues, leaving the class to eavesdrop. That was how he learned 'Jenny kissed me'. These lines were from Wordsworth, he thought:

> That best portion of a good man's life,
> His little, nameless, unremembered acts
> Of kindness and of love.

'Aye,' his Uncle Charlie said. 'That was Michael. But then ye'll no' need me tae tell ye that. Ye'll have yer own sense of him.'

HE IS STANDING IN THE DOORWAY of John Dalton's house. He is wearing short velvet trousers which have shoulder straps. He is three. John, who is seven, stands beside him. They have just finished a spell of digging for Australia in the back door. They have not been successful, although John exclaimed at one point, 'Ah can see the sky.' Now they are smoking Capstan Full Strength cigarettes, which John has stolen from his father's cigarette drawer. He is looking up at John admiringly, as he always does. It is then that he glimpses his mother's face at the window of his own house opposite. It is the most frighteningly distorted face he has ever seen.

He throws away the cigarette and runs towards the door of his house, reaching it just as it is opened by his mother.

'Ah'll never do it again, Mammy,' he shouts hopefully.

'No, by God, ye'll no'. Get in here.'

She unstraps his trousers and beats his bare bum all the way up the stairs. He is put immediately to bed, to wait for his father coming home. As he lies alone in the room, wondering what horrors may result, Michael puts his head round the door.

'Looks bad, Thomas,' he says. 'They're sendin' for the polis.'

MICHAEL'S HANDS ARE NO LONGER THERE. A moment of panic comes over him like a blackout which clears magically and instantly into blue sky and leaves. A cow is mooing somewhere. He hears Michael laughing. His mother and his father and his sister are part of him and they are not. They are waving. He can go back to them if he chooses and not if he chooses. The freedom he feels gives him the day as if it were his personal property. The grass is greener than he had noticed. The leaves are audible. The water of the Soldier's Hole, which has frightened him for weeks, is now his friend, supportive. He likes its rusty taste. He can swim, he can swim.

'HERE, TAM.'

He looks up from where he sits beside the cooker in the kitchen. The room has become his study. He sits there in the evenings with the cooker lit for warmth and does his homework. But this is a Saturday afternoon. The cooker isn't lit and sunlight is coming strongly through the window. His big brother, Michael, is standing over him.

'Here,' Michael says. 'Ye're not the ugliest bastard Ah've ever seen. Ah think ye're gonny need this.'

He hands Tam a slim book with hard covers. The covers are bright red. Tam opens the book and looks at the title page. He looks up at Michael. Michael is smiling at him with kindness.

'Ah don't think Betsy and Conn'll have told ye too much about it, eh?'

Tam smiles embarrassedly.

'Keep it in yer drawer,' Michael says. 'Beside yer Hank Jansen books.'

Michael goes out. The sun from the kitchen window shines like the light in a holy picture upon the book and Tam feels like a medieval knight who has been given a magic key but has no idea how to find the door the key might open. His mother walks into the kitchen. He slips the red book inside the cover of the book he has been reading, which is a book about an English public school called *Carry On, Rippleton*, one Allison gave him for his Christmas. The title of the book inside the book is his secret – *The Technique of Sex*.

I KNOW NOT WHITHER I SHALL HIE
When I at last am dead.
I only know as now I lie
On this, my own death-bed,
That I have sinned 'gainst God and man,
That I have slain my friend,
That I must die by my own hand
And thus must meet my end.

I have the knife, I have the will.
My tale is left untold.
I have the right myself to kill—
Our friendship's bond I sold.
I face my falsehood with the true.
My soul is calm within me.
I drive the blade my body through
And all is calm within me.

He holds the paper in his hand like a piece of some extra-terrestrial substance. Can such things be? (Afterwards, he would wonder, 'Should such things be?') He looks across the living-room at his mother reading and thinks what a weird thing is a newspaper. His lips silently mouth the words on the sheet.

He has written a poem. He can't believe it. He needs some kind of confirmation of what has happened. He finds Michael in the back green, sawing a piece of wood laid across a kitchen chair.

'Michael,' he says. 'Look at this.'

He hands his brother the poem as if it is something he has found and can't identify. Michael blows wood-chips from his left hand and takes the paper from him. He reads it sternly, looks up carefully at Tam. He seems to be checking Tam's face for something. He reads the poem again. His face relaxes and he tilts his head appreciatively.

'You didn't write this, kid? Did ye?'

'Uh-huh.'

'What age are ye? Fourteen? That's great, Tam. That's absolutely great.'

He gives Tam back the paper and returns to his sawing.

IN THAT CASUAL MOMENT, with the rasp of saw on wood and a light wind blowing, one kindness has helped to congeal a passing fancy into a compulsion and the smell of wood-shavings will always be for him like new hope coming to him on the wind and he will sometimes think that the epigraph to anything he writes should be: Michael's To Blame.

MICHAEL SITS UP IN HIS BED. He is drawing on a sketching-pad. The cold he has makes the skin around his nose bright red. Tam sits on the bed and puts down the two books he has been carrying. He lifts the top one and shows Michael the flyleaf of the back cover. Michael looks up from his drawing at the book. He shrugs.

'Think ye can draw him?' Tam says.

'Hemingway? Why?'

'Ah'd like a drawin' of him. Bigger than that, like.'

'Ah'll try. What's with the coat an' scarf?'

'Ah'm goin' out.'

'Ah didny think ye were goin' to yer bed. But it's a nice day.'

'Ye think so?'

'Jesus. What's up wi' you? Is it a funeral ye're goin' to? Where ye goin'?'

'Just out.'

'But where?'

'Just out.'

To avoid further questions, he gets up and walks to the door.

'Condolences to the bereaved,' Michael says.

IT WAS A SOLEMN MAN who came to Mrs Fitzpatrick's door. Little did she know that the ordinary-seeming person who approached her house had made deep and irrevocable decisions about his life. Had she but realised that he was setting out on a lifetime of unbroken celibacy, she might well have been amazed. She might even have tried to dissuade him. So young, she might have thought, and so determined to deny his very nature. But all expostulations would have been in vain. (Expostulations is a good word.) Words do not bend iron. His measured walk was going where no one could stop him. His level gaze saw far beyond these grey-stone houses, this gravelled driveway, this manicured garden, the imposing door with its beaded panel of coloured glass. His hand on the button rang the knell of all possibility of physical love for him. He would become a recluse, he had decided, something like that ancient mystic he read about. Saint Simeon. Lived on top of a pillar. Let the world try to bother you in those circumstances.

> (Dear Saint Simeon Stylites,
>
> Room for one more up there?)

'Hullo, Tom,' she says.

Her face is like a festival on a dull day. Graithnock's in black and white, she's in Technicolor. Her eyes are so vivid and so elusively hued. You could write an essay on trying to define their colour. Her mouth's amazing. She has enough black hair for twins. Maybe it's the way the sunlight catches the opaque panel on the door, making it look like the stained-glass window of a church, or maybe it's the thin floral dress she wears, but she looks like something out of one of the William Morris poems she read to him at the party. This can't be Graithnock. She seems genuinely pleased to see him. But this can't be him. Who was it supposed to be who turned up at the door?

'What an opportune visit! Come in, come in.'

Opportune visit. She might as well have opened the door into a book by Jane Austen. He would be as much at home there. His feet on the wooden floor of the hallway make him feel as if he's wearing hobnailed boots.

('Aarh, Mistress. Ah just be here to see if 'appen Maister be wishin' me to plough the nether field.')

Having closed the front door, she walks ahead of him into the living-room. She is bare-legged and wearing strapless, high-heeled white shoes. The way he's dressed, he feels like an Eskimo parachuted into the Riviera. She must have blood as thick as treacle. Do rich people live in a different climate from the rest of us? Do they order the season they want like new wallpaper? In Dawson Street just now, you moved four yards from the fire and you could feel winter limbering up, practising to freeze your back and put an ice-clamp on your nose. Here, they still seem to be dressing for summer.

'Here, let me take your coat and scarf,' she says.

She goes out to the hall with them. Feeling intimidated by the place, he stands waiting aimlessly. He can barely remember this room from the party. It feels so different. He must have been blind with nerves that night, for now he notices for the first time why she is dressed so lightly. The room has central heating. How could he have spent a few hours here and not have seen that there are radiators? Perhaps they were hidden by furniture. The room does look rearranged. Also, the fireplace, which was covered by a wooden screen during the party, is now revealed and glowing warmly.

'Sit down, Tom. Sit down.'

He heads for the nearest armchair and sinks so far into its soft upholstery he thinks he may need a block and tackle to get back out. She chooses the end of the couch near him, kicks off her shoes and tucks her legs under her. Her skirt flurries slightly as she settles herself. Her pants are blue. He feels like a creep for having noticed.

'Well. To what do we owe the honour?'

'Oh, yes. That's right. I brought your book back. Excuse me, where's my coat?'

He has managed to get out of his chair with all the ease of a fallen climber emerging from a crevasse. John Garfield that wasn't.

'Hanging in the hall.'

He goes into the hall, trying not to make his steps reverberate too much. He finds his coat, puts his hand in the right-hand pocket, puts his hand in the left-hand pocket. He freezes. He starts to pat his coat all over with both hands. There's no book there. He can't believe it. Where is the bloody book? He laid it out before he left the house. How could he have forgotten to bring it with him? What does he do now? She will think the book was only an excuse. Maybe she's right. If his sole reason for coming here was just to give her back the book, how has he managed to leave it in the house? (On Michael's bed, that's where it is.) But he didn't know she would be alone. Yes, he did. How many husbands are at home during the day? You would expect Eddie Fitzpatrick to be at his hosiery at this time. He doesn't know what to do. He stands with his hand on his coat, wondering if he should just take it and leave.

'Tom?'

He could leave now. He wouldn't have to face her, have to explain. They don't exactly move in the same circles.

'Tom? You see your coat?'

THE HERO MAKES A LIFE-AFFECTING DECISION.

HE WENT BACK IN. And it was like boarding a random express train that was going he didn't know where and they talked and she opened a bottle of wine and he didn't tell her he had never tasted wine before and the word Frascati kept rising in his mind like a curl of smoke that was confusing him about where he was and they talked and she seemed to recede before his eyes and then come unnaturally close, all without her moving, and the room seemed drifting and he had no idea how much time had passed and she opened a second bottle and she stared at him and said she would make some coffee and he should come through to the kitchen with her so that they could continue talking and he stood vaguely watching her move about the kitchen.

'WHY DON'T YOU TOUCH ME?' she says.

He knows he has fantasised the question. He will have to keep better control of his imaginings. He actually *heard* what she cannot possibly have said. The sound vibrated in the room, passed through the air like an electric charge. Yet she cannot have said it. That is not what people say. He must maintain his hold on reality. It must be the wine. Maybe the coffee will help.

They are in the kitchen now. She has filled the whistling kettle and put it on the cooker and ignited the ring with a gas gun. She is spooning chicory essence from the Camp bottle into two cups. This is a very ordinary scene. Remember that. This is Mrs Fitzpatrick making coffee in her kitchen. There is a calendar on the wall. The picture for October is English Bay, Vancouver. Perhaps she has relatives in Canada. The window lets in dazzling sunlight. The venetian blind has been pulled up until only a few slats show at the top of the window. This is the first house in which he has seen venetian blinds.

The sunlight is hypnotic. Is that what wine does to you? He is in a kind of trance where time seems to have stopped. He feels as if he has been in her house for days. He can hardly imagine being anywhere else. Maybe he was born here. He can see himself standing at the kitchen window. He can see her standing with her back to him. He feels strangely diffuse, as if the edges of his body have become blurred. This is a dangerous relaxation. He misses his inhibitions. They are old friends who have deserted him. Anything is perhaps possible. But anything is not possible. He is imagining the freedom of this moment as he has imagined her question. This is a very ordinary scene.

'Why don't you touch me?'

She *is* saying it. She is saying it again. She screws the top back on the bottle. She licks the spoon and lays it on the work-surface beside the bottle. She doesn't turn round.

'You know you want to touch me,' she says. 'You've been

wanting to touch me since you came in. Why don't you do it?'

Her voice has become different. It is raw and husky. There is no gloss of social inflection to it. It has a basic, primal sound. It is a voice gone naked. The timbre of it makes this not a kitchen, just a place, receptacle for two people and some sunlight.

He looks at her and sees not Mrs Fitzpatrick but a woman. She assumes a deeper identity before his eyes. The voice has dispelled the obfuscations through which he has been seeing her – friend of his uncle, wife of a man he knows, sophisticated older person, middle-class intellectual – and the social mists have cleared. Her body palpitates before his eyes, breathing through the thin dress. He is aware of its beautiful solidity, the contours of it, as if the heat of the flesh is melting the cloth that contains it. Her legs are blonde with sunlight, astonishingly vivid, the calves tensed from the high heels she is wearing. The dress moulds itself to her buttocks and thighs. Her back is firm and strong. He wants to smell her hair.

She clasps her hands on the edge of the worktop on either side of her. She lowers her head and the suddenly cascading hair reveals the nape of her neck. The sight of that normally hidden place, white and vulnerable, is surprisingly and shockingly erotic. It is as if she has stripped herself before him.

'Do it. Do it now.'

It hardly seems to be herself that is speaking but a force passing through her. The command comes from some potency of feeling which they have created in the room. It is not to be denied. It galvanises him beyond his own control. It walks him across the floor towards her. She still stands with her head lowered.

He very gently touches the back of her neck, awed by its smoothness. A shiver goes through her. He traces the shape of her buttocks with his hands. Slowly, very slowly, his hands move up her back and sides, feeling the flesh ripple across the rib-cage. She is leaning back towards him. His hands slide gradually round until, incredibly, they are cupping her breasts. The soft weight of them scalds his palms with passion. His erection is prodding at her thighs. He bends and sucks her neck. That action, so simple yet so unimaginable until it has happened, makes a vortex of sensation in him. He seems to be spinning, detached from the solidity of the floor. Strange images eddy with him in a swift whirlpool that throws up and sucks down debris of perception, shipwrecked pieces of himself: his mother's thoughtful face, a page with his handwriting on it, the Grand Hall full of dancers, Eddie Fitzpatrick staring, Dusty Thomas standing vaguely in front of his class. The unthinkableness of what he is doing flashes before him, how irretrievable all this is, and then it is atomised in an explosion of feeling.

The room goes seismic and they are caught in the sensation. He does not know what is happening or how it is happening. She turns towards him and closes on him like a trap. Their hands have become a riot, moving madly of their own volition, out of anybody's control, looting touch from each other's body. The sunlit window expands to a vast brightness. Vancouver seems to be in the room with them. The coffee cups are dancing. He and she have been moved across the room by something.

Her left leg is raised – the foot, still with the white shoe on, is resting on a kitchen chair. The tensed thigh overwhelms him like amnesia. What identity, what world? There's only this. He is a witless devotee of the muscular hollow formed where leg and body meet, as if he were seeing God's thumbprint on beautiful flesh still warm from the making. Her blue pants are crumpled round her right ankle. The skirt of her dress is an impromptu belt, ruched round her waist. The top of her dress is unbuttoned and one breast has spilled out over the brassiere, the nipple like an antenna. Her hair seems impossibly wild, threatening to fill the room. Her eyes are dark as tunnels, sucking everything into them. Her mouth is wide. Her back is to the wall.

He stands against her. She has not so much unbuckled his belt as torn it apart. His trousers are wherever he has kicked them, to be left until called for. His shirt is unbuttoned. Skin ignites against skin. Somewhere in him there remains the amazed awareness that she had started to make coffee. He came up behind her and put his hands round her and held her breasts. A tremor became a subsidence. How did they come to be here? He is easing her up and on to him. How does he know to do this? He is talking a language he has never heard before and does not understand. She is making a noise that comes from somewhere he has never been, as if her mouth is a shell that knows the sound of the sea.

Then she speaks. Her voice comes small and dirling from some far distance, as weird and irrelevant as a crossed line on some very long-distance call.

'Have you got any protection?' she says.

He does not know what she means. He thinks she must be referring to her husband. A gun? A suit of armour? Then he remembers Harry Walker going into a chemist's boldly one afternoon while the rest of them waited outside. She must mean an FL.

DID YOU COME PREPARED? HAVE YOU GOT A DUREX? HAVE YOU GOT ANY PROTECTION?

No matter what form the question took, he would realise, it was to acquire in time for him a certain irony. He had always been lucky enough to avoid strange night sweats – at least for that reason – or panicked contemplation of genitals in the toilet. But it didn't mean you didn't pay. As his mother used to say, there's more ways to kill a dog than choke it.

Maybe the biggest damage we do each other in attempting to make love isn't through the body but through the head and heart – those ways in which we dismantle each other's sense of ourselves without knowing how to put the pieces back together again. Penicillin won't cure that. And when will they invent a condom for the head?

(Dear Casanova,

I still feel ambivalent about my attitude to your promiscuity. I imagine you must have given the women pleasure. So what's the problem? I suppose my misgivings are not so much moral as experiential. I mean, the crap you must have talked, the fake promises, the lies, the improvised nonsense, saying whatever you had to say to unlock the next corset. And presumably the crap you must have listened to. Didn't that do something to you? I suspect there is a kind of mental clap with which lovers can infect the purity of the act and which they can pass on to each other. If so, you must have been raddled with it, finally gibbering disconnected phrases, from where and to whom you didn't know any longer, trapped in a kind of paralysis of the socially insane. No?)

'NO,' HE SAYS.

'Oh,' she says.

There is a stillness while he wonders what will happen. Perhaps she is waiting for her misgivings to march past in protest. Her objections seem to dwindle. Their mouths leap at each other, pulling them after them. They make the edge of the table a place for a different kind of meal. This is a kitchen? It might as well be a clearing in a wood and them alternating nymph and satyr, pursuer and pursued. They are both completely naked now. They eat, they touch, they knead. She is discovering places in him he hadn't known he had.

They fall off the edge of the table on to the floor. She is underneath him. What in Margaret Inglis might as well have been a hedgehog has mysteriously turned into a hairy flower. Its petals part so gently and its soft, moist interior receives him. He moves in and out incredulously. She arches herself off the floor and he is rocking in a human cradle, bucking on an unbroken horse, riding lost in a coracle of self across an unknown sea. His mind seems to be expanding as if it will burst. Then it explodes like a Catherine wheel. Who will collect the pieces? He seems to come through his whole body. He is afraid she will ingest his pelvis into her. She claws his buttocks to her and holds him there while he judders as if he's strapped to a machine. Some animal of a species he doesn't know is moaning in him. She wriggles madly on the end of him still in her. She stiffens suddenly, yowls delicately like a cat with a gag on, collapses on the floor. Maybe he has killed her. Maybe she has killed him. He slumps across her.

THE KETTLE SCREAMS AS LOUD AS A FACTORY WHISTLE.

AS HE MADE THE COFFEE AND THE BOILED-EGG SANDWICHES, he would worry again, as he did several times a day, about his inability to cook. Why was he so incompetent in the kitchen? It was pathetic at his age. He would love to be a decent cook. It wasn't for want of trying. He remembered his most recent, determined attempt.

He had gone to the William Low supermarket nearby and bought brisket. That was his first mistake. It wasn't until he got back to the flat that he realised it wasn't brisket he liked but silverside. In the vagueness that always afflicted him when shopping, a state of mind analogous to looking at a huge menu printed in a language he didn't understand, he had mixed up the names. Staring at the lump of brisket and chastising his lack of concentration, he wondered what you were supposed to do with this. He had intended to casserole (impressive word) the silverside but he had no silverside.

He phoned a woman friend for advice and she suggested that he boil the meat but he told her his heart was set on having a casserole. That was his second mistake. She wished him well, in the manner of someone responding to an armless man's stated ambition to become a juggler.

He put on the butcher's apron Gus's girlfriend had bought him (presumably regarding it as appropriately macho kitchen wear for a man). He opened a bottle of wine, filled himself out a glass and began.

Externally it was a fine performance. He pre-heated the oven, put the brisket in a casserole dish and basted it with butter as it warmed. He peeled potatoes and would try to time their boiling to coincide with the readiness of the meat. He emptied a tin of butter beans into a small pot, to be heated quickly just before the meat was ready.

For two hours he performed the role of cook as he had seen on television. He was good at it. He walked up and down in his apron, sipping from his glasses of wine and checking things. He must have looked the part. At one point he sliced up part of the brisket to make it more tender. Having started before six, he waited until after eight o'clock before he decided to eat. The timing of things became a little frenetic towards the end but he managed to sit down to hot brisket, boiled potatoes and warm butter beans. The wine was almost finished.

The first sign that all was not well was the whiff of butter beans from the plate. Jesus, he thought, I didn't know that butter beans could defecate. The taste confirmed the smell. He retrieved the can from the waste-bin and read it. The beans had been in brine, which should have been drained off. The butter beans were out.

The potatoes had been mistimed. They were raw inside. That left the brisket. But he couldn't cut it. He sat for a while gesturing at it with his knife and fork but the meat refused to co-operate. He was miming having a meal. Suddenly he was shouting at the plate. 'You brisket bastard! What's the point of meat like you?'

He began to rave at the room. His head was spinning from no food and too much wine. He found two slices of stale bread and dipped them in the casserole where the melted butter was flavoured with the meat. The pretence of culinary sophistication collapsed into atavistic frenzy. The bread, impregnated with the ghost of what should have been his meal, was stuffed into his mouth with his fingers. He dumped the plateful of the inedible into the bucket, washed and dried his hands, filled out the last glass of wine. He stood briefly in the doorway with his wine, stared round the kitchen like King Lear looking at his daughters, and went to bed. He lay with the duvet up to his chin, trying to make his wine last, staring ahead, cursing the world and daring it to come near him until he sent for it. The discarded apron lay on the floor of the bedroom like the costume for a part he would never be able to play convincingly. It was 8.15 in the evening.

Now he settled for boiled-egg sandwiches, two chocolate biscuits and coffee. Know your limits. He carried them through to the table by the window in the living-room. From here he could look out at the old Warriston Cemetery across the road. He sometimes walked there. He liked cemeteries. Paradoxically, they recharged him, seeming to remind him that he was still outrunning the headstone. His favourite was probably Père Lachaise in Paris, a real city of the dead with streets and monuments like little houses where the famous and the unknown had addresses beside each other, still at home to visitors. But Edinburgh had a graveyard almost as good – Dean Cemetery, a lesson in Scottish history set in stone, what happened when Scottishness as a way of life gave way to Britishness as a career. Home is the Scotsman who has been on the make.

He sipped. The coffee now was made from granules, not chicory essence as it had been that day in Maddie's kitchen.

He could still see her crawling away from him across the floor to reach up to switch the kettle off, beautifully naked. He watched her flesh move, not quite like a sea-anemone, but near enough. This was a respectable woman in her kitchen, moving as a wonderful beast, without shame or self-consciousness. His sense of things had been irrevocably altered and he was glad. The socially practical contained the wildly sensual. The wildly sensual contained the socially practical. In the tension between the two you had to learn to live. Well, he would try. Life could be rugged but there it was.

She turned round and smiled a soft, wet smile and stood up slowly, letting him see what he had been allowed to enjoy. Maybe she knew it was the first time he had seen a fully naked woman, for she stood watching him watch, letting his eyes graze on her body. She seemed to him the most perfect being he had ever seen. They can make people like that?

(And the Lord beheld His work and He saw that it was good. And He looked upon Maddie that was called Fitzpatrick and He spake thus. 'Yes!!! That's what I meant by a woman. I knew I would get it right some time.')

She started to laugh at his wonderment and walked towards him. She reached down and took his head gently and pulled it into her thighs. It was furnace-warm in there and he thought he might suffocate but there were worse ways to die. It must have been then, he would decide, that he knew he was in love with her.

He was not to remember the rest of that time at her house too clearly. Too many strangenesses had fallen on his head. First wine, first naked woman, first annihilation of inhibition, first making of full, physical love. Not only had he entered into a different and much deeper relationship with her but with everything else, it seemed. He was calling her 'Maddie' and it was as if he were on first-name terms not just with her but with the world. He felt oddly at home in himself and things took on a settled shape and colour and were there for his personal enjoyment – the floral curtains in the sitting-room, the warm wood of the table where they laid their coffee cups (she said it was yew), the print of *Peasant Digging* on the wall.

> (*Dear Camille Pissaro,*
>> *How is it you can paint the air?*)

Other things happened, unimagined but with a natural and undeniable rightness. She put on a red silk dressing-gown and he, not knowing the form in a situation like this, put his clothes back on. He found it astonishingly erotic to sit clothed and drinking coffee with a woman whose breasts kept almost appearing and whose naked legs invaded every thought. It was the ordinary transformed into the endlessly exciting, a dream of what life should be like that had often haunted him.

They talked about what he could never remember. All he would remember was the effortless pleasure of the talking, as if they had always been sitting in this room. The exotic and the practical embraced in their words, like long-lost friends. 'Lapis lazuli' was like the meaning of life in a poem, Eddie was on business in Holland and Tom would come back the day after tomorrow. She had friends coming tomorrow. He felt jealous about that.

When he had reluctantly put on his coat to go and was standing in the hallway, she pulled him back into the doorway of the sitting-room and undid his trouser-front. (Strange how trousers used to button at the front. Maybe the invention of the zip was the prophetic heralding of a freer attitude to sex.)

As she knelt there sucking him voraciously, the dressing-gown slipped off her shoulders and the doorbell rang. Someone was there. He could imagine the shadow against the coloured glass. He panicked. But she looked up at him, her shoulders hunched, her hands cupping him, her mouth opening around him like a flesh-eating flower, and her opaque eyes hypnotically commanded him to do nothing but submit to being devoured. He did, some part of him realising that he was having his very own dangerous liaison. Here was fantasy made flesh in the sperm that creamed on her smiling lips. The doorbell had rung twice more and whoever it was had gone away, like his inhibition.

Out in the street eventually, he moved through the town on a private escalator. This must be what euphoria meant. Life seemed spread before him, a banquet to choose from. The town was his own in a way it had never been before. Life was not to be worried about but enjoyed. Even the recent past was transformed. Times that had been ordinary in their happening were now sauced with present well-being and made piquant with a new-found sense of self, to be savoured as he chose.

LET IT BE MORNING. Let the sun be up but still too feeble to have softened yet the mild chill of the night, so that you can taste the crispness of the air. Let Hilly Brown and Jack Laidlaw be walking beside you.

You're grubby from a night-shift at the brickwork and pleasantly tired from your exertions. You've been working nine hours in the dark, while everybody slept, and now you know you have earned every fresh, clean breath you take. The air, it seems, belongs to you personally. Don't anybody challenge your right to the pleasure of it.

You're going home and everybody else is walking past you, poor zombies, their heads still fogged with sleep, moving towards a day that's not their own. You'll buy twelve rolls in Ingram the Baker's and six of them you'll eat when you get in, spread thick with white butter and washed down with two cups of strong, sweet tea. You'll have a long, slow bath. You'll take a book to bed with you. You probably won't read much of it. When you fall asleep, the book will be beside you, comforting as a child's teddy bear, dreams to share.

Sometime in the afternoon you'll waken and you'll do whatever you want to do. You might read some words, you might sit in the darkness of a cinema, you might just walk the streets of your familiar town and watch the passing girls. For she's there, the unknown woman, waiting to be made flesh by chance or circumstance or unforeseen event.

Anything you choose to do will be good, for you are seventeen and you are going to university at the end of the summer, and you are probably going to be a writer, though nobody knows that but you, and you feel you have enough energy to populate a small country.

THAT DISCOVERED POTENCY OF SELFHOOD, he would remember, stayed with him even in the house. He had a phase of feeling almost condescendingly tolerant towards his family. His mother and father could be forgiven for not noticing the difference in him. It must be so long since they had been where he was. He could allow Marion and Michael their illusion that he didn't understand what happened between them. Allison's tendency to treat him as an intermittently tolerable nuisance now amused him. He wondered if he had arrived at this new place before she had. He remembered an incident that had happened between them a long time ago, when he was fifteen.

He was sitting in the living-room, leafing through a dictionary, asking Allison the meaning of random words. She was putting in her curlers at the mirror above the fireplace. He had asked her 'causeway' and 'chalice' and she had got them both and he felt the need for something more difficult. He came upon a word he had never seen before. It looked a cracker.

'Chancre,' he said, pronouncing it as a French word.

There was silence.

'You've got me there,' Allison said. 'Ah give in.'

But by now he had read the meaning, which made him blush instantly: 'the hard swelling that constitutes the primary lesion in syphilis'. 'Lesion' he wasn't sure of but 'syphilis' would do.

'No, that's not the one,' he said quickly. 'Sorry. This is it. Wait till ye hear this one. Chaparral. Eh?'

'What?'

'Chaparral.'

Fortunately, he was boring her so much that she noticed

neither that he was blushing nor that an abandoned word had been unexplained.

'Spell it,' she said.

He did.

'No.'

'Dense tangled brushwood.'

'Hm,' Allison said. 'That's a handy word for Graithnock. Ah must remember it the next time Ah'm in the main street.'

What a quaint boy that had been, sitting with a dictionary on his knees, trying to find the meaning of experience in a book when it was growing wild all around him, ripe fruit just waiting to be plucked. He could sigh now for the folly of wasted time.

He could now sit among the same old conversations, smiling to himself, holding his secret as if it were uncountable wealth they didn't know he had. But he soon discovered the inverted alchemy of secrets, how they can tarnish in the dark and begin to corrode the holder.

MAN WITH BUNION DIES IN HOSPITAL. The incidental, ludicrous headline would come back to him in Edinburgh, showing him how old news can be a source of memory clusters, a public troopship from which the piquancy of individual memories can disembark.

HE HAS COMMITTED ADULTERY. *He has committed adultery*. Suddenly, the Bible which he used to read so keenly feels as if it is personally addressed to him. Jehovah, twiddling his cosmic thumbs through many millennia, stirs in the heavenly regions. His eyes flash fire.

(And the Lord spake and he was exceeding wroth. 'I knew somebody was going to do it, I just knew it. It doesn't matter how often you warn them. You can carve it in stone. No. It still won't work. There's always going to be one. Well, he can't say

I didn't warn him. Thou shalt not commit adultery. Did he think I was kidding?')

There is no escaping from this. You have done it. It is there, final, irrevocable. It is you who have done it, nobody else.

('Tam Docherty? 14 Dawson Street? Right. We've got a real one here. No mercy. What justification could he possibly have for this? I'll tell you. None. For the Lord thy God is an angry God.')

'What's wrong with you, boay?' his mother says. 'You liked macaroni and cheese last week.'

'Maybe he's went vegetarian,' his Auntie Bella observes.

She is arranging her headsquare in front of the oval mirror that hangs on a chain from the living-room wall. She has refused her tea, saying, 'Ah've the five thousand tae feed up there.' (The biblical reference gives a new and sharp pang of guilt.) But she has still been sampling a few chips from his plate. She ruffles his hair as she does so.

'What part of an animal does macaroni come fae?' his father asks.

He is looking up, puzzled from his newspaper where Tam has noticed the headline 'Man with Bunion Dies in Hospital'. He probably thought he had problems. If that's what happens to you for having a bunion, what could be in store for him?

'The cheese!' his Auntie Bella says, as if she finds it wearisome having to explain everything to humbler intelligences. 'The cheese. That's from a cow, intit? Milk. To butter. To cheese.'

She pats the knot on her headsquare with the complacency of the well informed. His father is staring at her. His mouth shapes itself a couple of times towards speech. But whatever he is thinking appears to be inexpressible. He goes back behind his newspaper. From there his final comment is issued.

'Bella,' he says. 'See when you die? See if ye donate yer brain to medical science? Gonny leave directions? So they can find it?'

His Auntie Bella laughs, happily impervious to his father's lack of appreciation. Her nature, as his father has said before, 'come intae the world dressed in elephant hide.'

'Tom,' his mother is saying. 'How can ye work in a brickwork if ye don't eat?'

'He's left the brickwork,' his father says.

'Oh, so that means he should stop eating?' his Auntie Bella says.

('Silence, ye little people!' saith the Lord.)

Their voices bicker distantly. He is alone with His wrath at his wrongdoing. He has committed adultery. Adultery. The word has attached itself to him like an incurable disease. But nobody else knows he has it yet. He carries it around with him secretly, a sickness that estranges him from normalcy and breeds debilitating questions in him like diseased corpuscles. How can he claim to be a Socialist if he can betray Eddie Fitzpatrick in this callous way? What is the point of trying to write when the pen droops in your hand like a lost erection? What would his family think? Is the day before yesterday the land of lost content? He sees it shining plain.

The three boys in the Queen's Café seem to be living where he used to live. He's in exile now. And Cain went out from the presence of the Lord, and dwelt in the land of Nod, to the east of Eden. (James Dean would have understood. He wishes, maybe for the hundredth time, he hadn't piled up in his Porsche a few days ago. He misses him like a friend he was only just getting to know.)

The three of them are laughing a lot. The table they sit at is in the same room as he is but he feels as if it could be a scene from another world. He is sipping a cup of aloes. They seem to have been drinking euphoria, though the empty cups would suggest tea. The one in the middle is conducting their mood. The other two are just following his lead. He holds up his hands. They give him the silence he wants.

'Expeliment on pledictability of human nature,' he says

He takes the silver paper from a Player's packet which is lying empty on the table and very carefully pares the lining of rice-paper from it. Taking the rice-paper, he kneads, tears and twists it into an elongated, vaguely human shape, like a figure by Giacometti. He does it all with that exact, fanatic concentration with which Hollywood scientists bend over hissing beakers. The paper man is laid ceremoniously on his side in a saucer from which the cup has been removed. Then the cup, containing dregs of cold tea, is poised precisely above the figure, angled on the axes of the thumb and forefinger. He pauses, looking around with manic mischief in his eyes.

The moment freezes for Tam as he looks. He sees the boy who is holding the cup smiling in his arrogant handsomeness. He sees the other two watching the boy intently. They are bathed in dull sunlight, like figures in an old painting where the pigment has dimmed. They seem so brief and so poignantly unconscious of their brevity. They are turned in on one another, simultaneously declaring the importance of themselves and concentrating on nonsense. As if he has become an instant geriatric, Tam contemplates the joyous wastefulness of youth.

'Observe,' the boy says. 'Confucius, he say: what happen when man pee the bed?'

He delicately tilts the cup until some drops of cold tea fall on the paper figure. With just the right degree of languor, the figure turns gently in its saucer until it is facing the other way.

'All clear?' he says. 'No more confusement? Man loll away from plish. Plish velly wet.'

They all laugh until it seems that medical attention may have to be summoned.

Oh, very good. Is that all they have to do with their time? Do they know nothing of the griefs to be endured? Can they imagine having committed adultery? Have they ever wandered through a world blighted by their own evil, a self-made and permanent winter, and found not the solace of one friend? For John Benchley wasn't in.

The housekeeper has come to the door wearing that perpetual hat she presumably goes to bed in. It is fused for ever to her head as if it has been surgically attached. Maybe it has a religious significance, like that skull-cap Jewish men wear. The cap of devout respectability. No bad thoughts may enter here. It may be raining evil but, behold, it touches me not. Her face looks like one of the prunes they served so often at school dinners. You took them like penance and later, in the lavatory, they purged you of impurities.

'Yes?' Mrs Malone says, staring at him.

This is not a red carpet. He feels as welcome as a drunk man at a Rechabite meeting. She has never liked him, perhaps because once, when she was in the room clearing away the tea things,

he said, 'God is dead.' He was quoting from his skim-reading of
Nietzsche at the time.

(Dear Friedrich Nietzsche,

*If God is dead, how could he ever have been God
in the first place? And if he ever was God, how could he be dead? Did you
find a body? Any photies?*

Puzzled Reader, Graithnock.)

But he doesn't think such niceties would matter to Mrs Malone,
even if you explained them to her. Quoting would still be
blasphemy. (The teacups had rattled like forewarning of an
earthquake. John Benchley had smiled at him. Mrs Malone
hadn't.) Or perhaps she dislikes him because she knows that
John and he secretly drink sherry. Or perhaps her hat is an
evil-detector and she had always instinctively known about him
then what has now been proven to be true, that he was destined
for bad things.

'Ah'm sorry tae bother you, Mrs Malone,' he says. 'But is
John in?'

Her face wrinkles even more, from prune to raisin. Maybe those
who have become wicked betray themselves in every subsequent
act. She has found him out.

'The minister,' she says, and pauses. He understands the
meaning of the pause: thou shalt not take thy minister's
name in vain, which means familiarly. He has disrespected
the sanctum. He has entered the mosque with his shoes on.
Thou shalt honour the man with his collar back to front. 'The
minister is at a funeral.'

(Why do you want to interrupt the solemn duties of the great
ones with your trivia?)

'Any idea when he'll be back?'

'He's a busy man. Mrs MacPherson's not very well. There's an
elders' meeting. He has things to do.'

The door shuts in his face. He imagines more bolts being shot
home than the door of the Bastille had. He stares at the door for
some time, absorbing its symbolic significance. He is despised and
rejected of men. He turns away, disappointed and relieved.

For what could he have said to John anyway?

('Hullo, John. Good to see you. What it is. I've just been riding the wife of a friend and I thought we might have a chat about it. Any chance of a sherry?')

It is hopeless. There is nobody he can tell about this. There is nothing to do but pace out the dimensions of his loneliness. He decides he will commit suicide.

The woods of Bringan take his mood into theirs. He has stopped on the Swinging Bridge and watched the waters writhe below, brown as beer and frothing white across the rocks. Recent rains have deepened the river but not enough. These aren't the waters of a grand oblivion and an abiding mystery thereafter, the insoluble grief of family and friends for the drowned. These are the waters of an embarrassing unconsciousness, maybe a fractured skull and three weeks in the hospital and the puzzled disgruntlement of his family ('Whit the hell were ye tryin' to do?' his father asks) and the need to pretend that you fell while trying to walk the parapet of the bridge.

Now he has passed on into the trees. This place is mythic for him. Bringan is where his boyhood came to commune with its dreams of a secret greatness only he knew about. This was his Chiron, a wild and living entity that taught him impossible possibilities and the strange, dark power of imaginings, that contradicted, every time he came, the banality of his daily life, that cured him, with leaves, of petty wounds the town had given him. Here his short trousers had become hose and kilt and buckskin chaps. Here his woollen jersey had been medalled jacket with braided epaulets and toga and doublet. Here his hair had grown piratically long in an hour. Here, still hiding out among the trees, like outlaws waiting for their time to come when he would finally identify with them, were Robin Hood and Wat Tyler and Robert the Bruce and William Wallace. Their ghostly presences shame him now.

For what has he become? A seedy adulterer, a betrayer of himself and everyone else. He senses his heroes, who were him in hiding, dead all around him in the dark places of Bringan, starved from the lack of the provisions he should have brought them. This place is haunted for him today, and not just by famous names or the possible versions of himself he had imagined. He is suddenly awed by stumbling upon memories much more immediate and real, as tangible as ancestral bones which embarrass his smallness by the size of them. These are his father's woods, his grandfather's woods.

He cups his hands and drinks from Moses' Well, a hidden spring his father showed to him, and the bad taste of him in his mouth has turned pure water sour. The thread of luminous liquid still runs as clear but when he breaks it with his flesh it is defiled. He spits it out.

The Soldier's Hole, the deep pool where Michael taught him to swim, is polluted by his presence. He feels that, if he stripped and dived into it now, his body would turn it to sludge.

He has made his decision. He will go home and collect the book Maddie Fitzpatrick gave him at the party. He will return it to her. He will say a final goodbye, no matter what desperate appeals she may make. Nothing will make him so much as pause in his purpose.

'DON'T EVEN IMAGINE IT,' his mother says.

The voice, coming from another room, sounds eerily preoccupied. It does not know that he is here, standing in the hallway outside the closed door of the living-room. He has in his hand the book he intends to return to Maddie Fitzpatrick. He has slipped into the house silently, using the key that hangs from a string inside the letter-box, wishing to talk to no one in his mood of grand despair. He has gone upstairs and found the book and tiptoed back down when the voice arrests him with his hand on the Yale lock.

'Ah'm tellin' you. Don't even imagine it.'

He takes his hand off the lock and stands very still in the lobby.

'Oh, Ah think Ah can imagine it, Betsy,' his father says.

'Can ye? Well, Ah can't.'

He is transfixed. He knows himself to be eavesdropping and he doesn't like to be doing that. But he is compelled. This is news of something he doesn't know, he senses. News of what? He waits. A child's voice shouting in the street outside comes and goes without meaning, hieroglyphic as a bird blown past on the wind. The sunshine refracted through the frosted glass at the top of the front door steeps the hallway in soft light. The hanging coats and jackets seem instinct with an unknown future, waiting to be worn.

'Why not?' his father says.

'Because it isn't what's goin' to happen.'

'You know that, do ye?'

'Yes. Ah do.'

'But it was good enough for Michael an' Allison.'

'Who says it was? It's what happened to them. That's all. Does that mean it was good enough?'

'They seem to be doin' alright.'

'Aye. Ah think so. It wid seem so. Maybe they have what they were wantin'. But it's not what Tom wants.'

The realisation that they are talking about him gives him a strange sensation. He feels himself existing outside himself, as if he were somehow an event, happening in ways he doesn't know and can't control. He is aware of the solidity of his life in a way he hadn't imagined.

'Ye know that, do ye?'

'Don't you?' his mother asks.

'Ye're sure it's no' what *you* want? Tryin' to make him somethin' he's not. For yer own sake.'

'Ye know me better than that, Conn. If ye don't, who have Ah been sleepin' wi' all these years?'

'He seems happy enough in the brickwork. An' it's money comin' in.'

'Happy? Were you happy in the pits? Are you happy now? An' Ah'm not tryin' to make him what Ah want. Just tae give him the chance tae decide what *he* wants. If he's a happy dustbin man, Ah'll be happy. But he'll be a dustbin man wi' vision. An' nothing'll curtail that, if Ah can help it.'

'An' the rest of us can plod on.'

'What he does'll no' detract from the rest of us. Just be an extension of it.'

He realises that his father has been suggesting they forget about his going to university and his mother is insisting that he will go. He feels strangely neutral about the question. He has thought about staying on at the brickwork. He has thought about taking up the place he has been offered at university. Both seem equally acceptable or unacceptable.

What intrigues him now, what holds him there – listening in the lobby with open-mouthed concentration – is the significance of the choice, not just for him. He realises, awesomely, that he is part of the quarrel that is the shared experience of his parents.

'Yer own father would have wanted him to go,' his mother says. 'He wanted you to go on at school.'

The silence is a man swallowing the bitter taste of his own past. Tam suddenly feels great compassion for his father. He remembers with sudden poignancy a moment he once shared with him. He thinks about himself there.

'THE COLLEGE,' his father says. 'You could go there.'

It is bright sunlight. His father is sitting on the step at the back door. He is dressed in old trousers, collarless shirt. Tam is standing maybe six feet away from him, between two of the clothes-poles on the back green. The clothes-poles are goalposts, for Tam is practising to be a goalkeeper. He has decided that he has discovered what he is going to be when he grows up. He will keep goal for Scotland's football team. He is nine.

He has just solemnly informed his father of his final decision about his future and the training that will lead to the fulfilment of the ambition has already begun. His father has unearthed the size-five leather stuffed with paper, which has recently replaced the paper balls bound with string Tam has been using for years to play football with him in the house. His father has been throwing the ball to Tam, varying the angles cunningly to test his reflexes. Tam has been diving in all directions with outrageous abandon, no matter how close the thrown ball comes to him.

He is sweating heavily since, in spite of the heat, he is wearing his yellow polo-necked sweater knitted by his Auntie Bella, for that is what goalkeepers wear. His short trousers are standing in for football pants. His black sandshoes give him a supernatural agility. His actions are compulsive as a dance to music no one else can hear. Indians did rain dances. His is a dance to the future, a series of twists and turns and mysterious acrobatic leaps in his improvised costume which will oblige to happen what he wants to happen. Self-absorbed as a dervish, he spins in the sunshine, whirling beyond Dawson Street. The back green becomes Hampden Park. The random noises of the day become the roar of the crowd. Somewhere in a certain future a radio commentator's voice is talking with urgent reverence.

'And Docherty makes another amazing save . . . I can't believe this . . . The crowd is going wild . . . Just listen to them . . . And again . . . And again . . . Now he is diving to the left . . . This is the most amazing goalkeeper I have ever seen . . .'

'Ye don't fancy being a centre forward?' his father is saying. 'They score the goals.'

Tam rejects the idea with an impatient shake of the head. It isn't just that he is too fiercely concentrated on the task of saving Scotland to deviate into speech. It is that one wrong ingredient may spoil the charm. What you wish for you must wish for utterly. They score the goals? 'Not against this amazing young goalkeeper, Docherty, they don't,' the commentator says.

'The college,' his father talks on while he patiently throws the ball to Tam and receives it back from him in a rhythm that becomes hypnotic, freezing a casual episode inexplicably into a shining moment that will stay with him.

NOW STANDING IN THE LOBBY ILLUMINED BY ANOTHER DAY, he feels the moment still turn dazzlingly in his mind, faceted and polished by memory, a diamond hewn from sunlight, an unbreakable image in which both of them are held, the man and the boy inextricably together.

'Ah made a choice,' his father says in the living-room, 'an' because of it Ah'm who Ah am. Ah'm sorry if Ah've disappointed ye. Maybe ye should've married an office worker. Or an insurance man. Would ye like me to go to night school?'

Tam hears the coldness of the distance that is between his parents. The living-room might as well be the Antarctic Ocean and them floating past on separate ice-floes. In this small house where they have all been living in such close proximity there has been such loneliness. How can such a small space encompass such isolation?

He would like to interrupt his parents and tell them that their positions have a false finality. For that day, playing with the ball, his father had spoken of university as if it were the promised land. He had made Tam see a wonderful place of great learning and fascinating conversations and sports. Out of his own ignorance of such places, he had created a blueprint for an ideal college. Where had that vision come from? Perhaps, it now seems to Tam, his father was not so much talking to him as dreaming an alternative life for himself. And in that dream his son had seen the possibility of his own life. It was his father who had first made Tam think, so long ago, of going to university.

Why had he done that? Why does he speak against it now? Was he then, in a moment of generous self-abnegation, inviting his son to conspire against him? I won't always be able to encourage such hope in you. Take this brief gift of openness and use it against me when you must. For I will close and it will be up to you to subvert my hopelessness with the hope I am giving you now.

Hearing his father try to close his future, Tam feels not the meanness of the present but the generosity of the past when his father sat that day dreaming, clumsily, like Plato on a step. In his personal hopelessness was multiplied the kindness of his giving of hope to Tam, a hope he could never share in. Tam sees the essence of his relationship with his father in that day.

'Conn,' his mother says in the living-room. 'Ye're as good a man as Ah know. Ah'm not askin' ye tae be different. But ye're less than ye can be. An' Ah am, too. Maybe that's what happens tae everybody. But we don't need deliberately tae arrange for it to happen to our weans.'

Tam remembers coming home from the dancing once to find his mother, the housework done, sitting by the fire reading the Rubaiyat. It wasn't the likeliest phenomenon where they came from. He is suddenly flooded with an awareness of the horizons his mother can still see, no matter how enclosed her circumstances. It seems to him a remarkable achievement. At the same time he understands his father's determined inhabiting of where he is. He feels love for both of them. The feeling makes him all the more certain that he must no longer be involved with Maddie.

HE STOOD IN FRONT OF MADDIE'S HOUSE. It wasn't her house now.

They had painted the woodwork of the windows yellow. A green Rover stood in the driveway. A young woman came out of the house in a blue sweater and black ski-pants. She was retrieving what looked like a small, leather weekend bag from the boot. She was attractive but not as attractive as her self-regarding manner suggested and not as attractive as Maddie. Maybe if she had been Garbo, she might just have got away with it. The haughtiness of her head suggested she was balancing something there. Maybe it was her bank account. With her hand on the raised boot, about to close it, she stared at the strange man standing across the street. She stared for maybe twenty seconds. She wanted him to know that she was staring. She closed the boot with vehemence and went back inside.

Don't phone the police, he thought. He was just a ghost passing through her life as she was a ghost passing through his. She wasn't to know that she was living in an important part of his past and him a compulsive revenant.

He hadn't intended to come here. When Michael's funeral was over he had gone back to his mother's with Marion and Allison and some people and they had talked for a while and he had left them there and come out for a walk. The walk had led him here without his being aware of it until the house ambushed him.

But he couldn't cross the street and go in as he had on that day of mental turmoil. What was it he really thought he was doing then? What had been his true intention? He would never know. He was returning the book, of course. But how necessary was that? She had invited him back anyway. And he also had in his inside pocket the poem he had written for her the day before. It wasn't exactly a demand that they part. He hated what he had done and he wanted not to do it again. He loved what he had done and he had an overwhelming desire to do it again. His memory, like a zoom lens, followed his past self across the road and up the driveway towards the door which, it had seemed to him, would open on to a bewildering confusion of possibilities.

'HHHHMMMMMMM,' she says. She has told him he must lie absolutely still, do nothing, say nothing. He must leave everything to her.

'Nice cock.'

You can *say* words like that? And the building doesn't fall about your ears? You don't have to lock them away in some dark drawer and bring them out only when you're alone at night?

She is saying them to *him*. The ectoplasmic woman whose features have always been blurred and shifting, for whom he has been writing and rewriting the script for years, trying to get it excitingly right, is here, solid with flesh. The hair that has graduated from blonde to brown to red to blonde has become vividly black, veined subtly with silver, experiential treasure. The wild and tumbling mass of darkness is more exciting than anything his imagination has ever conjured up.

The eyes that have been blue and brown and green are staring at him and they are olive now with weird shards of light in them that seem to find passing reflections of many other colours. Tunnelled with lust, they draw him into their disorientating dark.

The flesh is so sheer in close-up. The brown hollows of her slightly hunched shoulders seem as distant as valleys. The mole on her hanging right breast is monumental. The raised curve of her arse is part of a continent of body he feels he could spend the rest of his life exploring. He feels as if maybe he's seeing for the first time in his life. His eyes have found a true perspective. She defines his horizons.

And the mouth – curling with delicious wickedness, sometimes smiling abstractedly as if sharing a secret with another darker self, sometimes open and poised as if waiting for instructions only some distant part of her can hear, its lips writhing sensuously – ferociously soft, those muscular petals. And what it says.

'Nice cock.'

Her stiffened protruding tongue traces the length of it from where it is rooted in the shrub of hair to the pink, cleft tip of it.

'Sweet cock,' she says

She swings her breasts against it, letting their weight push it sideways until she raises herself and it springs erect again. She takes it gently in her hand.

'Look,' she says. 'You've finally come out to meet me.'

She looks up at him with savage gentleness.

'So this is who you are, shy boy. Pleased to meet you.'

As she bends again, her hair falls, obscuring everything but itself.

'Thomas,' she murmurs.

Then she flicks her hair into a new chaos through which her watching eyes look strangely disembodied, dryad in a dark wood.

'John Thomas.'

Her amusement is eerie, like laughter in a far room.

'John Thomas! You've read Lawrence?'

The name jars him the way an alarm clock would. There's another world besides the one he is in? Lawrence? Who the hell is that? Lawrence Sterne? He's heard of him. Is she so familiar with his stuff, she calls him by his first name? Lawrence of Arabia? A small and boring brain cell somewhere continues to concentrate on the problem, like some workaholic still at his desk while the office party is going full swing downstairs. D.H. Lawrence. By the time the answer arrives, there is no one there to receive it. He's glad he doesn't have to say no, he hasn't read him, except for *The Man Who Died*.

She is licking him again without taking her eyes off his face. Is she checking his expression? The way he feels, he can't imagine that he has one. His features appear to be floating on his face. He must look like anybody, or nobody.

'You look like Billy Budd,' she says.

What is this? The Graithnock Literary Appreciation Society's sexual outing? This at least is a reference he knows, the only book of Melville's he has read. It's lucky she didn't compare him to *Moby Dick*. The only thing he knows about that book is that the title sounds like a social disease. Billy Budd. Angelic. Beatific. (That's a good word.) That must be what she means. Well, given the right conditions, who can't look beatific?

THAT TIME WITH MADDIE, he would think, was probably when his adolescence ended. That afternoon was a crash course in growing up. Summertime was officially over. He learned that intensity of feeling doesn't automatically generate itself in the other and that making love doesn't necessarily mean making soul-mates. This surprised and saddened him.

His initial purpose of renouncing his feeling for Maddie had evaporated within seconds of entering the house. She kissed him at the door and led him to the bedroom. After two hours of making love in ways that had been unimaginable even to someone as imaginatively preoccupied with the subject as he was, he knew that they must spend the rest of their lives together. He explained this to her as they were drinking wine again at the yew table.

Smiling, she explained that she was married.

He understood that but they would tell Eddie together.

That was hardly necessary.

There couldn't be any way to keep it from him.

They wouldn't have to.

He didn't understand.

Eddie knew already.

He didn't understand.

She had spoken to him on the phone.

The muffled nature of that conversation had always haunted him, like attempts to communicate from different planets. And when the line finally cleared, the realisation was suddenly deafening. He sat with his love poem in his pocket and understood that this was something Maddie had done often enough before and would do often enough again. It was something Eddie agreed to. Strange rules they played by in the adult world.

His departure was not too fast, at least not as fast as he would have wanted it to be. At the door she had kissed him lightly on the cheek and her lips felt searing, as if they might burn that place and leave it for ever numb. She told him to keep the book as a memento of her but he couldn't imagine that he would.

HE WALKED ON, away from the house where she had lived. She died of a massive stroke before she was fifty. Allison had told him the news on the telephone. He was glad they weren't face to face or she might have noticed the effect her words were having on him, how personally he was taking her voice. Bright images of Maddie came and dimmed and everything seemed a little darker.

He had never given her the words he had written for her, his first, brief love poem. They were written on the back of a Monet painting of water-lilies, a page he had cut carefully from one of Michael's art books, hoping that Michael would never notice. As he walked home that day from her house, feeling stupid and infantile, he had taken the painting from his pocket and, without even glancing at his words, he tore it into very small pieces and dropped it in a litter-bin. But, if he had managed to erase the evidence of his embarrassing folly, he had never been able to erase the words from his memory.

> These water-flowers, as in a glass,
> Can watch their own brief beauty pass
> And envy you your loveliness
> That ages but does not grow less
> And cuts the heart as sharp as when,
> A woman new, you wounded men,
> Immortal dagger – mortal sheath—
> That brightens more the more you breathe.

Nor could he forget the few lines he had written a couple of days later, sitting alone in Michael and Marion's room feeling his life blighted by an insurmountable and unrequited love.

> In rooms where I shall never be
> She is. Each day's a perfect glass
> My breath can't fog and where
> The bright impossibilities beck and pass.
> I stroke the falling absence of her hair.

That must have been my mirror-and-breathing period, he thought.

HE WOULD STILL HAVE THE BOOK. He felt sure of that. He didn't think he had read it since that summer. For a time after Maddie had given it to him, it was all he read, again and again. It was very short. He loved the poetry but perhaps the intensity with which he read it over and over might have had something to do with trying to find Maddie Fitzpatrick in it, a breach by which feeling might get into her fortress of sophistication. It was certainly passionate poetry.

(Is she putting a secret key in his hand? Is she giving him a sign? Is he mad?)

It was strange that a book which had once meant so much to him hadn't been looked at again. Perhaps he had been afraid that opening the book would be like opening a wound and he might find blood on the pages. Certainly, the book had followed him around like an old letter resealed to quarantine its contents. It had been in his digs during his last year at university. It had been in the house Gill and he had had in Glasgow. Where was it now?

He sat staring at the painting Phil and Jane had put above the fireplace, a ship that looked becalmed. The Ancient Mariner's ship. Maybe they were trying to tell him something. Each his own albatross. He was sure the book must be here in Edinburgh.

Most of his books were still in the coalhouse of his mother's place in Graithnock, in boxes and plastic bags. They had been there for years, since Gill and he split up. He realised it was a ludicrous place to keep books but he hadn't been able to find anywhere else at the time and he had been moving around so much since then. Also, he had been able to raid the coalhouse occasionally for iron rations.

And, he had to admit, there seemed something genealogically appropriate in his storing his books in a coalhouse. Coal had been his father's chosen way of life. Books were his. There was a kind of symbolic continuity in the arrangement. He also had a strong suspicion that books were destined to become as marginal a form of social fuel as coal now was. For coal, read gas and electricity. For books, read television and the Internet. His chosen occupation was becoming, if not obsolete, a lot less central.

Most of the books he had brought with him were dumped in the spare bedroom of the flat, where Phil and Jane had put all the old furniture which had been Phil's mother's and which they hadn't worked out what to do with yet. He went through there. He felt a little guilty about pushing the debris of an old woman's life around – dusty lampshades, a small dresser, boxes of what looked like curtains, an old ribbed washing-board. A pram?

Phil and Jane had been very apologetic about not giving him the use of this room. What would he have done with it? Hire it out as a disco? He smiled as he thought of them. They didn't exactly fit the contemporary image of grasping landlords. Jane dropped in every so often to check that he was eating properly, bringing pots of homemade soup and food in cellophane, like Red Cross parcels. Phil arrived irregularly, not asking directly for the rent so much as making enquiries about whether he could afford it. There had never been the slightest question of raising the rent he paid.

He had almost given up when he saw, at the bottom of a box, the three gilt faces embossed on the brown cover of the thin book – Pushkin, Lermontov, and Tyutchev. Three friends from an old summer. He lifted the book, amazed at how light it was, and went through to the living-room.

The first shock of the old was the number of pages: fifty-six, a continent of imagined experience in a microchip. Then there was the simplicity of the title page: Pushkin, Lermontov, Tyutchev. Poems. Lindsay Drummond Limited, London 1947. Then it was the drawings by Donia Nachsen, endearingly corny. They looked like woodcuts. But the greatest surprise was to see the words. 'Translated from the Russian by Vladimir Nabokov'. He had no memory of that. The name had meant nothing to him at the time. It was as if he had met someone famous before he was famous and was only now realising that they were the same person. In the introductions to the poets he thought he could catch echoes of that familiar later tone of aristocratic eccentricity.

He read the poetry again, cover to cover. His favourites then were his favourites now. Was that a good sign or a bad? Youthful perceptiveness or a failure to mature? Maybe it was yet another example of repeated behaviour. But that's how it was. Pushkin's 'Exegi Monumentum' ('Not all of me is dust. Within my song/Safe from the worm, my spirit will survive.') Tyutchev's 'The Journey', which seemed to him now like some darker, Russian cousin of Frost's 'Stopping by Woods on a Sunday Evening' – darker because it was less philosophically civilised than Frost's poem. And, best of all, was Lermontov's 'The Triple Dream', so passionate and so controlled.

He sat, after two in the morning, remembering how much this book had meant to him and wondering if even the way people read had changed. Was that possible? He seemed to have been reading all his life towards a sense of continuity, a desire to find what stays true of our lives. Perhaps that was why he could still remember phrases of these poems after all this time. He suspected that more and more people read as an end in itself, something you did that was expressive of the moment and nothing more. The ability to make lasting judgments was disintegrating. Books were becoming process, not event, fashion not identity, market not morality. Or had it always been like that and his belief in something more just his personal mirage?

He decided to go to bed. He was tired and couldn't make up his mind if times really changed or if, through aging, we simply lost our ability to engage with them, locked ourselves in a past to which the present couldn't gain entry unless it had a ticket of admission it couldn't have, since it was out of date.

He lay, thinking that for him the key to any serious understanding of life must lie in some kind of unity between the present
and the past, a marriage of equals. He wondered despairingly if
he would ever find such a key.

MYTHIC REALISM (he would write): a way rationally to depict
the irrationality of experience. Since we can't escape the mind,
we must find a way to use its own power against it. Mind is the
tyrant that never abdicates. Even in madness it will remain the
lunatic director and judge of all we do. Like a Chinese emperor
who has no serious perception of what is happening even in the
adjoining chambers of his court, it will presume to judge and
pretend to control an empire of experience vast beyond human
imagining. We must never accept its assumptive authority but
constantly challenge it with the intractable realities of our lives.
While mind seeks to vet our behaviour, the mind itself must be
always on probation and must give itself up constantly to have its
own behaviour vetted. The mind must be used always partly as
a neutralising agent against itself so that it does not merely give
us a self-defining cerebral version of ourselves but may restore
to us, by acknowledging its limitations, our total nature, which
is our only absolute and which, by the fact of being living, must
remain a continuing mystery. The key to that depiction lies in the
subversion of time, the ultimate tyrant. If we could escape every
accident or evil which life may offer, time would still try to define
us finally by eroding us to death through the sheer exercise of its
own power. Time means death and death is our final enemy, the
apparently unconquerable. When the rational mind accepted the
authoritativeness of historical time, it volunteered for oblivion.
But what if time past and place past are not merely past? What if
they live still? What if what has happened still happens in some
way, its essence resurrected in other places, other times? Then
we will live on in one another, transubstantiated each into us
all, ego marrying into species. That was the dark and awesome
power myth knew, the defeat of the gods, the Promethean theft
of eternal fire. Chronological time is monolithic but mythic time

is relative. Whoever has lived will live on in us whether we want them to or not. The gods may be there for all we know and we will parley with their imagined presences but, deceitful as they are, we can outwit them. We will survive without their intercession. The mythic hero teaches us that we are more than time would have us be. Myth is the story of humanity learning to become itself. To partake of time is to be always a part of it. To embrace evanescence utterly is to be humanly immortal. Who were the most alive are the least dead.

He looked up suddenly from the white, bobbled paper of the table napkin on which he was writing. He saw three separate couples at three different tables in the restaurant, staring at him. One couple were apparently discussing him with some concern. The others seemed to be sitting in four separate amazements, too stunned as yet to share the bizarreness of what they were seeing.

He wondered why. Then he realised with a shock that he was on his fifth napkin. The other four lay covered with his hieroglyphics on the table around him. The pursuit of what he had thought was a significant insight had driven him through acceptable social behaviour like a runaway horse. For the first time, he was conscious that the people in the restaurant must have seen him get up four times and go to the adjoining table, set for four but unoccupied, and steal a napkin. Thank God he was finished for the moment or he might have found himself grabbing extra napkins out of people's hands. He was briefly and irrationally annoyed with the waiter for clearing the cutlery and the three napkins from his own table because he was eating alone. Worse than the man from Porlock. O Philistine, thou wouldst steal the paper from beneath the writer's hand.

He was momentarily so embarrassed that he almost wiped his lips with the last napkin and crumpled it up, as if the purely practical action might erase their belief in what they had seen. But the impulse didn't last long. That would be taking social conformity a bit too far. Instead, he gathered his five napkins like Sybil's leaves and arranged them in order of writing. As discreetly as he could, he slipped them into his inside pocket. But his dark and unnatural action was observed. He had revealed himself to all as that worst of social misfits, a secret napkin-writer.

One of the women in particular, the one who had been seemingly talking about him, looked positively outraged. Attractive and middle-aged, she was more or less making a display of her attentiveness, as if she wanted him to know that she knew what he had been up to. She was also glancing round the restaurant, whether seeking support from a lynch-mob or wanting to complain to the management, he couldn't tell.

He wondered what she thought he was. An eavesdropper kinky for other people's conversations? But he was too far away from everybody else to hear what they were saying and in her case he was glad. A stringer for a good-food guide? A modern revolutionary equivalent of Marx in the British Museum? A hopeless neurotic let out of his institution for the day?

The last one was maybe not so far away. How unneurotic was it to sit in an Italian restaurant in Hanover Street and write on napkins about how history is a decadent form of mythology? People had been taken away for less.

No wonder he often felt alienated from the lives of others. He often felt alienated from his own life. He was sometimes surprised when people recognised him as someone they knew.

'I HOPE YOU'LL FORGIVE ME, TOM,' the voice said. 'I fully appreciate you're a man endeavouring to have a quiet beverage.'

He looked up. It was Sanny Wilson.

'I would never wish to intrude on a person's privacy. God knows it's rare enough in these troubled times to find a halcyon moment.'

It didn't take Tom long to remember one of the basic mechanisms of Sanny's nature. If you met him when he was sober, Sanny might say, 'Aye, Tom.' If you met him several whiskies into a night, he was more likely to say something like, 'Hail, Tom. And where have your peregrinations taken you this evening?' He seemed to drink out of a thesaurus. This Sunday afternoon he must already be approaching zed.

'I'm also cognisant of your present sad situation. Michael

was a prince among paupers. And your grief is no doubt commensurate with such a sad loss. Therefore, I am naturally hesitant to intrude.'

'Sanny,' Tom said. 'What is it?'

'There's a gentleman at the end of the bar deeply desirous of making your acquaintance. I said I would enquire re your state of mind. Apropos confabulation with a stranger.'

'Certainly, Sanny. No problem. Tell him to come down.'

'Gracious as ever. I shall instruct him accordingly, Tom.'

With his right hand, Sanny made a gesture towards Tom, almost like a papal blessing, and moved back up the pub. The Bushfield was busy with lunchtime drinkers. The man who emerged from the ruck at the end of the bar was someone Tom had noticed earlier, talking to Sanny. At one point he had left the bar briefly and returned, carrying a small holdall, which he still held as he came towards Tom. The holdall was ominous.

'Hullo there,' the man said, and shook hands.

He sat down without introducing himself. He was middle-aged and balding, with a slightly disconcerting fixity in the eyes. He had put the holdall at his feet. Tom assumed that the calculated brusqueness of his manner was a way of making it clear that he wasn't exactly impressed by meeting Tom. But then nobody had assumed he would be. Tom began to feel as if he was the one who had asked for the conversation. He began to feel that, as Sanny might have said, the omens were not propitious.

'Well,' the man said. 'Ah've been wanting to meet you for some time.'

'Oh.' That seemed safe enough.

'Aye,' the man said. 'Ye're not very highly thought of in Onthank.'

Onthank was a district in the north of Graithnock.

'Sorry?'

'Ah'm sayin'. They don't think too much of you in Onthank.'

'Why would that be?'

'Well, we've got a writers' club up there. And you've never been to visit us.'

The fixed stare might as well have had a judge's wig round it.

'Actually, you're wrong,' Tom said. 'I've been to Onthank

Writers' Club. Did a reading. Answered questions for an hour and a half, two hours.'

The eyes were still in no mood for an acquittal.

'Well, Ah wasn't there,' the man said.

'Well,' Tom said. 'Ah don't really think that's my problem, is it?'

Some strangers are stranger than others, Tom thought.

'Anyway,' the man said. 'How would you go about getting a novel published?'

'Well, first of all, you would write it.'

The man was staring at him.

'Ah mean, you've written a book?'

The man smiled. He reached down and Tom had never before realised what a dread sound the unzipping of a holdall could be. He couldn't believe it was happening but it was. The man took out about six or seven pages of handwritten words and passed them to Tom. What was he supposed to do? Put them on the table in front of him and genuflect? He was supposed to read them. The man was waiting. Instinctively, since he carried his spectacles in his left-hand inside pocket, Tom patted the right-hand side of his jacket. The jacket pluffed emptily beneath his hand.

'Sorry,' he said. 'I haven't brought the bins with me.'

He was congratulating himself on quick thinking when the man took the sheets back and started to read aloud.

'It was raining in Copenhagen when Manson's flight came in. Gustavsen wasn't there to meet him. This could mean one of two things. This was a double-cross. Or Gustavsen was dead . . .'

Lucky Gustavsen. There were people shouting orders at the bar, two men were playing the fruit machine, piped music surrounded them, the multiple conversations sounded like the monkey-house at the zoo. And a man was reading the first six pages of his novel to him. There were no books of etiquette that told you how to handle this. Tom had a poignant moment when he noticed what could have been beer or coffee stains on some of the pages. He thought of the lonely compulsiveness of his own attempts to write. The man was in full flow now, locked into the compulsive readability of his own words.

'Excuse me,' Tom said. 'Excuse me.'

It took a moment for the man to pause and drag his eyes irritably away from the page.

'I'm sorry. But this is hopeless. I can't hear you. I mean, this is a pub we're in.'

The man stared at him and shook his head slowly and sadly. He put the sheets back in the holdall and zipped it shut. He stood up, carrying the holdall. He looked down at Tom.

'You are an arrogant bastard,' he said.

'Sure,' Tom said. 'And you must visit Planet Earth some time. It'll make a change for you.'

The man stormed out. Tom was aware of the people looking at him, perhaps wondering how badly he had behaved towards the man to make him leave like that. Thank you, Sanny Wilson. You can't disown your past without becoming no one. But there can come a time when your past disowns you. This could be one of those times. A bad day at the Bushfield.

He had already had some bad moments before the arrival of the manic novelist. He had met Ted Hayes. The meeting had been blessedly brief. Ted and the man he was with had had to get back to Ted and Sandra's, where the man and his wife had been invited for a meal. The thought of several hours trapped at table with Ted seemed to Tom a dangerous prospect, during which the will to live might be lost. Sunday lunch with the Borgias. Hearses at four.

Since Gill and Tom had gone to Grenoble, Ted had suffered a heart attack. He was apparently fully recovered and Tom was glad for him. But, listening to Ted, it again struck Tom how much crap was talked about the transforming effect near-death experiences had on people. It was his sense of it that, once the danger was over, most people became even more confirmed in the natures they had had.

(Yea, though I walk through the valley of the shadow of death yet shall I change not a whit. For my prejudices are with me and mine adamantine self-satisfaction that is an hugeness nought can diminish and they comfort me. And though death rage at mine ear and the fire burn with great noise yet shall I emerge therefrom as big a shit as in I went.)

In Ted's case, it seemed to Tom, this meant that he had become a bigger bore than ever. Never mind articulated lorries, he could now tell you his experience of the big one. It was a subject that would last him all his life. It was all they talked about in the brief time they had together. Michael's death became an excuse for Ted to describe to them in endless detail how he had *nearly* died. He had finally discovered the theme that allowed him to make an art-form of his boringness, to become mind-numbingly self-absorbed. He had turned himself into an oral *Finnegans Wake*. And Finnegan was still alive. Even the final point of the boringness didn't exist. Hell is Ted Hayes.

And then he saw Sammy Clegg peering in the window.

'Jesus,' somebody said. 'A Clegg on the horizon. Sew up your pockets. Look at 'im. Like a piranha checkin' out an aquarium.'

When Sammy came in, Tom understood the remark. He bummed a drink off Tom and one other person. Then he left, presumably to prospect pastures new. Their attempted conversation had been nothing. Once Sammy had the drink from him, he had nothing else to ask of him. Tom felt sad. All that sweet innocence of the past had converted to cynicism. What the world did to people.

One man he had met before he came to sit alone had redeemed a little the darkness of his thoughts, infiltrated them with a faint light. His name was John Kellner. He was an Englishman who had lived in Graithnock in the twenties and travelled a lot since then and come back to Graithnock in old age. His talk of the values he had found here and which had brought him back had brightened Tom's day briefly.

But, sitting alone and reflecting on John Kellner's words, Tom had saddened again. He sensed those values under constant erosion all around him. Michael's death began to feel for him like the end of more than a private era. The lessons of previous generations in solidarity and mutual concern were being forgotten.

IT'S NOT TRUE THAT WE LEARN FROM OUR MISTAKES. If we did, he would be wiser than the British Museum. He'd made enough of them.

He lay in bed at Warriston and wondered why he never seemed to learn. Not just him. The world itself was a fair old dunce. Look at Britain. For the last fifteen years or so it had been rushing forward into the nineteenth century. He couldn't believe how quickly a largely decent society had been conditioned to prey on itself. The misgivings he had felt that day in the Bushfield had hardened into bleak realities. One woman, with all the vision of a soldier ant, had managed to screw up the UK. Dehumanisation by statute. There is no such thing as society. A self-fulfilling idiocy.

He supposed, in the face of that, you should at least try to continue to live on your own terms. He had been doing that. But he was being ambushed by the same old patterns of behaviour. What did you do to cure that? Even that thought was itself a repeated pattern.

He had been here before often enough. He remembered being here when Brian and Elspeth Alderston had gone home after the night of the Sandra Hayes beauty contest.

Brian had started to lecture him paternally about his behaviour. It seemed that he lacked self-control, that he was hypersensitive, that he should learn to take things more easily. He wasn't too receptive. He wasn't in the mood for a lecture. He rarely was. He hated monologues – better a dialogue of any kind, even spears of hurt hurled at each other. At least what Gill and he had been up to was some form of life, however undomesticated. Brian sounded like a recording of a gravestone, everything settled, neatly buried in certainty.

Tom told him so. He told him that doubt was the most fructifying thing in the world and that, by that criterion, Brian's head was a desert. There was more of the same.

THE EVENING DIDN'T SO MUCH COME TO AN END AS IT BROKE UP. Tom had the impression Gill didn't feel things had gone well. Not that she said. The evening went into its coda, one of those haunting adagio movements you seem to have experienced a thousand times, in which you imagine you can maybe hear an echo of your own dying. Gather ye debris while ye may. Collect the sticky glasses. Put the uneaten peanuts in the bin. Make a formal composition of the scattered furniture. He aimlessly rearranged some apples in a bowl. It is the apple we didn't eat that poisons us to death. He felt that residual taste of malice in his mouth from bad things said. His rage had turned to acid in his guts.

They were both in bed before Gill spoke, with a Grand Canyon of cold space between them. She lay on her usual left-hand side of the bed. His eyes were open towards the curtains, a negative of their pattern showing in the light from the lamp-post outside. The room had a dim, subaqueous glow. It was one of those moments when night-thoughts scull among their own strange, sunless vegetation.

They might as well have been lying exhausted on the shore of their separate desert islands, watching the wreckage of their dreams float in the bay. So many ambitions shared, so much time travelled to be lying here in mutual loneliness. Any attempt to communicate had as much hope of arriving as a message in a bottle. But Gill was trying.

'I still don't believe it,' she said.

The stillness took her quiet voice without a ripple.

'I don't believe it. Why? That's all I ask. Then we can leave it. Why?'

He let the question pass him by like someone he didn't recognise.

'Nobody would believe that. Out of nothing. The man was just giving his opinion. You attacked him like a mugger. He's your headmaster. That's all. That's all I'm asking. Just tell me why? Then I'll take my overdose and you can get some sleep.'

He thought that maybe the question wasn't entirely unrecognisable. It had the kinship of impossibility with so many of the questions we ask each other. It was a mutant relative of that question people in love ask, 'What are you thinking?', though it was a long time since they had asked each other that one.

'Oh boy,' Gill said. 'I thought Elspeth was going to have a heart attack. Did you notice her face? You bastard. You nearly gave her a cardiac arrest. What gives you the right to do that to people?'

She was right. For too long now he had been disrupting what

were supposed to be pleasant social occasions with noisy opinions, sometimes roughly clad in swear-words – John the Baptist of the sitting-room.

'Your headmaster. And you come on like Tarzan of the Apes. What must they have thought? Why?'

He was doing things he no longer believed in, he thought. Perhaps that was it, or at least part of it.

'Don't tell me. I really don't want to know. I couldn't stand to listen to one of your boring lectures about working-class life. Still, maybe it would put me to sleep.'

He recognised a familiar tactic, the calculated use of insult to provoke a response. He reflected dispassionately that it was one of Gill's favourite techniques to attribute to him something so out of context that he would deny it and she would have him involved in one of those interminable exchanges of inaccurate venom, dance of the blind, spitting cobras.

'All he does is write a report about you every year.' Returning to the theme of 'career consolidation', she had left him behind. He was still thinking of what she had said earlier. 'All you did was volunteer for a letter-bomb. Maybe when we come back from France you can get a job helping the janitor.'

The silence reformed like icicles in the air. They lay back to back, book-ends with no books. The gathered significance of their relationship was emptiness.

It's not that the evening with the Alderstons was so significant in itself. In the scale of his life's failures it ranked small. It was simply when it came. The last step of a pilgrimage is no different from any other but after it you know that you've arrived. He had reached some sort of destination, some terminus of exhaustion. So had Gill. No matter how long it took them to admit it to each other, they both knew that they eventually went different ways from here.

He lay working on and abandoning makeshift maps. Career was out. Career had always been out. He didn't believe in turning the sequential mystery of his days into currency and buying his future in bulk.

He had a sudden memory of standing on the steps of Glasgow University Union, haranguing a group of his friends. It was not as bad as it sounded, though maybe nearly. They had been walking down from a lecture. Their final examinations were near and they had all been talking about what they were going to do, the jobs they might get.

He had an irresistible vision of potential being wasted. He had spent several years among these friends. They had sat at tables in the Union café while countless afternoons peeled from the calendar like a 'time passing' sequence in an old film. They had converted one another to many crazy ideas of the moment, sung choruses to the genius of Shakespeare, vast as the steppes, been unable to believe the stupidity of some literary criticism, while the spilled coffee fused the cups to the saucers. They had conjured up so many dangerous ideas that the haze from their cigarettes had sometimes seemed to him like the smoke-trail of a summoned devil. They had lived inside one another's heads so much that they often came out on to the street not knowing who was who. The sense those meetings always engendered was of so many things to be done, of almost infinite potential.

Yet here they were approaching the place where their minds had been broadened to continents, and approaching for near enough the last time, and they were discussing which village of the spirit they would spend their lives in. A few were going to be teachers. One was going into industrial management. One – O Marco Polo, lives thy spirit still? – was thinking of being a journalist.

He couldn't take it. There, on the steps of the Union, his vision cleft him. In the not quite blinding Glasgow sunlight, he stood and spoke. (Perhaps not just lately but all his life he'd been auditioning for John the Baptist.) It must have been a strange sight to a passer-by: a group clustered unevenly around the steps with briefcases while one of them, tall and lean and with his own briefcase abandoned at his feet, demanded they be true to themselves, frothing with urgency. He didn't say 'the end is nigh', although that's largely what he meant. His idea was that there was a conformist fate in store for all of them – to be devoured by their own unacknowledged reality – if they succumbed to social pressures. He had some effect. They all trooped into the Union, brooding on the need not to become stereotypes.

Then he went into teaching. He didn't go into teaching in the same way as everybody else did, of course. He had a secret plan, infallibly cunning. He would only teach for two years, during which time, making effective use of his weekends and such evenings as he wasn't out on the skite looking for girls, he would write a masterpiece and the world would beat a path to his door. The plan didn't work.

There were several reasons for this, he thought. First of all, the world took a wrong turning. He did finish a novel of some forty thousand words but nobody would publish it. A few publishers made encouraging noises which kept him fairly buoyant for a time until he realised all that the noises translated into was 'write something else'.

Secondly, he discovered to his amazement that he liked teaching. He had entered the profession with no missionary zeal whatsoever. The fools – didn't they realise who had come among them? Were the tweed jacket and slacks enough of a disguise to delude them? But within a month or two he realised this was something he could do and that tended to be a seductive realisation. He remembered passing the boys' cloakroom and hearing two third-year boys who had just been in his class when he taught Saki's 'The Open Window'. 'Jesus Christ,' one of them said. 'That was one terrific period.' 'The best,' the other replied. 'I'm for another read at that story the night.' He decided not to chastise them for swearing. Who knows what accidental, drifting feathers of experience land to add their weight to decisions that affect our entire lives?

Thirdly, he had met Gill. He was in Graithnock railway station, waiting for a train to Glasgow on a late Saturday afternoon. He was going to the dancing at the University Union. He hadn't been back there since he started teaching and he fancied casting the mature eye of a man of the world upon the scenes of his youth. He was talking to a porter he knew since he had spent a summer there working as a temporary porter himself. He had borrowed his cap to try it on, mainly because he felt a porter's cap made him look like Marlon Brando in *The Wild One*. A girl was walking towards the barrier, fair, well breasted and wearing the stiletto heels of all his fantasies. O foolish man, is that all it takes? On impulse, he smiled at her and said, 'Excuse me, madam. Carry your ticket?' It was so witty he was crying still.

It wasn't that he blamed Gill for any failure of ambition or for his not writing more. You takes your choices and you pays in blood. It was perhaps just that marriage has a hard way with those delicate reaches of the self where creativity grows, those inexplicable feelings that we have no names for – those vagrants of our social conditioning that sleep in the doorways of the heart and the empty spaces of the mind, accosting our preoccupations without warning. He found that marriage kept shaking its head at them: sorry, nothing to spare. When Megan and Gus came along, those vagrants were even less tolerable. Time seemed to chase them away with sticks. He had always been determined that nobody connected with him should suffer because of his writing ambitions. The compulsion to write was his, not theirs. But that determination had taken its toll. He wondered if it had reached its limit.

It had brought him to this bed where he lay feeling as if there wasn't enough of him left to spread on a sandwich. He suspected from Gill's breathing that she was asleep. He stared at the curtains, their pattern archipelagos of boringly regular islands in the lamplight, and he pondered the morality of where he was. Being a proselytising agnostic (what other position is humanly tenable?), the only source of morality he could find was existential honesty. He knew why he had let his ambitions withdraw whenever they encroached on his family's lives, threatening to rule them. He had seen the wilful control of anybody else's life as immoral because it was an existential lie against your knowledge of your own weakness, your certain death. It was like abrogating God. But that night, like the other side of the moon, there loomed up before him the converse of that principle. What of the point at which concern for others becomes erosion of the truth of self, denial of self-need? He thought maybe he was lying now at this point.

He remembered the story of St Martin and the beggar. St Martin was travelling on horseback through a storm. A beggar appeared before him, clad only in a loincloth, asking for covering. St Martin took his cloak from his back, divided it in two with his sword, threw the beggar half of his cloak and galloped on. Later, at an inn, St Martin sees the beggar, who is Jesus. Jesus tells him he did well. It would have been false charity to give away all his cloak. He had been true to his own needs as well as those of the beggar.

He felt the truth of the story as strongly as if it had ridden through the bedroom. What could you give your children if there was nothing of you left? As it was, he couldn't be sure that there was any of him left. Perhaps he was already too late. Dozing fitfully, he kept surfacing into terror. Every time he woke, another monster of despair blocked the path of his desire effectively to find himself.

Was he drinking dangerously too much? He certainly had considerable expertise in swallowing the stuff. It had become a kind of three-string fiddle for his various moods: beer for bearing the banal, wine for the trivial convivial, but whisky for soul talk. They reckoned you never knew when you were becoming an alcoholic. Also, the search for himself he was vaguely planning would put even more pressure on his already frazzled nerves. Could he withstand the pain without the aid of some familiar anaesthetic? One of the signs of alcoholism was wild behaviour. He surely fulfilled that requirement. But then he had fulfilled it, as far as he was aware, since his teens, when he hardly drank at all. And the dark, sub-cranial journey he saw as becoming necessary – could the hero undertake that lonely task without some magic potion by his side? No. Fidus Achates in a bottle, come with me. He would maintain his friendship with the dancing juice for now. He could handle it. It would be all right. Rest, rest, perturbed spirit. Behold the ceiling.

His frazzled nerves? That was true. It had been true for some time. Was he going through an unofficial nervous breakdown? That sounded possible. Presumably you didn't have to be staring at the same wall for ten days or coming on like a Pentecostalist to be having a nervous breakdown. There must be subtle forms, as there were subtle forms of cancer that were only discovered a fortnight before you died. Anyway, lately he had done enough mad things to fill a psychiatric ward. What about when he was dancing with Flora Benson at the school disco? 'What are you thinking?' she had shouted intimately. 'I'm thinking I'd like to fuck you,' he had whisperingly bellowed back. Incredibly, instead of summoning the constabulary, she had smiled, raising her eyebrows, and screamed, 'I like your style.' He had subsequently been avoiding her eyes in the staff-room as they tracked him like laser beams. How could that be sane? And if he was going mad, how could he ever hope to find the sense of himself he was looking for? How do you make a journey of the mind when the mind is a warren of contradictions? But then how could he so logically work that out if he was cracking up? No. He was all right in the head – so far. But he wouldn't remain so if he didn't get some sleep. Sometimes if you rolled your eyes up under the closed lids, it helped you to lose consciousness.

A psychiatric ward? Perhaps he needed psychoanalysis. No, that was something he wasn't having. His reading of old Sigmund had left him with unassuageable misgivings in that area. His hackles had risen steadily, page by page. He admired Freud as a brave man fighting against the shit his society gave out but he couldn't help feeling that he took the shit too seriously. Much had been made of the fact that his observations were largely drawn from the behaviour of neurotics. What was more important, it seemed to him, was that they were bourgeois neurotics. In other words, they were recruited from that part of society which took most seriously external morality, the social forms, which came closest to finding the definition of itself in current mores. Therefore, they were those who feel most strongly the failure to conform, to measure up to the norm. When you thought of some of the trivial things that gave those poor sods neuroses, you wondered why they bothered coming out of the womb.

('I don't think I'll bother, Mummy. It's all too distasteful.')

Even the cures, assuming there were any, he was suspicious of. Events create a temporary truth. You become your role in the event. Just as the process by which you examine a phenomenon can affect the phenomenon or limit its truth, so the means by which you comprehend experience are condemned to be another experience in themselves. You don't escape from process. Because of that, he saw psychoanalysis as the induction of a kind of rational hysteria, precipitating a compulsive role. It created a theatre in which 'reality' could posture. No, he decided, it was just another part of social conditioning, and that's what he was trying to escape. No psychoanalysis. His neuroses were his own. That was one thing sorted out anyway. Now maybe he could get to sleep.

And no career. A career is a poor substitute for a life. All right, careerless sane man who will never be psychoanalysed. Let's bed down here. He dozed again.

But how did he make his inner journey? With his ubiquitous agnosticism, what guides could he possibly have? He doubted the success of human relationships. That was the main impulse behind the need for the journey. He had no religion or, if he did, it wasn't nameable. He didn't trust psychoanalysis. He didn't trust philosophy. In his teens he had written:

> Philosophers have talked but we
> Are only people and must be.

Philosophy had always seemed to him to be like letters on a headstone, at best a description of the corpse of truth. He wanted to live with it. He suspected history as a kind of decadent mythology. Perhaps only art answered, the honest fictionalising of himself.

With Gill asleep, he stared around the dimness of the room. Only one guide hovered phantom-like in the gloom. It was himself, whoever he honestly was, not fully shaped, shifting and insubstantial, as unable to merge with the recumbent figure on the bed as that figure was unable to merge with it. Between the two a long way lay. He had to travel it. His guide was himself. When the certainties outside perish – he made his motto – you must scour yourself to the bone and find them there.

EACH OF US REMAKES THE WORLD WE LIVE IN, he would think. But in his case, he sometimes thought, the process had turned into an assembly-line of replica experience. From cottage industry to Henry Ford.

He lay insomniac at Warriston as he had lain insomniac that night with Gill. The most significant difference he could see was that this time he lay alone. Was that progress or regress? It certainly didn't *feel* like progress. Separate insomnias, please. *Une nuit blanche.* He liked that French expression. A white night. The problem with insomnia was that you couldn't switch the light off in your head. There were too many things you'd rather not look at. But you couldn't avoid them. And at this time of the morning every mote in the mind's eye had pretensions to be a Zeppelin. You saw an Andes of molehills.

In the glare he realised that old griefs were still with him. You didn't live beyond them, you just found out how to live round them. They were like bad lodgers you learned to accommodate. In that repeated scouring of himself, he had yet again been trying to rebuild his world around them. Wasn't that what everybody had to do in the light of changing experience? To live in the world was to remake it daily.

Even our parents, he thought. In a way, we are all our own parents. Just as they create us, we recreate them. The choice of materials we have to work with in that act of recreation may be limited. If our parents are cruel to us, for example, honesty should forbid us from turning them into saints. But even here the inventiveness of the human spirit in rendering malleable what may seem to be intractable experience could be quite remarkable. Just as he had known parents who seemed to him to have tried with every observable sinew of their nature to parent well and had seen them condemned as parental failures by their grown-up children, so he had known adult children take a mother or a father – whose selfishness differed from the act of Thyestes in eating his own offspring only in that they did it in the full knowledge of what they were doing – and transform them into a revered object of nostalgic love.

He supposed what happens is that, out of the almost infinite complexity of parental behaviour, we choose those elements we need to reaffirm our sense of ourselves. We choose, within the limitations we are offered, the parents we need, to effect a birth beyond our physical selves into our spiritual selves.

Perhaps not the least horror of child abuse was that it crippled the child's freedom of choice of spiritual parenthood. It demonised the child's sense of his or her own origins. It left the child with only broken and rotten materials with which to attempt the utterly necessary process of constructing the individual reality of being for herself or himself. It left the child's nature to some extent stillborn.

Outside of that abyss, which none could fully know but those who had to live in it, the rest of us were as responsible for our parents as they were for us. Most parents needed our forgiveness as we needed theirs. What we made of them was what we would become.

That was why he despised the contemporary fashion for grown-up children to wail against their parents, to exaggerate imperfection into abuse, to blame their individual problems on 'dysfunctional' families. All human beings were dysfunctional. Otherwise, they wouldn't die. If there was a God, depend on it: if this was His universe, He was dysfunctional, too. Perception is a choice.

You had to take responsibility for your own experience and not be intimidated by the abstractions others might try to impose on its reality. All his life, he had to admit, he had probably been writing letters in his head to an unknown woman. No doubt psychologists could have had a field day with that impulse in him – emotional inadequacy, inability to sustain a mature relationship, prolonged adolescence. If he thought they were wrong, one reason was because he believed he had had relationships as full as any psychologist had had.

Relationships that endured to the death could be impressive but they might merit more than sanctimonious paeans to the true nature of love. They might merit also questions. Constancy was a portmanteau in which could sometimes be found, among other things, the senile decay of habit, the drug of comfort, the fear of change.

He believed in fidelity. But final fidelity required some kind of final arrival. He was still travelling.

If the journey seemed to repeat itself at times, perhaps that fact wasn't of purely negative significance. There were two ways to see repeated behaviour, it seemed to him. It could mean that you merely repeated initially learned responses in subsequent situations that did not justly evoke them but had them superimposed through habit. Or it could mean that your initial response was a kind of primal discovery of your true instinctual self (before rationalisation) and, therefore, was something which you continued justly to obey. Your continued failures might not be merely personal but an expression of the failure of your experience to match what your nature needed. It remained possible that your refusal to accept might be the truth of your experience, the most honest expression of yourself. To cure you of yourself was a way of killing yourself. Why should the definitive actions of your nature be regarded as necessarily a limitation of that nature? They were just as likely to be its ultimate expression.

The attempted discovery of a new self appeared to him a good way to lose yourself and pretend to be someone else. The best you could do was to redynamise who you were, not try to reinvent it. Not who were you but what would you do with who you were, how would you use it, with what honesty, what integrity, what justice? Not where do you come from but where are you travelling to? You had to keep travelling. He would.

(Dear Saint Simeon Stylites,
Please cancel my order for a pillar. And oblige.)

HE SAT IN THE TRAIN from Graithnock to Glasgow, on the first stage of his return journey to Grenoble. He was moving from the certainty of Michael's death towards the uncertainty of his future with Gill and Megan and Gus. The familiar names of the stations they stopped at renewed in him an old innocence.

SITTING BLEARY-EYED AT BREAKFAST, he feels a slight pain in his ribs. This is a strange part of a strange day. He was wakened by his mother at six in the morning, an achievement roughly equivalent to resurrecting a corpse.

'Ma ribs are murder, Mither,' he says.

'They will be, son. Ah had tae punch ye tae get ye wakened. Where is it you go when you sleep? Anither planet?'

He eats the ham and eggs slowly, gradually re-evolving to the stage of being able to masticate. It is still dark. The brightness of the familiar kitchen seems somehow poignant, a banal Eden from which growing up is expelling him. The gas cooker is lit and its door has been left open, deputising for a heater. He remembers how often he sat at that lit cooker in the evenings when he was at school, doing his homework. He learned a lot of Greek verbs here, French phrases, the history of the Restoration. He read *Far from the Madding Crowd* in this room and here he was stolid, dependable Gabriel Oak and rakish Sergeant Troy and haunted Boldwood and here he fell abstractly in love with Bathsheba Everdene.

Here he discovered, unexpectedly, that his favourite homework was translating Livy. He used to take a sensuous pleasure in opening the book at the next passage for translation and having his jotter and pencil ready and his Latin dictionary and the piece of scrap paper where he would try to decipher the nuances of what Livy was telling him. Everything else would recede to a far place: the endless, only sometimes unpleasant argument that was his family, the hard, frosty streets of Graithnock, the wondering who he would be when he grew up, the dreams of beautiful and compassionate and understanding women, the goals he would score for Scotland.

There would be only him and the words and the ghostly, shifting presence of a man called Livy. He would make sure of literal meanings first. Then he would wait, doodling variants on the scrap paper. What was Livy *really* saying? He would coax the strange words towards a modern idiom. It amazed him how thrilling it could be. He was conversing with a dead man. When it worked and he thought he could hear Livy talking in a modern voice, he felt such awe, as if he were a necromancer. For there, in the kitchen of a council housing scheme in Graithnock, transubstantiated across almost two thousand years, was a Roman. He felt as if he could have touched his toga.

But, washing down the ham and eggs and buttered bread with hot, sugared tea, he thinks he regrets those monastic evenings. This is where they have led, to his first day at the University of Glasgow. He is terrified. He wants to stay in this small brightness, among objects so familiar he could live here by braille. But it is already too late. The strangeness of what is happening to him has transferred itself to everything else.

The oilcloth table-cover is scuffed with numberless lost moments. He would wish them back again if he could. But the shapes they make are the hieroglyphs of a strange language, seeming more ancient and less decipherable than anything Livy ever wrote. The burning lines of gas jets on each side of the oven seem as ceremonial as processional candles. The room reflected in the dark window is as haunting as the vivid painting of a place where he has never been.

Even his mother, the most continual presence of his life, moving about the kitchen to do the things he has always seen her do, seems mysterious. She washes a cup and puts it on the draining-board and suddenly he imagines the action multiplied a million times, an infinity of small selfless deeds with which she has sustained their lives, in which she has immured herself. And he realises that he has merely assumed he knew this woman. He remembers an old photograph of her he saw recently, taken by a street photographer. She hadn't known it was being taken. She was just walking in the street. She looked so young and attractive and separate from any sense of her her family might have. Walking on out of that photograph, where might she have gone if it hadn't been for them? What longings, what possibilities has she quietly entombed in the daily tasks of living?

She turns and looks at him. She laughs and lifts the towel, coming towards him. She is drying her hands.

'Ah don't think Ah'm up to this, Mither,' he says.

She laughs again. She says what she used to say to him every morning before an examination at school.

'You do the best you can, son. Nobody can ask ye to do more.'

He breathes out noisily.

'Whit d'ye think, Tom? If ye fail, we'll disown ye? Ye've earned yer right to go. Go as yerself. Whitever you make of it will do us fine.'

She puts her hand on his shoulder and it feels like an accolade: arise, Sir Thomas. He does. He washes his dishes in the warm, soapy water of the basin. He puts them on the draining-board. He reaches for the dish-towel.

'Here,' his mother says. 'Away an' use yer head.'

It *is* time to go. He has to catch the 7.25 train if he is to make his first-ever lecture at nine o'clock. He brushes his teeth again, keeping his new university tie close to his chest with his left hand as he leans over the hand-basin. Maybe cleanliness is next to braininess. He puts on the university blazer and the thin university scarf he bought from the money he earned at the brickwork, the bizarre result of sweating over hutches in the rain and a wild, confused night in a kiln and sweary conversations about women and football and the state of the world. He stares at himself in the mirror. He can't believe in the image he sees there. He might as well be going to a fancy-dress party. Still, maybe appearances, by sympathetic magic, can create the reality. He collects his coat from the lobby.

'Hey, Big Yin.'

His father is speaking from the living-room. Tam is surprised. He had thought everybody else was still in bed.

Tam looks round the door. His father is sitting in his armchair in old trousers and a zip-necked sweater. His feet are bare. He is smoking in front of the dead-ash fire. He will kindle it soon. Tam wonders if his father has left the kitchen to Tam and his mother deliberately, as if this morning has needed a special ceremony. His father looks tired and thoughtful. Maybe he hasn't slept much.

'You feart?' his father says.

Is his fear so obvious?

'Well. Ah don't feel great.'

'Everybody's feart. At least you're facin' yours. Yer grandfather wanted me to go on at the school. Ah didny want tae. Ah told maself it wis because Ah had more important things to do. But Ah think Ah wis just feart to learn ma limits. An' Ah've had to learn them anyway.'

Standing in the doorway, he is embarrassed. His father looks so dismayed with himself. He shouldn't be.

'Son,' he says. 'We're all feart o' the world. We lie in bed at night an' dread the things that might happen. The biggest man in the world, if he's got a brain, will live in fear. He just learns to control it. You'll have to do the same. Sometimes, son, ye just have to shout Geronimo and jump.'

They smile at each other.

'Cheers, Feyther.'

'Good luck.'

His mother opens the outside door for him. He lifts his Uncle Josey's briefcase from the floor of the lobby. It has new notebooks in it and some pens and the first textbooks he will need. It feels like a talisman in his hand. (You may be Johnny Appleseed in the stone groves of academe but you've got your own lineage. You once had an uncle that owned a briefcase.)

'Good luck, Tom,' his mother says.

'Thanks, Mither.'

He hears her close the door behind him. It is still dark and it is cold. He buttons up his raincoat with one hand, awkwardly.

'Hey, Einstein!'

It takes a moment to locate the voice. Michael's head is dimly visible projecting from the upstairs bedroom window. The hair is rumpled.

'Go slaughter them.'

The window closes and he walks on. The briefcase still feels like a prop in his hand. He never used it at school. He had carried a canvas, ex-army satchel with a shoulder-strap. That way, he didn't look pretentious passing through the housing scheme. A lot of workmen used them for carrying their pieces to work. He could still feel he belonged to where he came from. But, though the coat covers the blazer, the briefcase seems to him to be flashing ostentatiously in his hand. It was given to him after his uncle's death because his uncle had more than once said to other members of the family, 'Tam's going to achieve something. Wait and see.' It was passed on to him like a posthumous commission. Now the responsibility of it is heavy to him.

THAT WAS THE SUMMER OF THE KILN. He knew it over then. No other summer would be the same as that.

THAT WAS WHEN Senga gave him the gift, so precious at the time, of her kind silence. It didn't matter how roughly it was wrapped. That was when he had a summer passion for Margaret Inglis. That was when he had an affair with Maddie Fitzpatrick for three days and decided to commit suicide for two hours. That was when his mother had the strength to shape his life towards more freedom, when his father respected his strangeness, when Michael and Allison and Marion hovered protectively but inconspicuously around his days.

THAT WAS WHEN he made many fools of himself but in the end didn't want to disown any of them. They had been ways of trying to come nearer to himself – gestures in search of actions – and, therefore, ways of trying to come honestly nearer to others. Afterwards, he might laugh at them but it would be laughter between friends, for the boy he had stupidly been was related to the man he would spend the rest of his life hoping wisely to be. The boy had been earnestly trying to emulate an adult the man would probably never manage to become. The man might constantly change the forms the attempt would take but the content for those forms would always have its source in the energy of the boy.

THAT WAS WHEN he had his first awareness of experiencing the kiln, an accidental place which became a mythic centre in the mind – action in which you discover you, the self learned in happening beyond the lies of the word and beyond prevarication of the thought, the repeated point where existence hardens into being or breaks down into flux. The kiln had been the shifting nucleus of his summer. The kiln was not only in Avondale Brickwork. It was between Maddie Fitzpatrick's legs. It was in his head. It was where you found who you were. It was where he divested Cran Craig of his fearsomeness through the intensity of his own fear, where, by seeing Maddie Fitzpatrick clear, he saw himself more clearly, where a partial truce with his family earned him a partial truce with himself, where he began to compact into who he was.

• William McIlvanney

THAT WAS WHEN he began to see the justice of his father's baffled rage, the quiet and gracious stature of his mother, to understand at last his uncle's refusal to the death to surrender his love for others. That was when he learned he came from people and a place that were enough, when the uncommemorated names he lived among seemed to give him all the genealogy he needed.

THAT WAS WHEN he found for the first time the generous giving of a woman's body and the darkness of its hunger. She had taken what she needed from him but she had given him in return some edges of himself, a compass for his lostness, a map of longing. He had received from her more than he knew how to give but he might learn and he was grateful. Even the first sound of his own voice she had given him in a few lines that might matter to no one else but mattered to him.

He heard faint within the words he had written to Maddie a strange voice talking and was amazed to think it was his own, the first time of its hearing. It was his own not because it spoke well or wisely but because it said what it was totally compelled to say, an utterance that grew undeniably out of his own experience. It was querulous and lost, like a cat long in the cold, but it was there and he might find it again.

THAT WAS WHEN he knew what Pushkin meant. 'Not all of me is dust.' It seemed to him one of the bravest and most human things that anyone could say. It refused to be more precise than it could honestly be. There is more than this because I have experienced so. But the more there is will in no way denigrate what has been. Unless it includes without reservation all that has been, it cannot be more. QED.

THAT WAS WHEN a seeming infinity of situations and conversations and people and feelings and ideas and sights and places and sounds and thought fused slowly out of fragmentary chaos into a shifting and volatile and dynamic coherence of experience, an imperfectly grasped significance that still tremored on the edge of transformation with each approaching happening, became a past whose only purpose was to be the future in embryo, a future which only the perpetual present could deliver. Now. And now. And now.

AND NOW HE WOULD PAUSE THERE. Tom stood up from the table and put down his pen. The book is as good as finished.

He can remember when he had finished what he was sure would be his last book of poetry. He had known that the poetry was the sum of something in him and he had to admit to himself that it didn't seem to add up to a lot. His poetry had been a thirty-odd-year gamble. He thought, even before the book was published, that he had lost, so that he wasn't surprised when it sank without trace. But at least he had ridden with the bet. That was his last wager on the same old number and he could feel himself walking out before the croupier called.

This was just another bet. This time he could imagine himself saying to the croupier, 'Hold the wheel still. Don't call just yet. There's something Ah have to do first.'

Okay, Tam, he says to himself. Let's do it.

He goes through to the small kitchen and opens the door of the refrigerator. One heel of cheese is all it shows. But in the door of the fridge is the bottle of champagne he has been saving for this moment. The coldness of its neck almost sticks to his hand as he takes it. He elbows the door of the fridge shut. As he crosses to the sink, he rips off the foil, drops it on the draining-board, unwinds the wire. His thumbs jockey the cork up the neck of the bottle till it pops and fires itself into the curtain. It is darkening outside.

He loves the gushing of the juice that wants out and lets some of it splatter into the sink. Where there is spontaneity, there will be waste. This stuff is like good moments. When they come, you have to take them there and then. There is no postponing. You can't put the cork back on champagne.

He licks the neck of the bottle. He lifts an upturned glass from the draining-board and goes through to the living-room. The sun is setting on this side of the house and it glows in the room. He fills a glass as he walks and goes to the table at the window and puts the bottle down there. The sunlight makes jade of it. Tangled among trees and dripping red, the sun lays its warm light on his papers and seems briefly to bless their irrelevance as it blesses everything indiscriminately.

He looks across at the old graveyard of Warriston where the cluttered headstones are casting darkness before they become it. He holds up his glass to the dead.

He drinks off his glass and fills out another.

One thing he hopes he has got right is how the social life seems to him a farce and how the individual life seems a tragedy. And, since all of us are individuals first, it would seem to follow that life is a tragedy performed by farceurs. Enjoy the play.

He drinks to that. He has spoken to Phil. He will be leaving here soon. He will go somewhere else, catch another train, stoke up the kiln. Impossible to get in touch with Vanessa now. But he must have Grete's number somewhere. It would be good to talk to her.

He raises his glass above where the dead are, to the sun that still smoulders dimly among the trees.

As he drinks, he imagines he can hear the whir and clatter of a spinning wheel. He'll abide the outcome. He fills out another glass and drinks to the self he has met again in the summer of the kiln.

THAT WAS WHEN he walked in the air of early morning through the town towards the railway station. And the self-conscious and solemn progress of his purpose was waylaid by the remorseless and dynamic irrelevance of the moment.

'Aye, Tam,' Hilly Brown shouted from across the street, on his way home from the brickwork. 'What's wi' the briefcase? Takin' yer case to a higher court?'

Suddenly, he felt released by Hilly's irreverence. He laughed. He waved with exaggerated panache.

'To the higher court of human understanding,' he bellowed in a ludicrously portentous voice. (Valentine Dyall would have been proud of him.)

'That'll fuckin' do me,' Hilly shouted back. 'Put in a word for me.'

He burst out laughing. He would try. For all of them.

GERONIMO, his mind is shouting.